RATTLESNAKE CROSSING

By J.A. Jance

Joanna Brady Mysteries

DESERT HEAT
TOMBSTONE COURAGE
SHOOT/DON'T SHOOT
DEAD TO RIGHTS
SKELETON CANYON
RATTLESNAKE CROSSING

J. P. Beaumont Mysteries

UNTIL PROVEN GUILTY
INJUSTICE FOR ALL
TRIAL BY FURY
TAKING THE FIFTH
IMPROBABLE CAUSE
A MORE PERFECT UNION
DISMISSED WITH PREJUDICE
MINOR IN POSSESSION
PAYMENT IN KIND
WITHOUT DUE PROCESS
FAILURE TO APPEAR
LYING IN WAIT
NAME WITHHELD

and

HOUR OF THE HUNTER

J.A. JANCE

RATTLESNAKE CROSSING

A JOANNA BRADY MYSTERY

AVON BOOKS  NEW YORK

AVON BOOKS, INC.
1350 Avenue of the Americas
New York, New York 10019

Copyright © 1998 by J.A. Jance
Interior design by Kellan Peck
Visit our website at **http://www.AvonBooks.com**
ISBN: 0-380-97499-1

Library of Congress Cataloging in Publication Data:
Jance, Judith A.
Rattlesnake crossing : a Joanna Brady mystery / J.A. Jance.—1st ed.
p.   cm.
I. Title.
PS3560.A44R38   1998   98-10952
813'.54—dc21   CIP

First Avon Books Printing: August 1998

◆

For Richard Guerra,
whose encouragement fanned a tiny spark.

RATTLESNAKE
CROSSING

PROLOGUE

High on a cliff, the shooter panned the nightscope back and forth across the San Pedro Valley. It took a while for him to locate his chosen target across almost a mile of intervening desert. At last, though, he found it. After first putting on his ear protection, he pulled the trigger. In his hands the fifty-caliber sniper rifle roared to life. He felt certain he had nailed the pump, but there was no way to tell for sure. The pump didn't collapse. It just stood there, hit perhaps and with its interior guts shattered, but outwardly the machinery remained unfazed.

Frustrated, the shooter looked around for some other possibility. That was when he saw the cattle. Taking a bead on a dozing cow, he pulled the trigger again and was gratified to see her legs collapse under her. The shooter smiled in satisfaction. There was something god-like in being able to kill from that far away, to be able to strike without warning, like a thunderbolt. The other cattle, alarmed and frightened, milled about, trying to escape from this unseen threat. Laughing in the face of their stupidity and panic, he dropped another one, just to prove he could.

Letting the others go, he pulled off his ear protection and was starting to take down the tripod when he heard someone shouting at him, screaming up at him in fear and outrage. "What are you, crazy? Stop it before someone gets hurt!"

The shooter could barely believe his ears. Someone was out there in the desert, a woman, standing somewhere between him and the dead cattle. Someone who had heard him shooting.

"Sorry," he called back. "I was just doing some target practice. I didn't know anyone was here. Where are you?"

He ducked back down to the tripod. Once again he sent the nightscope scanning across the desert floor. A minute or two passed before he caught sight of the green-hued figure. Moving determinedly, she was trotting away from him, heading toward the river. It stunned him to realize that she must have been on the mountain the whole time he was. Maybe she had seen him and could even identify him. Reaching a spot of fairly open desert, she darted forward with all the grace of a panic-stricken deer. The green image in the high-powered night-vision scope smeared as she accelerated.

Without pausing to consider, the shooter covered his ears once more and placed a firm finger back inside the trigger guard. The woman was much closer than the cattle had been, so he had some difficulty adjusting his aim. The first shot caused her to trip and duck. As she limped forward, he realized he had winged her, but it wasn't enough to stop her. The second shot did, at least momentarily. She dropped to the ground, but even then, desperate to get away, she scrambled to her feet once more and staggered forward, cradling one arm.

"Damn!" the shooter exclaimed. "Missed again."

His third shot did the job. The bullet caught her in the middle of the back. She pitched forward and plummeted facedown on the rocky ground. This time she stayed down. He watched for the better part of a minute, but there was no sign of movement. None at all.

Up on the mountain, the shooter was barely able to contain his glee as he gathered equipment and shell casings. Killing people did something for him that killing animals didn't. It made him feel all-powerful and all-knowing.

He didn't rush, though. He took his time. After all, there was no reason to worry that she'd somehow get up on her hands and knees and crawl away from him. No, people shot with fifty-caliber shells weren't mobile enough for that. He had no doubt that by the time he found her—by the time he and his trusty knife arrived on the scene—the woman would still be there, waiting for him.

Stopping at her mailbox after work on a Monday evening in mid-August, Sheriff Joanna Brady surveyed the heat-shimmering landscape of southeastern Arizona. Off across the mesquite-covered Sulphur Springs Valley, she counted eleven separate dust devils weaving dances and leaving their swirling tracks on the parched desert floor. It had rained hard late the previous afternoon. Now all that remained of that gully-washing downpour was elevated humidity and the vague hope that another storm would blow through eventually. The dust devils and a few fat puffs of cloud on the far horizon were the only visible hint that another summertime monsoon might soon be in the offing.

Rolling up the window of her county-owned Blazer, Joanna retreated into air-conditioned comfort. Quickly she thumbed through the mail, hoping to see a postcard from Jenny, her daughter. Finding none, she tossed the mail—bills and advertising circulars—onto the seat beside her. Then she put the Blazer in gear, rumbled across the cattle guard, and headed up the narrow track that led to her home on High Lonesome Ranch.

Usually the road wound through a forest of mesquite sprouting out of hard-packed red clay that resembled adobe far more than it did dirt. But that summer's rainy season had broken all previous records, and it had turned High Lonesome Ranch into a jungle of waist-high weeds. The desert greenery was a life-affirming miracle that left Joanna Brady fascinated. All her life she had heard about how in the early days, when Anglos first came west, that part of the Arizona desert had been a lush grassland. When overgrazing gave rise to water-greedy mesquite, the native grasses had all but disappeared. One of Andy Brady's lifelong dreams had been to clear away the forest of mesquite on High Lonesome and restore the depleted grassland. Unfortunately, Deputy Andrew Brady had fallen victim to a drug lord's hit man long before that dream came true.

The herculean task of clearing the mesquite was something Joanna and Andy might well have tackled together, but on her own—with an eleven-year-old daughter to raise alone and with a demanding, time-consuming job—the stand of mesquite on High Lonesome Ranch was safe. At least for now.

Within a quarter mile of the cattle guard, Tigger and Sadie, Joanna's two dogs, came galloping down the road to meet her. Sadie was a long-legged bluetick hound who ran with all the easy grace of a greyhound. Tigger, a stocky half pit bull/half golden retriever, had to struggle to keep up. Twenty yards from the Blazer, their noisy approach rousted a long-eared jackrabbit out of the undergrowth. When the rabbit exploded from the brush and set off cross-country, the dogs forgot about welcoming Joanna and pounded after him. That oft-repeated nightly ritual chase—a contest the dogs always lost and the rabbit always won—never failed to make Joanna smile.

By the time she had pulled up and stopped next to the gate of the fenced yard, the dogs were back. Tongues lolling, they raced around the parked Blazer, searching frantically for something they were convinced must be hiding somewhere in the car.

"You can look all you want to," Joanna told the dogs. "Jenny's still not here."

Eva Lou and Jim Bob Brady, Joanna's in-laws and Jenny's paternal grandparents, had taken Jenny with them on a two-week trip that included a Brady family reunion in Enid, Oklahoma. Eva Lou and Jim Bob had wanted to show off their only grandchild. They had offered to take Joanna along as well, but she had declined: time was doing some of its healing work. Over the past few months, the curtain of grief and hurt of Andy's loss had gradually begun to lift. Still, Joanna had feared that being tossed into a virtual army of her dead husband's sympathetic relatives would cause a relapse. Pulling herself out of the suffocating morass of grief had been far too hard for her to risk falling into it once more. Against her better judgment, she had let Jenny go on the trip without her, mostly because Jenny herself had wanted to.

From the corral, Kiddo, Jenny's horse, voiced his whickered objection. He was looking for Jenny, too. With the dogs gamboling around her, Joanna went over to the corral and pulled a sugar cube out of her blazer pocket. Clayton Rhodes, her octogenarian neighbor and handyman, was good about feeding the animals, but he wasn't long on socializing with them. After giving Kiddo the sugar, Joanna scratched the sorrel gelding's nose. "You're not the only one who's lonesome," she told the horse. "I miss her, too."

When she finally headed into the house, the phone began ringing as she unlocked the back door. Dropping her brief-case, keys, and mail on the washer/dryer, Joanna raced into the living room to pick up the receiver. The name on the Caller ID box belonged to Melvin Unger, Andy's second cousin's husband. Joanna knew that while the Bradys were in Oklahoma, they were staying on the Ungers' farm a few miles outside Enid.

"Hi, Mom," Jenny said. "Did you just get home?"

Phone in hand, Joanna kicked off her heels and dropped onto the couch, where she could stretch out with her stock-inged feet up on the cushioned armrest. "Yes," she an-swered. "Just now. I was unlocking the door when I heard the phone ring."

"Why so late?" Jenny asked.

"It's not late," Joanna corrected. "Just six. You're in Okla-homa. There's a time zone difference, remember?"

"Oh," Jenny said. "That's right. I forgot."

"So how are you?" Joanna asked. "Was the reunion fun?"

"I guess so," Jenny said.

Joanna heard the uncertainty in her daughter's voice. "What do you mean, you guess so?"

"It's just that some of the kids were . . . well, you know . . ."

"I don't know," Joanna said as Jenny's voice trailed off. "They were what?"

"Well, mean," Jenny said finally.

"Mean how?"

"Rodney and Brian, from Tulsa. They kept making fun of me the whole time. They said I talked funny and that since we go to a Methodist church instead of a Baptist that I'd probably go to hell when I die. Is that true, Mom? Is

Daddy in hell and not in heaven? And how come Baptists are so mean?"

Joanna felt a sudden surge of anger rise in her breast. Had she been at the reunion, she might well have told Rodney and Brian a thing or two. "Who are Rodney and Brian?" she demanded. "Isn't their dad's name Jimmy?"

"I think so," Jenny said.

"That figures, then," Joanna said. "Your dad used to tell me how, whenever he was back in Oklahoma visiting, his older cousin Jimmy always made his life miserable, too. Remember, 'Sticks and stones will break your bones, but names will never hurt you.' " Joanna knew those words of consolation weren't entirely true, but they were worth a try. Predictably, they were greeted by dead silence on the other end of the line. "That is all, isn't it?" she asked then. "The boys saying mean things?"

"Well . . ." Jenny said.

"What else?"

"You know, just stuff."

Joanna sighed. "Rodney and Brian aren't mean because they're Baptists, Jenny. Most likely they're mean because that's how they were raised. And then, too, they're boys. Remember that old nursery rhyme Daddy used to read to you, the one about what boys and girls are made of? Girls are sugar and spice and everything nice and boys are frogs and snails and puppy-dog tails."

"I know," Jenny said. "Are frogs in there because of the legs?"

"Legs?" Joanna asked. "What do you mean?"

"That's something else Rodney and Brian do—they catch frogs and bugs and pull their legs off. And then they watch to see what happens."

Joanna felt suddenly sick to her stomach. She was a mother, but she was also a cop. She knew about the kinds

7

of profiling done by investigators of the FBI. She knew how often things like torturing small animals had been dismissed as harmless little-boy stuff, when in fact it had been a clear warning signal that something was seriously haywire and the little boy was actually taking his first ominous steps on a journey that would eventually lead to serial homicide.

Joanna's biggest concern right then wasn't so much that Rodney and Brian Morse were already junior serial killers. But it did seem possible that, bored with verbal abuse and tiring of helpless animal victims, the boys had turned their propensity for physical torture on Jenny. If so, Jenny wasn't saying.

Joanna was careful to keep her voice steady. "How long are Rodney and Brian going to be there?"

"I don't know for sure," Jenny answered. "I guess the rest of the week."

"And are they staying out there on the farm?"

"No. They're at a motel in town each night, but they come out to the farm during the day."

Mentally, Joanna closed her eyes and tried to remember the school photos accompanying letters in Christmas cards past. It seemed as though the boys were close to Jenny's age, but she couldn't be sure. "How old are they?" she asked.

"Rodney's twelve. Brian's eleven."

"Listen," Joanna said. "And I mean listen carefully. The rest of this week, I don't want you to spend any more time alone with those boys than you absolutely have to. But if you end up with them and they give you any more lip about being a Methodist or whatever, I want you to go after Rodney and punch his lights out. Use that thumb hold Daddy taught you for starters."

"But is that okay?" Jenny asked. "Don't I have to forgive them? Aren't I supposed to turn the other cheek?"

No, you're not, Joanna thought. *And you don't have to be a victim, either.* She said, "They've pulled these name-calling stunts more than once, haven't they?"

"Yes," Jenny replied. "The whole time they've been here."

"Then you've already turned the other cheek as much as you need to," Joanna assured her daughter. "The next time they look at you cross-eyed, let 'em have it."

"But what will Grandpa and Grandma say?" Jenny objected. "What if they get mad at me?"

"They won't, not if you tell them what's been going on."

Joanna heard a sound in the background. "That's Grandma Brady now," Jenny said. "It's time for dinner. Do you want to talk to her?"

Joanna took a deep breath. "Sure," she said. "You go eat, and I'll talk to Grandma." Moments later, Eva Lou came on the line. They chatted for a few minutes before Joanna brought up Rodney and Brian. "What's going on with those boys?" she asked.

"That's it," Eva Lou said. "They're just being boys."

"It sounds to me as though they're out of control."

"Well, maybe a little," Eva Lou agreed.

Joanna didn't want to step over any lines, nor did she want to make it sound as though Jenny was being a tattle-tale. "Try to keep an eye on them," Joanna said. "Some extra adult supervision never hurt anybody."

Long after she put down the phone, Joanna lay on the couch, staring up at the ceiling, her heart seething with a combination of worry and anger. *Why do kids have to be such monsters?* she wondered. The incident reminded her of the little flock of leghorns Eva Lou used to keep out in the chicken yard. Among chickens, even a small difference from the rest of the flock would be enough to provoke an unrelenting attack. After a while, the different one would just give up. It wouldn't even bother to fight back.

From that standpoint, Joanna had no doubt that she had given Jenny good advice. The last thing bullies like Rodney and Brian expected was for a helpless victim to turn on them and beat the crap out of them. Which Jenny was fully capable of doing. Andy had seen to that. He had taught his daughter both offensive and defensive moves, making sure she knew how to use them.

Shaking her head, Joanna rolled off the couch. Carrying the phone with her, she made her way into the bedroom and stripped off her clothes. Only when she was standing there naked did she realize that her favorite set of summer attire—sports bra, tank top, shorts, and undies—was still in the dryer, where she had left it on her way to work early that morning.

Eleanor Lathrop, Joanna's mother, had done her utmost to inculcate Joanna with the same kinds of repression and overweening modesty in which she herself had been raised. In Eleanor's scheme of things, walking naked through her own house—even a good mile from the nearest neighbor— would have been utterly unthinkable. But Eleanor was out of town this week, on a belated Alaskan honeymoon cruise with George Winfield, Cochise County's new medical examiner and Eleanor's new husband of some three months' standing. No, if Joanna happened to walk around naked in her own home, who was going to give a damn? Certainly not the two dogs.

With that Joanna flung open the bedroom door—closed out of habit—and strode through the living room and kitchen and on into the enclosed back porch that doubled as a laundry room entryway. There she pulled the clothes out of the dryer and put them on. Then she went back to the kitchen and switched on Jenny's boom-box CD player. Patsy Cline's distinctive voice came wafting through the speakers in her trademark song of falling to pieces, a road-map for how not to move beyond the loss of a love.

The CD was new, a birthday gift from Butch Dixon, a friend of Joanna's from up near Phoenix. It was a never-before-released recording of a concert Patsy Cline had given shortly before the plane crash that had taken her life. Listening to Patsy sing from across all those years was like hearing from Andy as well. Patsy Cline was dead and yet, through the magic of her work, she lived on in much the same way Andy was still a part of High Lonesome Ranch and of Jenny's and Joanna's lives as well.

Joanna had been taken aback by her strong emotional reaction to the music. *She* had been surprised. To her dismay, Butch Dixon hadn't been surprised in the least.

With the music still swirling around her, Joanna opened the refrigerator door and stared at the contents, wondering what to fix for dinner. It came to her all at once. Closing the refrigerator door and opening the cupboard instead, she plucked out the box of Malt-o-Meal. She had always wondered what it would be like to have hot cereal for dinner.

That night, with no one there to criticize or complain—with no one to consider but herself—Joanna Brady found out. She cooked the cereal in the microwave, covered it with milk and brown sugar, and then ate it standing there by the counter. Eleanor would have been aghast.

For the first time, a fragile thought slipped across Joanna's consciousness—flitting briefly through her mind on gossamer butterfly wings—that maybe living alone wasn't all bad.

CHAPTER ONE

"So what went on overnight?"

Morning briefing time the next day found Sheriff Joanna Brady closeted in her office at the Cochise County Justice Complex with her two chief deputies, Dick Voland and Frank Montoya. For a change, the burly Voland and the slight and balding Montoya weren't at each other's throats.

Montoya, deputy for administration and a former city marshal from Willcox, had been one of Joanna's several opponents in her race for sheriff. Voland, chief for operations, had been chief deputy in the previous administration and had actively campaigned for another losing candidate. Joanna had confounded friends and critics alike by appointing the two of them to serve as her chief deputies. Almost a year into her administration, their volatile oil-and-water combination was working. The constant bickering didn't always make for the most pleasant office environment, but Joanna valued the undiluted candor that resulted from the two men's natural rivalry.

"Let's see," Voland said, consulting his stack of reports.

"Hot time up in the northwest sector last night. First there was a report of a naked female hitchhiker seen on Interstate 10 in Texas Canyon. Not surprisingly, she was long gone before a deputy managed to make it to the scene."

"Sounds to me like some long-haul trucker got lucky," Montoya said.

"That's what I thought, too," Voland agreed. "Then, overnight, somebody took out Alton Hosfield's main pump and two head of cattle over on the Triple C."

CCC Ranch, referred to locally as either the Triple C or the Calloway Cattle Company, was an old-time cattle ranch that straddled the San Pedro River in northwestern Cochise County. The family-owned spread had historic roots that dated all the way back to Arizona's territorial days. Alton Hosfield, the fifty-three-year-old current owner, was waging a lonely war against what he called "enviro-nuts" and the federal government to keep his family's holdings all in one piece. Meanwhile, neighboring ranches had been split up into smaller parcels. Those breakups had caused a steady influx of what Alton Hosfield regarded as "Californicating riffraff." Most of the unwelcome newcomers were people the rancher could barely tolerate.

"Does that mean the Cascabel range war is heating up all over again?" Joanna asked.

Voland nodded. "It could be all those rattlers are getting ready to have another go at it."

In high school Spanish classes Joanna had been taught that *cascabel* meant "little bell." But in Latin American Spanish it meant "rattlesnake." No doubt Voland wanted to impress Frank Montoya with his own knowledge of local Hispanic place-names.

"Deputy Sandoval checked to see if maybe Hosfield's cattle had broken into Martin Scorsby's pecan orchard again," Voland continued. "As far as he could tell, the fence was intact, and both cattle were found on the Triple C side of the property line."

Scorsby, Hosfield's nearest neighbor, was a former California insurance executive who had planted a forty-acre pecan orchard on prime river bottom pastureland Alton Hosfield had coveted for his own. During an estate sale, he had attempted to buy the parcel from the previous owner's widow. Years later, Hosfield still read collusion into the fact that Scorsby's offer had been accepted by the former owner's son—yet another Californian—in place of his. In addition, Joanna knew that on several previous occasions, when Triple C cattle had breached the fence and strayed into Scorsby's pecan orchard, Hosfield had been less than prompt in retrieving them.

"It's not just that the cattle are dead," Voland added ominously. "It's how they got that way. This isn't in the report, because I just talked to deputy Sandoval about it a few minutes ago. He managed to recover a bullet from one of the dead cattle. He said he's never seen anything like it. The slug must be two inches long."

"Two inches!" Joanna repeated. "That sounds like it came out of a cannon rather than a rifle."

"Sniper rifle," Frank Montoya said at once. "Probably one of those fifty-caliber jobs."

Both Joanna and Voland turned on the Chief Deputy for Administration. "You know something about these guns?" the sheriff asked.

"A little," Montoya said. "There's a guy over in Pomerene named Clyde Philips. He's a registered gun dealer who operates out of his back room or garage or some such thing. He called me a couple of months ago wanting to set up an appointment for his salesman to come give us the whole sniper-rifle dog and pony show. He said that since the bad guys might have access to these things, our Emergency Response Team should, too. He sent me some info. After I looked it over, I called him back and told him thanks, but no thanks. Maybe the crooks can afford to buy guns at twenty-five hundred to seven thousand bucks apiece, but at that price they're way outside what the department can pay."

"What can fifty-calibers do?" Joanna asked.

"Depends on who you ask. After I talked to Philips and looked over the info he sent me, I got on the Internet and researched it a little further. Fifty-calibers were first used as Browning automatic rifles long ago. Remember those, Dick? Then the military in Vietnam tried a sniper version. The farthest-known sniper kill is one point four-two miles, give or take. Not bad for what the industry calls a 'sporting rifle.' "

"Sporting for whom?" Joanna asked.

"Probably not for the cattle," Voland replied.

"We'll be running forensic tests on the slug?"

Voland nodded. "You bet."

"I don't suppose there's any way to tell who some of Clyde Philips' other local customers might be," Joanna suggested.

Montoya shrugged. "You could ask him, I suppose, but I don't know how much good that'll do. Fifty-calibers may be lethal as all hell, but they don't have to be registered. Anybody who isn't a convicted felon is more than welcome to buy one, including, incidentally, those Branch Davidian folks from over in Waco. But just because felons can't buy them doesn't necessarily mean they don't have them. All the crooks have to do is steal one from somebody who does."

"Great," Joanna said. She glanced at her watch. "I guess I'll take a run over to Pomerene later today and have a little chat with Clyde Philips. Anybody care to join me?"

"Can't," Montoya said. "I've got a set of grievance hearings with jail personnel lined up for this afternoon."

"I've got meetings too," Voland said, "although if you need me to go . . ."

"Then I'll make like the Little Red Hen and do it myself," Joanna said firmly. "While I'm at it, I may stop by and visit both Hosfield and Scorsby. Maybe I can talk sense into one or both of them. The last thing we need is for all those wackos up around Cascabel to choose sides and start throwing stones."

"Or bullets," Frank Montoya added.

"Right," Joanna said. "Now, what else is going on?"

"Just the usual," Voland replied. "An even dozen undocumented aliens picked up on foot over east of Douglas. A stolen pickup down in Bisbee Junction. Two domestics, one in Elfrida and another out in Palominas. A couple of DWIs between Huachuca City and Benson. In other words, no biggies."

Joanna turned to Montoya. "What's happening on the administration side?"

"Like I said before, those grievance hearings are set for this afternoon. I should have the September rotation and vacation schedules ready for you to go over by tomorrow morning, and next month's jail menus by tomorrow afternoon. Also, there are two new provisioners, one from Tucson and one from Phoenix, interested in bidding on becoming our food supplier. I'm trying to set up meetings with their sales reps for later this week. You should probably be in on both of those."

Joanna nodded. "All right. Anything else?" Both deputies shook their heads. "Okay, then," she told them. "Let's go to work."

Voland and Montoya left Joanna's office. Running one hand through her short red hair, Joanna contemplated the hard nut of uncompleted paperwork left over from the day before when her private phone rang. It was a line she had installed specifically so family members—Jenny in particular—could reach her without having to fight their way through the departmental switchboard.

"Hello, Joanna," Butch Dixon said as soon as she picked up the phone. "How are things with the Sheriff of Cochise?"

Blushing, Joanna glanced toward her office door and was grateful Frank Montoya had closed it behind him when he went out. She didn't like the idea that anyone in the outer office, including Kristin Marsten, her secretary, might be listening in on her private conversations.

"Things are fine," Joanna said. "But I've barely heard from you the last few days. What's going on?"

"I've been as busy as the proverbial one-armed paper hanger," Butch replied. "Or maybe a one-legged flamenco dancer. What about you?"

Joanna recognized that his joking response was meant to gloss over the lack of real information in his answer, and that tweaked her. On the one hand, she couldn't help wondering if his being so busy had something to do with some other woman. On the other hand, since she and Butch had no kind of understanding, Joanna realized she had no right to question him, and no right to be jealous, either.

"Just the usual," she said, matching the vagueness in his answer with her own.

"The usual murder and mayhem, you mean?" he asked. She could almost see the teasing grin behind his question.

"More meetings and paperwork than murder," she admitted with a laugh.

That was one of the things that had dismayed her about being sheriff. Her officers often balked and complained at the amount of paperwork required of them. Joanna found that she certainly had more than her own fair share of it, but what seemed to chew up and squander most of her time, what she resented most, was the never-ending round of meetings. She despised the necessity of attending one mindless confab after another—endless, droning conferences where little happened and even less was decided.

"What are you doing tonight?" Butch asked.

"Tonight? Nothing, but . . ."

"How about dinner?"

"Where?" Joanna asked, trying not to sound too eager. Several times in the past few months, she and Butch had split the two hundred miles between them by meeting in Tucson for lunch or dinner, but she wasn't sure she wanted to make that trip on a weeknight.

"Eight o'clock in the morning comes mighty early," she said.

Butch laughed. "Don't worry," he returned. "I promise I won't keep you out late. I'll pick you up at the ranch at seven. I've got something I want to show you. See you then."

"Wait a minute," Joanna interrupted before he could hang up. "What kind of dinner are we talking about? How should I dress?"

"Casual," Butch said. "Definitely casual."

"This doesn't include going someplace on your motorcycle, does it?" she asked warily. Butch Dixon was inordinately proud of his Goldwing, but riding motorcycles was something Joanna Brady didn't do. And she didn't intend to start.

"No," Butch answered. "We won't be winging it. I'll have my truck. See you then."

Just as Joanna put down the phone, her office door opened and Kristin marched up to her desk carrying that morning's stack of mail, which landed on top of the previous day's leftovers. Shaking her head, Joanna dived into it. She wondered if she'd ever achieve the kind of organizational skill where she handled paperwork only once without having to sort it into stacks and piles first.

Kristin stood for a moment watching Joanna work, then she turned to go. "Do me a favor if you would," Joanna called after her. "Look up the number for Clyde Philips over in Pomerene. Call him and ask if I can stop by to see him for a little while early this afternoon, say around two o'clock. And then double-check with Marianne Maculyea and see if we're still on for lunch."

The Reverend Marianne Maculyea, pastor of Canyon United Methodist Church, was not only Joanna's minister, she was also her best friend. The two had known each other from junior high on, and once a week or so, they met for a girl-talk lunch at which they could let down their hair. In Bisbee, Arizona, the two friends were well known for their nontraditional jobs. As women doing "men's" work, both were often targets of small-town gossip, jealousy, and criticism. Set apart from most of the other women in the community, they used their weekly get-togethers as sounding boards and pressure valves. Huddled in the privacy of one of Daisy Maxwell's booths, they could discuss issues neither could mention to anyone else.

While Kristin went to make the calls, Joanna settled in to answer the correspondence. Over the months, Kristin had finally accepted the fact that Joanna preferred to type her own letters on her own computer, rather than going through what she regarded as the cumbersome process of dictating them and having them typed. Dictation might have been fine for a hunt-and-peck typist like Sheriff Walter V. McFadden. For Joanna, however—a former insurance-office manager whose personal typing speed was about one hundred and twenty words a minute—dictation simply didn't make any sense. Whenever possible, the sheriff typed her own correspondence.

One after another, Joanna ripped through the letters, keying one letter in, printing it, and signing it before going on to the next. All Kristin would have to do when they landed on her desk was type the envelopes, stuff the letters inside, and run the stuffed envelopes through the postage meter.

An hour and a half passed with blinding speed. Later, on her way to the coffeepot in the outside office, Joanna stopped at Kristin's desk. "Any luck with Clyde Philips?" she asked.

Kristin shook her head. "I can keep trying, but so far there's no answer at his place."

"What about Marianne?"

"She says it's Cornish Pasties Monday at Daisy's, so she wouldn't miss it for the world."

By eleven-thirty, Joanna was settled into one of the worn Naugahyde booths in Daisy's Cafe. Arriving ahead of Marianne, Joanna sat and waited, stirring her iced tea and replaying her conversation with Butch Dixon. There was a part of her—the old, loyal to Andy part—that enjoyed his company immensely but still wanted to hold the man himself at arm's length. Then there was the other part of her—the new Joanna—who didn't want to run the risk of losing Butch to someone else.

That was one of the reasons she was looking forward to this particular lunch with Marianne. She wanted to have the opportunity to discuss the Butch Dixon dilemma. Marianne Maculyea was a skilled minister and counselor as well as a trusted friend. Joanna hoped Marianne would help sort through some of her jumbled emotions and make sense of what she was feeling.

Unfortunately, the possibility for the two women to have an intimate little chat disappeared the moment Marianne opened the door. She arrived with her two-year-old twins in tow.

Months earlier, Marianne and her husband, Jeff Daniels, had adopted Ruth Rachel and Esther Elaine from an orphanage in China. Ruth had quickly bounced back from the inhumane deprivations of her infancy, while Esther continued to suffer lingering health difficulties, one of which had placed her on the waiting list for a heart transplant. That painful subject was one Marianne and Jeff seldom discussed with anyone outside their immediate family, Joanna Brady included. It was easy to understand why. For one thing, doctors hadn't held out much hope. Potential donors who might match Esther's ethnic background were few and far between. Without the transplant, Esther would inevitably die, but a successful transplant for her would automatically mean a lifetime of heartbreak for some other devastated family.

Ruth's plump arms and legs as well as her constant tornado of activity stood in sharp contrast to Esther's wan lethargy. Crowing with joy at seeing Joanna, Ruth ran headlong into the restaurant and scrambled eagerly up onto the seat beside her. Marianne followed, carrying Esther, a purse, and an enormous diaper bag—one Joanna had given her on the day the twins arrived in Tucson.

"I hope you don't mind," Marianne apologized, slipping Esther into a high chair the busboy quickly delivered to the booth. He returned a moment later with a booster seat. Beaming up at him, Ruth climbed into that. "Jeff had to make a run up to Tucson to pick up some parts, and in this heat . . ." Marianne continued.

For years Jeff Daniels had served solely as househusband and clergy spouse to his full-time pastor wife. The arrival of the twins, along with Esther's ongoing medical problems, had put an extra strain on the couple's already meager finances. Faced with the real possibility of financial ruin, Jeff had taken his hobby of restoring old cars and turned it into a thriving business, Auto Rehab Inc. Most of the time he was able to keep the girls with him, but Joanna agreed with Marianne: in the scorching heat of mid-August Arizona, a two-hundred-mile round-trip jaunt in a vehicle without air-conditioning was no place for even healthy two-year-olds. For an ailing one, that kind of trip was absolutely out of the question.

Moderately disappointed at having her plan for an intimate chat scuttled, Joanna didn't have to struggle very hard to put a good face on it. "Don't worry," she replied, pulling the irrepressible Ruth into a squirming hug. "Jenny's been gone for over a week now. Being around the girls will help bring me back up to speed in the motherhood department."

Gratefully, Marianne sank into the booth and began opening the cellophane wrapper on a package of saltine crackers. By the time the crackers were peeled, Ruth was demanding hers in a raucous squawk that sounded for all the world like a hungry, openmouthed nestling screeching for its mommy's worm. As soon as Marianne put the crackers down on the table. Ruth scooped them up, one in each hand, and stuck them both in her mouth at once. But Esther's lone cracker had to be placed directly in her hand. Even then, she sat holding the treat, watching Marianne with a wide-eyed, solemn stare, rather than putting the cracker into her mouth.

The lack of that instinctive gesture worried Joanna. So did the grayish tint to the little girl's pale skin. Having missed church on Sunday, Joanna had gone more than a week without seeing either one of the girls. It shocked her to realize that Esther seemed noticeably weaker. Meanwhile, the usually well-composed Marianne appeared to be utterly distracted.

Daisy Maxwell, owner of Daisy's Cafe, appeared just then with her towering, beehive hairdo as well as a long yellow pencil and an outstretched order pad. "What'll it be today, ladies?" she asked. "We've got pasties, you know. They'll probably go pretty fast."

"They always do," Joanna said with a smile. "Sign me up for one."

"Me, too," Marianne added, pulling two empty and spill-proof tippy cups out of her diaper bag. "And a grilled cheese divided into quarters for the girls. A grilled cheese and a large milk."

"Sure thing," Daisy said, slipping the pencil back into her hairdo.

Watching the woman walk away, Joanna struggled to find something inconsequential to say. "That's a magic time to be a mommy," she said finally. "You walk into a restaurant and all you have to know is how to order a grilled cheese sandwich. Believe me, once little kids get beyond their love for grilled cheese, it's all downhill."

Joanna had meant the comment as nothing more than lightweight conversational filler. She was dismayed when her friend's gray eyes clouded over with tears, which Marianne quickly wiped away.

"Esther's worse, then?" Joanna asked.

Marianne nodded wordlessly. Joanna reached across the table and grasped her friend's wrist. "It'll be all right," she said comfortingly. "I know it will."

"I hope so," Marianne murmured.

Daisy chose that moment to reappear, bringing with her the girls' milk and an extra glass of iced tea. "You didn't order this," she said, setting the tea in front of Marianne. "I figured you probably just forgot, but if you don't want to drink it, there'll be no charge."

Instantly Marianne's tears returned. This time they came

so suddenly that one of them raced down her cheek and splashed onto the tabletop before she had a chance to brush it aside.

"Thanks," she said.

"Think nothing of it, honey," Daisy Maxwell told her. "Believe me, if I had anything stronger back there in the kitchen, I'd give you some of that. Just looking at you, I'd say you could use it."

CHAPTER TWO

Driving toward Benson after lunch, Joanna called in to the
department to let the staff know where she was going and
when she'd be back. For the rest of the fifty-mile drive, she
thought about Marianne and Jeff and Esther. Compared to
her friends' life-and-death struggles, her concerns and conflicts about Butch Dixon seemed downright trivial. She felt
guilty for even thinking about bothering Marianne with
something so inconsequential.

Between Tombstone and St. David, Highway 80 curves
through an area of alkaline-laced badlands. To Joanna, that
stark part of the drive usually made her think of what she
had once imagined the surface of the moon would be. But
this year the summer's record-breaking rainy season had
made moisture so plentiful that even there a carpet of wild,
stringy grass had caught hold and sprouted, softening the
harsh lines and turning the rugged desert green—a mirror
and a metaphor for the miracle of life itself—clear, visible
evidence of an unseen Hand at work.

"Look, God," Joanna Brady said aloud, as if He were

right there in the Blazer with her—a concerned civilian, maybe, doing a ride-along. "Surely, if You can make grass grow here, You can figure out a way to save Esther Maculyea-Daniels. Please."

Beyond that, there was nothing Joanna could do but let go and let God.

A few miles later, at the traffic circle in Benson, she turned east off Highway 80 and followed the I-10 frontage road until she reached the turnoff for Pomerene. There, crossing the bridge across the San Pedro, she slowed enough to observe the awesome effect of water in the desert. Over the hum of the Blazer's powerful engine, she could hear the chatter of frogs. And above that, she heard the water.

Since an earthquake in the late 1800's the modern San Pedro usually carried little more than a trickle of mossy water in a wide expanse of dry and sandy riverbed. On that hot August day, however, the rushing tumult below the bridge was running almost bank to bank in a reddish-brown, foam-capped flood. Unfortunately, people accustomed to the river's usually placid guise often failed to give this transformed San Pedro the respect it deserved.

Summer rains had come early and often that year, starting in the middle of June. In the course of the past two months the renewed San Pedro, with its deadly change of personality, had claimed four separate victims. One carload of Sunday-afternoon picnickers had been washed away up near Palominas in the middle of July. That incident alone had resulted in three fatalities. A mother and two preschool children had died, while the father and two older children had been hospitalized. Then, in early August, a seventeen-year-old St. David youth had bet his buddies ten bucks that he could swim across the rain-swollen flood. He had lost both the ten-dollar wager and his life.

Joanna could see why. More than twenty-four hours after

the last rain, a torrent of silt-laden water still churned north-ward. Seeing it reminded her of the stories she had heard at her father's knee—stories D. H. Lathrop had heard from Cochise County old-timers. They had claimed that before the earthquake, there had once been so much water running in the San Pedro, they could float on rafts from Palominas north all the way to Winkelman, where the San Pedro River met up with the Gila. For years Joanna had privately scoffed at what she regarded as nothing more than tall tales on the order of Paul Bunyan's blue ox, Babe. Now, though, the raging river made those claims seem much more plausible.

Pomerene, a few miles on the other side of the bridge, seemed to have little justification for its continued existence. A few people—several hundred at most—seemed to live in the near vicinity, but for what reason, Joanna couldn't fathom. Some of the houses were fine, but the good ones were interspersed with tumbledown shacks and moldering mobile homes surrounded by rusted-steel shells of wrecked vehicles. The cheerfully sparkling and still brand-new street signs, assigned with ironic artistry by some bureaucrat locked up in the county addressing department, were wildly at odds with the sad reality of their surroundings.

It seemed to Joanna that Pomerene should have been a ghost town—that it should have been allowed to die the natural death of fading back into the sandy river bottom. Instead, it stubbornly persisted, hanging on like some punch-drunk fighter—hurt badly enough to be beyond help, but too far gone to have sense enough to lie down and die.

The down-at-heels hovels on Bella Vista Drive and Rim-rock Circle in particular made places in Bisbee's Tin Town neighborhood seem prosperous by comparison. And Clyde Philips' tin-roofed shack at the far end of Rimrock could easily have been thrown together by the same turn-of-the-century carpenters who had built the mining-camp cabins that still clung like empty, dry locust husks to the red-rocked sides of Bisbee's B-Hill.

Climbing up onto the rickety front porch, Joanna knocked firmly on the grime-covered door. Even though she knocked several times, no one answered. Leaving the front door, she went to the side of the house past a dusty, faded blue Ford quarter-ton pickup. At the back door she knocked again—with similar results. No answer.

Trying to decide what to do next, Joanna glanced around. At the end of the driveway, in place of an ordinary garage, was a slump-block building that looked like an armed fortress. Or a jail. Rolls of razor wire lined the tops of the walls. The only windows were narrow slits on either side of a steel door, barred in front by a heavy-duty wrought-iron grille. Approaching the door, Joanna could tell that the slits were covered by one-way glass that allowed whoever was inside the building to see out without offering even a glimpse of what was on the other side of the wall.

Fastened to the grille was a hand-lettered sign that announced, NO TRESPASSING. THESE PREMISES GUARDED BY A LOADED AK-47. GO AHEAD. MAKE MY DAY.

Great, Joanna thought as she stepped forward and punched a doorbell that had been built into the casement of one of the windows. *Just what we need. A gun nut with a Clint Eastwood complex.*

Pressing the button, she strained to hear whether or not the bell actually worked. Up on the roof, an air-conditioning unit of some kind rumbled away. Over the din of that, it was difficult to tell if the bell did indeed function, but between the grille and the concrete-block construction, knocking on either the door or the wall wasn't an option.

While waiting for someone to answer, Joanna studied her surroundings, expecting to find some kind of electronic monitoring equipment focused on the door. As far as she could see, however, Clyde Philips counted on old-fashioned armory kinds of protection rather than newfangled gadgets. She rang the bell a second time and waited once more. Still no one came to the door. She was about to give up and walk away when a woman's gravelly voice startled her.

"Clyde's pro'ly over to Belle's. His truck's here, so he musta walked."

Joanna turned to see a sun-baked old woman standing on the sagging back porch of the house next door. "Where's that?" she asked.

"Belle's?" the old woman asked, and Joanna nodded. "It's his ex-wife's place. Uptown." The woman pointed vaguely to the left with a gnarled cane. "Over on Old Pomerene Road."

"Will I have any trouble finding it?"

"Hell's bells," the woman said. "Hardly. It's the only restaurant in town. But you'd better hurry if you want to catch lunch or Clyde, either one. Belle closes her doors at three sharp. After that, people have to go all the way into Benson if they want a bite to eat."

The woman was right. Belle Philips' place on Old Pomerene Road wasn't at all hard to find. Of the dozen or so storefronts on what passed for Main Street, only three still functioned as businesses. One of the three with lights on was the ground floor of a decrepit two-story building that looked as though a strong wind would blow it to smithereens.

At some time in the distant past, someone had gone to the trouble of covering the exterior with cedar shingles. Sun and heat had leached all the natural oils out of the wood, leaving it gray and brittle and almost charred around the edges. On the north and east sides of the building, the shingles sagged in crooked, weary rows. On the west side of the building—the one that took the brunt of the sun—most of the shakes were missing completely, revealing in their stead a ghostly layer of faded red tarpaper painted to look like bricks.

The rest of the building didn't look much better. In both grimy front windows, chipped gold letters announced "Belle's Donuts and Eatery." Under one sign was a three-by-five card. On the card along with a hand-drawn ballpoint arrow that pointed to the word "Donuts," was the added notation "One hundred thousand two hundred served."

When Joanna pushed open the wood-framed glass door, a bell tinkled overheard. A heavyset woman, wearing a faded bandanna babushka-style on frizzy gray hair, stood leaning against what looked like a soda fountain counter. Under a massive apron she wore a sleeveless tank top. Folds of loose flesh dangled from upper arms a good eighteen inches around. Stubbing out a cigarette in a brimful ashtray, she quickly stowed it under the counter.

"Howdy," the woman said. "Saw you lookin' at my sign. I make 'em all myself—the doughnuts, I mean—and keep track of every dozen, although I only change the card once't a month or so."

"That's still a lot of doughnuts," Joanna said.

The woman grinned, showing several missing teeth, both lowers and uppers. She nodded sagely. "Yup, you bet it is. Don't just sell 'em here, of course. Take 'em to places like the county fair and Rex Allen Days and Heldorado over to Tombstone. That's always a good gig, Tombstone is. Most likely 'cause it's in October and colder'n a witch's tit by then. I hire me a couple of young kids, good-lookin' girls if I can find 'em, to do the actual sellin'. What can I get for you?"

Joanna was still more than pleasantly full from downing Daisy Maxwell's Cornish pasty, but she knew that ordering something from Belle would help smooth things along. "How about a cup of coffee?" she asked.

When the coffee came, it smelled acrid and old—as though it had been sitting in an almost empty pot on the burner for the better part of the day or maybe even longer. Usually Joanna drank her coffee black, but this strong stuff definitely called for making an exception.

"Cream?" Joanna asked hopefully.

Belle nodded. "Sure. What kind of moo-juice you want? We got regular cream, half-and-half, canned, and cow-powder. Take your choice."

In that dingy, fly-speckled place, Joanna worried about the age and possible contamination of anything requiring refrigeration. She opted for Coffee-mate. When Belle delivered the jar, the crust of dry powder lining the bottom was so old and hard that Joanna had to chip it loose with her spoon before she could ladle the resulting lump into her cup. Further examination of the almost empty jar showed no sign of any expiration date and no sign of a scanner barcode, either. Not good.

"You must be Belle Philips," Joanna said, stirring the brackish brew to dissolve the lump.

"That's right," Belle said. "And who might you be?"

Joanna reached into her blazer pocket and pulled out her ID. "Whoee," Belle exclaimed, holding the card up to the light and squinting at it. "Don't guess I've ever met a sheriff before, leastways not in person. You're not here on account of somethin' I've done, are you?"

"I was actually looking for your former husband."

Belle grimaced. "It figures," she said. "Clyde's always up to some fool off-the-wall thing. Me an' him split the sheets about six years ago now, and I say good riddance. Best thing I ever done. If I'da known how things would work out, I would of done it a lot sooner. Still see him most every day, though. Comes in here and has me cook him his breakfast, but, by God, he pays me for it. Cash. Every day. None of this running-a-tab crap. If I'da had a brain in my head, I woulda done that the whole time we was married, too—charged him, that is. And not just for cooking his meals and washing his damned underwear, either." She grinned slyly. "If you get my meanin'."

Joanna nodded. She got it, all right. "So has he been in today? I tried stopping by both his house and his shop. His truck was there, but he didn't answer at either place."

Belle shrugged. "He hasn't been in so far, and once I close the doors at three o'clock, he'll be out of luck. Probably got himself a snootful last night and he's sleeping it off today. He does that, you know—drinks to excess. That's one of the reasons I divorced him—for drinking and carousing both."

"Well," Joanna said, "since he isn't home, is there anywhere else in town he might be?"

"My guess is he's in the refrigerator he calls a bedroom, sleeping the sleep of the dead, and can't hear you over the sound of that damned room air conditioner of his. That's another thing about him. The man's so tight his farts squeak. He's cheap as can be about everything, but not air-conditioning, no, ma'am. Keeps his shop and bedroom so cold they're like as not to freeze your butt. Us'ta be, I'd walk in there to go to bed in the summertime and my nipples would turn to ice. Now that I'm alone, I sleep upstairs here with just a single fan. Sometimes, even in the summer, I don't bother with that."

"Getting back to Clyde . . ." Joanna hinted.

"Want me to go over and wake him up for you?" Belle Philips offered. "We've been divorced a long time, but I still have a key. He coulda changed the locks, but like I said, he's so damned cheap . . ."

Glad of an excuse not to drink the awful coffee, Joanna pushed the still brimming cup aside. "That would be a real favor, if it's not too much trouble."

"No trouble at all," Belle said. "All's I got to do is turn out the lights and lock the door. Since I'm my own boss, I can come back later on and finish cleaning up. I do that sometimes, anyway, especially if it gets too hot of an afternoon."

While she waddled over to the door and turned the CLOSED sign to the front, Joanna put a dollar bill down on the counter. The sign over the cash register said coffee cost seventy-five cents. After a moment's consideration, she added a quarter to the single.

Belle returned and plucked a huge, fringed leather purse out from under the counter. "Ready," she said, jangling a ring of keys. "My car or yours?"

"Let's take mine," Joanna told her. "It's parked right out front."

When Belle Philips clambered into the Blazer, the seat springs groaned under her weight. She had to struggle with the seat belt to get it to reach all the way around her. "Nice car," she commented, once she was finally fastened in. "Not like one of those little foreign rice buckets. That's mine over there." She pointed to an enormous old white-finned Cadillac. "That one's real comfortable. That's one thing Clyde does for me, and I 'preciate it, too. Twice't a month or so, he goes down to Naco or Agua Prieta and brings me a couple of jerricans of regular old gas. You know, the leaded kind, the kind you can't buy on this side of the line no more. If it weren't for that, I wouldn't be able to keep that old Caddy purring along. I just love that car. Couldn't stand to give it up."

Joanna knew what she meant. In fact, to a lesser degree, she felt the same kind of attachment to the county-owned

Blazer. She remembered when the vehicle had been severely damaged by a dynamite explosion down near Douglas. The blast had blown out the windows and then sent a hail of shattered glass into the air, shredding both the head liner and the upholstery. After surveying the damage, the county insurance adjuster had totaled the vehicle. For months the damaged Blazer had languished in the departmental lot waiting to be cannibalized for parts, while Joanna had been forced into using one of the department's new, two-wheel-drive Crown Victoria cruisers. Two-wheel drive and a sedan-type construction, however, were a poor match for Cochise County's miles of rural back roads.

After seeing some of Jeff Daniels' auto restoration handiwork, Joanna had prevailed on Frank Montoya to find a spot in the budget to pay for repairs. For far less money than the adjuster had estimated, Jeff Daniels had put the Blazer's interior back in almost perfect condition. There were still occasions when Joanna used one of the Crown Victorias, but usually she drove the Blazer, preferring that over anything else.

Less than three minutes after leaving the restaurant, Joanna stopped again outside Clyde Philips' house. Belle opened the car door and lumbered out. Standing on the decrepit front porch, she spent the better part of a minute digging through her capacious purse and finally extracting both a cigarette and a lighter. With the cigarette dangling from one corner of her mouth, Belle selected an old-fashioned skeleton key from her key ring, stuck it in the lock, pushed open the creaking door, and stepped inside.

Wrestling with probable-cause issues, Joanna hesitated, thinking it would be better if she remained outside until Clyde himself invited her into the house.

"It's okay if you wan'ta come on in," Belle called back to her.

Joanna considered. As far as she knew, no crime had been committed. She was there to talk with Clyde. The man certainly wasn't a suspect in any ongoing investigation.

"So are you coming or not?" Belle urged.

Shrugging, Joanna stepped over the threshold. Her first impression upon entering the hot and stuffy little house was that a goat lived there. The place stank. It smelled of dirty socks and dirty underwear, old shoes, stale beer, and cigarettes. Even though the unscreened windows stood wide open, without air-conditioning, the heat inside the room was overwhelming. The room was tall and narrow with a rust-stained tin ceiling. A single light fixture dangled from the center of the room. Ratty, broken-down furniture was littered with a collection of beer cans, paper trash, garbage, and bugs.

"That's the other thing about Clyde," Belle said. "His mama never taught him about cleanliness bein' next to godliness and all that, and he never did learn how to pick up after hisself, either. As you can see, once't I quit doing for him, the whole place went to hell in a handbasket. Hang on," she added. "If you think it's bad out here, you sure as heck don't want to see the bedroom. He allus sleeps in just his birthday suit with hardly any covers."

Joanna nodded. "You go on ahead," she agreed. "I'll be happy to wait out here."

Belle lumbered toward a short hallway. Beneath filthy, chipped linoleum, the aged plank floor groaned in protest with each passing step.

"Clyde?" Belle said tentatively, tapping on a dingy gray door that might once have been painted white. "You in there? It's me—Belle. There's somebody here to see you. A lady, so don't you come wanderin' out with no clothes on, you hear?"

There was no reply. In the answering stillness of the

house, there was only a faint but insistent mechanical sound that Joanna assumed had to be coming from the bedroom air conditioner Belle had mentioned earlier.

Belle knocked on the door again. "Clyde?" she said insistently. "Listen here, you gotta wake up now. It's late. After three, but if you're very nice to me, I might consider whipping you up an omelet just because. Okay?"

Again there was no answer. Belle glanced apologetically over her shoulder in Joanna's direction. "Sorry about this. The man always did sleep like a damned log. Guess I'm gonna have'ta go give him a shake. If you'll just wait here . . ."

With that Belle opened the bedroom door. As soon as she did so, a chilly draft filtered into the room, carrying with it an evil-smelling vapor, one that totally obliterated all other odors. That putrid smell was one Sheriff Joanna Brady recognized and had encountered before—the awful scent of death and the rancid stench of decaying flesh. Without even seeing it, Joanna guessed what kind of horror lay beyond that open door, but for a time, Belle seemed oblivious.

"Clyde?" she said again. "Wake up, will you?"

Then, after a moment of silence with only the air conditioner humming in the background, the whole house was rent by a terrible, heart-wrenching, wordless shriek. Hearing it, Joanna cleared the living room in two long strides. When she reached the doorway, she stopped long enough to observe a scene that might have been lifted straight from some grade-B horror movie.

With her cigarette still in her mouth, Belle had crossed the room to where a male figure lay on an old-fashioned metal-framed bed with a sagging single mattress and no box springs. Just as she had predicted, the man was naked. Above him swirled a cloud of flies.

As Joanna stepped inside she saw Belle lift the man up by the shoulders. Belle began shaking him back and forth the way a heedless child might shake a loose-jointed Raggedy Andy doll. It was only then, when she raised the man off the pillow, that Joanna realized Clyde Philips wasn't entirely naked. A black plastic garbage bag covered his face and was fastened tightly around his neck with a belt.

Seeing the way the head flopped back and forth, there was no question in Joanna's mind that the bag had already completed its awful work. No amount of shaking would awaken him. Clyde Philips. He was dead.

"You gotta wake up, Clyde," Belle Philips was sobbing as she shook the body back and forth. "Don't joke with me now. It's not funny."

Fighting to control her gag reflexes, Joanna ventured far enough into the room to lay a restraining hand on the distraught woman's shoulder. "It's too late," she said gently. "Leave him be now, Belle. You'll have to leave him be."

Still holding her dead husband in a sitting position, Belle Philips swung around and glared at Joanna. The look on her face was one of such baleful rage that for an instant Joanna thought the other woman was about to take a swing at her. Warily trying to move out of range, she stepped back. And it was that one full step that saved her.

After a second or two, Belle seemed to lose interest in Joanna. Instead, she let go of the body. As the dead weight of Clyde Philips sank back onto the bed, she threw herself on top of it.

Watching from a few feet away, Joanna was mystified by the gesture. There was no sense to it. There was no way to tell if Belle hoped her smothering, all-enveloping embrace might warm the chilled body or somehow force breath back into the lifeless corpse. Suddenly, under the combined weight of both bodies, the frail old bedstead could bear no more. With a creak and a groan, it gave a lurch. Next, the two ends—head and foot alike—seemed to fold together like someone trying unsuccessfully to shuffle a gigantic deck of cards. Then the whole thing listed to one side, crashed to the floor, and disappeared as the wooden floor disintegrated beneath it.

Almost a minute went by before the dust cleared enough for Joanna to see what had happened. Coughing and squinting through tear-filled eyes, she found herself standing on the edge of a jagged wooden cliff. The aged floor, weakened by generations of hardworking termites, had simply collapsed into the earthen crawl space under the house.

Gingerly, Joanna edged over to the musty abyss and looked down. As the dust cleared, she could see a rough dirt surface five or six feet below. In the dim, dusty gloaming she could see Clyde—at least she caught a glimpse of one naked leg. She could also see the glowing end of the cigarette. Belle, however, was nowhere in sight.

"Belle?" Joanna called. "Are you there? Are you all right?"

No answer.

Joanna knew that the cool, moist earth underneath the house could very well be a haven for any number of unwelcome critters from black widow spiders to scorpions, centipedes, and worse. In her old life, Joanna Brady wouldn't have ventured into that crawl space on a bet. But now it was her job. Her duty. Belle Philips was down there, possibly badly hurt and most likely unconscious.

Looking around, Joanna located a bedside table that had been far enough from the hole that it hadn't tumbled in. Finding a floor joist that still seemed sturdy enough to hold her weight, Joanna lowered the table down as far as she could reach into the crawl space. She had to drop it the last foot or so, but fortunately, it landed upright and stayed that way. Thankful that her skirt and blazer were permanent press, she lowered herself onto the table and climbed down. Once in the crawl space, she spent a few minutes adjusting to the dim light so she could find Belle.

When the bed crashed through the floor, it had spilled Belle off and sent her rolling away from the hole. Fighting an attack of claustrophobia, Joanna finally located the unconscious woman lying with her head against the foundation. By then, Clyde Philips' ex-wife seemed to be coming around.

"Where am I?" she mumbled dazedly. "What happened?"

At the sound of Belle's voice, Joanna went limp with relief. She was grateful, too, for the woman's forgetfulness.

"You fell," Joanna said. "Don't move, because you may be hurt. I'm going for help."

Unfortunately, Belle Philips' blessed forgetfulness didn't last. "What about Clyde?" she demanded, reaching out and clutching at Joanna's arm before she managed to make her escape. "Where is he?"

"You can't help him, Belle," Joanna said firmly. "It's too late for him. I've got to get help for you. Promise me that you'll stay right here. That you won't move. Promise?"

There was a long moment of silence. "I promise," Belle said finally, and then she began to cry.

CHAPTER THREE

Two separate fire departments responded to the 9-1-1 call Joanna placed from a creaky rotary-dial phone on the wall in Clyde Philips' kitchen. One truck arrived from the Pomerene Volunteer Fire Department, as did another engine and an ambulance from Benson. One by one, Belle Philips' would-be rescuers disappeared into the house. Meanwhile, Sheriff Joanna Brady went out to the Blazer and radioed back to the department. Larry Kendrick, head of the department's dispatch unit, happened to be on duty.

"Put me through to Detective Carpenter," she said. Ernie Carpenter was her department's lead homicide investigator. "When I'm done speaking to him, I'll need to talk to Dick Voland as well."

"This isn't exactly your lucky day," Larry told her. "Ernie just went home with a migraine headache, and Deputy Voland is locked up in the conference room with the guys from the MJF."

The Multi-Jurisdiction Force was a group of officers from various jurisdictions that had banded together to deal with crime along or near the U.S./Mexican border. Cochise County's eighty-mile stretch of international line made Joanna's department the natural headquarters for such a group working what law enforcement had dubbed Cocaine Alley.

"What about Detective Carbajal?" Joanna asked. "Is he in?" Jaime Carbajal was Cochise County's newly minted homicide detective. His promotion from deputy to detective had happened on Sheriff Brady's watch.

"Jaime's in," Larry said. "I can patch you through to him."

"Good. By the time I finish with him, maybe you can pry Dick free from the MJF long enough for me to talk to him. We have a situation up here in Pomerene that could be either a homicide or a suicide."

"But I thought . . ."

"You thought what?"

"I understood the nine-one-one call to say that the incident in Pomerene involved a woman with injuries. Something about a bed falling through the floor."

"Right," Joanna said grimly, "but that's only half of it. She and the bed fell, all right, but so did a body. The dead man happened to be on the bed at the time."

"Oh, boy," Larry said. "Okay, then, here's Detective Carbajal."

Jaime came on the line. "What gives, Sheriff Brady?"

"I need you up here in Pomerene," Joanna told him. "ASAP. We've got a dead man with a garbage bag on his head and cinched tight around his neck." Looking down at her tan suit, Joanna caught a glimpse of the grime running down the front of her skirt, blouse, and blazer. "Not only is he dead," she added, "the bed he was on fell into the crawl space under his house. It's a mess down there, so whatever you do, don't show up wearing good clothes."

"Whereabouts in Pomerene?" Jaime asked.

"Four-two-six Rimrock. Do you know where that is?"

"Not exactly," Jaime said, "but I'll find it. Pomerene isn't that big, and Dispatch has the new county emergency map. Larry Kendrick can give me directions over the radio while I'm on my way. Will you still be on the scene when I get there, or do I need to get the details from you now?"

Joanna glanced first at her watch and then at the waiting ambulance. It was now almost twenty minutes since the six firemen and two EMTs had disappeared through Clyde Philips' front door. It seemed likely that they were having some difficulty strapping Belle's oversized body to a stretcher and then hauling her up out of the crawl space.

"Believe me," Joanna said, "I'll be here."

"Okay," Jaime said. "I'm on my way. You want me to send you back to Dispatch?"

"Please."

"I called Chief Deputy Voland out of his meeting. He's right here," Larry told her. "Hang on while I put him on the line."

"I understand you've got a homicide up there?" Dick Voland demanded at once. "Where? Who?"

"Clyde Philips, that gun dealer Frank was telling us about earlier this morning. I went by his house in Pomerene to see if he might have any idea who would be shooting up Alton Hosfield's Triple C with a fifty-caliber sniper rifle. The trouble is, Philips was already dead when I got here—dead in his bed."

"You're saying somebody killed him?" Voland asked.

"I don't know for sure. He had a garbage bag fastened around his neck, so it could be a homicide or a suicide, either one."

"Have you notified Doc Winfield yet?" Voland asked.

As of the first of July, Dr. George Winfield, former Cochise County Coroner, had taken on the revised title of

Cochise County Medical Examiner. And as of several months prior to that, by virtue of marrying the widowed Eleanor Lathrop, he had assumed the role of stepfather to Sheriff Joanna Brady. Under ordinary circumstances, Joanna's call to 9-1-1 would have been followed immediately by a call to Doc Winfield. Right that minute, however, the pair of newlyweds was out of town.

"He's away, remember?" Joanna said. "On his honeymoon."

"Oh, that's right. The cruise to Alaska. I keep forgetting. So I guess somebody needs to call Pima County and have them send in a pinch hitter."

"Bingo," Joanna said. "That was the arrangement. I was hoping we'd manage to skate through without needing to do that. Since we haven't, I'd like you to make the call. I'm stuck here in Pomerene for the duration, waiting for the EMTs to haul the victim's injured ex-wife out of the crawl space under the house."

"So what is it, then?" Voland asked. "Some kind of domestic?"

"I'm not sure what it is, although I don't think DV is too likely," Joanna told him. "Anyway, once you settle things with Pima County, I'll need you to do something else. Clyde has a locked gun shop out behind his house. It isn't necessarily part of the crime scene itself, and neither is his truck. We'll need to go through both of those in order to find out whether or not robbery is part of the motive for what happened here."

"You want me to stop off and pick up a warrant?"

"That's right."

"Okay, then," Voland replied. "I'll be there as soon as I can."

Just as Joanna ended the call, Clyde Philips' front door opened. First one and then another of the firemen emerged.

For more than a minute the two stood conferring, studying the door. The old-fashioned door was narrower than expected, and working Belle Philips' stretcher out through it was no easy task. It took several minutes of back-and-forthing before the EMTs finally managed to squeeze the heavily laden stretcher out onto the porch. As they loaded the gurney into the waiting ambulance, one of the firemen, red-faced and mopping grimy sweat from his brow, came over to where Joanna was standing. "How do you guys do it?" he demanded.

"Do what?" she asked.

"Stand the smell," he replied. "Do you get used to it, or what?"

Joanna shook her head. "I don't think anybody ever gets used to it."

The fireman shuddered. "Well, give me a fire any day of the week. In fact, give me two or three."

Just then the ambulance started to move. With siren blaring, it made a quick U-turn and started back up Rimrock. "Where are they taking her?" Joanna asked.

"University Medical Center in Tucson," the fireman replied. "One of the EMTs said he thought she probably broke both her hip and her shoulder. Although I'd say broken bones are the least of her problems."

"What's the matter?" Joanna asked, giving him a searching look. "You think she has internal injuries as well?"

The fireman—the name embroidered on his shirt pocket said "Lt. Spaulding"—shook his head. "Somebody said the dead guy was her husband, right?"

"Ex-husband," Joanna replied.

"So if she's the killer, her bones'll be the least of her troubles."

Moments before, Dick Voland had instantly assumed Clyde Philips' death had something to do with domestic

violence. Now Lt. Spaulding was making the same assumption. "What makes you say that?" Joanna asked.

Spaulding shrugged. "Isn't that the way it usually
works? Somebody gets murdered and the killer turns out to
be either the wife or the husband, or the ex-wife or ex-
husband."

Closing her eyes, Joanna recalled Belle Philips' inane
chatter as she headed into the bedroom, as well as her desperate attempts to awaken her presumably sleeping former
husband. Was it conceivable that Belle Philips was that accomplished an actress? Could she possibly have murdered
Clyde herself and then put on a such a flawless performance
when it came to finding his body a day or so later? As far
as Joanna was concerned, it didn't seem likely, but still those
preconceived notions—backed by statistics—carried a lot of
weight. There could be little doubt that when it came time
for a homicide investigation, Belle Philips would be a
prime suspect.

"Ex-wives do kill ex-husbands on occasion," Joanna conceded, "but I'm not at all sure that's what happened here."

Spaulding shrugged once more. "I read a lot of true
crime—just for entertainment. And I watch those forensics
shows on The Learning Channel. It's kind of a hobby of
mine. That's how I know about some of this stuff. I hope
we didn't do too much damage to your crime scene, Sheriff
Brady. We had a hell of a time lifting her up and out of
there."

"I'm sure it'll be fine," Joanna assured him.

"I guess we'll be on our way, then," he said. "It looks
to me as though the boys have pretty much gathered up all
the equipment. I have to keep on their cases to pick up all
their stuff—the bandage wrappers, plastic bags, and packag-
ing. Otherwise they just rip 'em and leave 'em."

Once the firemen had taken their trucks and left, Joanna

made her way back inside the house. She moved gingerly now, careful not to touch anything, even though she knew it was far too late for that. Despite her reassuring comment to Spaulding, she saw at once that damage to the crime scene was considerable.

For one thing, the entire floor, from the bedroom out through the front door, was covered with literally dozens of grimy footprints—hers included—left behind by dirt that had come up from the crawl space on the soles of shoes and on the firemen's heavy-duty boots. If Clyde Philips had been murdered, and if the murderer had left behind some trace evidence of a footprint, it would be gone now, obliterated by everyone else's tracks.

Standing in the doorway to the bedroom, fighting off the all-pervasive odor, Joanna was shocked to see that the hole in the floor was much larger than it had been when she left. At first she thought that maybe the firemen had used saws to enlarge the hole in order to facilitate maneuvering the stretcher through it. On closer examination of the jagged-edged break, she realized that more of the floor had given way under the combined weight of several firemen and the two EMTs. What was even more disturbing was the fact that the new breakage in the termite-infested wood had occurred at almost the same spot where Joanna herself had climbed in and out of the crawl space.

Seeing it now, Joanna realized how very near she had come to falling. Wanting to get to the injured woman, she had crawled down after her without taking the time to call for backup or even to notify 9-1-1. Had the floor collapsed under her then, both she and Belle might have been trapped in the crawl space for hours before anyone noticed or came to help. Joanna had a cell phone, but she had left it plugged in in the Blazer when she and Belle had gone into the house.

She was still berating herself for her stupidity when Detective Carbajal showed up behind her. "Jesus Christ!" he exclaimed, peering over her shoulder. "It looks like a war zone in here. What happened? Did somebody blow the place apart with a stick or two of dynamite?"

"Termites, not dynamite," Joanna answered. "What you see is the case of the collapsing bed. Once it broke, it went right through the floor, taking two people along with it."

Jaime grinned. "How old were these people?" he asked. "If the bed broke, they must have been getting it on."

Gradually Joanna had become accustomed to crime-scene black humor. That was one of the tools homicide cops used to maintain their sanity. In spite of herself, she smiled.

"It wasn't like that," she explained. "Clyde Philips was already dead when Belle Philips, his ex-wife, tried to get on the bed with him. She's not exactly a lightweight. Having both of them on the bed was more than the frame or the floor could handle. She went right through the floor with him and got hurt pretty bad in the process. The firemen just finished lifting her out a few minutes ago."

"That's where all the footprints came from?" Jaime asked. "From the firemen?"

Joanna nodded. "Mine are in there, too," she said.

Jaime busied himself taking notes. "Where is she now?"

"On her way to Tucson—University Medical Center."

"And the body?"

"As far as I know, nobody's touched it. Clyde is still down in the crawl space," Joanna said.

"From what Dispatch said, you and the ex-wife were the ones who found him?"

Joanna nodded again.

"What exactly were you doing here, Sheriff Brady?" Detective Carbajal asked. "Somebody call you, or did you just happen to be in the neighborhood?"

"No," Joanna said. "I came here on purpose—to talk to

Clyde Philips. There's a shop out back where he ran a gun dealership. I was hoping to find out whether he could put me in touch with some of his sniper-rifle customers."

"Because of the Triple C case?"

"That's right. I stopped by earlier, between two and three. His truck was here, just like it is now. When he didn't answer the door, I checked with his former wife to see if she could help me locate him. Belle and I came here together. She was sure he was sound asleep and just didn't hear my knock. Instead, it turned out he was already dead."

"And the bed?"

Joanna shrugged. "When she realized he was dead, she went haywire—hysterical. She piled onto the bed with him, and it broke."

"You said Philips was a gun dealer?"

"That's right. Registered and everything."

"Any chance of a robbery motive?"

"I already thought of that," she said. "Dick Voland's picking up a search warrant before he comes."

"Good." Jaime stuffed his notebook back in his pocket and prepared to enter the bedroom. First he donned both face mask and gloves. Then he removed a camera from his pocket, taking the first crime-scene shot from the doorway of the bedroom. Knowing how vital those photographs would be, Joanna stepped aside.

"I'll wait outside," she told him. "But remember, termites have turned most this floor into so much sawdust, so be careful."

With apparent unconcern, the young detective lined up his camera and took another shot. "Any idea when the victim was last seen alive?"

"None," Joanna replied. "His next-door neighbor—I don't know her name—is the one who told me he might be at his ex-wife's—at her cafe. That's why I went there looking for him. But once we found the body, I never had a chance to ask her when the last time was that she saw him."

"And the ex-wife didn't give you any kind of alibi?"

"No," Joanna said.

Making a deliberate circle around the perimeter of the room, Jaime clicked the camera again. "Don't worry," he said. "Either Ernie'll check her out or I will."

"Sheriff Brady?"

She turned to find Deputy Eduardo Sandoval standing behind her. Of all Joanna's deputies, Eddy Sandoval—a beefy man in his mid-to-late forties—was the one with whom she had the least personal contact. Because he both lived and worked in the far northwestern sector of the county, he was the most physically removed from her office. And when he came to Bisbee to drop off a prisoner or make a court appearance, Sandoval wasn't one to hang around the Cochise County Justice Complex shooting the breeze.

"Hi, there, Eddy," Joanna said. "How long ago did you get here?"

"Just now," he said. "Sorry it took me so long. I was up at Cascabel taking a missing-person report when this call came in. I got here as fast as I could."

"Missing person?" Joanna asked. "What missing person?"

"About this time yesterday afternoon, a lady wandered off from that oddball dude ranch just up the road from the Triple C," Eddy answered. "You know the place I mean— the ranch they've started calling Rattlesnake Crossing."

Joanna frowned. "Isn't that the dude ranch where all the guests dress up like Indians and camp outside?"

Sandoval nodded. "Right," he said. "That's the one."

"So who's missing?" Joanna asked. "One of the campers? The last thing we need about now is to have some tenderfoot who thinks she's a born-again Apache go wandering off in the desert. It's the middle of August, for God's sake. Depending on where she's from, she'll die of heatstroke before we can call in Search and Rescue."

"Her name's Katrina Berridge," Sandoval replied. "And she's not one of the guests. She's more of an employee, I guess. Employee or partner, I'm not sure which. She's the owner's sister. As I understand it, the missing woman and her husband work there at the ranch. Katrina handles paperwork—reservations, finances, payroll, that kind of thing. Her husband's the handyman—does a little of everything. According to him, his wife went out for a walk yesterday afternoon and never came back."

"Any trouble on the home front?" Joanna asked.

Sandoval shook his head. "Not that I could tell. At least, none that the husband happened to mention."

"If she wasn't driving a vehicle when she left, does anyone have an idea of where she might have gone?"

"Nobody knows for sure," Sandoval replied. "According to the husband, each afternoon Rattlesnake Crossing has sort of a free period. All the people pretty much go their separate ways for a time—a few hours. I guess they're all supposed to use that time to get back in touch with nature. Anyway, when dinnertime came around and Katrina didn't show up, people weren't too worried, because I guess she's done that before—gone out for a walk and stayed out later than the others, watching a sunset or a moonrise or something. When she still wasn't home this morning, though, her husband—his name's . . ." Sandoval paused long enough to consult his notes. "Dan . . . no, Daniel Berridge—he said he went looking for her. He claims she has some favorite hangouts up in the cliffs alongside the river. Mr. Berridge said he looked up there for her this morning, but he couldn't find any trace of her."

"Wait a minute," Joanna said. "Aren't those cliffs just on the west side of the river?"

"Yes," Sandoval nodded. "They are."

"And isn't Rattlesnake Crossing Ranch on the *other* side?"

Sandoval nodded. "That's right, too."

"The river's been running like crazy ever since that storm the day before yesterday. If Katrina Berridge was going over to play on the cliffs, how did she manage to cross the river?"

Eddy Sandoval shrugged. "That's what I asked her husband. He said maybe she swam."

"Or maybe she never crossed it at all," Joanna said. "Maybe, for some reason or another, he's interested in having us look in one place and not in another."

Eddy Sandoval frowned. "You're thinking maybe the husband had something to do with whatever happened to her?"

The irony wasn't lost on Joanna. She had been disturbed by the fact that everyone seemed fully prepared to jump to the conclusion that Belle Philips had murdered Clyde. Now here she was, jumping to the same kinds of conclusions about Daniel Berridge.

"I'm not saying that, one way or the other," Joanna replied. "But if we're bringing in Search and Rescue . . ." She paused. "We *have* called them in, haven't we?"

He nodded. "That's right. They should be on their way."

"Good," she said. "When Search and Rescue gets here, or when Dick Voland does, tell whoever's in charge of the search that I want them to look on *both* sides of the San Pedro. You got that?"

"Got it."

"Where are you meeting them?"

"I told Dispatch I was coming here and that Search and Rescue should catch up with me here. In the meantime, is there anything else you need me to do, Sheriff Brady? I'll be glad to help out."

"As a matter of fact, there is," Joanna told him. "You stand right here in this doorway and watch Detective Carbajal like a hawk. That floor he's walking on is made of so much Swiss cheese. If it caves in under him, I want to know about it right away. Now, I'm going to go outside and start talking to the neighbors. We need to find out where and when's the last time someone saw Clyde Philips alive."

CHAPTER FOUR

Joanna soon discovered that when it came to Clyde Philips' neighbors, there weren't all that many for her to talk to. There were three other houses on the short, unpaved block, but two of them were empty. The only other one that was occupied belonged to Sarah Holcomb, the cane-wielding lady who had directed Joanna to Belle's restaurant.

Minutes after leaving Eddy Sandoval to watch over Jaime, Joanna found herself in Mrs. Holcomb's old-fashioned living room, seated on an overstuffed sofa in front of a doily-covered coffee table. It turned out that getting Sarah Holcomb to talk was easy; separating important details from the old woman's meandering conversation was considerably more difficult.

"I never saw a thing out of line," Sarah declared in answer to one of Joanna's questions. "Course, I was gone a good part of the weekend. Went up to Tucson to see the doctor and visit my daughter and son-in-law," she said. "I left about midmorning on Sunday and didn't come back until just a little while before you showed up this afternoon.

My doctor's appointment was yesterday. Anymore, seeing a
doctor just takes the starch right out of me. I don't like to
make that drive on the same day as my appointment, not
at my age. I'm eighty-three, by the way, and still driving,"
she added. "And I'm proud to tell you that I've never had
an accident or a ticket, either one."

"When's the last time you saw Clyde, then?" Joanna
asked.

Sarah frowned. "Musta been last week sometime, although I don't rightly remember when. He wasn't the best
neighbor I ever had. A real ornery cuss, if you ask me. When
Belle finally up and left him a few years back, I thought it
was high time. Belle, now, she's all wool and a yard wide—
maybe even more than a yard wide, come to think of it."
Sarah grinned at the joke. When Joanna didn't respond, the
woman resumed her story.

"Anyways, what went on between them was none of my
business, although I always did think Clyde took terrible
advantage of the poor woman. Belle never was much of a
looker, and ol' Clyde always acted like he done her a great
big favor by marryin' her. I can tell you that the man never
lifted a finger around the place long as he had her to do all
the cookin' and cleanin'. You'da thought she signed up to
be his slave 'stead of his wife. Poor Belle'd spend all week
workin'—she used to cook up three meals a day over to that
rest home in Benson. You know which one I mean—the one
that had that electrical fire and burned to the ground a
few years back. That's where Belle worked, right up until
the place burned down. As I remember it, she got burned
in that fire, too, somehow. When all was said and done, I
think she got some kind of little insurance settlement.
Pro'ly wasn't all that much, but it was enough, and it was
money that belonged to her, not him. The way I heard it,

that's what she used to open that little doughnut place of hers.

"Anyways, gettin' back to how things were afore that. Here she was working five or six days a week. But still, come Sunday afternoon, she'd be out there in the yard pushin' that big old mower around, while Clyde'd be sittin' there on his backside on that porch of his like King Tut hisself, tellin' her what part she mighta missed and where she maybe needed to go over it again. If he'da been my husband, I think I woulda found a way to drive that mower right smack over his big toe. Maybe that woulda shut him up."

"About the last time you saw Clyde . . ." Joanna urged.

Ignoring Joanna's polite hint, Sarah continued her tirade. "On the other hand, I always say it takes two to tango. Much as I'd like to, I can't lay the whole thing at Clyde's door. Not all of it. I figure if'n a woman sets out to spoil a man like that, she pretty much deserves what she gets. You can't hardly blame the man for takin' advantage. And Belle's no fast learner. Matter of fact, believe it or not, even after all these years, she's still doin' Clyde's wash. Up till a few months ago, every once in a while he'd fill that camper shell of his plumb full up with dirty clothes and drag the whole mess over to her place. Next thing you know, he'd be comin' back with it all washed, ironed, and folded neat as you please. Lately, though, Belle's been pickin' it up and bringin' it back. Some people never do learn."

Joanna remembered what Belle had said about not allowing Clyde to run a tab for his meals. Maybe the woman had turned doing her ex-husband's laundry into a money-making enterprise as well. Considering the dirty clothing scattered all over the dead man's house, Clyde must have been closing in on another laundry trip when he died.

"Mrs. Holcomb," Joanna urged again, "about last week. Did you see any strange comings or goings?"

"Well, Clyde always did have people in and out at odd times of day, although that's slowed down quite a bit lately. It wasn't like he ran a store with reg'lar hours or anythin' like that. And then sometimes he'd go on the road and be gone for a week or more. I always tried to keep an eye on things whilst he was gone that way—on his house, I mean— not 'cause I liked the man so much, but just 'cause it was a neighborly sort of thing to do."

"Could you give me the names of any of the people who might have dropped by?" Joanna asked.

"His customers, you mean?"

Joanna nodded. "We're going to need to speak to as many of them as possible."

"Why's that?"

Joanna sighed. "Solving a homicide is a lot like unraveling a knot of yarn. You have to take each single strand and follow it all the way to the end. As far as an investigation is concerned, all the people who knew the victim are separate strands of yarn. We'll be talking to all of them—friends, neighbors, customers—the same way I'm talking to you."

"I see." Sarah became thoughtful. "When is it that you think old Clyde croaked out?" she asked.

"Sometime over the weekend," Joanna replied. "We won't have more detailed information until after the autopsy. That's one of the reasons I'm trying to learn when you last saw him alive."

"You mean he didn't just die last night or this morning?"

"I'm not sure. Why?"

Sarah grimaced and pursed her wrinkled lips. "I pro'ly shouldn't even say this," she said, "but Belle was here bright and early Sunday morning when I was getting ready to leave for Tucson. I was mighty surprised she come by at that hour. Clyde was one of them night owls and a real late sleeper as a consequence. Right after Belle moved out on him, that just got worse and worse. Like he got his days and nights all turned around. He partied a lot back then. When he wasn't workin', he'd stay up most of the night, drinkin' and carryin' on; then he wouldn't never show his face much before early afternoon. The partyin's pretty much dropped off the last year or two, but he still slept real late. Them kind of habits is tough to break."

"Do you remember what time it was when Belle came by?" Joanna asked.

"Not exactly," Sarah returned. "But it musta been right around nine o'clock or so. I remember I was out gettin' my clothes in off the line. I got up early to wash up a few things to take along to Tucson. I musta put 'em out on the line about seven—I put 'em in as soon as I woke up. I wake up at six-thirty on the dot. Always have, and I put on the coffee and turned on the clothes washer about that same time. The clothes had been out long enough to dry, and I wanted to get 'em packed and in the car so I could hit the road before the sun got much hotter. That's one of the bad things about gettin' old. Just can't take the heat the way I used to. It must have been about eight-thirty then. Maybe a quarter to nine. I'da thought she'd be on her way to church by then."

"What was Belle doing when you saw her?" Joanna asked. "Anything out of the ordinary?"

"Nope. She drove up and parked that big ol' Cadillac of hers right there behind Clyde's truck. Belle's car is so big that I'm always surprised it makes it through that narrow little gate. Once it's inside, it takes up half the driveway. Anyway, Belle couldn't have been inside the house more than a minute or two, because I was just rollin' my clothes basket back into the house when she came tearin' out of the house and took off again."

"You didn't talk to her?"

"No," Sarah said. "And that wasn't like her—not stopping off long enough to say hello or chew the fat. Didn't give much thought to it, though. Figured maybe she was on her way somewhere or had her mind on somethin' else and didn't even see me standin' out there in—"

Stopping abruptly in mid-sentence, Sarah pursed her thin lips again. "You don't suppose . . . ?" Then, as if in answer to her unfinished question, she shook her head. "Certainly not," she announced. "It's not possible."

"What's not possible?" Joanna asked.

"That Belle had somethin' to do with all this—with what happened to Clyde. No, I've known the woman all her life. She wouldn't hurt a flea. Fact of the matter is, some of the neighbors and I used to laugh at her when we'd see her move things out of the house—bugs and centipedes and such—rather than kill 'em. Surely someone who literally wouldn't hurt a fly couldn't kill a person, could they?"

For the third time in the space of a half-an-hour, someone had raised the possibility that Belle Philips was somehow responsible for her former husband's death.

"That's why we have homicide detectives," Joanna said soothingly. "To find out whether something like that *is* possible."

All the while Sarah had been droning on and on, Joanna had been paying close attention to what was happening outside the lace-curtained windows and beyond the two cottonwood trees that shaded Sarah's front yard. Sitting where she was, the sheriff had an almost unobstructed view of the street. In ten minutes' time, a series of cars had come and gone as Mike Wilson's Search and Rescue detail assembled, collected Deputy Sandoval and then left again. Dick Voland's Bronco had also pulled up. It was parked directly behind Joanna's Blazer. Voland and one of the deputies had marched off toward Clyde's shop at the back of the property. Realizing her chief deputy must have arrived with a search warrant in hand and trusting that he knew what he was doing, Joanna hadn't bothered to traipse after them.

Now, though, she watched as a van with Pima County's logo emblazoned on its door pulled up and parked behind Dick's Bronco. The pinch-hitting medical examiner had arrived from Tucson, so Joanna decided to go.

She stood up and held out her hand. "Thank you so much, Mrs. Holcomb. You've been a great help. One of my detectives or I may need to talk to you again, but in the meantime, I'll have to be going."

Rather than taking Joanna's proffered hand, Sarah simply stared at it without moving. "If I'da known where all this was headed . . ." she said, "that you might end up goin' after Belle . . . I'da kept my big mouth shut. That's what I shudda done."

"Mrs. Holcomb," Joanna said reassuringly, "depending on the actual time of death, what you've told me may or may not have any bearing on this case. Regardless, let me assure you that you've done the right thing by telling us everything you know."

Sarah Holcomb shook her head. "I always did talk way too much," she muttered morosely. "From the time I was just a little tyke. You'da thought that by the time a woman gets to be my age she'd know better."

"But—" Joanna began again.

Sarah waved her aside. "No," she said. "You go on now. I don't want to talk no more. Not to you and not to nobody else, either."

Feeling as though she'd botched things somehow, Joanna let herself out the front door. She hurried back to Clyde

Philips' house in time to see a tall, beefy woman with bleached blond hair disappear through the front door.

Joanna arrived at the bedroom doorway as the woman slammed a heavy brown valise to the floor just inside the room. Planting both hands on her hips, she turned to survey her surroundings. "I'm Fran Daly of the Pima County Medical Examiner's office," she told Jaime Carbajal. "*Doctor* Fran Daly. Who are you?"

At five-four, Joanna couldn't see over Dr. Daly's broad shoulder, but she peered around the other woman in time to catch sight of a grimy Jaime Carbajal using a metal ladder to climb up and out of the crawl space. Gingerly, he eased himself onto what seemed to be a relatively stable part of the bedroom floor.

"I'm Detective Carbajal," he replied. "I'm a homicide detective with the Cochise County Sheriff's Department."

"All right. So where's the body?"

Jaime nodded back toward the hole. "Down there," he said. "The victim was lying on a bed that collapsed and fell through the floor into the crawl space."

"Great," Fran muttered irritably. "Just what I need. The body's fallen into the basement. What else? It looks like a damned army's been in and out of this room. What the hell happened here?"

"Well," Jaime explained, "a woman fell through the floor right along with the victim. As I understand it, she was seriously hurt in the fall. We had to call for help. All told, it took six men—four firemen and two EMTs to get her out—and—"

"You're telling me six men have been tracking through my evidence? Who the hell's the dimwit who authorized that? The least those clowns could have done was worn booties over their shoes so they wouldn't have left these god-awful tracks all over the place. Are you responsible for this mess, Detective Carbajal?"

Joanna couldn't see the superior sneer Fran Daly leveled at Jaime Carbajal, but she heard it well enough.

"No," Joanna said quietly. "I am."

Dr. Fran Daly spun around and glared at her. Built with all the grace and delicacy of a tank, she wore a cowboy shirt and jeans. Her only pieces of jewelry were a man's watch and an immense, turquoise-encrusted silver belt buckle on a wide leather belt.

"And who might you be?" Fran Daly demanded.

"My name's Joanna Brady."

"Well," Fran said, "I was directed to report to someone named Voland—Chief Deputy Richard Voland. Where's he?"

"Outside," Joanna said. "Chief Deputy Voland is busy at the moment, but you're welcome to talk to me."

"What are you?" Fran Daly asked. "His deputy?"

"As a matter of fact," Joanna said deliberately, "it's the other way around. Dick Voland is my deputy. I'm *Sheriff* Joanna Brady, Dr. Daly. And I'm also the person—I believe you used the term 'dimwit'—who made the decision that it was more important to effect a timely rescue of a seriously injured woman than it was to tiptoe around preserving evidence. When it comes to handling injury situations, the possibility of losing some trace evidence must take a backseat to emergency medical care. What was done here seemed like a reasonable trade-off to me. If I had it to do over, I'm sure that I'd reach the exact same conclusion."

Fran Daly sighed and rolled her eyes. "All right then," she said. "Just show me where the body is and let me get started. And for God's sake, somebody turn off the damned air-conditioner."

With that she picked up her valise from its spot in the doorway and started into the room.

"I'd be careful if I were you," Joanna warned. "The floor in here collapsed because the whole thing's been rotted out by termites. Underneath the roll flooring, what's left of the wood is little more than powdery cardboard."

Once again the medical examiner swung around to face Joanna. "Excuse me, Sheriff Brady," she snapped. "My boss sent me here to do this job because I happen to be a trained technician, the senior trained technician in our department. I don't know what that means in *your* bailiwick, but in mine it means that I know what I'm doing. It also means that I'm qualified to do my job without any unnecessary supervision from you or anyone else. So if you'll excuse me—"

Reaching the center of the room, she slammed the heavy valise down once more. The thud of the case on the floor was immediately followed by a loud, ominous crack. What had appeared to be flat flooring up to then tilted sharply downward. In slow motion, the valise began to move, sliding down a ski slope of worn linoleum toward the jagged-edged and ever-expanding hole into the crawl space.

As the bag of equipment slid away from her, Fran Daly reached down and made a desperate grab for it, but she missed. Eluding her fingertips, the still upright valise slipped out of reach and then dropped majestically from view. When it landed in the dirt of the darkened crawl space some five feet below, it did so with a distinct splat—one that included the muffled tinkle of breaking glass.

"Shit!" Fran Daly exclaimed.

Joanna had a sudden, vivid remembrance of her father, D. H. Lathrop. "What goes around comes around" had always been one of his favorite expressions. Those words came back to his daughter now with such clarity and meaning that it was all Joanna could do to keep from laughing.

With some difficulty she managed to contain herself. "If this is your idea of crime-scene preservation, Dr. Daly," Joanna said sternly, "then it would appear supervision is very much in order. I'll leave Detective Carbajal here to keep an eye on you. He can give you any assistance you might need."

Glancing at the young detective, Joanna saw that he was having almost as much trouble keeping a straight face as she was. "Is that all right with you, Detective Carbajal?" she asked.

Sobering quickly, he nodded. "Sure thing, Sheriff Brady," he managed. "I was just on my way out to the van to pick up some lights. I've been taking pictures this whole time, but it's really dark down there in the crawl space. If Dr. Daly and I are going to do any kind of meaningful work, we'll need more light. If that's okay with you, that is." He turned deferentially to Dr. Daly.

She waved him aside. "If you say we need lights, we probably do. Go ahead and get them."

"And Sheriff Brady is right about this floor, Dr. Daly," Jaime added. "It's extremely treacherous. In fact, I don't think it would take much for the whole house to cave in to the crawl space. That being the case, on your way over to the ladder, it might be wise if you stick as close as possible to the outside wall. And if you can wait long enough for me to come back with the lights, I'll bring along a couple of hard hats as well. We probably shouldn't be down there without them."

"All right, all right," Fran Daly grumbled reluctantly. "I'll wait right here until you get back."

Smiling to herself, Joanna backed away from the door. "I'll leave and let you two get to it, then," she said sweetly.

"And if you need anything else, Chief Deputy Voland and I will be right outside."

Out on the porch, Jaime Carbajal convulsed with laughter. "What planet did *she* come from?" he demanded when he was finally able to talk.

"Pima County," Joanna replied. "As long as Doc Winfield's out of town, we're stuck with her."

"Let's hope it's for this case only," Detective Carbajal said. "I wouldn't want to make a career of it."

Joanna nodded. "Me, neither."

"Did you see the expression on her face when she finally figured out that you were in charge?"

"I saw it, all right," Joanna said. "Unfortunately, I don't think I handled the situation in the best possible fashion. Dr. Daly got under my skin almost as much as I got under hers. While you're down in the crawl space working with her, Jaime, see what you can do to smooth things out."

"I'll try," Jaime Carbajal replied cheerfully, "but I'm not making any promises. From what I saw of Fran Daly, she doesn't look like the kind of person where smoothing is going to work."

"Sheriff Brady?"

Joanna turned to see who had called. Lance Pakin, the deputy she had seen arrive with Dick Voland, came jogging toward her from the back of Clyde Philips' property.

"Did you get the door open?" Joanna asked.

"Yes, ma'am," Pakin replied. "But Chief Deputy Voland wants you to come there right away."

The urgency in Pakin's voice made Joanna's heart fall. She had visions of another previously undiscovered victim rotting on the gun-shop floor. "Not another body," she said.

"No," Pakin said. "Nothing like that."

"What, then?"

"They're empty."

"What's empty."

"The shop out back and the truck, too. If either one of them used to have guns in them, they don't now. Chief Deputy Voland thinks you'd better come take a look."

CHAPTER FIVE

Compared to the harsh August heat outside, the interior of Clyde Philips' fortresslike gun shop was downright cold. Consisting of two rooms, the shop had a large showroom and a back room with a door marked OFFICE. The place was lit by ceiling-mounted shop lights. The outside walls of the showroom area were lined with glass-enclosed, locking gun racks. Now all of those glass-doored cabinets stood wide open, with the slots inside them totally empty. In the middle of the room stood a series of glass-topped display-case counters, also open and empty. In the dust left behind on the glass shelving were the imprints of missing handguns and holsters as well.

Seeing the ghostly shadows of those missing weapons, Joanna felt a wave of gooseflesh spread across her body. That icy reaction owed far more to simple dread than it did to the droning presence of Clyde Philips' air-conditioning unit up on the shop's roof.

Joanna glanced away from the missing guns and caught Dick Voland staring at her with a look of undisguised longing on his face. In the months since the collapse of Dick Voland's marriage, Joanna's working relationship with her chief deputy had become more and more complicated. At this point, she would have welcomed a dose of Voland's early and outspoken opposition, rather than the puppylike (if unspoken) devotion with which he now sometimes regarded her. Clearly, the fifteen years' difference in their ages and the fact that his feelings weren't reciprocated made no difference.

Joanna had no quarrel with the man's professionalism. He had never once said anything out of bounds. In the easy give-and-take of the office, he was fine. In public, in fact, he still tended to be overbearing and patronizing on occasion. But in private, unguarded moments like this one, the man wore his heart on his sleeve. Joanna sympathized with him, but she needed a working, full-fledged chief deputy far more than she did a lovesick schoolboy suffering from an unrequited crush.

Joanna's eyes met his over the top of one of the display cases. Quickly, Dick Voland looked away. "How many guns do you figure walked out of here?" she asked.

Blushing visibly in the sallow light, he shrugged his shoulders. "No way to tell for sure," he said gruffly. "But even if the cases held only one or two guns apiece, it's way too many to have them running around loose. They would still amount to enough guns to supply a small army."

"Peachy," Joanna said. "Any sign of a break-in?"

"None whatsoever," Voland replied in a brisk, business-like fashion. "Whoever did this came in with a key to the front door and with keys to all the individual cabinets as well. None of the locks have been damaged in the slightest. Not only that, whoever did it also knew he or she had plenty of time. This place was cleaned out in a methodical and very thorough manner, probably in the middle of the night and probably in dead silence. Any kind of noise or breakage might have aroused suspicion."

"To say nothing of Sarah Holcomb," Joanna added.

Voland frowned. "What was that?"

"Never mind," Joanna told him. "What about paperwork or a computer, maybe? Any kind of customer lists?"

"Not so far."

"What about inventory, sales, or billing information? If we had some of those details, we'd know where to start in order to estimate what's actually missing."

"That could be a problem. Come take a look," Voland said, gesturing toward the office door. "It's a combination office/storeroom, and from the looks of things, there's not much left there, either."

Joanna walked as far as the office doorway and stopped. Inside, the drawers to the file cabinet lay scattered around the room, spilling loose papers on the floor in all directions. Other drawers still sat in place in file cabinets, but they appeared to be completely empty, as though someone had simply dumped the contents into a bag or box and carted them away.

"If there's been a conscious effort to destroy paper trails, we could be dealing with some kind of insurance fraud," Joanna suggested, musing more to herself than to anyone else.

"It could be," Voland agreed.

"We'll need to dust the whole place for prints," she added, glancing at her chief deputy.

"Right," he said. "I've already asked Patrol to send over anyone they can spare to help out with crime-scene investigation. It probably won't do much good, though. I have an idea whoever did this was probably smart enough to wear gloves."

Joanna looked around the room again. "What about letting ATF in on this? Considering the possible number of weapons involved, we probably should."

As expected, any suggestion of involving another jurisdiction, especially a federal agency like Alcohol, Tobacco, and Firearms, elicited an immediate frown of annoyance from Richard Voland. An old-timer with the department, the chief deputy jealously guarded all possible jurisdictional boundaries.

"Why include them until we have to?" he asked.

Through working with the MJF and with Adam York of the Drug Enforcement Agency, Joanna was coming to understand that in the new world of law enforcement, cooperation was the name of the game. *I wonder if anyone's ever explained that fact of life to the lady from the Pima County Medical Examiner's office,* Joanna wondered wryly.

"Their guys run as much risk of going head to head with whoever took these guns as ours do," she said. "So even though reporting it may not be strictly required, we're going to tell them all the same. Out of courtesy, if nothing else."

"All right, all right," Voland agreed grudgingly. "I'll take care of it once we get back to the office. So tell me, what all's going on back at the house?"

"For one thing, Detective Carbajal is working with that lady buzz saw from Pima County, Dr. Fran Daly," Joanna said. "Incidentally, since Dr. Daly fully expected to report to you, she wasn't at all pleased to have me involved."

"I'm sorry," Voland apologized. "When I was talking to the woman on the phone, I told her as plain as day what the deal was. Where she got the idea that I was in charge, I don't—"

Joanna cut him off in mid-apology. "It doesn't matter. What Dr. Daly did or didn't think makes no difference. Whatever her misapprehensions, we've worked them out."

Trying to change the subject, Joanna glanced around the room and said:

"It looks to me as though poor old Clyde was a far better shop owner than he was a housekeeper. The house is a pigsty. You maybe wouldn't want to eat off the floor in here, but it's a whole lot cleaner than the house was. With the added advantage that the shop feels like it's built on a concrete slab."

At once Voland turned solicitous. "You didn't get hurt when the floor collapsed, did you? Even with an injured woman down there, you never should have climbed down there by yourself without waiting for backup."

Cops are always concerned about the well-being of other cops. Had there been someone else present, Voland's comments probably would have passed unnoticed and unremarked. Unfortunately, Joanna knew the man too well. She read the worried look of concern in his eye; heard the undiluted caring in his voice. Not wanting to make things worse, Joanna decided to treat the subject lightly.

"The only thing hurt is my pride," she said, reaching out in another futile attempt to brush some of the grime from her skirt and blazer. "Ernie Carpenter's always on my case about grunging around crime scenes in good clothes. My problem is, I just can't seem to take a hint."

"You'll catch on eventually," Voland said.

Ignoring the slight but unmistakable quaver in the man's voice, Joanna tried to turn the conversation back to business. "Speaking of catching on, how about bringing me up-to-date on what's been happening back in the office? I've been out of the department all afternoon. Anything else interesting going on?"

"We found the trucker," Voland said. "The trucker and his truck, both."

"What trucker?" Joanna asked with a frown.

"Remember that naked hitchhiker from last night, the one we didn't catch?" Joanna nodded. "Well," Voland continued, "she may have been naked, but it turns out she wasn't alone. A guy in an eighteen-wheeler picked her up and drove her as far as that rest area east of San Simon. The driver and the girl were up in the over-cab sleeper and just getting it on when the girl's accomplice burst in on them. The two of them held the driver up at gunpoint. They took all his cash and credit cards. Afterward, they hogtied him with duct tape, drove him as far as Portal, and left him there—stark naked, miles from anywhere. Then the two of them drove the poor guy's truck as far as Lordsburg, New Mexico, where they abandoned it at a truck stop."

"So the trucker's all right?"

Joanna had learned that talking cases with Dick Voland always seemed to help put the proper distance back between them. This time was no exception. The chief deputy grinned at her. "Same as you," he said. "The only thing hurt is his pride and some missing hair where the tape pulled it out. He managed to get loose and walk as far as Mabel Lofgren's place. She keeps a collection of men's clothing around just in case somebody shows up who might need them."

"You mean, in case a passing UDA showed up and happened to need work clothes," Joanna remarked. In INS circles, the Widow Lofgren was notorious. Mabel had been cited countless times for employing undocumented aliens. No one was sure exactly how she did it, but she always somehow managed to skate free of the charges.

"In this case, though, it was probably a good thing that she had those extra clothes and shoes. I sent Deputy Hollicker out to interview both her and the trucker. According to Dave, by the time the guy could get to a phone and call his bank, the bandits had already used his ATM card to lift a chunk of money out of his account. And they were going through his credit cards like a dose of salts."

"Any other incidents reported with the same kind of MO?" Joanna asked.

Voland nodded. "I'm afraid there are. Sheriff Trotter, over in Hidalgo County, New Mexico, claims this is the third one his department has seen this month. So far no one's been hurt, but with handguns involved . . ."

"It's only a matter of time," Joanna finished.

"That's right," Voland said.

"Do we have a description?"

"Yes. Since the other two incidents both happened on Trotter's watch, he's talking about having Identi-Kit sketches done for all three. He said he'll pass them along to us."

"Good," Joanna said. "When he does, I'll have Frank Montoya make sure those pictures are posted at every truck stop and rest area in Cochise County. Pima County, too, for that matter."

"Good idea."

"And what about the missing woman up at Rattlesnake Crossing? Have you heard anything from Search and Rescue?"

Voland shook his head. "Not so far," he said. "One of us should probably go up there as soon as possible to see how things are progressing."

"I will," Joanna volunteered. "That was where I was headed to begin with. With everything that's happened this afternoon, I still haven't had a chance to talk to either Alton Hosfield or Martin Scorsby."

"Better you than me," Dick Voland said. "If those two are going to start taking potshots at one another, I'm likely to try knocking some sense into them first and asking questions later. Actually, if you want to head over there now, I can stay here and supervise the crime-scene guys."

Joanna thought about it, but not for long. "You can also oversee Fran Daly," she added with a smile. "Compared to dealing with her, Scorsby and Hosfield should be duck soup."

The sun was dropping behind the Little Rincons as Joanna headed north from Pomerene along the San Pedro. The angle of the setting sun exaggerated the jutting angles and deep crevices in the black-shadowed cliffs to the west of the river. She remembered her instructor in a college-level class in Arizona Geology explaining how three different periods of down cutting had dug three separate levels of terraces along both sides of the San Pedro, creating two matching sets of steep canyon walls. At some time in the distant past—a time of supermonsoons when llamas and turtles had populated a far wetter Arizona landscape—a massive flood had washed away the entire eastern side of the canyon. Left behind, the cliffs to the west still thrust skyward, but their rugged outline was nothing more than a muted echo of the same natural forces that had carved the monumental Grand Canyon.

The rough brown cliffs stood out that much more due to the striking contrast between them and the unaccustomed greenery on the steep flanks of hillside beneath them. Water had been so plentiful that summer that even in the high heat of mid-August, the hillsides were dressed in lush green robes of grass and waist-high weeds.

As Joanna drove north, she turned her thoughts from one case to the other. In Cochise County, crimes involving gunshot livestock were fairly commonplace. Ordinary murders—the kind of crime where people kill people—usually occurred among folks who were known to one another. Killers and victims often turned out to be relatives, lovers or ex-lovers, former partners, or former friends. When it came to the unauthorized slaughter of livestock, Joanna had learned that was generally a stranger-to-stranger kind of crime. That was especially true during hunting season when good-old-boy city-slickers came down from Phoenix and Tucson to shoot up everything on four legs and occasionally a few things on two legs as well.

Losing a few head of cattle meant a financial loss, but to a farmer or rancher of Alton Hosfield's standing, the loss of two cows would be little more than an annoyance. The loss of an irrigation pump, however, especially at this time of year, could very well mean financial disaster. *Any other year but this one,* Joanna thought. *So why bother shooting up the pump now? What's the point?*

Joanna remembered a long-ago case in which her father, then Sheriff D. H. Lathrop, had dealt with a similar situation. A pump dealer from Willcox had lost patience with a melon farmer who had fallen behind in making payments. Two weeks before melons were due to be harvested, the pump dealer had gone to the melon farm to repossess his equipment. His wife, armed with a high-powered rifle, had ridden shotgun on that ill-fated trip. Once at the farm, the well dealer had hooked a come-along around the pump and was preparing to pull it out of the well when the farmer showed up with his own gun. The incident had ended with the farmer and the pump dealer's wife both dead of gunshot wounds and the pump dealer shipped off to the state penitentiary in Florence on two charges of second-degree murder.

Such a tragic outcome was exactly what D. H. Lathrop's daughter was trying to prevent. The Hosfields and the Scorsbys weren't exactly the Hatfields and the McCoys, but with unknown persons running around armed with a fifty-caliber sniper rifle, they were close enough.

Twenty minutes later, just north of Sierra Blanca Canyon, Joanna pulled off onto the washboarded private dirt lane that led to Martin Scorsby's Pecan Plantation. The road snaked between two fields planted with lush, leafy, twenty-foot-tall trees. Winding up into the low foothills of the Winchester Mountains, Joanna found the roadway teeth-jarringly rough.

At the end of the primitive track, however, Joanna discovered a modern white stucco building with a red-tiled roof nestled inside a grove of towering cottonwoods. Seeing the house for the first time, as well as the manicured grounds surrounding it, Joanna was amazed to discover a California-style mansion plunked down in the middle of the Arizona desert. It always surprised her to find someone going to all the trouble and expense of living in the lap of luxury in the dead middle of nowhere at the far end of an almost impassable dirt road. Since there weren't any nearby neighbors to impress, what was the point of all that conspicuous consumption? Joanna's own modest home on High Lonesome Ranch had a lot more to do with old-fashioned, hard-scrabble farming and ranching than it did with some insurance company's overly generous golden handshake to a departing executive.

Martin Scorsby himself came to the gate of his well-manicured yard to greet her. Dressed in white shorts, socks, and shoes and with a cockily brimmed hat perched on his head, Scorsby looked as though he had just stepped off a tennis court. His spotless attire made Joanna painfully aware of the gray crawl-space grime on her own clothing.

"What can I do for you?" Scorsby asked.

"I'm Sheriff Brady," Joanna said, stepping out of the marked Blazer and showing him her badge. "Do you have a minute?"

Scorsby glanced at his watch. "Not much more than that," he said, standing just inside the gate to the yard and making no move to open it. "What do you want?"

Without having had anything to drink since her iced tea at Daisy's hours earlier, Joanna would have welcomed an invitation to come inside and have something to drink—iced tea or even water. If anyone had attempted to teach this boorish, newly transplanted Califorian the rudiments of Arizona-style hospitality, the lessons had not yet taken root.

"I came to talk to you about what went on over at the Triple C last night—"

"I already talked to your deputy," Scorsby interrupted brusquely. "Sandoval or Sanchez or whatever the hell his name is. I told him I had nothing whatsoever to do with that incident. I also told him that any further discussion of same would have to be conducted through my attorney."

Martin Scorsby may have expected Joanna to retreat in the face of that first volley, but she did not. "I'm here to help rather than make any kind of accusations," she said evenly. "And to listen," she added. "If I'm not mistaken, this isn't the first time we've had similar problems in this particular neighborhood."

Taking off the little white hat, Scorsby glowered at her while running a handkerchief across his perspiring brow. "Yes, yes, yes. I know I *said* that I'd shoot Hosfield's damn cattle if they ever came near my trees again. I said it and I meant it, too. But they haven't—come within a hundred yards of my orchard, that is. The electric fence I installed around the place is doing wonders at keeping the cattle out. Deer, too, for that matter."

In the eighteen-eighties, a pioneer rancher named Henry Hooker had run huge herds of cattle on a thirty-square-mile spread that had started somewhere near the current boundaries of Martin Scorsby's Pecan Plantation. To an old-timer like Henry Hooker, someone who had specialized in moving his livestock on and off federal land at will, the idea of barbed-wire fencing would have been anathema. Joanna smiled, thinking he probably wouldn't have liked electric fencing, either.

"Mr. Scorsby," Joanna said patiently, "I'm not implying that you're in any way responsible for what happened at the Triple C. What I am saying, however, is that right now, with feelings running so high, it's important to keep things in perspective."

"What 'things' do you mean?" Scorsby asked.

The Ten Commandments, Joanna thought. *Starting with "Love thy neighbor."* She said, "I don't want this to escalate into a range war."

"A range war!" Scorsby exclaimed. "Are you kidding? Didn't those go out with *High Noon?*"

"Unfortunately, no," Joanna said. "As sheriff of Cochise County, I can tell you that as long as weapons—particularly high-powered weapons—are involved, people can still die."

"When it comes to weapons, I don't have anything much stronger than a cue stick," Scorsby said. "That's what I shoot mostly—pool. Guns aren't my style."

"But you said—"

"I *said* guns aren't my style," Scorsby insisted. "And if you're still determined that I had something to do with what went on, I can assure you that I was right here in the house all night long. If you don't believe me, ask my wife. We were never apart for even a moment, except for maybe the time I was in the bathroom. She wasn't with me then. Would you like me to call her?"

Joanna might have missed the snide put-down in the comment had not Scorsby's tone of voice made his superior attitude blatantly clear.

"No, thanks," Joanna replied, matching her tone to his. "That won't be necessary. Not just now, anyway. Let me suggest, however, that in the meantime, until we clear up this matter, you stay away from the Triple C."

"Believe me," Scorsby told her, "that'll be my pleasure. The last thing I need to do is to get into some kind of beef with Alton Hosfield or one of his hired thugs—excuse me, I mean one of his hired hands."

Turning, Joanna stepped back into her Blazer.

"And Sheriff Brady?" Scorsby added.

Closing the car door behind her, Joanna opened the window. "Yes?"

"As I said to Deputy . . . What's his name again?"

"Deputy Sandoval," Joanna answered.

"As I told Deputy Sandoval earlier, if this matter requires any further discussion, my attorney is Maximilian Gailbrathe with Gailbrathe, Winters and Goldman in Tucson."

"Of course, Mr. Scorsby," she said sweetly. She gave the window control button a forceful jab. "Like hell," she added to herself once the window was safely closed, shutting him out of earshot.

If it turned out that Martin Scorsby had indeed had something to do with Alton Hosfield's dead cattle and wrecked irrigation pump, Scorsby's attorney would be doing a whole lot more than simply handling "incident" discussions.

Plea bargains would be a lot more like it, Joanna thought. With that she threw the Blazer into gear. In the process of driving away from Scorsby's yard, she caused the speeding Blazer to leave behind a rooster tail of fine red dust that powdered the man's spotless white tennis outfit. The last glimpse she had of him in the mirror was of his arms flailing in a futile attempt to brush himself clean.

"Pardon my dust," Joanna muttered to herself.

Despite that little bit of deliberate revenge, she was still seething from the encounter with Scorsby some twenty minutes later when she drove up the entrance to Alton Hosfield's Triple C Ranch. She stopped long enough to read an almost billboard-sized sign that had been erected next to the cattle guard marking the boundary line.

PRIVATE PROPERTY, the sign announced in no uncertain terms. ENTRANCE IS PERMITTED TO THE GENERAL PUBLIC, BUT THAT PERMISSION MAY BE WITHDRAWN AT ANY TIME. NO SMOKING. NO HUNTING. NO FISHING. NO TRESPASSING IS ALLOWED FOR EMPLOY-EES OF THE FEDERAL GOVERNMENT, SUBCONTRACTORS OF THE FED-ERAL GOVERNMENT, OR ANYONE GIVING INFORMATION TO THE FEDERAL GOVERNMENT. NO EXCEPTIONS.

At the last meeting of the Arizona Sheriffs' Association, several of the law enforcement officers gathered there had spoken of hairy encounters with their own particular juris-diction's version of the tax-and-government-protesting Free-men Movement. Most of the run-ins with Randy Weaver wannabes had ended peacefully, but that wasn't always the case. Especially not when the protestors had weapons readily available.

At the time of the meeting, Joanna had been only too happy to have nothing to report in that regard. Now, though, seeing the sign, and in light of all the weapons miss-ing from Clyde Philips' gun shop, she wondered how much longer that would be the case.

She reread the sign once more, paying particular atten-tion to the places where it referred to the federal govern-ment. *Maybe Dick Voland was right,* she thought. *Maybe the best thing for all concerned is to leave the ATF out of this.*

CHAPTER SIX

The dirt road leading onto the Triple C Ranch was almost as badly washboarded as the one leading to Martin Scorsby's Pecan Plantation, but compared to the Scorsbys' almost palatial digs, Alton Hosfield's house was far more modest. The gingerbread-frame construction topped by a steep tin roof had Joanna wondering if this larger house and her turn-of-the-century bungalow on High Lonesome Ranch weren't closely related cousins. As she studied the exterior, it seemed to her that, like hers, this was a mail-order Sears Roebuck kit-house that had been shipped west from Chicago by train. Some assembly required.

The woman who came to the gate to meet Joanna's Blazer was a plain-faced blonde with streaks of blatantly untinted gray showing in a utilitarian ponytail. She looked to be in her late forties or early fifties, but under a ruffled apron was a youthfully trim figure in a pair of snugly fitting jeans. Her single best feature—bright blue eyes—sparkled out of a face lined as much by laughter as by the sun.

She smiled, holding out a hand in welcome. "I'm Sonja Hosfield," she said. "Can I help you?"

The woman's firm handshake as well as the unfeigned friendliness in her welcome immediately put Joanna at ease. She held up her badge. "I'm Sheriff Brady," she said. "Joanna Brady. I was hoping to speak to your husband."

"He and my stepson are still out working in one of the fields," Sonja said. "They're cutting hay. It's dry right now, and they need to get it cut, baled, and stacked before it rains again, but it's just about time for them to come in to supper. If you don't mind waiting, I could send my son to tell Alton you're here. I'm sure he'll want to speak to you."

Sonja pulled open the gate. "Come on in," she said. "We can have some iced tea while we wait."

Inside the house, she went to the bottom of a flight of stairs. "Jake?" she called. "Are you up there?"

"Yeah, Mom, I'm here."

"Come down, then," she said. "Somebody's here to see your dad. I need you to go get him for me."

Sonja Hosfield was old enough for Joanna to expect a hulking twenty something son to come down the creaking stairway. Instead, the red-haired boy who bounded down into the entryway was scarcely older than Joanna's Jenny. He started to dart straight past them and out through the front door, but Sonja stopped him.

"Just a minute, young man," she said. "Where are your manners?"

Jake Hosfield stopped in mid-flight, turned, and skulked back into the house, blushing sheepishly as he came. "This is Sheriff Brady, Jake," his mother said.

Flushing to the roots of hair that was almost as red as Joanna's, he wiped one hand on his pant leg, then reached out awkwardly to shake hands. "Glad to meetcha, ma'am," he said.

"I'm glad to meet you, too," Joanna returned.

With the obligatory handshake over, Jake stood for an awkward moment or two and then backed away. "I've gotta go now," he said. "See you later."

"That's better," Sonja called after him. "Hurry, now. Tell your father supper's almost ready, too."

She turned back to Joanna. "He's a little shy," she said. "That's what happens when you raise kids out in the country. Now, I hope you don't mind sitting in the kitchen. You caught me right in the middle of cooking dinner. I was just chopping up some tomatoes and onions to put in the salsa."

As they started away from the entry, Joanna heard the whine of what sounded like a motorcycle starting up outside. "Don't worry," Sonja said over her shoulder. "That's only Jake's ATV. He prefers that to horses, and he only rides it when he's on our property. As far as helmets go, believe me, he knows that if he doesn't wear one, I'll kill him."

Following Sonja Hosfield into her warm and fragrant kitchen, Joanna found the combination of smells utterly tantalizing. There was no mistaking what was for dinner—roast beef, a vat of simmering pinto beans, and a slab of freshly baked corn bread cooling in a thirteen-inch cast-iron skillet.

"Sit right here," Sonja said, shifting aside one of the four place settings already laid out on a pillared round table made of solid, well-worn oak. "Help yourself. The tea's right there in the pitcher," she added, "and here's a glass with ice. Supper isn't going to be anything fancy, but you're welcome to join us if you like."

Gratefully sipping her tea, Joanna couldn't help comparing Sonja Hosfield's openhanded hospitality with Martin Scorsby's lack of same. Much as she would have loved to sample some of Sonja's cooking, Joanna knew that in order to maintain a sense of impartiality between the two families, she would have to decline the invitation. Only belatedly did she remember that she also had a date for dinner—with Butch.

"Thanks just the same," she said. "I'm sure I won't be able to stay that long. I happened to be in the neighborhood and wanted to stop by to assure you and Mr. Hosfield that we're taking last night's shooting incident very seriously. My department is doing everything it can to find the culprit. The last thing any of us wants is for this situation to escalate out of hand."

"Isn't that the truth!" Sonja exclaimed. "I know exactly what you mean. When Alton saw that wrecked pump this morning, I thought he was going to come unglued. By the way, Sheriff Brady, call him Alton. If you call him Mr. Hosfield to his face, he'll blush deep purple, the same as Jake. Like father, like son, I guess. The two of them are two peas in a pod, although I tease Alton that his forehead seems to be getting longer these days."

She laughed then—in a gust of straightforward, bell-like laughter—that made Joanna want to laugh right along with her. Moments later, Sonja had to pause in her chopping long enough to dab at her eyes with one corner of the ruffled apron.

"Onions," she explained. "Crying's the best part of making salsa. If there aren't a few tears mixed in, it's not real salsa."

Looking around the room, Joanna saw the usual kitchen clutter and homey counter stuff—a can opener and coffee-pot; an aging toaster oven; an old gray-and-blue crock holding a selection of spoons and spatulas. Across the room sat an old Tappan gas range and a Frigidaire refrigerator, both of which looked like they belonged on the 1950s-era set of *I Love Lucy*. There was no dishwasher, only a drainboard with an empty wire dish rack sitting to one side of the double sink.

On the ledge of the window stood a series of several handmade clay pitchers. Roughly formed and out of balance, they struck a familiar note—the kind of handiwork that childish hands might create in a Bible school arts and crafts session. Well-used pots and pans dangled from a metal framework attached to the high ceiling. Old-fashioned wooden cupboards complete with white knob handles went all the way to that same ceiling. A worn step stool in one corner of the room hinted that it might be the secret to making Sonja's top shelves more accessible.

Next to the cupboard at the far end of the table was a wall-mounted phone—the old-fashioned dial type. Next to that hung two framed diplomas from the University of Arizona. One listed the recipient as Sonja Marie Hemmelberg. The other had been issued to David Alton Hosfield. Both of them dated from the mid-sixties.

Sonja glanced in Joanna's direction and caught her studying the diplomas. "Looking at the artifacts, are you?" she asked with a smile.

"Artifacts?" Joanna repeated, ashamed to have been caught snooping.

Sonja laughed again. "I was a Home Ec major," she said. "I don't think they make those anymore. Since I was in Home Ec and Alton was an Aggie, everybody thought it was a match made in heaven. We met at a mixer between my dorm and his fraternity the first week of school our freshman year. I was in Pima Hall—sort of an honors dorm for poor but smart girls." She shrugged. "What can I tell you? It was love at first sight."

They've spent more than thirty-five years together, Joanna thought. The stab of hurtful jealousy that passed through her might have been Sonja Hosfield's paring knife plunged deep in her heart. She and Andy never had a chance to come near twenty-five years, much less thirty-five.

The words burst out of Joanna's mouth before she could stop them. "You're lucky to have had so much time together. My husband died on the night of our tenth anniversary."

Sonja stopped chopping. "I'm sorry," she said.

"I'm sorry, too," Joanna said guiltily. "I shouldn't have brought it up."

"No, it's fine. But you're wrong about the timing—ours, that is. We haven't had that many years together, either. Alton and I went together all through college, but then we broke up during spring semester of our senior year. We had a big fight over something stupid, and I gave Alton back his engagement ring. He wanted me to take birth control pills, you see. They were fairly new back then. He said he didn't want us to, as they called it back then, 'get in trouble and have to get married.' But birth control pills were against my religion—or at least they were against my *parents'* religion. I told him if he really loved me he wouldn't even ask me to do such a sinful thing."

Sonja scraped the pile of finely chopped onions across the cutting board into a mixing bowl. Then she absently stirred the contents of the bowl with the blade of her knife. "I'm not sure how I came to all those erroneous conclusions," she said finally. "Here we were sleeping together—had been for years. It seems to me now that risking an unwed pregnancy should have counted as more of a sin than taking birth control pills, but then Home Ec majors always were strong on cooking and short on philosophy."

She stopped stirring and brought the dish of freshly made salsa over to the table. The combination of chopped tomatoes, onions, and cilantro was enough to make Joanna's eyes water as well.

"With everything that's on TV and in the movies nowadays," Sonja continued, "the whole thing sounds ridiculous—almost quaint, doesn't it? But it wasn't ridiculous back then. Not at all, and we broke up over it. Alton and I each married other people and spent the next eighteen or nineteen years in hell. I found someone who didn't want a stay-at-home wife, and Alton married someone who wasn't one. By the time we met again, at our twentieth class reunion, we were both divorced. In our case, it was re-love at first sight. So we haven't been married very long, either. More tea?"

As the jasmine-laced tea poured over Joanna's partially melted ice cubes, she was astonished at the ease with which she and Sonja had fallen into this conversation. They were strangers, and yet they might have been friends forever. Joanna suspected that a good deal of Sonja's volubility had to do with plain, ordinary loneliness. Stuck out here on the far fringes of civilized Cochise County, Sonja Hosfield probably didn't have many people to talk to outside the confining circle of her own small family.

"Do you have any children?" Sonja asked.

Sipping her tea, Joanna nodded. "A daughter. Her name's Jenny—Jennifer Ann. She's eleven."

"So she's not all that much younger than Jake," Sonja said. "He just turned twelve this past March. He's ours together, Alton's and mine, but we both have other kids besides. He has a son, Ryan, and a daughter, Felicia, from his first marriage, and I have two boys—men now—Matt and Jason. When I divorced their father, the boys couldn't understand why I was leaving. They opted to stay with the big bucks—with the house and the cars and the swimming pool. Living in a ratty little two-bedroom apartment wasn't for them. I don't think they've ever forgiven me. Not for leaving then, and certainly not for being happy now."

Taking another knife from a wooden block on the

counter, Sonja began to slice up the cornbread. "What happened to your husband?" she asked. "Was he ill?"

Joanna steeled herself to tell the story once again. "He was a police officer," she said. "He was shot."

"In the line of duty?"

Even though Deputy Andrew Roy Brady had been officially off duty at the time of the incident, the county commissioners had ruled his fatality as line of duty. "That's right," she said.

Sonja nodded. "I remember now. He was running for office at the time, for sheriff."

"Yes," Joanna said. "After the funeral, some of his supporters asked me to run in his stead, and here I am."

"I've never been one of those women's libbers," Sonja said. "Being a woman in a man's job must be difficult at times."

Joanna glanced around Sonja Hosfield's old-fashioned and industrious but nonetheless spotless kitchen. It was Sheriff Brady's turn to smile. "I don't know," she said. "I'm not so sure being a woman in a woman's job isn't just as hard."

Sonja shrugged. "Maybe it is."

For a little while it was quiet in the kitchen, except for the noisy hum of a teapot-shaped electric clock on the wall over the stove. The sound of it served as a reminder to Sheriff Brady that she was neglecting her responsibilities. "About last night . . ." Joanna began.

"I heard them," Sonja told her. "The gunshots, that is. There were several of them, one right after another. Then, after a pause, there were several more. They sounded like the M-80 firecrackers my boys used to like so much when they were kids. It's not the first time I've heard them in the last few weeks. I figured they were just leftovers from somebody's Fourth of July. Now, though, I'm thinking Martin's not much of a shot and this was the first time he's actually managed to hit something."

Noting that Sonja Hosfield immediately assumed that Martin Scorsby was the person responsible, Joanna let that slide for the moment. "You said you heard shots. Does that mean your husband didn't?"

"Right," Sonja said. "Alton went to Vietnam, you see. A land mine blew up close enough to him that it knocked him out. He wasn't badly hurt. Unlike some of his buddies, he didn't lose an arm or a leg, but he came home with a severe hearing loss. Without his hearing aids, he's deaf as a post. According to the VA, his deafness isn't service-related. He's been fighting the benefits people about it for years, but it hasn't done any good. I guess the people in charge of claims are just as deaf as he is."

"I noticed the sign down by the road. No feds allowed. Is that why he's mad at them, because he thinks they mismanaged his VA claim?"

Sonja shook her head. "He's mad at them because every time he turns around, there's some other federal regulation or requirement that gets in the way of his being able to run his ranch. He's sick and tired of governmental interference, and as far as I'm concerned, the man's entitled to his opinion."

"Does that opinion extend to the Cochise County Sheriff's Department?" Joanna asked.

Sonja smiled. "I shouldn't think so, especially since you're here to help straighten out this mess with Scorsby."

Somewhat reassured, Joanna resumed her questioning. "So, getting back to that, what time did you hear the shots?"

"Ten-thirty, maybe? The ten o'clock news had just gone off and I was getting ready for bed. Alton was already asleep."

Just then there was a rumbling outside the house. It

sounded like several vehicles arriving at once. When Joanna glanced out the window, however, she saw only two—Jake Hosfield's ATV and a 1980s-era Ford pickup. While she watched, Jake jumped off the ATV, pulled off his helmet, and dashed toward the house. Two men climbed out of the other vehicle. After what looked like a brief conference across the bed of the pickup, one of the two walked away and disappeared into a barnlike structure, while the other— the driver—limped toward the house.

Sonja Hosfield peeked out the same window. "I'd better go let him know what's what," she said. With that she slipped off her apron and hung it on one peg of a hat rack just to the left of the back door.

Feeling a little like a voyeur, Joanna watched as Sonja darted out the back door and hurried up the path to meet her husband. Tall and angular, Alton Hosfield doffed his cowboy hat and had to lean down to kiss the top of his wife's head. Then, holding hands, the two of them continued on toward the house.

Except for the hearing aids Alton wore in each ear, he was exactly what Joanna would have expected of an Arizona rancher. Hard physical labor meant that there was no fat on his spare, lean body. His features were as craggy and deeply tanned as the rockbound cliffs overlooking the San Pedro. His dusty boots were worn down at the heels, but even after a day out in the field, his threadbare Levi's still showed a hint of the crease some loving hand had ironed into them, while the back hip pocket bore the unmistakable imprint of a round tobacco can. The sleeves of his plaid cowboy shirt— tan with pearlescent snaps—were rolled up almost to the elbows, exposing bare, work-hardened hands and sinewy forearms. The moment he walked into the house, he re-moved his sweat-stained Resistol hat, revealing a head of hair every bit as red as his son's—although, as Sonja had mentioned, Alton's hairline was definitely receding.

With practiced ease, he tossed the straw hat onto an empty peg next to his wife's apron. Then he came striding across the faded kitchen linoleum with his hand extended. "Sorry to kick up such a fuss around here today, Sheriff Brady," he said in a soft-spoken drawl. "But if somebody doesn't put a stop to Martin Scorsby's nonsense, I will, and I guarantee you, he won't like it."

"Now, Alton," Sonja cautioned. "Please . . ."

"Don't you 'Now, Alton' me," Hosfield returned. "I mean what I say. That man and that little Birkinstar-wearing bimbo of his—"

"Birkenstock," Sonja corrected smoothly.

"Whatever you want to call 'em," Alton said, "those two have been a pain in my backside ever since they showed up here. Before that, even. And if Scorsby thinks he can sit over in those trees of his and take shots at my property . . ."

"Did Deputy Sandoval take pictures this morning?" Joanna asked.

"Pictures?" Alton Hosfield repeated. "Of my dead cattle? Why would he? Most everybody with a lick of sense can tell a dead cow when he sees one. Why would anybody want to take pictures?"

"If Deputy Sandoval was following proper procedure, he would have," Joanna said. "Photos would have shown exactly how the cows were situated in the field. They would also give us the positions of entrance and exit wounds. With that kind of information, we can begin to develop a sense of trajectory of the bullets. Knowing where the shots came from will help us identify who the shooter is."

"Well," Hosfield conceded, "your deputy may have— taken pictures, that is. I just don't remember."

"What about the pump?"

"When Sandoval got here, I gave him the smashed housing, but I had already replaced it by then. I'm not going to sit around all day with a broken pump while I'm waiting for a cop to decide whether or not he's going to show up. Sometimes they don't, you see. You call and maybe the deputy will turn up that day and maybe he won't.

"Still, the new housing is the same as the old one. They had discontinued that model when I bought them. I was able to get the two—one and a replacement—for almost the same amount of money as a new one would have cost. So if you look at the one that's on the pump now, you should be able to get a pretty good idea of what happened."

Outside, a vehicle started. Joanna looked out the window in time to see an old panel truck, a rust-spotted blue one that looked as though it might have once belonged to a dairy, rattle out past the gate. "Where's Ryan going?" Sonja asked her husband with a frown.

"Into town, I guess."

"What about dinner?"

"He said he had plans."

For the first time since Joanna had met Sonja Hosfield, she saw a look of real annoyance wash across the other woman's face. "He didn't have plans this morning," she said. "Don't you remember? I asked him at breakfast because I wanted to know how much meat to get out of the freezer."

"Well, I don't know where he's going," Alton Hosfield said. "All I know is he said he was going."

With her lips set in a thin, angry line, Sonja came over to the table and removed one of the four place settings, slamming the plate back in the cupboard, dropping the silverware into the drawer. "It would have been nice—it would have been good manners—if he had told *me*," she said pointedly.

"I'm sorry, hon," Alton said. "I should have made him . . ."

"You shouldn't have done anything, Alton," she told him. "It's not your fault. He's twenty-two years old. He should have thought of it himself."

"Now, Sheriff Brady, getting back to this pump business . . ."

At that precise moment, Joanna's cell phone rang. While Sonja and Alton Hosfield looked on in some surprise, Joanna reached into her purse, removed the phone, and answered it. "Sheriff Brady here. I'm in the middle of an interview. What's up?"

"Sorry to interrupt," Larry Kendrick said. "We tried several times to raise you on the radio. I finally decided we'd better try the phone."

"Why?" Joanna asked. "What's happened?"

"Search and Rescue just found a body," Larry Kendrick said. "A woman who's been shot. I thought you'd want to know."

A knot, like a sudden, sharp cramp, gripped Sheriff Brady's insides. Sonja Hosfield claimed that she had heard several shots. The pump and the two dead cattle accounted for three of the several bullets. She wondered if the dead woman accounted for another.

Larry, the chief dispatcher, sounded as though he wanted to add something more, but Joanna cut him off without giving him a chance. "Tell them I'm on my way, Larry. Where do I go?"

"Where are you now?"

"With Mr. and Mrs. Hosfield at the Triple C."

"Search and Rescue set up a command post just inside the gates to Rattlesnake Crossing Ranch. It's another three miles or so up Pomerene Road from where you are."

"I know where Rattlesnake Crossing is," Joanna said. "I'll be there just as soon as I can make it."

"Detective Carbajal's still in Pomerene and tied up with the lady from the Pima County Medical Examiner's office," Larry continued, "so I called Ernie Carpenter at home. He's still a little woozy from whatever medication he took for his migraine, but he said to tell you that he's on his way."

Sighing, Joanna ended the call and slipped the phone back into her purse. "Sorry," she said to the Hosfields. "There's been an emergency. I have to go."

"They must've found that woman," Alton said, turning to his wife. "I probably forgot to tell you. Her husband came around looking for her right after breakfast this morning. He came by while Ryan and I were working on the pump. Said she'd been missing since yesterday afternoon."

"Is she okay?" Sonja asked.

"No," Joanna told them. "She's not okay. She's dead."

CHAPTER SEVEN

As she heeled the Blazer around and headed back for Pomerene Road, Joanna glanced at her watch. Six o'clock, straight up and down. She had stayed at the Triple C far longer than she had intended, and time had slipped away from her. Now, with exactly one hour before her date with Butch and with more than an hour's worth of driving between the Triple C and High Lonesome Ranch, she was headed for Rattlesnake Crossing, which lay in the opposite direction.

Rather than hightailing it for home and a relaxing evening of fun with someone whose company she had come to value, Sheriff Joanna Brady was, instead, off to investigate her second crime scene of the day—her second homicide of the day.

Slowing almost to a crawl on the rough, washboarded surface, she pulled her cell phone out of her purse once again and checked the roaming light to be sure she still had a signal. Then she punched in the memory code for Butch's Roundhouse Bar and Grill up in Peoria, near Phoenix. Obvi-

ously, since her date with Butch was scheduled for Bisbee—
a minimum of four hours by car from the Phoenix area—he
wouldn't be at the Roundhouse to take the call himself, not
at the bar and restaurant downstairs or in his bachelor apartment upstairs. Nevertheless, Joanna knew from past experience that Butch Dixon was a conscientious business owner
who never left town without leaving behind a telephone-
number trail to let people know exactly where he'd be staying. That way, in case of any unforeseen circumstances or
emergencies at his place of business, the daytime bartender
and relief manager would have no difficulty in reaching
him.

Punching SEND, Joanna waited, listening for the phone to
ring. Then, because there was so much road noise, she held
the phone away from her ear long enough to punch up the
volume. When she put the phone back to her ear, an operator's recorded announcement was already well under way.
". . . you feel you have reached this number in error, please
hang up and dial again. If you need help, hang up and dial
the operator."

Puzzled, and scowling at the phone, Joanna punched RE-
CALL. She studied the lit display long enough to verify that
the number she had dialed was indeed that of the Roundhouse. Once again she pressed SEND. This time she was careful to hold the phone to her ear, only to hear the familiar
but irritating sequence of a disconnect announcement. She
listened to the message from beginning to end.

"The number you have reached has been disconnected.
If you feel you have reached this number in error, please
hang up and dial again. If you need help, hang up and dial
the operator."

Disconnected! Joanna thought dazedly. *How on earth could
Butch's number be disconnected? And why wasn't there a forwarding referral to another number? How could that be?*

The Blazer bounced across the cattle guard at the edge of the Triple C and lurched to a stop at the intersection of Triple C with Pomerene Road. Her stopping there had far more to do with a need to think than it did with the stop sign posted there. *What on earth had happened?*

Joanna waited while first one car and then another rumbled past. The second one she recognized. Seeing Detective Ernie Carpenter roar by in his private vehicle, the Mercury Marquis he called his "geezer car," was enough to shock Joanna out of her reverie. Not wanting to be left out of the loop, she quickly turned onto the road and followed him, maintaining just enough distance between his vehicle and hers to avoid most of the cloud of dust kicked up by his tires.

Following Ernie and operating on autopilot, Joanna continued to grapple with the puzzling problem of what had happened to Butch Dixon and his restaurant. She remembered how, during the past few weeks, he had told her over and over how busy he was. More than once she had allowed herself the smallest possible qualm that perhaps another woman had arrived on the scene. Now, though, other scenarios marched through her head. Maybe something terrible had happened to him, something Butch hadn't wanted to burden her with. What if his place had burned down? What if he had somehow landed in financial trouble and had simply run out of money? And if he hadn't left a forwarding phone number, how did he expect anyone—her included—to be able to get in touch with him?

For a few minutes she toyed with the idea of calling Dispatch and asking them to send an officer out to her place to meet Butch and tell him exactly what was going on. She considered the idea, then dismissed it. Prior to her arrival on the scene, the Cochise County Sheriff's Department had operated like a little fiefdom, with on-duty officers running personal errands on behalf of their supervisors. Under Joanna's administration, that practice had been expressly forbidden. And as someone who wanted to lead by example, Sheriff Brady couldn't afford to fly in the face of the very rules she herself had created.

No, she decided finally as she turned in under the arched gate marked "Rattlesnake Crossing." *We'll have to let the chips fall where they may. I'll stop just long enough to make an appearance. Since Ernie's here to take charge, I won't have to hang around. With any kind of luck, Butch will wait at the house until I get there.*

Once again Joanna found herself driving on a mile-long dirt track. The Triple C holdings were situated along the river bottom. Rattlesnake Crossing, however, like Martin Scorsby's Pecan Plantation, was located on the other side of the road—upland and away from the river itself. What Joanna knew about Rattlesnake Crossing was more countywide gossip than anything else.

Under the name The Crossing, the place had come into existence in the mid-seventies as a residential psychiatric treatment center for patients of Dr. Carlton A. Lamphere. Dr. Lamphere, a New York native and a devotee of R. Buckminster Fuller, had bought up a tract of land, sunk a well, and then created his treatment facility by building a massive main ranch house in the center of the property and scattering the rest of his hundred and twenty acres with twenty or more Fuller-inspired geodesic domes.

Lamphere, operating on the theory that his patients lacked the self-esteem that came of self-reliance, insisted that his clients stay in these individual "cabins," as they were called. There they were expected to live alone, commune with nature, and learn to face their personal demons. The patients' nonpenal solitary confinement was broken each day by the arrival of golf-cart-riding orderlies who delivered trays of proper macrobiotic vegetarian meals and clean lin-

ens. Other than the orderlies, the only visitor to the individual cabins was Dr. Lamphere, who came by regularly for
counseling sessions and to make sure the patients were staying on course.

Everything was going fine at The Crossing until one pa-
tient, a twenty-two-year-old schizophrenic, returned home
and immediately came down with severe flulike symptoms.
Her mother correctly diagnosed morning sickness, and a
court-ordered blood test established that Dr. Lamphere himself was most likely the father of the young woman's baby.

A subsequent investigation—one that had set the entire
San Pedro Valley on its ear—had revealed that Dr. Lamphere's course of treatment had routinely included drugging
and raping his female patients—with particular concentration on the younger and more attractive ones. Not only had
he victimized the women, he had also managed to maintain
such a high degree of mind control over them that not one
of them had told. None of the other victimized patients had
become pregnant, so had it not been for that single alert
mother, Lamphere might never have been caught.

In the aftermath of the investigation, The Crossing was
shut down. For years the geodesic domes sat empty and in
danger of crumbling back into the desert. Then, surprisingly,
in the early eighties, Rattlesnake Crossing had risen Phoenix-
like from the ruins. Locals had scoffed at the idea of somebody running a summer camp for well-heeled grown-ups
pretending to be Apache, but it seemed to be working. Almost fifteen years later, the place was still going strong with
guests that purportedly came from all over the world.

Off to the right, sheltered behind a lush mesquite tree,
Joanna caught sight of a tepee. "A tepee?" she wondered
aloud. "Since when did Apaches use tepees?"

Fifty yards farther up the road, she caught sight of her
first cabin, sheltered under a towering mesquite. The geode-

sic dome shape still remained, but it was concealed under a layer of woven ironwood and mesquite branches that gave it the look, at least, of the domed shelters the nomadic Apache had once called home. *That's more like it*, Joanna thought.

Up ahead, but just before a cluster of buildings that included the main house, barns, and corrals, Joanna saw a string of vehicles lining the right-hand side of the road. She pulled in and stopped directly behind Ernie Carpenter's Marquis. She had barely stepped out of the Blazer when a woman materialized in front of her.

The woman was dressed in a buckskin squaw dress and high-topped moccasins, both of which had been dyed black. Her whole body dripped with silver and turquoise, from the concha belt cinching in her narrow waist to the heavy squash-blossom necklace, the bottom of which disappeared into the shadowy crevasse of an extravagant décolletage. Her hair, black but showing telltale gray at the roots, was pulled into a heavy bun at the nape of her neck. With her tan, windblown skin and dark, smoldering eyes, the fifty-something woman might have been an Indian. Until she opened her mouth. As soon as she spoke, the accent was pure New York.

"So what's the deal here?" she demanded.

"Deal?" Joanna repeated.

"Yeah. I mean, what's going on? That guy up there . . ." She pointed toward a group of men that included Ernie Carpenter. "The tall one, right there. He told me the woman in the next car would tell me what was up. After all, it's my sister-in-law they found up there. I want to see Katrina. I'm one of her closest relatives. Why the hell won't somebody let me through?"

Joanna pulled out her badge and flashed it. "I'm Sheriff Brady," she said. "And your name is?"

"Crow Woman," was the reply.

Joanna had to bite her tongue to keep from repeating that as well. "Is that a first name or a last name?" she asked.

"It's my name," Crow Woman replied. "Legally. I changed it after I got my divorce. I went to court and it cost me four hundred bucks. Now tell me, Sheriff Brady, what the hell is going on?"

"I don't know," Joanna said truthfully. "As you saw, I just arrived myself, but if you'll excuse me for a moment, I'll go see what I can find out."

Leaving Crow Woman where she stood, Joanna approached the group of men congregated around the white Bronco that served as Search and Rescue's command vehicle. Detective Ernie Carpenter broke away from the others as she approached.

"The lady back there wants to know what's going on," Joanna told him. "Did Search and Rescue find a body or not?"

"Yes, they did," Ernie replied.

"Where is it?"

"About two miles west of here," Ernie said, pointing. "The boys from S and R tell me that she was on a shelf of cliff on the other side of the river. According to Mike Wilson, they've cordoned off the area and left Deputy Sandoval to guard it. Mike says there's a place where the river widens out enough that we should be able to drive across in the Blazer. If we follow him, Mike'll take us to the crime scene."

"So it *is* Katrina Berridge, then," Joanna said with a resigned sigh. She had hoped S and R would find the woman alive. "I guess I'll go get Crow Woman. The three of us can ride up together."

"Who's Crow Woman?" Ernie asked.

"Her," Joanna said, pointing back to the woman who still stood leaning on the Blazer's fender. "That's her legal name—Crow Woman. She also happens to be the dead woman's sister-in-law."

"I don't think so," Ernie said.

"Well, of course she is," Joanna returned impatiently. "She just told me so herself. She wants to know what's going on and she wants to view the body. I know that's not standard procedure, but why not? We could just as well let her do it now as later. Since Doc Winfield is out of town, we'll be working with Fran Daly on this case as well as the one in Pomerene. The body will be up in Tucson, so it'll take a lot less time if we get the whole identification thing done now, rather than waiting until later."

"I don't think that's such a good idea—"

Impatiently, Joanna rushed on without giving Ernie a chance to finish what he was saying. "All right, then, I suppose you're right. We shouldn't drag her along to the crime scene, but when it's time to transport the body, maybe we could stop here long enough to get the job done. Once the body's in Tucson, what'll take a few minutes tonight will take all day tomorrow. Either you or Detective Carbajal will have to come all the way out here, pick up Crow Woman or Katrina's husband, take them up to Tucson for the ID, and then bring them back again. I say let's do it now and get it over with, once and—"

"It's not her," Ernie Carpenter interrupted.

Joanna stopped. "Not her? But I thought . . ."

Knitting his bushy eyebrows together, Ernie shifted his considerable weight back and forth. "Katrina Berridge disappeared from Rattlesnake Crossing sometime yesterday afternoon," he said. "According to Mike Wilson, the body they found today has been dead much longer than that. Several weeks, anyway."

"You're saying somebody else is dead?" Joanna asked.

"Some other victim is here, one that we didn't even know about?"

Ernie nodded. "That's right."

"Who is it, then?"

"No way to tell. No ID was found, and very little clothing, either. She was buried under a pile of rocks, which pretty well rules out natural causes. One of the dogs found her."

"Any idea what she died of?"

Ernie shook his head. "Not yet anyway, not without an autopsy."

Joanna tried to come to grips with the dynamics of this new situation. Someone else was dead, someone no one had even bothered to report as missing. In the meantime, the initial object of the Search and Rescue mission still hadn't been located.

"What about the Berridge woman, then?" she asked.

"That's what I was discussing with Mike Wilson and the S and R guys just as you showed up. Finding this other body and dealing with it has pretty much put a wrench in the works. Also, the crime scene is right in the middle of the area they were searching. Between preserving evidence and the sun going down, I'd say they're pretty much out of business for tonight. Mike says they can be back here first thing in the morning and take another crack at it then."

Nodding, Joanna looked back up the road to where Crow Woman still stood waiting for an answer. "I suppose I'd better go tell her," she said. "The news was awful enough to begin with, and this is that much worse. I'll also have Dispatch contact Fran Daly."

"You mentioned her before," Ernie said. "Who is she?"

"Dr. Fran Daly," Joanna replied. "She's Doc Winfield's pinch-hitting investigator from the Pima County ME's office. She and Jaime have spent the afternoon locked up in a collapsed crawl space back in Pomerene on another homicide. I don't believe Dr. Daly was happy to be working with us on that first case. When she finds out about this one, I doubt she'll be thrilled."

"So what?" Ernie said. "In this business, them's the breaks."

Walking back toward the Blazer, Joanna tried to think of what to say to Crow Woman. For someone who had prepared herself for the worst, would she regard this reprieve as a blessing or a curse?

"Well?" Crow Woman demanded impatiently.

"There's no point in your seeing her," Joanna said. "The dead woman isn't your sister-in-law."

"Not Katrina?" Crow Woman echoed faintly. "But I thought . . . I understood . . ."

"So did we all," Joanna replied grimly. "But my investigators say that the body that was found has been out in the desert far longer than your sister-in-law has been missing."

"So you're saying Trina may still be okay?"

"She may be. Let's hope, anyway. It isn't like she's been out in the boonies in the dead of winter. Then we'd have to worry about hypothermia. It's not cold at all, and currently there is water available."

"But you said they found a body." Crow Woman sounded anxious. "Who's dead, then?"

"We don't have any way of knowing," Joanna answered. "Not yet. That's what we're trying to find out."

"Was this person murdered? Is it a man or a woman?"

"Please," Joanna said. "We're just starting our investigation. What I'm telling you is that the victim is *not* your sister-in-law. Beyond that, I can't tell you anything more."

Crow Woman wasn't interested in taking no for an answer. "Look," she said, "I have a business to run here. If people are being killed on or near my property, I need to know about it. I have guests to protect. And if one person has been murdered, then that's probably what's happened to Trina as well."

Joanna hesitated, puzzling over exactly how to address Crow Woman. *Is Crow her first name and Woman her last?* Joanna wondered.

"Ms. Crow Woman," Sheriff Brady said finally, assuming her most official-sounding tone, "please don't leap to any unfounded conclusions. Until Detective Carpenter and I actually visit the crime scene, there's no way for us to know whether or not it's on your property. I can assure you that, as the investigation progresses, you will be kept informed. And as for your sister-in-law, the Search and Rescue team will be going back out first thing in the morning to look for her."

"In the morning," Crow Woman echoed. "What's the matter with them going back out right now? It won't be dark for a while yet."

"We're doing the best we can," Joanna replied gently. "For your sister-in-law and for the dead woman as well. Why don't you just go on back home and let my people and me do our jobs."

She turned away from Crow Woman, reached into the Blazer, and pulled the radio microphone off the hook. She radioed through to Tica Romero at Dispatch.

"Tica," she said, "I need you to reach Chief Deputy Voland or Detective Carbajal back in Pomerene. Tell them that as soon as they finish with the Clyde Philips crime scene, they'll need to bring Dr. Daly up here to Rattlesnake Crossing. Tell Detective Carbajal there's another homicide on tap that we'll need Fran Daly to investigate."

"Does that clear the missing-person case, then?" Tica asked.

Joanna looked back at the black-clad figure of Crow

Woman striding away toward the cluster of buildings that made up the core of Rattlesnake Crossing. She wanted to be sure Katrina Berridge's sister-in-law was well beyond hearing distance before she spoke again.

"No," she said with a sigh. "I almost wish it did, but it doesn't. Trina Berridge is still missing. It's somebody else who's dead."

Tica Romero whistled. "What's happening around here?" she demanded. "Two murders in one day? Isn't that some kind of record?"

"It's a record, all right," Joanna answered. *It sure as hell is!*

CHAPTER EIGHT

While Ernie Carpenter set off to find Mike Wilson, Joanna went to the rear of her Blazer and hauled out the small suitcase she kept there, packed with what she called her "just-in-case clothes"—a Cochise County Sheriff's Department T-shirt, jeans, and hiking boots. Sitting inside the vehicle, she managed to change from her skirt, blazer, and heels into something more appropriate for a crime-scene investigation. Still, looking at the ground-in grime already on the skirt and blazer, she realized the change of wardrobe had come far too late. The damage from climbing in and out of Clyde Philips' crawl space had already been done—a bit like locking the barn door long after the horse was gone.

Joanna was dressed and out of the Blazer when Detective Carpenter returned with Mike Wilson in tow. "Did you get hold of Jaime?" Ernie asked.

She nodded. "According to Dispatch, he's on his way and bringing Dr. Daly with him. We could just as well wait here until they show up. That way we'll have only one caravan going in and out rather than two or three."

"It's getting late," Ernie remarked, glancing at the sun falling low in the west.

"You have lights in the van, don't you?"

Ernie nodded. "That's all right, then," Joanna said. "We'll wait."

And they did. Considering the distance involved, Detective Jaime Carbajal and Dr. Fran Daly arrived at the rendezvous on Rattlesnake Crossing within twenty minutes—far less time than it should have taken. As Dr. Daly and Jaime stepped out of their respective vehicles, Joanna handled the introductions. "So where's the new body?" Fran Daly asked.

"Across the river and up on those cliffs," Mike Wilson told her. He turned around and gave her van a critical onceover. "Is that thing four-wheel drive?"

"No," Fran answered. "Why?"

"Because it's pretty rough terrain between here and there," he said. "And we have to cross the river besides. If I were you, I'd leave the van here and ride with someone else, someone who has all-wheel drive."

That wasn't a suggestion Fran Daly was prepared to accept without an argument. "What about my equipment?" she demanded.

"Depending on how much you have, we could probably load it into one of our vehicles," Ernie offered.

"All right, then," Fran agreed. "I suppose that will have to do."

While she supervised the transfer of necessary equipment, Joanna eased up to Detective Carbajal. "How did it go?" she asked.

Jaime shrugged. "She's into bugs."

"Bugs?"

"That's right. Especially flies and maggots. She just took a course in forensic entomology. She thinks she'll be able to use the stage of development of maggots found on the body to help estimate time of death."

"I see," Joanna said, although she wasn't eager for more details. "So when did Clyde Philips die?"

"Beats me," Jaime replied. "If she's figured it out, you don't think she'd bother to tell me, do you? After all, I'm just a lowly detective, and I'm not from Pima County, either. It turns out our guys aren't even good enough to come pick up the body. I offered, but she insisted on calling for a Pima County van to collect it."

"What a surprise," Joanna said. "That way they'll be able to charge us time and mileage for the driver, too. It'll probably cost a fortune."

Moments later, Dr. Daly asked, "We're finally loaded, so who do I ride with?"

Joanna glanced at Jaime Carbajal's face. He'd already spent several long hours with Dr. Daly that afternoon, and it showed. She decided to give the man a break. "Detectives Carpenter and Carbajal can ride together in their van," she said. "You come with me in the Blazer."

"Let's get going, then," Dr. Daly said. "What are we waiting for? The sun's almost down."

"We have lights along," Joanna told her.

Fran Daly grunted in reply, climbed into Joanna's Blazer, and slammed the door.

The three vehicles sorted themselves into a line with Mike Wilson leading the caravan, Joanna behind him, and Ernie and Jaime bringing up the rear. Wilson led them back down the road that wound away from the main buildings at Rattlesnake Crossing. Instead of turning onto Pomerene Road, though, he took them across that and onto an even narrower dirt track that meandered first through a fenced grassy pasture and then into mesquite-tangled river bottom.

Approaching the San Pedro, Joanna grew apprehensive.

In the Arizona desert, crossing a monsoon-swollen stream or river can be dangerous, even in a four-wheel-drive vehicle. The last time she remembered seeing the river had been hours earlier, when she had crossed the bridge outside Benson. There, within the confines of fairly narrow banks, the water had been a roaring flood. Here, though, hours later, and in a spot where the banks were half a mile or so wide, the flow had spread out, calmed, and slowed.

As liquefied sand filtered out of moving water, it settled to the bottom, covering the river's floor with a firm, hard-packed layer that made for relatively easy driving. The Blazer was almost across and Joanna was about to breathe a sigh of relief when Mike Wilson's lead vehicle dropped into an invisible but still deep channel. It took all of Joanna's considerable driving skill to fight the Blazer through the swiftly flowing current and to bring it up and out on the other side.

It was only then, after they had emerged from the river and started negotiating the steep foothills on the other side, that Fran Daly spoke for the first time. "Mind if I smoke?"

With the other woman's nerves showing, Joanna could have rubbed it in. After all, the county's required NO SMOK-ING sign was posted on the glove box. But right then, with two people dead and Doc Winfield out of town, Joanna needed Fran Daly's help. Instead of hiding behind the sign, Joanna opted for reasonableness.

"Not if you roll down the window," she said.

Moments later, after exhaling a cloud of smoke, Fran leaned back in the seat and closed her eyes. She looked tired.

"What's this new deal now?" she asked. "Who is it this time? Do we have a name?"

Joanna shook her head. "Not so far. Our S and R guys have been out here most of the afternoon looking for a woman who wandered away from home yesterday. Her name's Katrina Berridge and she lives back there on that ranch, the one where we all met. According to her sister-in-law, Katrina left home sometime after noon yesterday, and she hasn't been seen or heard from since. Once the twenty-four-hour missing-persons deadline passed, my guys started conducting an official search. It was one of the Search and Rescue dogs that turned up this other body."

"So you're saying the body we're going to investigate isn't hers?" Fran Daly asked. "It isn't the missing woman?"

"Right."

"How do we know that for sure?"

Joanna bristled at what sounded like the snide suggestion that her officers were most likely incompetent—as though they weren't smart enough or well trained enough to differentiate between an old corpse and a new one. It took a real effort on her part to keep from snapping.

"We know that because Mike Wilson said so," she replied evenly.

"I see." Fran Daly shrugged. "Maybe he's right," she added, "but your people aren't exactly batting a thousand, you know."

"What do you mean by that?"

"When whoever it was called me up in Tucson . . ."

"Dick Voland," Joanna reminded her once more. "He's my chief deputy."

"Right. Mr. Voland told me that the guy in Pomerene, Clyde Philips, was a homicide victim. Where he got that idea, I don't know."

He got it from me, Joanna thought. She said, "You're saying he wasn't murdered?"

Fran blew another cloud of smoke. "I doubt it," she said. "I think he got himself all liquored up, put the bag over his head, cinched it shut with a belt, and then waited for the combination of booze and lack of oxygen to do the trick."

"You're saying he committed suicide. Did you find a note?" Joanna asked.

"Good as," Fran said.

"And what would that be?"

"You saw the body, didn't you?"

Joanna tried to recall the chaotic scene in the bedroom with the dead man lying naked on the bed and Belle Philips shaking him, shaking and shrieking.

"Yes," Joanna replied.

"So you saw the lesions?"

Reminded now, she recalled that one detail, the series of angry red marks on the man's white skin—on his chest, belly, and thigh. She had noticed them only long enough for them to register as some kind of surface wounds, but that was just before Belle had leaped on the body, collapsing both the bed and the floor into the darkened crawl space below. In all the confusion that followed, that single detail had slipped out of Joanna's consciousness.

"I saw something," Joanna admitted. "They looked like wounds of some kind, stab wounds, maybe."

"Not stab wounds," Fran Daly insisted. "Lesions. Whenever I've seen lesions like that before, they've been on AIDS patients. I can't be sure without blood work, of course, but I'm guessing that the autopsy will bear me out on this. Clyde Philips might still have been able to get around on his own, but he wouldn't have been able to for long. He was suffering from AIDS—full-blown AIDS. Instead of hanging around to fight it, he used the bag and his belt and took the short way out. I don't know that I blame him. If I were in his shoes, I might very well do the same thing."

"But without a note," Joanna objected, "how can you be sure? And what about his guns?"

"Guns? What guns?" Fran Daly asked.

"The guns in his shop," Joanna explained. "Clyde Philips

was a gun dealer. He had a shop out back, behind his house. It should have been full of guns. But it wasn't. From the way it looks, sometime in the last few days somebody's cleaned the whole place out. Taking an armload of stolen weapons into consideration, I would have thought we were dealing with a robbery/murder."

Fran ground out the remains of her half-smoked cigarette into the ashtray and then, before Joanna could stop her, the medical examiner removed the ashtray from the dashboard and tossed the contents out the window. Joanna watched in the rearview mirror, hoping there were no live embers left to start a fire.

"That's what happens when people who don't know what they're doing jump to erroneous conclusions," Fran said as she slammed the ashtray back into place. "From that point on, the accuracy of the whole investigation goes right out the window."

Joanna could see that once Fran Daly herself made an assumption—erroneous or otherwise—there was no changing her mind. Sheriff Brady considered volleying back some smart-mouthed response to that effect or raising hell about her tossing out her smoldering cigarette debris, but after a moment, she decided not to. *Save your breath,* Joanna told herself. Dr. Fran Daly was the way she was. No amount of crystal-clear argument on the sheriff's part was going to change the woman. Instead, Joanna concentrated on her driving and considered the implications of what Fran had said.

Who knows? Maybe she's right about Clyde Philips. Maybe he really did commit suicide. And if it turns out one of today's two murder victims wasn't murdered, maybe the second one—whoever she is—wasn't, either.

After leaving the river, the three-vehicle caravan traveled up and up through deepening twilight and steep, trackless terrain. Finally, Mike Wilson stopped his Bronco directly behind Eddy Sandoval's. Putting the Blazer in park and switching off the engine, Joanna stepped outside and stood staring at a solid wall of sheer and forbidding cliffs that jutted skyward far above them.

Just then a low rumble of thunder came rolling across the valley behind them. *Here we go again,* Joanna thought. Here was yet another crime scene where investigation and evidence collection would most likely have to take a backseat to Mother Nature.

Deputy Eddy Sandoval had been sitting out of the heat in his idling Bronco. Now he came slipping down the steep hillside to meet them as Fran Daly heaved herself out of the Blazer. "Let's get a move on," she said. "Where's this body supposed to be?"

Once again Dr. Daly succeeded in tweaking Joanna. Cochise County was *her* jurisdiction, not Dr. Daly's. As the ranking officer on the scene, Sheriff Brady should have been the one calling the shots. That detail of line of command wasn't lost on Deputy Sandoval, who, without responding, glanced briefly at Joanna. She was gratified that he checked with her before answering the other woman's question.

"Right, Deputy Sandoval," Joanna said, nodding her okay. "Tell us where we're going."

"It's up there." He pointed toward the cliffs. "There's a narrow rock shelf that runs along the base. Most of the way it seems solid enough, but just beyond the body it breaks off into a gully. From the looks of it, that's the spot where most of the water drains off the upper cliffs. There's been enough runoff the last few weeks that some of the cliff broke away. When it slid down the mountain, it took a big chunk of the shelf right along with it."

"A landslide?" Fran asked, pausing from the task of unloading her equipment from Ernie and Jaime's van.

Deputy Sandoval nodded. "I went down into the wash and checked to see if it looked safe for people to walk out there. I don't think the bank is undermined, but . . ."

Having just witnessed the collapse of Clyde Philips' floor, Joanna wasn't taking any chances. "Show me," she said.

Obligingly, Eddy turned and started back up the hill, past the two parked Broncos. Joanna followed on his heels. "Wait," Dr. Daly yelped after them. "You can't go rushing over there without me. You're liable to disturb evidence. Let me get my stuff first."

Joanna didn't bother to stop, but she did reply. "It's been raining for weeks now," she called back over her shoulder. "If there ever was any evidence lying around loose up there, it's long gone by now."

Eddy led Joanna to the spot where he had climbed in and out of a sandy creek bed. They slogged through damp sand for some fifty yards. By the time they reached the place where the slide had come down the mountain, Joanna knew they were close to the body. She could smell it. *No wonder the dogs focused in on this instead of Trina Berridge,* she thought. *They could probably smell it for miles. And no wonder, either, why Eddy Sandoval was waiting in his Bronco when we got here.*

For the next several minutes she examined the walls of the arroyo. In the end, she agreed with Deputy Sandoval's assessment. As long as another gully-washer of a storm didn't break loose another several-ton hunk of cliff face, the shelf was probably safe enough. After that, they retraced their footsteps out of the wash and then made the steep climb up to the shelf.

Once they were out on the ledge, footing was somewhat more solid than it had been on the hillside, but it was still a long way from foolproof. Here and there, loose rocks and gravel lay along the surface, waiting to trip the unwary. The shelf was five to six feet wide and not more than three to four feet tall. The problem was that beneath that three-foot sheer drop, the rocky flank of the mountainside fell away at an impossibly steep angle. Anyone tumbling off that first three-foot cliff probably wouldn't stop rolling for a long, long way.

Picking her way south along the cliff face, Joanna was thankful she wasn't particularly frightened of heights. She did worry, though, about the possibility of tripping over a dozing rattlesnake.

"Here you are," Eddy Sandoval said at last. He stopped and stepped aside, allowing Joanna to make her way past him and into the awful stench of rotting flesh. Fighting the urge to gag, she found herself staring down at a pile of rocks. Considering the broken cliff just above them, one might have assumed the pile had appeared there as a result of that slide. Except for one small detail. These were the wrong kind of rocks. In the wash below, Joanna had seen how the sandstonelike cliff had broken apart in long, rectangular brown chunks that looked almost as though they had been hacked apart with a saw blade. The round, smooth rocks forming the pile, colored a ghostly gray, were river rocks that someone had hauled up the mountainside one at a time.

The far end of the rock pile was where the slide had roared through, taking with it the rocks at that end. And there, where the river rocks were missing, lay two partially skeletalized human legs. On one of them most of the foot was still attached, while the other one was missing. At the ankle joint just above that remaining foot was a thick length of knotted rope that bound one leg to the other.

Joanna swallowed hard. Clyde Philips might have committed suicide. This person hadn't. She turned back to Eddy.

"You told Ernie it was a woman," she said. "But if that little bit of leg is all you can see, what makes you think it's a female?"

Eddy Sandoval had been hanging back and holding a handkerchief over his mouth and nose. Now he switched on his flashlight and shone it on something at Joanna's feet, near what had to be the head of the burial mound.

"I guess we still don't know, not for sure, but I think it's a pretty good guess. Look at this."

Peering down, Joanna found herself standing over a short, makeshift cross. The marker had been crafted by using two twigs of mesquite bound together with what appeared to be strips of cloth. Taking Eddy's flashlight, Joanna squatted beside the cross in order to examine it more closely. It took several seconds before she realized the bindings—what she had assumed to be strips of material—were really articles of clothing: a sports bra and a pair of nylon panties. Both pieces of underwear appeared to have been white originally. Now they were stained with blotches of some dark substance.

In the dim glow of the flashlight, Joanna couldn't tell for sure what that substance was, but still she knew. The underwear was stained with blood. Lots of blood.

In Sheriff Brady's previous life, that awful discovery would have sent her reeling. Now she simply took a deep breath—took one and wished she hadn't. "You've photographed all of this, Deputy Sandoval?" she asked.

"Yes, ma'am," he said.

"Good, but I suspect the detectives will probably want to take their own pictures before we start bagging and inventorying evidence."

As she turned to look at the bier once more, another low growl of thunder rumbled across the valley. "We'd better hurry," she told him. "There's a storm coming. Go back down and see if there's anything you can help carry. And then you should probably round up as many plastic tarps as you can find just in case we get rained out before we have a chance to finish gathering evidence."

Nodding, Eddy Sandoval hurried away down the narrow shelf. Meanwhile, Joanna turned back to the mound of rocks and stared at the pair of protruding bones. Joanna's law enforcement studies had taught her that there is often a message in the position of the body, especially if the murderer has gone to the trouble of posing his handiwork.

This is posing, all right, Joanna told herself, gazing down the mountainside from this sheltered yet desolate spot, one that commanded a view of the entire river valley. It had taken time and effort to bring the rocks here, and the victim as well. *This was posing, all right. With a capital P.*

CHAPTER NINE

For the next few minutes, standing there alone, Joanna turned her attention once again to the bones, which were visible from just below the knee down. The rope that bound the two limbs together was tied in a clumsy half hitch that would have been easy to undo—if, that is, the victim's hands had been free and she had known anything about ropes and knots.

If he kept her tied up, how did he get her up the mountain? Joanna wondered. *Dead or alive, she couldn't have been carried. The mountain was too steep, the path too treacherous. So did he lure her here or did he force her at gun- or knifepoint? Or did they simply meet, expectedly or by accident, up here on this ledge? Perhaps the meeting was unexpected on the victim's part, but the presence of the rope shows advance planning on the killer's.*

Premeditation was a necessary ingredient for a case of aggravated murder. If that was what her detectives were dealing with here, Joanna would have to make certain that every procedure was followed, every *t* crossed and every *i* dotted.

Ernie Carpenter, lugging two cumbersome equipment cases, came huffing and puffing up the ledge. "What do we have?" he asked, setting down his load near Joanna.

"A sicko," she answered. "A male sicko."

"You've already decided the killer's a male? What makes you say that?"

Joanna was startled to realize he was right, that she had decided, but she also understood that Ernie's question wasn't necessarily a criticism. He wanted to understand her rationale while at the same time drawing his own conclusions.

"Look at the rocks on the mound for starters," Joanna told him. "Some of them went tumbling down the mountain when the slide hit, but there must be more than a hundred or so left. How much do you think each of those little hummers weighs?"

"Ten pounds," Ernie guessed. "Some of 'em might go as high as fifteen to twenty."

"Right," Joanna said. "And look at the kind of rocks they are. They aren't from around here. They didn't come from the cliffs themselves. Those are river rocks, Ernie. Somebody went to the trouble of picking them out, one by one, and then hauling them all the way up here from down by the river. Even if the killer was strong enough to pack them two at a time, it still took a major effort on his part—effort and time both. So did piling them together all nice and neat.

"Next, take a look at this." Using the toe of her hiking boot, she pointed to the cross. "Once the rocks were in place, he manufactured this little grave marker and planted it at the head of his burial mound."

Ernie squatted and peered intently at the marker. "Underwear?" he asked.

Joanna nodded. "Bloodstained underwear."

Ernie sighed. "We'll bag this first thing."

"So call me a sexist if you want," Joanna continued, "but I can't see a woman doing this kind of thing—not the rocks and not making a trophy out of bloody underwear."

Ernie rubbed his chin. "I suppose you've got a point," he allowed.

"A point?"

"Right," he said. "The killer probably is a man. The next question is, was he a smart man or a dumb one?"

"What do you mean?"

"Like you said, it must have taken him a hell of a long time to drag all those rocks up here. What I'm wondering is whether he was smart enough to wear gloves the whole time he was doing it. And if not, is there a chance we've got some decent prints hiding in there out of the weather?"

"You're saying we should dust all the rocks for prints?"

"You've got it."

"But how? With a storm coming we can't possibly take the time to do that now . . ."

"The first thing we do is bring Deputy Sandoval's Bronco as close to the bottom of the ledge as we can get it. Then we load in as many rocks as it will carry and drag them back to the department."

That was the moment Fran Daly and Jamie Carbajal arrived with their own loads of equipment. Mike Wilson from Search and Rescue, also drafted into the role of pack animal, brought up the rear.

"You're kidding!" Fran Daly objected at once. "You want to haul all these rocks out and dust them for prints? That'll take for damned ever—all night long, probably. And I just saw a flash of lightning off over the Chiricahuas. If there's another storm rolling in from the east, we don't have time to catalog this whole pile of rocks."

The threatening storm was a legitimate concern. Still Ernie shot Joanna an exasperated look. Around the department, Detective Ernie Carpenter was known for his easygoing, long-suffering ways. In less than five minutes' worth of contact, Fran Daly had managed to outrun the man's considerable capacity for patience. That, too, had to be some kind of record.

"We'll take the time," Joanna insisted. "I heard thunder, too, and I've already taken precautions. Deputy Sandoval went back down the mountain to gather up some tarps. We'll go as far as we can before the rain gets here, cover whatever we haven't managed to accumulate in the meantime, and then come back for the rest when the weather improves. Sandoval has already taken some pictures, but you'll probably want your own. So while you three set up lights and start taking photos, I'll go down and help Eddy and Mike position the Bronco for loading."

"All right," Fran Daly said. "First we collect bugs. After that we take pictures."

Bringing the Bronco into position turned out to be far easier said than done. Parking it directly next to the mound would have placed it too close to the slide and to the edge of the gully as well. Rather than risk it tumbling down into the arroyo, they were forced to leave the vehicle some distance from the ledge. Only after considerable maneuvering did they finally settle on parking it with the hood facing down the steep mountainside and with the tailgates as near as possible to the ledge and rock pile for ease of loading.

As soon as the Bronco was in place, the group formed into a line and began dismantling the pile of rocks. Grunting with effort, they passed the small round boulders firebrigade-style, hefting them from one pair of gloved hands to another. Joanna, the last link in the human chain, took the rocks Mike Wilson handed down to her. Then she pivoted and heaved them into the waiting Bronco, letting them roll across the carpeted floorboard and come to rest against either the back of the seat or each other.

It was slow, painstaking, sweaty, and labor-intensive work. When they started, a resigned but still grumbling Fran Daly took charge of removing each boulder. Just because she didn't approve didn't mean she wasn't prepared to do a good job. Not only did she take photos prior to removal of each rock, she also labeled each one after first sketching its relative position to its neighbors. That way, if it became necessary to reconstruct the mound later on in a laboratory or courtroom setting, the evidence technicians would have a blueprint for reassembling the rocky pieces of the puzzle.

From her station near the Bronco's tailgates, Joanna was too far below the ledge and the action to be able to see exactly what was going on. Each time she turned to await the next boulder, she watched the grotesque play of shadows on the lamplit cliff face far above her. Since she had no direct view of the burial mound, her only way of accessing the work crew's progress was by seeing the load of rocks grow inside the creaking Bronco. At last, when the overloaded Bronco could hold no more, Joanna called a halt. While Mike Wilson and Deputy Sandoval went to remove the loaded vehicle and replace it with an empty one, an exhausted Joanna Brady hauled her sweaty body back up onto the ledge.

Ernie Carpenter met her there and handed her a bottle of water. "You'd better have something to drink before you drop," he said.

Joanna took the bottle, twisted off the lid, and gratefully swilled down most of the contents. The ounce or two left in the bottom of the bottle she poured over the top of her head, letting the water run through her hair and down her shirt. She hoped the water might help cool her, but it didn't do very much.

Joanna stared off to the horizon, where periodic flashes of lightning continually backlit a towering cloud bank. "Evidence or no evidence," she muttered, "I say bring on the rain."

"Don't let her Highness hear you say that," Ernie said, nodding toward Fran Daly, who was crouched on all fours next to what remained of the burial mound. "We're pretty well down to the body now. If it starts to rain before she finishes up, I'm afraid she'll go nuts."

"She already *is* nuts," Joanna said. "But what's going on? From down where I've been standing, I couldn't see a thing."

"You didn't notice that Dr. Daly got awfully quiet all of a sudden?" Ernie asked.

"Well, I did, but . . ."

"Maybe you'd better come take a look."

With the body almost totally uncovered, the stench of carrion was far worse than before. Joanna had been working far enough from the body to have to reacclimate herself to the awful odor and fight down her gag reflexes all over again. Approaching the site, she saw that Ernie was right. The majority of the rocks were gone and the corpse was mostly uncovered. Only the tops of the shoulders and head still remained hidden from view. What was visible lay pale and ghostly in a dark shadow that looked at first like it might be a pool of water.

It was only when Joanna was standing right over it that she realized what it was—saponification. That was the official, three-dollar word for the crime-scene reality of what happens to decomposing bodies. Body fluids and fat had rendered out, leaving behind a coating of fatty acid that spilled a black, greasy stain across the surface of the rock.

Joanna walked up to where Fran Daly was using a set of hemostats to pluck something off the ground. Whatever it was, it was so small that from where Joanna stood, she couldn't see what was going into the evidence bag.

"What are you finding?" she asked.

Dr. Daly didn't look up. "Bone fragments," she answered.

Expecting a more detailed answer, Joanna waited for some time. When the medical examiner said nothing more, Joanna nudged the woman again. "So how's it going?"

This time Fran Daly stopped what she was doing and stared up at Joanna. "You've got yourself a real son of a bitch here, Sheriff Brady," she said. "A real mean son of a bitch. I've found three separate sets of bullet fragments so far. As soon as I finish gathering these bits of bone, I'll go looking for the fourth."

"You're saying the victim died of bullet wounds? And how can you possibly know how many bullets were used?"

"This guy didn't shoot her to kill her; I believe he shot her so she'd be helpless," Fran said. "He shattered both kneecaps and both elbows and then left her here to die—to bleed to death."

Joanna felt sick. "What kind of an animal would do such a thing?"

"Animals wouldn't," Fran Daly replied. "Most animals I know are better people than that."

Minutes later, when Sandoval and Wilson finished trading Broncos, Joanna stayed up top while Eddy manned the tailgate position below the ledge. Enough of the rocks were gone now so that from the shoulders up only a single layer remained. Even so, Joanna fell into the rhythm of silently moving rocks without necessarily watching what was being uncovered by their removal.

"Dear God in heaven!"

On the ledge, Fran Daly's groaned exclamation brought

loading to a sudden halt. "What is it?" Joanna asked. "What's wrong?"

"Look."

Only the lower legs, exposed to sun, air, and animals, had been totally stripped clean of flesh. Under the protective layer of rocks, much of the rest of the desiccated body remained intact. The woman's tapered fingernails, covered with some kind of brightly colored enamel, still glowed purple in the artificial light. For some reason, the condition of those undamaged nails made Joanna think that the rest of the body would be pretty much whole as well. But that wasn't the case. Without a shred of either hair or skin, the back of the woman's skull glowed white and naked in the light.

"She's been scalped," Fran croaked.

The very idea was enough to take Joanna's breath away. "Scalped? How can that be?"

"Look for yourself."

For a moment Joanna stared at the bare skull in appalled fascination. Scalping was something ugly out of the Old West, something she suspected had happened far more often in the world of cheap fiction and B-grade movies than it had in real life. But still, here it was, staring back at her from the body of a murder victim in modern-day Cochise County. From the body of someone Sheriff Joanna Brady had sworn to serve and protect.

The Indian wars were long over in southern Arizona. Geronimo had surrendered to General Crook and had led his remaining ragtag band of warriors into ignominious exile in Florida. Cochise County might have been named after an Apache chief, but there were very few Apaches left in that part of the country. Real Apaches, that is.

But a few miles away from where Joanna stood at that moment, there was another Indian encampment, one made up of a band of self-declared "Apaches." She glanced back at Ernie and caught his eye.

"First thing tomorrow morning," she said, "you and Jamie and I will pay an official visit to Rattlesnake Crossing. I'm betting one of the warrior wannabes from there has declared war on the human race."

It was after midnight before Joanna finally headed for home. Miraculously, the threatened rainstorm had moved north into Graham County without ever hitting the crime scene. Once the body was loaded into a van—a second Pima County morgue van—Joanna had ordered the vicinity of the burial mound covered with tarps. That done, she and her weary collection of investigators had called it a job. If there was anything left to find, it would be better to search for it in daylight.

More than an hour later, when she was finally driving up the narrow dirt road that led to High Lonesome Ranch with Sadie and Tigger racing out to greet her, she saw two extra sets of tire tracks that had been left behind in the dirt.

Now who . . . Joanna didn't even finish framing the question before she knew the answer. Butch Dixon! Butch had come to take her to dinner and she had forgotten all about it—had forgotten all about him. She had stood the poor guy up. In typical homicide-cop fashion, she had become so embroiled with the body on the ledge that personal obligations had slipped her mind completely.

There was a note pinned to the screen door with a bent paper clip. "You must be tied up," it said. "Sorry I missed you. Butch."

Tired, dirty, and frustrated—pained by guilt and kicking herself for it—Joanna slammed her way into the house. She was mad at herself, but, unaccountably, she was also mad at Butch. After all, she hadn't *meant* to stand him up. She had tried to contact him. It wasn't her fault that he hadn't left a telephone trail so she could have caught up with him in a timely fashion and let him know what was happening.

She stopped in the laundry room, stripped off her soiled clothes, and stuffed them into the washer. Then she went straight to the phone to check for messages, hoping there would be one from Butch. There was a single message, a short one from Marianne, that had come in at eleven-fifty. "It's Mari. I'll talk to you in the morning."

And that was all. Disappointed that there was no further message from Butch and believing it was far too late to call Marianne back, Joanna headed for the shower. She stood under the steamy water, letting it roll off her stiff and aching body. And in the course of that overly long and what Eleanor would have regarded as an "extravagant" shower, Joanna Brady made a disturbing connection.

She remembered all the times her mother had been irate with her father because D. H. Lathrop had gotten himself entangled in some case or other and had missed dinner or one of Joanna's Christmas programs at church or a dinner date Eleanor had set her heart on attending. And there had been times over the years, while Andy was a deputy, that Joanna and he had played out that same drama, following almost the exact same script. Andy would come home late, and Joanna would be at the door to meet him and gripe at him for getting so involved in what he was doing that he had missed Jenny's parent/teacher conference at school or her T-ball game down at the park.

Turning off the water, Joanna stepped out of the tub, wrapped a towel around her dripping body, and stared at her image in the steam-fogged mirror. "I don't believe it," she told her reflection. "The shoe is on the other damn foot now, isn't it!"

And it was true. Joanna Brady had changed. Without realizing it, she had turned into a real cop, into someone for whom a homicide investigation became paramount and took precedence over everything else. Shaking her head, she staggered out of the bathroom. *How the hell did that happen?* she wondered.

Naked and still damp, she fell into bed. She was so exhausted that she should have dropped off right away. But she didn't. She kept seeing that bare, bony skull glowing up at her in the glare of Ernie Carpenter's battery-powered trouble light.

Finally, after an hour, she got up, went out to the kitchen, and poured herself a shot of whiskey, emptying the last of the Wild Turkey that Marianne Maculyea had brought her the night Andy died.

That, too, reminded Joanna of other times, of times Andy had come home work-exhausted, had gone to bed, but had tossed and turned and been unable to sleep. *How many times had she hassled him for that, too?* she wondered now. *How many times had she given the man hell for sitting in the kitchen in the dark late at night—for sitting and brooding?*

"Sorry, Andy," she said aloud, raising her glass in his memory. "Please forgive me. I didn't know what I was talking about."

Had there been more booze in the house, she might have been tempted to have another drink. As it was, though, she drank only the one, and then she went to bed. She might have tossed and turned some more, but the whiskey, combined with the hard physical labor of moving all those rocks, made further brooding impossible.

She lay down on the bed, put her head on the pillow, pulled the sheet up around her shoulders, and fell sleep. Not sound sleep. Not a deeply restful sleep, but sleep haunted by vague and disturbing nightmares that disappeared as soon as she awoke and tried to recall them.

Considering all she'd been through that day, maybe that was just as well.

CHAPTER TEN

The phone awakened her. Groggy from restless sleep, she almost knocked it on the floor before she finally managed to grasp the handset and get it to her ear. "Hello?"

"Joanna, I'm sorry," Angie Kellogg apologized. "I woke you up, didn't I?"

"It's all right," Joanna said, squinting at the clock. It was almost seven; the alarm would have gone off in a minute anyway. "What's up?"

"I'm at Jeff and Marianne's," Angie said. "I'm taking care of Ruth."

Joanna sat up in bed. "Esther isn't in the hospital again, is she?"

"She is," Angie replied. "And it's the most wonderful thing—wonderful and terrible at the same time. Jeff and Marianne got a call from the hospital last night. A heart became available. A little girl in Tucson drowned in her grandparents' pool. That's the terrible part, but for Esther, it's going to be wonderful."

As a wave of impatience washed over her, Joanna clambered out of bed. "If that's what was going on, why didn't Marianne say so when she called?"

"You talked to her then?" Angie asked.

"No, she left a message, but I should have known."

"Known what?" Angie asked.

"That something was going on. When I got the message I decided it was too late to call her back. What time did the hospital call?" Joanna asked.

"Right around midnight," Angie replied. "Marianne called me just as I was closing up at one, and asked if I'd come look after Ruth. I told them I'd be right over."

Helping rehabilitate Angie Kellogg, a former L.A. hooker, had been a joint project assumed by both Joanna Brady and Marianne Maculyea. After escaping virtual imprisonment at the hands of a sadistic hit-man boyfriend, twenty-five-year-old Angie had been totally without resources when she first landed in Bisbee.

Taken under Joanna's and Marianne's protective wings, Angie was making a new life for herself. Bartending for Bobo Jenkins was her first legitimate job. With Jeff Daniels' help, she had purchased her own car—a seventeen-year-old Oldsmobile Omega—which she actually knew how to drive. She owned her own little house, a two-bedroom, in what had once been company housing for Phelps Dodge miners. For topping on the cake, she also had a boyfriend—a real boyfriend—for the first time in her life. Baby-sitting on a moment's notice both for Jeff and Marianne and for Joanna was Angie's way of repaying her benefactors for all they had done for her and for all the many blessings in her new life.

"What can I do to help?" Joanna asked. "Who's going to look after Ruth when you have to go to work?"

"I already talked to Bobo about it," Angie said. Bobo Jenkins was the African-American owner of the Blue Moon Saloon and Lounge in Bisbee's famed Brewery Gulch, where

Angie worked as a relief bartender. "He said I could take both today and tomorrow off. And I talked to Dennis. He says he'll come to town early on Friday so he can take over when my shift starts."

Angie had met Dennis Hacker, a British-born naturalist, through a mutual interest in bird-watching. Originally, Angie had been fascinated by his Audubon Society-funded project to reintroduce parrots into their former habitat in the Chiricahua and Peloncillo mountains of southeastern Arizona.

Knowing that the man had spent years living a her-mitlike existence, Joanna had been concerned that Hacker's interest in the young woman didn't go far beyond her lush good looks. She had been reassured, however, by the fact that as time passed, Hacker continued to find any number of excuses for driving into Bisbee several times a week from his camp in the Peloncillos. She knew that the possibility of a blossoming romance between Angie and Dennis was anathema to some of the grizzled old-timers who frequented the Blue Moon. Having established what they considered to be squatters' rights around Angie, they regarded the lanky, blond Hacker as an unwelcome interloper, one who might very well carry Angie away with him.

Now, though, Joanna realized that the relationship be-tween Angie and Hacker was verging on serious. "You mean Dennis would do that?" she asked. "He'd come baby-sit a two-year-old in your place?"

"Of course he would," Angie answered confidently. "Why wouldn't he?"

Why indeed? *Most men wouldn't volunteer to do that on a bet,* Joanna thought. She said, "So you don't need any help from me? With Ruth, I mean."

"Not right now. Marianne left me a list of ladies from

the church who'd be willing to help out, but for the time being, I've got it handled."

Joanna glanced at her watch. "Did Marianne say what time they'd be doing the surgery?"

"This morning sometime," Angie responded. "That's all I know."

"I'll head into the office right away," Joanna said. "I'm hoping I'll be able to slip up to Tucson a little later today. Which hospital?"

"University," Angie said.

Joanna swallowed hard. That was the same hospital in Tucson where Andy had been airlifted after he was shot— the place where he had died the next day. Joanna had never wanted to go back there; had never wanted to set foot in another one of their awful waiting rooms. But still, for Jeff and Marianne—for little Esther—she would. She didn't have any choice.

"I'll be there," she said. "As soon as I can get cut loose from the department."

Ignoring the dogs and without even bothering to go to the kitchen and start coffee, Joanna headed for the bathroom. With everything that had happened in Cochise County in the past two days, there would be plenty to do, plenty to stand in the way of her getting out of the department on time, to say nothing of early.

By a quarter to eight, she was at her desk, mowing through the stack of unanswered messages that had come in the previous afternoon. By five after eight, she had corralled Dick Voland and Frank Montoya into her office for the morning briefing.

"I guess you heard about Clyde Philips," she said as Frank settled into his chair.

Montoya nodded. "If he's dead and his shop's been

cleaned out, I don't suppose we'll be buying sniper rifles from him, no matter what."

"When you talked to him, he didn't happen to mention how many of those things he had on hand, did he?"

Frowning, Frank considered a moment before he answered. "Now that you mention it, I believe he told me there were three individual weapons we could choose from, ones he had available for immediate delivery."

"Great," Joanna said. "That's just peachy."

Voland came in holding computer printouts of the previous day's incident reports. "So what all's happening, Dick?" she asked.

"Not too much. S and R's been up and out since six of the A.M.," the chief deputy replied. "Still no sign of Katrina Berridge. The evidence techs are on their way to the crime scene to pick up anything we may have missed last night. Detective Carbajal will meet them there and lead them in. Ernie is going up to Tucson to be on hand for the two autopsies. Dr. Daly has scheduled them back-to-back this morning, one right after the other."

Joanna didn't shirk from most law enforcement duties. One of the precepts of leading by example was that she didn't ask her officers to do things she herself wasn't prepared to do. The lone exception to that was standing by during autopsies. That was one official task she was more than happy to delegate to her detectives.

Joanna leaned back in her chair. "All right, then," she said. "Let's get started. We're having a tough time around here at the moment. Do we have any deputies we can spare from Patrol to augment Search and Rescue?"

Voland glowered at Frank Montoya. The Chief Deputy for Administration was charged with overseeing the budget. In that role, he had been conducting an unrelenting campaign to keep Dick Voland's Patrol Division pared to an absolute minimum.

"You're trying to get blood out of a turnip," Voland said. "Frank here has us running so close to the bone that I don't have anybody I can spare. And if I bring in off-duty officers, we'll be dealing with overtime all over again."

In these kinds of internal turf wars, Joanna often found herself agreeing with Frank and his budget considerations. This time, however, she had to come down in favor of Dick Voland's need for additional manpower.

"You're going to have to cut us a little slack here, Frank," she said. "Dick's going to have officers running two homicide investigations and conducting a search-and-rescue operation in addition to working our normal caseload. He has to have extra help. If that means overtime, that means overtime."

Frank nodded. "You're the boss," he said. "I'll see what I can do."

"Speaking of normal caseload," Joanna added, "what else went on overnight?"

"Not too much," Voland answered."We had somebody—teenagers, most likely—shooting up road signs out on Moson Road."

"Road signs but no livestock and no people, right?" Joanna asked.

"Right," Voland replied. "Two speeders, a couple of DWIs, a reported runaway from out east of Huachuca City, and that's about it. Nothing serious."

"No illegals?"

"Hard as it is to believe, nobody picked up a single one last night."

"Good," Joanna said. "What else? Any leads on that truck hijacking over by Bowie? Has anybody been in touch with Sheriff Trotter's office over in New Mexico?"

"I have," Frank volunteered. "No leads so far. The driver isn't exactly eager to talk about it. He's evidently married and doesn't want his wife to know that he stops along the road to pick up naked hitchhikers."

"That's hardly surprising," Joanna returned. "If I were in the wife's shoes, I wouldn't be any too thrilled, either." She addressed her next question to Frank. "How did the grievance hearings go?"

"Pretty well," he said. "At least they're put to rest for the time being. Some of the old-time jail guards still haven't figured out that women are in the workforce to stay. There were three different complaints, all of 'em about Tommy Fender. He's forever telling off-color jokes and making snide comments. The women finally had enough. After I heard what they had to say, I hauled Tommy into my office and gave him a second warning. I told him to cool it. I let him know if he wants to stay around the department long enough to see his retirement, he'd damned well better shape up."

"Do you think he will?" Joanna asked. "Shape up, I mean."

Frank shrugged. "Who knows? I wouldn't hold my breath. I tried to put the fear of God in him, but if he doesn't fly right and we have to fire him, we'll be stuck between a rock and a hard place. We are anyway. If we ignore what he's doing, the women take us to court for sexual harassment. And if we end up firing him over it, chances are he'll take us to court for wrongful dismissal. Either way, it's going to be a mess. And as for those two provisioners—"

"I don't have time to talk about the provisioners, Frank," Joanna interrupted. "And I don't want to talk *to* them, either. Since you and the cook are the ones most closely involved, it makes a lot more sense for the two of you to meet with them and make a decision. I have total faith in your ability to decide who we should go with and where we'll get the best deal."

"You're right about that," Dick Voland grumbled. "Montoya's such a cheapskate, you'd think every dime he spends comes out of his own personal pocket instead of the county's."

"And you should be properly grateful," Joanna told Dick, biting back the urge to smile. "After all, if you'd been in charge of the budget last year instead of Frank, there would have been approximately two weeks at the end of the fiscal year that we all would have been without paychecks, which wouldn't have been any too cool. Now, if that's all, you two clear out and let me get started on my paper."

Squabbling as usual, the two men left the office. For more than an hour Joanna whaled away at paperwork—proofing and signing off on typed reports, scanning through the agenda for the next board of supervisors meeting, reviewing two requests for family leave. Good as his word, Frank Montoya had delivered the September rotation-and-vacation schedules. Those had to be gone over in some detail and signed off on as well. It was boring, time-consuming, but necessary work. The better part of two hours had passed and Kristin had just come into Joanna's private office with that morning's collection from the post office when the phone rang. Without Kristin at her desk to intercept the call, Joanna answered it herself.

"Sheriff Brady," Ernie Carpenter said, "I've got news."

Joanna glanced at her watch. "Don't tell me Doc Daly's already finished up the autopsy."

"Hardly," Ernie replied. "But that doesn't mean she hasn't made progress. We've got a positive ID on the girl from the ledge. Her name's Ashley Brittany. She's a twenty-two-year-old oleander activist from Van Nuys, California."

"An oleander activist?" Joanna said. "What's that? And how did Fran Daly pull this one out of her hat? Considering the condition of the corpse, I figured this was one ID that would take months or even years."

"First things first. The Pima County ME is a big supporter of the FBI's National Crime Information Computer. They're on this program to make sure all their missing persons' dental records get registered. In fact, I think some professor at the University of Arizona finagled a federal grant to help them do it."

"I remember reading something about that."

"So in Pima County, it's automatic now. Once people go on the missing-person's roster, their dental charts go into the computer. This Ashley Brittany was reported missing a month ago, although she may have been gone longer than that."

"May have?"

"That's where the oleander comes in. She was part of a federal grant, which they call a federal study, sponsored by the USDA."

"The feds are looking for oleander? What's the matter?" Joanna asked. "Have people stopped smoking grass and started smoking oleander?"

"It's poison."

"Of course it's poison. But then, according to what my mother always told me, so are poinsettias. Maybe oleander's getting the same bum rap."

"I wouldn't know about that," Ernie replied. "But somebody back in D.C. came up with the bright idea that oleander is killing wildlife out in the wilds of California, Arizona, and New Mexico. They commissioned a study, and that's what Ashley was doing. She was working on a summer internship sponsored jointly by Northern Arizona University and the USDA. The Pima County Sheriff's Department found her camper and her pickup truck parked in Redington Pass three weeks ago, but they never found her."

"Because she wasn't anywhere near Redington Pass," Joanna said.

She was thinking about the sign posted outside the Triple C. About no trespassing for employees of the federal government or for people giving information to the federal government. And about the conflicting layers of regulation that, according to his wife, threatened to strangle Alton Hosfield's efforts to keep the Triple C alive and running.

"Who owns those ledges along the river?" she asked.

"I don't know," Ernie answered. "I'm not sure where the boundary lines are. That land looks as though it might belong to the Triple C, but that may not be true. Once I finish up with Doc Daly, I could check with the county recorder's office and see who the legal owner is."

"Don't bother," Joanna told him. "You stick with the autopsies. I can check with the county recorder's office. Give me a call, here or on my cell phone, when you finish up with Dr. Daly."

"Okay," Ernie said. "Will do."

"Speaking of autopsies, what's happening on that score?"

"Because of the dental chart deal, Dr. Daly decided to do the girl first. That one's done. She's taking a break and then she'll do Philips."

"She told you she thinks he's a suicide?"

"She said something to that effect, but we'll see."

"Good," Joanna said. "Keep me posted."

She put down the phone and sat staring out her office window at the lush forest of green grass and fully leafed ocotillo covering the steep, limestone-crowned hillsides behind the justice center. She had seen Alton Hosfield's No Trespassing sign, but was it possible he had made good on the implied threat by killing some poor girl out earning a college degree through doing an oleander survey? That seemed so silly as to be almost laughable. Still, Joanna knew enough about the supposed Freeman Movement to be worried. She had heard a few of them interviewed on television. A lot of what they had to say made sense—up to a point— but it was what went beyond good sense that worried her. Maybe Ashley Brittany's oleander study had been the straw that broke the camel's back. Maybe her very existence had pushed Alton Hosfield over the edge.

Joanna picked up the phone and dialed the county recorder's office. She was glad when she heard Donna Littleton's cheery "May I help you?"

Donna, verging on retirement, had worked in the recorder's office from the time she graduated from Bisbee High School. She knew more about county property parcels than anyone, and it was only a matter of minutes before Joanna had her answer. The property just across Pomerene Road from the turnoff to Rattlesnake Crossing definitely belonged to Alton Hosfield—and the Triple C.

"Thanks, Donna," Joanna said when she had the requested information. In truth she didn't feel especially grateful. The answer she had was one she hadn't necessarily wanted.

There were two phones on Joanna Brady's desk. She had just finished talking to Donna when the other one rang. This was the private line that came directly to Joanna's desk. Expecting this to be a call from Marianne, she snatched the handset up before the first ring ended.

"How about lunch?" Butch Dixon asked. "You name the place and I'll be there with bells on."

"Oh, Butch," Joanna said. "It's you."

"Yes, it's me," he said. "Don't sound so disappointed. Now that I get thinking about it, I could even use an apology. The dogs and I had a nice evening watching the stars and the moon, but it wasn't exactly what I had in mind."

"I'm sorry," Joanna said. "I got tied up with . . ." The beginning apology sounded lame, even to her, and Butch didn't give her a chance to finish.

"I know," he said. "I picked up a copy of the *Bisbee Bee* this morning and read all about it. I could see from the headlines that you had your hands full yesterday. No hard feelings."

The fact that Butch was so damned understanding about it made things that much worse. Joanna didn't remember *ever* being understanding about Andy standing her up. Eleanor hadn't been understanding, either—not as far as D. H. Lathrop was concerned. *Could that be a trait that was hidden away somewhere in maternal DNA?*

"Where do you want to have lunch?" she asked. "And when?"

"Seeing as how I missed breakfast, any time at all would be soon enough," Butch told her.

Now that he mentioned it, Joanna realized she hadn't eaten any breakfast that morning, either. "What about where?"

There was the smallest hesitation in his voice before he answered. "Daisy's."

"All right. See you there. In what, about twenty minutes?"

"That'll be fine."

She put down the phone, finished racing through the few holdover items on her desk, and put that day's crop of correspondence to one side. Then she picked up the phone. "Kristin," she said, "I'm going to lunch. After that, I'll be going up to check on things in Pomerene. When I'm done there, I may end up going on to Tucson as well, so don't expect me back in the office today."

Picking up her private phone once again, she punched in the code that would forward all the calls on that line directly to her cell phone. If Marianne and Jeff called her from the hospital, she didn't want to risk missing them.

Joanna's corner office had a private entrance that opened directly onto her reserved spot in the parking lot. She had picked up her purse and was on her way to the door when the regular switchboard line rang once more. She hurried back to her desk and snatched the receiver up to her ear.

"What is it, Kristin?" she asked impatiently. "I was just on my way out the door."

"I know, Sheriff Brady," Kristin Marsten said. "But I thought you'd want to take this call. It's from Detective Carbajal."

"Right. Put him through."

"I think we found her," Jamie said as soon as he came on the line.

"Found who, Katrina Berridge?"

"That's right," he said, but there was nothing in his tone that sounded like the usual elation and pride of accomplishment that follow a successful search-and-rescue operation. Joanna heard none of the triumph searchers exhibit when they've gone into the wilderness and returned with a living, breathing, formerly missing person.

She felt a sudden clutch of dread in her gut, a knowledge that the other shoe was about to drop. "She's dead, then?"

Jamie sighed. "Yes, she is."

"How did it happen? Where did you find her?"

"The body is only half a mile south of where we were last night. If we hadn't been delayed by finding the first one yesterday, we might have found this one then as well. The victim was shot to shit with something big."

"How big?" Joanna asked. "A fifty-caliber, maybe?"

"Possibly."

But there was something more in young Jaime Carbajal's voice—a pained reticence—that Joanna almost missed at first. "What else?" she demanded.

"This one's the same as the other one," he said.

"What other one?"

"The victim we found last night. Like I said, she was shot. That's probably what killed her, but afterward . . ."

There was a part of Sheriff Joanna Brady that didn't want him to go on, didn't want to hear what he had to say. But there was another part that already knew what was coming.

"Afterward, what?" Joanna demanded. "Was she scalped?"

"You got it," Detective Carbajal replied bleakly. "From the middle of her forehead to the back of her neck, there's nothing left but bare bone. Nothing at all."

Stunned, half sick, Joanna allowed her body to sink back into her chair. For the space of a few seconds she said nothing, letting the awful realization penetrate her being. Joanna's department had started out to investigate reports of someone shooting up local livestock. Instead, her investigators had stumbled into the deranged leavings of someone who was obviously a serial killer.

"Have you called Ernie?" she asked finally.

"Not yet, but I will."

"Do it right away. I talked to him just a little while ago from the Pima County Medical Examiner's office. If we're lucky, you may be able to catch him and Dr. Daly before she starts on the second autopsy. Where are you now?"

"Still at the scene. The S and R guys are roping it off. Evidence techs are up working on the ledge. There's no sense in bringing them here until after the ME does what she needs to do."

"All right," Joanna said. "Finish up as soon as you can, then meet me at Pomerene Road and Rattlesnake Crossing.

I want to be with you when you go to notify Katrina Berridge's husband and sister-in-law. In the meantime, get on the horn to the FBI and see whether or not this is an MO they've seen before."

"Will do," Jamie replied. "How soon do you expect to be here, Sheriff Brady?"

"Soon," Joanna answered. "I'm on my way."

CHAPTER ELEVEN

As soon as she turned the key in the ignition, Joanna remembered Butch. She also realized that if she went straight to Rattlesnake Crossing without either breakfast or lunch, her body would run out of fuel long before she finished what she'd have to do that day. Not only that, she didn't know when there'd be another chance to eat. Pulling her cell phone out of her purse, she punched in the number of Daisy's Cafe. Not surprisingly, Daisy herself answered the phone.

"Sheriff Brady," she said, "your gentleman friend is already here. I've got him stowed in a booth and drinking coffee."

"Good," Joanna said. "And that's why I'm calling. Something's come up. I'm going to have to go on a call, but I thought I'd try to eat and run. Put in my order for chorizo and scrambled eggs and then go ahead and pour my coffee. I'll be there in three minutes or less."

"What about O.J.?" Daisy asked.

"I'll have some of that, too."

"Good enough," Daisy said. "It'll be on the table by the time you get here."

When Joanna pulled into the parking lot, the first vehicle she saw was Butch's Goldwing. That struck her as odd, because she clearly remembered him saying that he *wouldn't* be Goldwing-ing it when he came to take her to dinner. *Oh well,* she thought, *he must have changed his mind.*

She climbed out of the Blazer and slammed the door. That was when she saw a little white Nissan Sentra sedan with the *Bisbee Bee* logo on the door and a windshield sunscreen with the word PRESS printed on the outside. Joanna recognized the vehicle at once. It was one usually driven by Marliss Shackleford, whose tell-all column, "Bisbee Buzzings," kept the *Bee*'s circulation humming with local gossip. Ever since Joanna's election to sheriff, she had often found herself chewed up and spit out as part of Marliss' journalistic fodder. The fact that the sheriff and the columnist were both parishioners of Canyon United Methodist Church had done nothing to blunt the difficulties between them.

In the small-town world of Bisbee and of Cochise County, Joanna Brady was regarded as a public person. What she did or didn't do was thought to be of interest to everyone—at least that was how Marliss seemed to view the situation. Unhappy with the constant scrutiny, Joanna had learned to dodge the woman whenever possible. In small towns and even smaller churches, that wasn't always possible. Just as it wouldn't be now, when Joanna would be seen having breakfast with an out-of-town visitor—a *male* out-of-town visitor.

Marliss had already been introduced to Butch Dixon once—on the occasion of Joanna's mother's wedding reception after her marriage to Dr. George Winfield. If Marliss saw Joanna and Butch having breakfast together in Bisbee, no telling what conclusions she would jump to or how those would play out in her next column.

For two cents Joanna would have climbed back into the Blazer and driven away. But she couldn't do that. It wouldn't have been fair to Butch or to Daisy, either one. Squaring her shoulders, Joanna marched into the restaurant. Walking inside, she clung to the faint hope that she and Butch would be seated close enough to the door so she could slip in and out without being noticed. Unfortunately, Butch waved to her from the far corner booth, two tables beyond where Marliss sat chatting with her boss, Ken Dawson, the publisher and editor in chief of the *Bisbee Bee.*

Because Daisy was already carrying a pair of loaded plates toward the booth where Butch was sitting, Joanna gave Marliss a wave and hurried past almost before the woman saw her and without pausing long enough to exchange any pleasantries.

"Good morning, sunshine," Butch said with a grin, toasting her with his newly filled coffee cup. "I understand this is going to be wham, bam, thank you ma'am. I'm glad you could squeeze me in, although you're probably here more for the chorizo and eggs than you are for me."

"I'm sorry to do this to you twice in a row," Joanna said, "but Search and Rescue just now found another body up by Pomerene."

The grin disappeared from Butch's face. "The woman who was missing?"

"You know about that?" Joanna asked.

Butch held up a copy of that morning's *Bee.* "I'd say the coverage was pretty thorough. I always wondered what happened to the guy."

"What happened to what guy?"

"To Danny Berridge."

"You mean you know him?"

"I don't know him *per se,* but I know *of* him. He's a former Indy driver. He won several races. Placed second or maybe third at Indy one year. Was named Rookie of the Year. The next year during the Indy 500, he wiped out one of the track people—one of the safety workers. He walked away from the wreck and the track. That was the last I ever heard of him until I read about him in this morning's paper. At least I'm assuming it's the same guy. How many Daniel Berridges could there be?"

"The article didn't actually *identify* him as the same guy?"

"No, but I just assumed. He's evidently had a hell of a life, and now with his wife turning up dead . . ."

Joanna covered her lips with a finger. "We probably shouldn't talk about this right now. We don't have a positive ID and nobody's notified the next of kin. That's where I'm going right now—to meet up with the detectives and then go talk to the husband."

"I can see why you're in a hurry," Butch said, picking up his fork. "You'd better go ahead and eat before it gets cold. You need to keep up your strength."

Joanna's heaping platter of scrambled eggs mixed with hot, spicy chorizo came with a helping of cheese-smothered refried beans, a dish of Daisy's eye-watering salsa, and a tortilla warmer stacked full of tiny, homemade flour tortillas fresh from the grill in the kitchen. Butch helped himself to one, slathered it with butter, and took a bite. As soon as he did, a beatific smile spread across his features.

"I didn't know it was possible to find a place that still served homemade tortillas."

Joanna took one herself. "You have to go pretty far out into the boondocks before that happens," she said.

For several moments they ate in silence. "If it wasn't in

the paper, how did you know all this about Daniel Berridge?" she asked.

"Didn't I tell you?" Butch returned. "I'm a big race-car
fan."

No, Joanna thought, *you didn't tell me.* There were obviously any number of things she didn't know about Frederick
"Butch" Dixon. Even so, she knew that she still owed him
an apology.

"Look," she said, "I really am sorry about standing you
up last night. As soon as the call came in and I knew it was
going to be a problem, I tried calling, but your phone—"

"Good morning, Joanna," Marliss Shackleford said, sauntering up to the table, coffee cup in hand. "I hope you'll
excuse the interruption, but I had to know if you've heard
anything about Esther's surgery."

Joanna had no intention of pardoning the interruption,
but there was no way of ignoring it, either. Butch Dixon
looked up quickly and caught her eye. "Jeff and Marianne's
little girl?" he asked.

Joanna nodded. "Esther's been on a transplant waiting
list almost as long as she's been here. Because of her ethnic
background, the doctors hadn't held out much hope of finding a tissue match, but now they have one. The hospital
called last night and told them a heart just became available.
The surgeons are expecting to do the transplant sometime
today. This morning, most likely."

"So who's taking care of poor little Ruth?" Marliss asked.

"Angie Kellogg," Joanna said.

Marliss Shackleford's face twisted into a disapproving
frown. "Not that girl who—"

Joanna cut Marliss off in mid-sentence. "Angie is a friend
of Marianne's, and she's also a friend of mine. She also happens to be a very capable baby-sitter. Ruth adores her."

Marliss wasn't easily dissuaded. "You'd think that, as a

minister and in a situation like this, Marianne would call on someone . . ." The steely-eyed look Joanna leveled in her direction caused Marliss to pause and rethink what she was about to say. "Well, on someone from church, for example. I'm sure any number of the ladies from the church would have been willing . . ."

"The call came through in the middle of the night," Joanna told her. "I'm sure most of the ladies from church— you included—were all sound asleep in your neat little beds. Angie, on the other hand, was still at work and wide awake."

Dismissing Marliss, Joanna turned her attention to her plate, stabbing her fork deep into the steaming mound of scrambled eggs and sausage. Rather than taking the hint and leaving, Marliss stood her ground and cast around for a more rewarding topic of discussion. In the process, her eyes settled greedily on Butch Dixon's smoothly clean-shaven head. "You're not someone from around town, are you?" she said to him. "But I seem to remember that we've met before."

"That's right," Butch agreed mildly, putting down his fork and holding out his hand. "You're a newspaper reporter, I believe. Frederick Dixon's the name, and yes, we did meet before. At Joanna's mother's wedding reception."

"Of course." Marliss summoned her sweetest smile. "That's right. You're Joanna's friend. Down from Phoenix, are you?"

"Peoria, actually. But Phoenix is close enough. All those towns seem to run together."

"What brings you down our way?"

Over another forkful of egg, Joanna sought Butch's eyes. There was no way to say aloud what was going through her mind. *This woman is a malevolent witch. Anything you say to her is going to wind up in print.*

Unspoken or not, Butch must somehow have gotten the message. He gave Marliss an engaging grin. "Just passing through," he said. "My business is up in the Valley of the Sun, and we have a little too much of that this time of year— sun, not business. So it's a good time for me to get out of town for some well deserved R and R."

"I see," Marliss said. "What kind of business are you in?"

Joanna groaned inwardly. *Oh, great,* she thought. *Next he's going to tell her he owns a bar up there. Just wait until the ladies from church get wind of all the latest. An ex-prostitute is baby-sitting Ruth Maculyea-Daniels and Sheriff Joanna Brady is hanging out with a guy who rides a motorcycle and owns a bar!*

"Hospitality," Butch replied blandly.

Joanna almost choked with relief. Meanwhile, Marliss sidled closer to Butch's side of the table. "Really. So are you down here checking out how Bisbee does in that department?" The question was asked with one eyebrow arched meaningfully in Joanna's direction. "Hospitality, I mean."

"It's great," he said. "I'm staying up at the Copper Queen this time. It seems to be quite satisfactory."

Visibly disappointed, Marliss turned back to Joanna. "Any inside scoops about what's going on up in Pomerene?"

Sure, Marliss. We've just figured out that we've got a serial killer loose in Cochise County, and I'm going to give you an exclusive on it.

"Not at this time," Joanna said. She finished the last morsel of chorizo and eggs. Something was making her nose run, and she wasn't sure if the heat came from the sausage or from the salsa. Taking one remaining tortilla from the warmer, she buttered it and then waved down Daisy.

"Any chance of getting a cup of coffee to go?"

"Coming right up."

"And the bill, please, too."

"Don't bother with that," Butch said. "I'm buying."

"Well," Marliss said, finally accepting the fact that the conversation was over, "I guess I'll be going." She headed back to her own table.

And not a moment too soon, Joanna thought, watching her go.

"Can I see you tonight?" Butch asked.

Joanna shook her head. She hadn't told Marliss about the serial-killer part, and she wasn't going to tell Butch, either. "I can't promise, what with everything going on at work and with Esther in the hospital in Tucson. Even if I did say yes, I couldn't give you any guarantees about what time I'd finish up. That's one of the reasons I feel so rotten about last night. You were stuck out there on the porch by yourself for all that time."

"After living up around Phoenix, I thought it was gloriously quiet. Believe me, I enjoyed every minute of it. I especially got a kick out of watching that storm off to the east, the one that put on such a light show and then never let loose with a smidgen of rain. 'Full of sound and fury' and all that jazz."

Daisy dropped off both a traveler coffee cup and the bill. Butch snagged the bill away before Joanna could touch it. "So how about it?" he added, not taking no for an answer. "How about if I show up at your house about the same time I did yesterday—say seven or so. And when you get home, we'll see what time it is and decide what to do then."

She wanted to say no, but he had come all that way and would be here for just a couple of days. It was only natural that he wanted to spend time with her. "All right," she agreed. "But if you come out to the house, don't wait on the porch. There's a key hidden in the grass. Use it to let yourself in. That way, if I get hung up, at least I'll be able to let you know what's going on."

"A key hidden outside?" Butch asked. "Are you sure that's safe?"

Joanna laughed. "It's in the grass just to the right of the front-porch step, hidden under a plastic dog turd—a very realistic-looking plastic dog turd. Believe me, with Sadie and Tigger around, nobody's going to suspect that dark brown pile lying there in the grass isn't the real McCoy."

"I suppose not," Butch said. "Come to think of it, maybe I'll double-check before I pick it up."

Finishing the last of her orange juice, Joanna stood up. "Sorry to have to eat and run like this."

He waved her away. "It's fine," he said. "But if you don't mind, I'm going to hang around and drink my last cup of coffee here. I'd take one with me but coffee and motorcycles don't necessarily go together."

Grabbing both her purse and the Styrofoam cup, Joanna dashed toward the door. She was in the Blazer and headed uptown when she realized Butch Dixon hadn't told the truth to Marliss Shackleford. He had said that his business was up in Phoenix. But the phone to the Roundhouse Bar and Grill had been disconnected. *His business used to be in Phoenix*, Joanna thought. *But it isn't anymore.*

By the time she was up over the Divide, however, she had stopped thinking about Butch and was back to worrying about the case. Picking up the radio, she asked Dispatch to put her through to Detective Carbajal.

"What's happening?" she asked.

"I've been on the horn to Maricopa County," he told her. "According to the sheriff's office up there, we've got a possible."

"A case with the same MO?"

"Unfortunately, yes. It's old—from two years ago—and

it's still open. A fourteen-year-old named Rebecca Flowers was found up near Lake Pleasant north of Sun City. Shot first and then . . . well, you know the rest."

"No leads?"

"None so far. And my guess is nobody looked very hard. Rebecca was a street kid, a drugged-up runaway from Yuma. And since it hadn't happened again as far as anybody could tell, there wasn't any reason to take it very seriously."

"Until now," Joanna said. She switched on her blinking red emergency lights and pressed the gas pedal all the way to the floor.

"Right," Jaime agreed hollowly. "Until now."

"You've talked to Ernie?"

"Yes, and her Highness, Dr. Daly, too," Jaime replied. "You were right. I managed to catch her between autopsies. They're both on their way right now. Depending on where you are and where they are . . ."

"I'm just south of Tombstone," Joanna said.

"Then you'll probably be here within minutes of one another."

"Where are you meeting them?"

"They're coming straight here. I gave them directions. It's the same little track we took last night, the one off Pomerene Road right across from Rattlesnake Crossing. You'll come to a Y where we turned right last night. Go left this time. It'll lead you right here."

Still wearing her work clothes, Joanna had come dressed for next-of-kin notification rather than crime-scene investigation. Still, if that was where everyone else was going, she would, too.

"Listen, Jaime," she warned Detective Carbajal, "this is going to be a high-profile case. We're going strictly by the book on this one. I don't want any procedures skipped or skimped. You got that?"

"Got it, Sheriff Brady," Jaime said. "I hear you loud and clear."

As she finished with Detective Carbajal, Joanna was fast coming up on Tombstone proper. She slowed slightly, but not much. Her next call was to Frank Montoya, still closeted in his office back at the department. "Frank," she told him, "I need your help. Get on the horn to Motor Vehicles and track down some information on Daniel Berridge."

"The guy who's wife is missing?" Frank asked.

"The guy who's wife is dead," Joanna corrected. "S and R just found the body. I want you to check out his date of birth and then compare it with a retired race-car driver by the same name, a guy who once drove in the Indy 500."

"You think they're one and the same? What gives you that idea?"

"A little bird told me," Joanna said. "Check it out. Let me know as soon as you can."

Even though it was summer, as she passed Tombstone's elementary and high schools, she slowed down some more just to be sure. Then, when she reached the Chevron station, she whipped across two lanes of traffic and pulled in, threading her way past two out-of-state minivans loaded to the gills with kids, dogs, and luggage.

Parking as close to the rest-room door as possible and leaving her lights flashing, she whipped her suitcase of freshly laundered just-in-case clothes out of the back of the Blazer. It would be far easier to change clothes in a restroom than it would be at the crime scene. Less than two minutes after ducking into the rest room, she was outside again. Dashing toward the Blazer, she almost collided with a little boy of about seven or eight who stood next to the door.

"Lady," he said, wiping an orange circle of soda onto his shirtsleeve, "how come you got those flashing lights on the front of this car? You a cop or something?"

Joanna unlocked the door with her remote key and stuffed her clothes and the suitcase back inside. She was in a terrible hurry. It would have been easy to ignore the kid, but in the interest of good public relations, she stopped long enough to answer him. "Or something," she said.

"What does that mean?" he persisted. "Are you or aren't you?"

"I'm a police officer," she said. "Actually, I'm the sheriff."

"No, you're not," he said. "My dad just took me to see the O.K. Corral. Wyatt Earp's the sheriff."

"Wyatt Earp was a marshal," Joanna corrected. "But that was a long time ago. Now I'm the sheriff." She reached into the Blazer and pulled one of her business cards out of the packet she kept on the windshield visor. "See there? That's my name. It says Sheriff Joanna Brady."

"Darren," a shorts-clad woman called. "What are you doing? Come get in the car."

Darren studied the card and then glanced briefly in his mother's direction, but he didn't move. "A girl can't be a sheriff!" he said finally. "They grow up to be mothers and stuff, not sheriffs."

"Darren," his mother called again, "come here this minute!" Still Darren didn't move.

"You'd be surprised," Joanna told him. With that she climbed into the Blazer and took off. When she looked in the rearview mirror, she saw him still standing there, gazing thoughtfully after her as though what she had told him was more than his young mind could fathom.

That was exactly when she turned on her siren full blast—when she did it and why as well, telling herself, *The devil made me do it.*

Darren's obnoxious image stayed with Joanna long after she had turned the curve and erased him from sight. He was only a couple of years younger than Jenny, yet he was being brainwashed into believing sexual stereotypes that sounded as if they had stepped straight out of the fifties—from one of the old sitcoms like *Leave It to Beaver* or from a *Little Lulu* comic book.

Let's hope Darren and Jenny never meet, Joanna thought. *If he ever tried spouting that stupid stuff to her, she'd probably punch the little twerp's lights out. And it would serve him right.*

CHAPTER TWELVE

As Joanna headed north toward St. David with Darren's image still fresh in her mind, she was struck by a sudden pang of loneliness. Missing Jenny terribly, she grabbed up the cell phone and let the auto dialer call the Unger farm outside Enid, Oklahoma. All she wanted to do was talk to her daughter, to reassure herself that Jenny was holding her own against her hooligan cousins. But there was no answer, and by the time the Ungers' answering machine was about to begin, a radio transmission was coming in from Chief Deputy Montoya.

"What do you have for me, Frank?" she asked.

"All I can say is, that little bird of yours is right on the money," Frank told her. "Katrina Berridge's husband, Daniel, is indeed retired Indy driver Danny Berridge."

"That's what I was afraid of."

"Ruby Starr and I were just finishing working over the menus for next month, but if there's something else you need me to do . . ."

"Actually, there is," Joanna replied. "You and Dick Voland both better hotfoot it over to this new crime scene on the Triple C north of Pomerene. There's going to be lots of media attention on this one, and I'll want you to be on tap from square one. I'll brief you both once you get there."

When Joanna herself reached the crime scene, Detective Carpenter and Dr. Daly were already on-site and on the job. In the sheltering shade of a thicket of mesquite just short of the river bed, Dr. Daly was using what looked like a finely screened butterfly net to capture flies. Meanwhile, Ernie had gone up to the first crime scene on the ledge to confer with the evidence techs who were there working on the previous night's burial mound. By the time Joanna was ready to approach the body, Fran Daly was bent over it, carefully tweezing what looked suspiciously like maggots into a small glass vial.

Lost in concentration on her grisly work, and wearing a mask over her mouth and nostrils, Dr. Daly seemed oblivious to the sheriff's approach. Joanna had tried to steel herself in advance for what was coming, but the effort was mostly wasted. One look at the dead woman's bloody, denuded skull and gas-bloated body was enough to leave Joanna feeling weak-kneed and nauseated.

"What do you think?" she asked at last, after once again taming her unruly gag reflexes.

Dr. Daly looked up. "Well, Sheriff Brady," she said, "it's like this. I think we're looking for some asshole who has delusions of grandeur. Thinks of himself as some kind of Ernest Hemingway-style big-game hunter. She was shot from some distance away. Look here." Dr. Daly pointed at the woman's sliced shorts where a shallow wound cut from back to front across the victim's right thigh.

"That looks to me like a shot that nearly missed, one that just barely grazed her. The same goes for this one that nearly severed her left hand. My guess is he was aiming for a body shot each time and missed. It must have taken him three shots or more to adjust for windage. After that first shot—the one on her thigh, most likely—she took off running. At least she tried to run, but she couldn't get out of range. The shot that actually killed her came from the back and exited through the front of her chest. From the looks of it, I'd say it took most of her heart and lung tissue with it. That one killed her instantly."

Joanna felt an involuntary chill as she remembered how the other victim—Ashley Brittany—had been rendered helpless by four deliberately placed close-range shots that had shattered her joints and left her stranded on her back as helpless as an overturned box turtle.

"In a case like this, I guess dying instantly is a blessing, isn't it," Joanna managed.

Dr. Daly gave her an appraising look and nodded. "Yes," she agreed. "I suppose it is."

"Can you tell what kind of bullet?" Joanna asked.

"From the size of the exit wound, I'd say we're looking for something one notch under a cannon."

"Something like a fifty-caliber?"

Fran Daly frowned. "Maybe," she replied. "Why do you say that?"

"Because night before last, we had reports from this neighborhood of shots being fired. Two cattle were killed and an irrigation pump was shot to hell, all of it done with what we've pretty well ascertained must have been a fifty-caliber sniper rifle."

"That happened right here on the Triple C?" Dr. Daly asked.

Joanna nodded. "This ranch, but not in this same spot. About a mile or so from here."

"But sniper-rifle kill ranges can cover that much ground and more," Fran said. "Are you thinking maybe a killer started out shooting up machinery and livestock just for the hell of it and then moved on to her?"

"Right."

Removing her face mask, Fran lit a cigarette. "It could be," she mused. "It just could be."

With that the medical examiner fell silent. The second-hand smoke from her unfiltered Camels helped to cut some of the awful odor. Somehow ignoring the gaping wound in the dead woman's chest, Joanna tried to understand exactly what had happened.

"Do you think this is where she fell?" she asked.

Fran shook her head. Using her cigarette, she pointed toward where two thin dark strands of stain wandered off across the rocky terrain. "If you follow that trail out about twenty-five yards, you'll find the kill zone. It's pretty much out in the open. He dragged her in here under the trees after she was already dead."

"So if we're going to find bullets, that's where they'll be," Joanna said. "Out there where she fell."

"That's right."

Joanna looked upward through the lacy canopy of mesquite leaves that sheltered the scene from the worst of the early-afternoon sun. "If he went to the trouble of bringing her this far, maybe he was worried someone would be looking for her. Maybe he thought someone might mount an airborne search. Bringing her under cover would make spotting her from the air almost impossible."

Fran Daly nodded thoughtfully. "Sounds reasonable to me," she said.

Basking in the doctor's mild but still unexpected approval, Joanna went on theorizing. "The scalping's the same, but there are some obvious differences between the two cases. This body is still fully dressed, while Ashley Brittany was naked. There's no cross here, and no rocks, either. But maybe the killer just hadn't gotten around to that part of it yet. With Ashley, he must have known he had plenty of time. Her pickup truck was found over near Redington Pass. He probably moved it there himself. At any rate, he most likely was fairly confident no one would come looking for her here. That's why he could shoot her and leave her to bleed to death at leisure. That's also how he could afford to spend God knows how long gathering up the rocks he used to bury her.

"With this victim, he's more rushed, more hurried. It's as though Ashley's death was premeditated, while Katrina's wasn't. Maybe she just happened to be in the wrong place at the wrong time. Maybe he came out here to shoot up the cattle and stumbled over her in the process."

When Joanna stopped talking, Fran Daly was staring at her, staring and frowning. "How long did you say you've been a homicide detective?" the medical examiner asked.

At once Joanna felt embarrassed and self-conscious, sure her blatant lack of experience was showing. "I didn't say," she said.

"Why not?" Fran Daly pressed.

"Because I never have been," Joanna admitted. "I've managed an insurance office and been a mother, but I've never been a detective."

"You could have fooled me," Fran Daly said. "It sounds like you've got a good head for it. Now, have you established any kind of trajectory on the shots that killed those animals?"

Surprised by this undiluted praise, Joanna had trouble answering. "Not yet," she managed. "We're working on it."

"Well, we'd better make that a top priority. If we can figure out where the guy was when he started pulling the trigger, maybe we can find something that will tell us who he is and how to find him. We've got to take this animal off the streets, Sheriff Brady," she added urgently. "If we don't, you'd better believe he's going to kill again."

With that the medical examiner resumed her work. Dismissed, but feeling a sense of connection to the brusque woman, Joanna returned to her assembled troops—the two detectives and the members of the S and R team, all of whom were still standing by at a distance to see what would be required of them. Something Fran Daly had said had raised a red flag in Joanna's brain—the idea that the killer might kill again. What if he already had? What if there were more than two slaughtered victims hidden here in the wilds of the Triple C? Maybe the ledge beneath the cliffs—maybe the cliffs themselves—held other cairns and other mutilated bodies.

She called Mike Wilson over to her Blazer. "How are your guys doing?" she asked. "Are they ready to call it a day, or are they willing to work some more?"

"They're a gung-ho bunch, Sheriff Brady," Wilson replied. "You tell me what you want them to do, and they'll do it."

"I want somebody to go up and search those cliffs from end to end," she said. "Both the tops of the cliffs and the ledges that run underneath them. I'm worried we may have other victims up there, ones we haven't even found yet."

"We'll get right on it," Wilson said.

"There's something else. I want this whole area combed for evidence of any kind—tracks, blood, fibers, whatever. Dr. Daly can tell you where the victim was hit. That area should be cordoned off and held in reserve for the evidence techs. I'm hoping that's where we'll find the bullet that killed her. But there were other shots as well, with bullets that went astray. With any kind of luck we'll find them. I can order out deputies and have them here doing the search within a matter of an hour or so, but if your guys wouldn't mind . . ."

"No problem at all," Wilson assured her. "I'll split the team into two groups. Half of them will go up the mountain. I'll get the others working down here on the flat."

As Wilson went off to issue orders and dispatch his people, Joanna turned to Detectives Carpenter and Carbajal. Ernie's face was screwed into a disapproving frown. "What the hell's the deal?" he asked. "Why send Search and Rescue to do something detectives and evidence technicians should handle? Those clowns may be fine at finding lost hikers, but they're not going to know real evidence from a hole in the ground unless it jumps up and hits them in the face. Send those guys home and wait for people who actually know what they're doing. We're going to have plenty of help from real detectives. I just heard Pima County is sending us a pair of investigators. So is Maricopa."

"I'm afraid we're going to have more than plenty of help," Joanna said grimly. "Which is why we need to do what searching we're going to do now, *before* the place is overrun with a bunch of outsiders."

"What do you mean, more than plenty of help?" Ernie asked.

"Has either one of you ever heard of a race-car driver named Danny Berridge?"

Detective Carbajal shrugged his shoulders. "Not me," he said.

"Danny Berridge." Ernie Carpenter repeated the name as a frown burrowed across his forehead. "That sounds familiar somehow. Wait—wasn't he that Indy 500 driver who dropped out of sight several years back, sometime in the late eighties or so? I seem to remember that he was involved in some kind of on-track accident and then . . . Wait . . . are you telling us Danny Berridge is Katrina Berridge's husband?"

"One and the same," Joanna replied.

"How did you find that out?"

"I just lucked into it."

"But is it confirmed?"

"Yes. Frank Montoya already checked it out. So that means we not only have a serial murderer on our hands, we also have a case that's going to arouse a good deal of national interest. With the other cases and other counties involved, it would be bad enough to just have the Tucson and Phoenix media breathing down our necks. This one will probably draw reporters from all over."

"Great," Ernie grumbled. After a moment he brightened. "Get thinking about it, this thing could have an upside."

"What's that?" Joanna asked.

"My mother-in-law loves the *National Enquirer*," he replied. "Phylis is always asking me when one of my cases is going to appear in *her* paper. If the Indy driver turns out to be our killer, maybe this is it."

"Don't even *think* such a thing," Joanna told him.

While Ernie and Jaime set off to join the S and R team in the ground search, Joanna stared up the road, wondering how long it would take for Dick Voland and Frank Montoya to arrive on the scene. It was early afternoon in the middle of August. As the desert heat bore down on her, she rummaged in the back of the Blazer for a bottle of water. She had finally succeeded in locating what was evidently her last one when the phone in her purse rang.

Joanna's cell phone had come complete with an option that allowed her to adjust and personalize the ringer. In order to differentiate her phone from others, she had chosen the ringer option that sounded for all the world like the early-morning crow of an enthusiastic rooster.

"Hello," she said, after finally pawing the instrument out of the depths of her purse.

"They're done," Marianne Maculyea said. "Esther's out of surgery and in the transplant intensive care unit."

Joanna breathed a relieved sigh. "Thank God," she said. "How are you and Jeff doing?"

"We're both pretty ragged," Marianne admitted. "Jeff's at a phone down the hall calling his folks. I decided to call you."

Joanna heard the unspoken subtext in that simple statement. Jeff Daniels could call his parents and tell them the news. Marianne couldn't. Marianne's parents had never recovered from their daughter's public defection from the Catholic Church and becoming a Methodist minister. Over the years, Marianne had given Joanna helpful hints about resolving the mother/daughter rifts between Joanna and Eleanor Lathrop. That didn't mean, however, that she had ever been able to heal the long-standing feud with her own mother.

"Thanks for letting me know," Joanna said, not commenting on the unspoken part of the message. "Angie called early this morning to let me know what was happening. I decided that it was better for me to wait for you to call me rather than the other way around. Are you staying in Tucson?"

"For tonight anyway," Marianne replied. "We've booked a room at the Plaza at Speedway and Campbell. Once Jeff gets off the phone, he'll probably head over there to catch a nap. He'll come back later and spell me. I don't know about tomorrow. One or the other of us will go home to be with Ruth, or maybe Angie or somebody can bring her up here for a little while during the day."

There was a pause. "You don't necessarily sound all that hot yourself, Joanna. What's going on with you?"

Jeff and Marianne were enmeshed in the all-consuming cocoon of their own little crisis, and justifiably so. Joanna could see no reason to trouble Marianne Maculyea with any of the grim details of what was happening right then on the Triple C.

"I'm overseeing a search right now," Joanna answered carefully. "And then I have some interviews, but I thought I'd try dropping by the hospital later on this afternoon if that's all right with you."

"Please," Marianne said. "That would be great. I'd really like to see you. So would Jeff."

Something in Marianne's tone bothered Joanna—something she couldn't quite put her finger on. "Esther is all right, isn't she?" she asked.

"Yes," Marianne replied, her voice cracking. "At least I think so."

"What's wrong, then?"

"That's just it. I don't know. Maybe I'm just tired. We were here all night long. Neither one of us has had any sleep . . ."

"No, Mari," Joanna countered. "It's more than that." A long silence filled the phone. "What is it?" she urged. "Tell me."

Marianne took a deep breath. "You remember that night Andy was here in the hospital?" she said at last.

Joanna remembered every bit of it. Too well. "Yes," she said.

"Remember when you told me you were trying to pray, but you couldn't remember the words?"

That moment was still crystal clear in Joanna's heart and memory, as if it had happened mere minutes ago. She squeezed her eyes shut against a sudden film of tears that threatened to blind her.

"You told me that it didn't matter," Joanna said. "You

told me that trying to remember the words was good enough because God knew what I meant. And then you offered to pray for me."

"I shouldn't have," Marianne said now. The black hopelessness in her friend's words wrung Joanna's heart, made her want to weep.

"What do you mean, you shouldn't have?"

"I had no right," Marianne said. "I didn't know what I was talking about."

"Of course you did. What are you saying, Marianne? What's wrong?"

"I've been here all night trying to pray myself, but I can't, Joanna. And it's not just the words that I've lost, either. It's more than that. Far more. How could God do something like this to us and to Esther? How could He make Esther so sick that the only way to save her is for some other mother's baby to die? That's not right. It's not fair."

Marianne lapsed into a series of stricken sobs. For several seconds Joanna listened and said nothing. There was nothing she could think of to say. How could she go about comforting someone who was a steadfast friend and pillar of strength to everyone else?

"You'll get through this," Joanna said finally.

"Yes," Marianne choked, "maybe I will. But how will I ever be able to stand up at the pulpit and preach about faith when my own is so totally lacking? How can I teach about a loving God when I'm so pissed off at Him I can barely stand it?"

Joanna smiled in spite of herself. Marianne Maculyea, the rock-throwing firebrand rebel she had known in junior high at Lowell School, was a firebrand still.

"If you're so totally lacking in faith," Joanna pointed out, "you wouldn't even acknowledge God, much less be pissed at Him. Now, have you had any asleep?"

Even as she asked the question, Joanna reminded herself of her mother-in-law. For Eva Lou Brady, a crisis of the soul was almost always rooted in some physical reality.

"No," Marianne admitted.

"What about having something to eat?"

"Jeff brought me a tray from the cafeteria a little while ago, but I couldn't eat it. I wasn't hungry."

"Is the food still there?"

"The tray is."

"Eat some of it," Joanna urged. "Even if it tastes like sawdust when you try to choke it down. You're going to need your strength, Marianne. If you don't eat or sleep, you're not going to be worth a plugged nickel when you'll want to be at your best. If you're strung out because of lack of food or rest, you won't have anything to offer Esther when she finally comes out from under the anesthetic. She's going to need you then, and you'd better be ready."

There was another stretch of silence and Marianne seemed to consider what she'd been told. "I'll try," she said at last.

Joanna saw two vehicles pulling up behind the Blazer—Dick Voland's Bronco and Frank Montoya's Crown Victoria. "Good," Joanna said. "You do that. And remember, I'll be there either later this afternoon or else this evening. All right?"

"All right."

"You hang tough."

As soon as the call ended, Joanna stood with the phone in her hand. She thought about calling the Copper Queen Hotel directly and telling Butch that she wouldn't be able to see him that night, but she was afraid he'd talk his way around her. Instead, feeling like a heel and a coward to boot, she punched in the code for the sheriff's department.

"Kristin," she said as soon as her secretary came on the

line, "I don't have much time. Please call the Copper Queen Hotel and leave a message for Mr. Frederick Dixon. Tell him I won't be able to join him for dinner tonight. Tell him I'm going up to Tucson to see Jeff Daniels and Marianne Maculyea."

"Got it," Kristin said. "Copper Queen, Frederick Dixon, and you can't make it for dinner. How're Jeff and Marianne doing, by the way? I had lunch with my mother. She was telling me about the transplant. I don't know who told her."

I can guess, Joanna thought. *And her initials are Marliss Shackleford.*

"They're okay," she said. "At least they're doing as well as can be expected."

Finished with the call, she tried to reassure herself that she had handled the Butch Dixon situation in a kind and reasonable fashion. He might be disappointed, but at least she hadn't just left him hanging for a change. Still, though—

Her thoughts were interrupted by an excited shout from one of the S and R guys a good quarter of a mile away.

"Sheriff Brady," Mike Wilson yelled, relaying the message. "Come take a look at this."

With Dick Voland and Frank Montoya both trailing behind her, Joanna hurried over to where Mike was standing. Several of the other S and R guys were already converging on the spot. Ernie Carpenter and Jaime Carbajal weren't far behind.

"What is it?" Joanna demanded when she finally reached Mike.

He pointed toward the ground. "Look," he said.

There, nestled between a pair of rocks and winking back the brilliant late-summer sunlight, was a watch—a gold-and-silver Omega. On the watch's pearlescent face behind the remains of a shattered crystal, the two hands stood stopped at 10:26. That was the time Sonja Hosfield had told her she remembered hearing shots. Around ten-thirty.

Looking around, Joanna saw the blood spatters and knew this was the killing ground—the place Katrina Berridge had fallen to earth. She looked up and caught Ernie's eye. "Have you found any bullets?" she asked.

"Not yet," he said. "But we're looking."

"Hey, Mike." Terry Gregovich's voice shrilled out of the speaker on a small walkie-talkie fastened to the collar of Mike Wilson's orange hunting vest. "I think we may have found something up here."

All eyes turned from the watch and the blood-spattered ground around it to the majestic cliffs rising from the valley floor. There, barely visible and clambering over the rock face like so many orange-bodied ants, were the other members of the Search and Rescue team.

"What have you got, Terry?" Mike Wilson asked.

"No shells or anything like that," Terry Gregovich replied. "But I've got some funny little marks here in the dirt. Looks like they might have come from someone setting up a tripod. And some footprints, too. A couple of them might even be good enough to cast."

Joanna closed her eyes. *Now we're making progress,* she thought. "Great," she said to Mike. "Grab one of the evidence techs from the burial mound and get him over to Terry to make plaster casts. On the double. We lucked out that it didn't rain here yesterday, but that's not to say a storm won't blow through today."

Joanna knew enough to be thankful. Considering the amount of space involved, it was more than luck that someone had stumbled across the possible footprints on top of the cliffs and recognized their importance. It also crossed her mind that Terry Gregovich's skills and talents might be underutilized by his being permanently sidelined in Search and Rescue.

"Hey, Mike," she said, "do your guys carry binoculars?"

"We all do."

"Ask Terry to look off the other side of the cliffs and see if he can see the ranch house at the Triple C."

A few moments later, Terry replied in the affirmative.

"Now look off to the left of that," Joanna continued. "To the north. There's a well with a big pump on it with two dead cattle nearby. Can he see those from there?"

This time the search took a little longer, but eventually it paid off. "I can see them clear as a bell," Terry said.

"That's it, then," Joanna said. "That must have been where he was when he started shooting. Good work, Terry. Great work, in fact. This may be exactly the kind of break we need."

"So what should I do now?" Terry Gregovich asked.

"Don't touch a thing," Joanna told him. "Stay right where you are until the evidence guys show up with their plaster. And when you get down off the mountain, make an appointment to see Chief Deputy Montoya."

"What for?" Terry asked.

"To put in for a promotion," Joanna said. "You've earned it. You can tell him I said to find a spot for you in Patrol with the possibility of working into Investigations."

CHAPTER THIRTEEN

Ernie Carpenter bagged the blood-spattered watch and Jaime Carbajal logged it. While they worked the actual crime scene, the S and R team continued to range over the river bottom and rising hillsides in search of evidence as well as the ugly, if unspoken, possibility of finding other victims. Within half an hour, Joanna's two detectives were joined by investigators from Pima County, Detectives Lazier and Hemming.

Hot, bored, and unable to make any real contribution to the task at hand, Joanna finally took Ernie aside. "I think somebody should go to Rattlesnake Crossing and let them know what we've found. I'd hate for either Crow Woman or Danny Berridge to hear the news on the radio or from some enterprising reporter before we deliver the notification in person."

"We've got three detectives working here now," Ernie said. "So if you'd like me to go along with you . . ."

Next-of-kin notifications always left Joanna with a hole in the pit of her stomach. Telling someone of the death of a

181

loved one, regardless of whether that news was expected or not, often took as much of a toll on the messenger as it did on the recipient. Whoever brought the word was automatically forced into the role of front-row spectator as someone else's entire existence imploded around him. Still, it had to be done, and this one would be worse than most.

"I'd appreciate that, Ernie," she told him gratefully. "I'd appreciate it more than you know."

Leaving the on-going crime-scene investigations under the overall direction of Dick Voland, Joanna took Ernie Carpenter along with her in the Blazer for the drive to Rattlesnake Crossing. Bumping up the rough, dusty road toward the main ranch buildings, Joanna had the sense that she was traveling through some kind of deserted movie set. No people were visible, anywhere, but she did notice for the first time that all the ersatz tepees and hogans had air-conditioning units attached to discreetly camouflaged platforms placed at the rear of each pseudo-Indian dwelling.

"If these guys want to pay good money to turn themselves into real Indians for two weeks at a time, you'd think they'd be tough enough to put up with real Arizona weather."

Ernie ignored the wry humor in her comment. "The scalping's real enough," he said grimly. "Whoever's doing this made damned sure he got that part right."

Joanna glanced in Ernie's direction. "Have you ever seen anything like this?" she asked.

"No," he admitted. "I never have."

"Since it's likely the killer's using a sniper rifle, is it possible all of this is connected to what happened to Clyde Philips?"

Ernie thought about that for a moment. "It could be, I suppose," he said finally. "The fact that a fifty-caliber may have been used in this latest case does point in that direction. We know from what Frank told us that Clyde was trying to demo a fifty-caliber, so he must have had one or more in stock."

"Frank told me this morning that Clyde claimed to have three different models available for immediate delivery."

"So he did have some, then," Ernie mused. "But which ones? And how do we know the killer's rifle is one of them? Without any serial numbers . . ."

"Wait a minute." Joanna reached for the radio clip. "Frank," she said once she had been put through to Chief Deputy Montoya, "how many companies manufacture fifty-calibers?"

"Not that many," he replied. "More than five but probably less than twenty nationwide."

"As soon as you get back to the department, and when you're not busy dodging reporters, I want you to call all those companies. ATF should be able to help out in locating manufacturers. Once you have them on the phone, find out if any of them were doing business with Clyde Philips in Pomerene. They should be able to come up with lists of serial numbers."

"Will do," Frank returned. "I'll get to it as soon as possible, although it may be a while. The first wad of reporters just drove up and they're clamoring for information. I told them to go to the Quarter Horse in Benson and wait for me there. How are you doing on the next-of-kin notification?"

"We're about to pull into the yard at Rattlesnake Crossing. "We'll check in with you as soon as it's done."

Joanna stopped the Blazer in front of a sprawling ranch house built of bulging gray river rock and gnarled, rough-hewn eight-inch timbers. She and Ernie stepped onto a spacious covered porch with flagstone flooring and a scattering of cushion-covered wooden rocking chairs. At the door, Joanna turned and took in the view. The house was built on a low rise. Anyone who had been seated on one of the porch chairs would have looked off across the San Pedro to the ridge of cliffs behind it.

"If a person had a strong enough scope," she observed, "he could have sat right here and seen the whole thing."

"That's a pretty big if," Detective Carpenter replied.

Nailed to the doorjamb was a wooden notice that said, PLEASE ENTER. Since there was no sign of either a bell or a knocker, Joanna and Ernie did as they were told. Driving from the crime scene to Rattlesnake Crossing, Joanna had used the Blazer's air-conditioning, but the two officers had been out in the unrelenting heat for so long that they were still overheated when they entered the ranch house and found it to be surprisingly cool. The room was spacious and decorated with the kind of over-stuffed furniture most often seen in old-time hotel lobbies. Directly across from the officers was what looked like an unmanned hotel check-in counter, complete with a silver bell and directions to PLEASE RING FOR ASSISTANCE.

Ernie picked up the small silver bell and gave it a shake. For a long time after that, nothing happened. While they waited, Joanna plucked an expensive-looking, all-color brochure off the counter. It was filled with tourist-grabbing photos of the ranch house, some of the tepees, and what looked like an Olympic-sized swimming pool. The pictures included one of a beautiful, raven-haired young woman wearing a squaw dress and weaving a green and white bear grass/yucca basket. Another shot showed a war-painted young man wearing little more than a loincloth and sitting bareback astride a pinto pony. Behind rider and pony was a vivid, saguaro-punctuated sunset.

Come to Apache Country, the bold-faced ad copy said. Live along the fabled San Pedro as Native American Peoples did for thousands of years before *the coming of the White Man. Give your mind and body the purifying cleansing that only a sweat lodge ceremony can provide. Find or renew your life's purpose by enduring your own personal Vision Quest. Return to your workaday world with the blessing and direction that can come only from the Great Spirit.*

She handed the brochure to Ernie and he read it, too. "Who dreamed this up?" he asked, handing it back to her. "Sounds like the Apaches meet the New Agers. A two-week stay probably comes complete with frequent-flyer miles and a free pass to the Happy Hunting Ground. And the restorative value of the purification ceremony will be directly proportioned to how much lighter the poor guy's wallet is."

Suppressing a chuckle, Joanna turned over the brochure. On the back was a paragraph that read:

THE LEGEND OF RATTLESNAKE CROSSING

Once, no rattlesnakes lived in the Land of the Apaches. They roamed the cliffs and hills on the far side of the river, but the water was so deep and swift that none could cross it. One day a great storm settled over the valley. From one full moon to the next, it rained and rained. It rained so long and so hard that some of the mountains tumbled down across the path of the river, leaving behind a wall of solid earth. Wise Old Rattlesnake took some of the younger ones and led them across the river. They have lived here ever since.

"May I help you?"

Joanna had expected Crow Woman to make an appearance. Instead, the person behind the counter was a tanned and handsome, blond-haired, blue-eyed man who looked to be in his early forties. His words were touched by the slightest trace of a New York accent.

"I'm Sheriff Joanna Brady," she said, bringing out her ID. "And this is Detective Ernie Carpenter. We're looking for either Daniel Berridge or someone named Crow Woman."

A quick flash of something that looked like hope passed across the man's chiseled features. "I'm Danny," he said. "Have you found her, then?"

"We're not sure, Mr. Berridge," Ernie put in. "We need to ask you a few questions."

"You *have* found her!" Daniel Berridge exclaimed as all hope disappeared from his face and was replaced by unmasked despair. "She's dead, isn't she? I knew it. What happened? Did she fall? Did a cougar get her? A snake? What?"

In this case, Joanna thought, *being dead is the least of it.* "We're not sure the person we found is your wife," she said kindly. "Detective Carpenter and I have been going over a copy of the missing-person report Deputy Sandoval took yesterday. It says Katrina was wearing a watch when she left home. Unfortunately, the report neglected to say what kind."

"An Omega," Daniel Berridge answered at once. "I bought it for her for Christmas years ago."

Ernie reached into his pocket and pulled out the see-through bag containing the remains of the shattered watch. "This one?" he asked.

Daniel Berridge looked at it and nodded numbly. "That's it," he said. "Where is she? Please, tell me what happened."

"Search and Rescue found her on the far side of the river," Joanna said. "She was shot—shot and mutilated."

"Oh, God," Daniel groaned as his face reddened and contorted with grief. He swallowed hard. "Was she . . . was she raped, too?"

"No," Joanna said. "To the best of our knowledge, she was spared that. From the looks of it, all her clothing was still intact."

"But I thought you said she'd been mutilated. What does that mean?"

"I'm sorry, Mr. Berridge. There's no easy or kind way to tell you this. Whoever murdered your wife also scalped her."

"Scalped," he whispered hoarsely. "You're kidding! This is the twentieth century, for God's sake. This has to be some kind of sick joke. You're making it up."

"No," Joanna said. "I wish I were."

Stumbling backward Daniel Berridge collapsed on a low, rolling stool. He buried his face in his hands, and sobbed. Several minutes passed before he was once again capable of speech.

"What kind of a monster would do such a thing?" he croaked. "It's awful. It's insane."

"Yes," Joanna said. "I couldn't agree more. It *is* insane and whoever did it is indeed a monster."

For a time the room was silent except for the ticking of an immense grandfather clock. Finally Berridge seemed to pull himself together. "Who did it?" he asked. "What kind of a person could do such a thing? And why?"

"We don't know," Joanna said. "We were hoping you might be able to help us answer some of those questions. Did your wife quarrel with anyone recently? Did she have any disagreements with some of the guests here, or maybe with one of the other employees?"

Daniel Berridge's teary eyes met Joanna's. "Only me," he said bleakly. "The only person Tina ever quarreled with was me."

"When?"

"Just before she went out Monday afternoon. She told

me then that she was going to leave me—for good. She insisted she wanted a divorce, and if I wouldn't give her one, she'd get one anyway. When she disappeared right after that, I thought that was what had happened. Even though she didn't take anything with her—no clothes, no luggage—I still thought that the next time I heard from her would be through a lawyer. I never thought she'd turn up dead. I still can't believe it. I can't."

"What was the quarrel about, Mr. Berridge?"

"Money," he said. "Money and racing."

Just then a door on the far side of the lobby opened, and Crow Woman swept in. She was dressed much as she had been the day before, except this time her hair was pulled back into a hair net and she wore a long white cook's apron over her almost floor-length squaw dress.

"Danny?" she called. "Are you in here? Somebody said there were cars out front—" Crow Woman stopped short when she saw Joanna and Ernie. "What are you doing here?" she demanded.

"They found Trina," Daniel Berridge said.

"Good. I'm ready to have her come home to the kitchen, where she belongs. That substitute cook we hired from Sierra Vista doesn't know up from down."

"Trina isn't coming home," Daniel Berridge said softly. "She's dead, Carol. Somebody shot her."

Now it was Crow Woman's turn to stumble in search of a place to sit. "Shot?" she echoed. "No. Are you sure?"

"It's Trina, all right. They found her watch."

Crow Woman stood up and went over to the man who was supposedly her brother, although the two of them were as different as day and night. "Oh, Danny," she murmured. "I'm so sorry. Who did it? Do they know yet?"

"No . . ." Joanna began.

"And she wasn't just shot, Carol. Sheriff Brady here says

she was scalped." Daniel Berridge's voice broke over the word. "Whoever killed her scalped her."

"My God. I can't imagine . . ."

"I can," he said fiercely. "It's probably one of the guests. I've been telling you all along, Carol. Some of these people are nutcases. Just because they've got enough money to come here and stay for two weeks doesn't mean they aren't crazy."

"Oh, no," Crow Woman gasped. "A few of them may be a little strange, but I'm sure they're not killers. That's utterly out of the question."

"What do you mean, strange?" Joanna asked.

"Strange?" Daniel Berridge repeated. "I'll tell you about strange. Most of the people who come here have been playing at being Indians for years. It's a big deal over in Europe, in Germany especially. Sort of like Boy Scouts, but for grown-ups. For adults. People have little bands that go on camp-outs together. They give themselves Indian names and dress in Indian costumes. Some of them learn to make baskets or do beadwork.

"They believe Indians still live close to nature, and they think that by coming here, they're getting the real thing. It's bullshit, of course. They'd be astonished if they saw 'real' Indians, if they went out to Sells or over to San Carlos or into one of the reservation gambling casinos. Our guests don't want to know that the Indians in this country aren't any better off than, say, Turkish immigrants are in Germany. And here at Rattlesnake Crossing, they don't have to. They're in no more danger of meeting a genuine Indian here than they are a genuine Turk—"

"We give them what they want," Crow Woman interjected. "We give them what they *expect* to find here."

"We make money and we give them a crock of horseshit," Danny Berridge countered. "We let them sleep on Posturepedic mattresses in air-conditioned cabins or spend the night cooking their brains out in a stupid sweat lodge. And when they go back home after this 'native' experience— when they go back to Düsseldorf or Frankfurt or Kempten— they're convinced that they've been touched by the Great Spirit. Give me a break!"

"Danny, please. What if one of them were to hear . . ."

"Let 'em," Daniel Berridge said fiercely. "Because when I find the son of a bitch who did that to Tina, I swear to God I'm going to return the favor!" With that he stood up, strode across the lobby and disappeared outside, slamming the heavy wooden plank door behind him.

Crow Woman gazed after him wonderingly. "I've never seen Danny like this," she said. "And he doesn't mean it, of course. He's the kindest, most gentle man I know. He wouldn't hurt anyone, but still . . ."

"Your brother told us that he and Trina quarreled before she left," Joanna said. "Is that true?"

Crow Woman looked at her. "I suppose so," she said. "I mean, I didn't hear them fighting myself, but Danny told me about it later. And I guess I knew it was coming."

"Knew what was coming?"

"That she'd leave."

"Why?"

Crow Woman shrugged. "She was tired. Tired of working so hard and getting nowhere. Struggling along with an operation like this is a lot different from being an Indy driver's wife. Cooking three meals a day for twenty-five or so fussy people isn't exactly glamorous, and I'm sure she thought she deserved better. She had this unrealistic idea that Danny could go back to racing any time he wanted; that he could pick up where he left off with cars and sponsors and all, and things would go back to being the way they used to be." Crow Woman stopped. "I don't suppose you know about any of that."

"We know your brother is a retired Indy driver," Joanna said.

"That news is out, then?" Crow Woman shook her head. "That means people around here are going to know who he is."

"People all over the country are going to know who and where he is," Joanna replied. "As soon as the wire services pick up on the murders, you can bet it'll go national."

Crow Woman stared questioningly into Joanna's face. "Did you say murders?"

Joanna nodded. "Your sister-in-law and at least two others. One of the other two victims was found here in the immediate area. The other one was a fourteen-year-old runaway from Yuma. Her body was found up near Phoenix."

"Then the killer couldn't possibly be one of our guests," Crow Woman said with what sounded like genuine relief.

"Why do you say that?" the sheriff asked.

"Our guests are booked in for two weeks at a time with a tour operator out of Munich. When they leave here, they get on a bus and go straight to the Grand Canyon. Do not pass Go; do not collect two hundred dollars. Between here and there one of them wouldn't be able to stop off in Phoenix long enough for visiting a Burger King, to say nothing of killing someone."

"If your sister-in-law worked here for you as a cook, what's your brother's function?" Ernie put in.

"Danny's my handyman extraordinaire," Crow Woman answered. "From the time he could walk he was taking things apart and putting them back together. It used to drive our parents nuts. He keeps the air-conditioning units running, fixes the pool filter when it conks out, looks after the grounds. But you're wrong about one thing. Danny doesn't work for me, and Trina didn't, either."

"But I thought . . ."

"We're all equal partners in this," Crow Woman said. "If it weren't for the money and effort the two of them sank into this place, I never would have made it. You see, the ranch belonged to my husband originally," she explained. "To my ex-husband, that is. You may have heard of him— Dr. Lamphere, Dr. Carlton Lamphere."

Joanna remembered the story well enough. The scandal surrounding Dr. Lamphere and the sexual exploitation of his patients had been big news in Cochise County. But she, along with everyone else, had been under the impression that the people who had taken over the place and renamed it Rattlesnake Crossing were unrelated to the previous owner. And Crow Woman had done nothing to disspell that notion. *No wonder she changed her name,* Joanna thought. *Under the circumstances, I would have changed mine, too.*

"I'm familiar with some of what went on," Joanna said.

"Some but not all," Crow Woman returned with more than a trace of bitterness. "After one paternity suit was followed by several additional malpractice suits, there wasn't much left for anybody, especially an ex-wife. By the time the attorneys finished picking the bones, the ranch here was all that was left to be divvied up by the divorce decree. The only reason I got this was that none of Carlton's creditors wanted it or could figure out what to do with it. Bottom line, I came out of a twenty-year marriage with nothing to show for my trouble but a relatively worthless chunk of Arizona real estate. But I was sitting around thinking one day and I came up with this crazy idea that maybe I could turn it into a moneymaking proposition after all. And I have. Not by myself, mind you, but with Danny and Trina's help. After Danny left racing, he wanted to find a place to disappear out of the public eye. This was as good a spot as any to do just that."

"Let me get this straight," Ernie said. "Your sister-in-law has been gone for two days now, but you've already hired a replacement cook. Is that right?"

"Danny and I had to do that," Crow Woman said. "I can boil water occasionally. I can even peel a potato or two, but I can't cook. I've never been able to cook. So of course we hired a cook—early yesterday morning. Too late for her to help with lunch, but time enough for her to cook dinner."

"How did you manage that so fast?" Ernie asked. "This doesn't seem like the kind of place where people would be lined up looking for work."

"Oh, that." Crow Woman waved a hand dismissively. "We already had a list of potential applicants. Danny told me weeks ago that it might come to this. That Trina might leave."

"If he expected her to go, why did he report her missing, then?"

"Because she didn't take anything with her. Trina wasn't a woman who traveled light. She wouldn't have left here without taking her stuff. So when she did go, it was more or less what Danny expected, but she didn't do it the *way* he expected. Besides, if the police brought her back, maybe he could talk her out of leaving. Does that make sense?"

The outside door opened and Danny Berridge slammed his way back inside. Earlier, he had been dressed in work clothes—a short-sleeved khaki shirt, shorts, and work boots. Now he wore a light blue sport shirt, a pair of nice slacks, and dress-up boots.

"Where is she, Sheriff Brady?" he demanded. "Don't you need someone to identify the body?"

"Yes, we do, but it might be better if you waited until we got her into the morgue in Tucson."

"No," he said. "I want to do it now."

"Danny," Crow Woman said, "you don't have to do that. I'll handle it for you if you want me to."

"No," Daniel Berridge insisted. "She was my wife. It's my responsibility. Let's go," he said to Joanna. "I want to get this over with."

CHAPTER FOURTEEN

With Daniel Berridge in the front seat and Ernie Carpenter in the back, Joanna drove the Blazer back to the crime scene. She could see as they drove up that they were just in time. Fran Daly and her two helpers were within bare minutes of loading the body into a waiting Pima County van.

Daniel and Ernie stepped out of the Blazer. Joanna was about to follow when her phone rang. "Go on, you guys," she said, wrestling the phone out of her purse. "I'll take this call and then catch up in a minute. Hello?"

"Mom?" Jenny's voice was bright and chipper. "How are you? Are you at home or are you still at work?"

The sudden shift between crime scene and domestic scene—between being a cop and being a mother—did its usual mind-bending trick.

"I'm still at work," Joanna told her.

"But you sound funny. Strange. Like you're in a well." The cheeriness drained out of Jenny's voice and was replaced by a certain wariness. "Maybe your phone is weak or something. Maybe the battery is tired."

"I'm out in the middle of nowhere," Joanna said. "East of Benson. The signal is probably weak. I tried to call you earlier this afternoon, but no one was home."

"That's what I wanted to tell you about. This afternoon."

Up ahead of the Blazer, a small procession moved toward the waiting van. The two technicians from the Pima County ME's office carried a loaded stretcher. Behind them walked Fran Daly. Not surprisingly, she was sucking on the smoldering stub of a cigarette.

When Ernie and Daniel Berridge met up with them, the little procession came to a sudden halt. Fran Daly stepped forward and nudged the lead technician out of the way. After a brief conference with Detective Carpenter, she unzipped the top of the body bag, then stood aside to give Daniel Berridge an unobstructed view.

"Mom," Jenny said insistently, "are you listening to me or not?"

"I'm sorry, Jenny. There's lots going on right now. What were you saying again? I must have missed some of it."

"We were out picking rocks in the field today, and Melvin let me drive the tractor. My very own self. Can you believe it? He let Rodney and Brian do it, too. I didn't think he was going to let me because . . . well, you know. Because I'm a girl. That's what Rodney said, anyway. But Grandpa talked to him—to Melvin, not Rodney—and the next thing I knew, there I was driving the tractor. It was great. Aren't you proud of me?"

"Yes, I am. Of course I am."

Over Jenny's excited prattle, Joanna watched the drama unfold in front of her. She saw Daniel Berridge glance briefly into the body bag; then she saw the way he shuddered and drew back. As the color drained from his face he nodded and his lips moved. "It's her." Even though Joanna couldn't hear him, she knew exactly what he had said. Then he turned and blundered blindly away from the others. Several feet away he settled heavily onto a boulder, and once again buried his face in his hands.

Watching someone else encounter the soul-killing death of a loved one always carried Joanna directly back to that awful time in her own life, to that sandy wasteland of a wash where she had found Andy's mangled and bleeding body.

In that respect, Jenny's phone call couldn't have come at a better time. It had kept Joanna inside the truck with the windshield and a few feet of desert creating a sort of emotional buffer between her own aching heart and Daniel Berridge's mind-numbing pain. Without the luxury of that distance, Joanna knew only too well that she would have been sucked down into Daniel Berridge's crushing whirlpool of grief right along with him.

". . . that's okay, isn't it?"

Again Joanna had no idea what was being said on the other end of the cell-phone connection. "Is what okay?" she asked stupidly.

"Mother!" Jenny complained. "Are you listening to me or *not*?"

"I'm trying to, sweetie," Joanna apologized. "As I said, there's lots of other stuff going on. What were you saying?"

"The Grandma and Grandpa want to take me into town tomorrow to buy school clothes. I told the Gs you wouldn't mind. Please say yes, Mom. They really do want to."

Joanna sighed. "If they want to spoil you, that's okay with me."

"Mom, are you all right?" Jenny demanded. "Your voice sounds so funny, and it's not just the phone, either."

For a second, it seemed as if their roles were suddenly reversed—as though Jenny was the mother and Joanna the daughter. "Esther's in the hospital," Joanna said. "She had her heart transplant this morning. That was one of the things I was going to tell you when I called. But you were out, and I didn't want to leave a message."

Jenny took a deep breath. "Is she going to be okay?"

"As far as we know. I talked to Marianne this afternoon. Esther's out of surgery and in intensive care."

"I'll bet Jeff and Marianne are really scared. Shouldn't we send them flowers or something?"

"What a good idea," Joanna replied. "I'm planning to go see them later on today. I'll be sure to take them some flowers. I know they'll appreciate it."

By now the body bag had been zipped back up and the stretcher loaded into the van. Daniel Berridge straightened up and stood for a moment as if uncertain of what his next move should be. Joanna was relieved when Ernie Carpenter took the man by the arm and led him back toward the Blazer.

"Jenny," she said, "I'm going to have to go."

"Will you call me tonight and let me know how Esther's doing?"

"Yes, of course I will."

"And Mom?"

"What?"

"What about poor little Ruthie? What will happen to her if Esther dies or something? What if she never comes back from the hospital? Daddy didn't. They took him away and he never came back. The same thing could happen to Esther."

With death there is no "or something," Joanna thought. "Don't worry, Esther will be fine," she said with as much conviction as she could manage. "But even if something awful did happen, Ruthie would still have Jeff and Marianne to love her."

"That's different," Jenny said. "That's not like having a real sister."

"No," Joanna agreed, "I don't suppose it is. I've got to go now, Jenny. I love you."

"I love you, too."

Ernie Carpenter was pulling open the back door to the Blazer. "We've got a positive, Sheriff Brady," he told her unnecessarily. "From the looks of things, the evidence techs and the detectives are going to be here for the next several hours. Probably right up until dark or until it rains again, whichever comes first. So if you wouldn't mind taking Mr. Berridge back to Rattlesnake Crossing, I'd really appreciate it."

Glancing to the east, she saw columns of fat thunderheads rising over the Chiricahuas. Quickly she folded her phone and returned it to her purse. "No problem," she said, motioning to the still ashen-faced Daniel Berridge. "I'll be glad to take you back."

The return trip to Rattlesnake Crossing was conducted in absolute silence. While a stricken Daniel Berridge stared stonily out the window, Joanna tried desperately to think of something to say that wouldn't sound either stupid or patronizing. Only when he opened the door to climb out did she finally find words.

"I'm very sorry about all this, Mr. Berridge. I lost my husband, too, so I know what you're going through. It's a bitch!"

He had started to slam the door shut. But when he opened it once more and stared back across the seat at Joanna, she was touched to see that trails of tears were still clearly marked on his pallid face.

"You warned me," he said, "but I didn't know how bad it would be to see her like that. I had no idea."

"We should have foreseen that. If I'd been thinking, we

could have waited and just used dental records. It might have taken a little longer, but not much, and it would have spared you—"

"No," he interrupted. "I wanted to see her. I wanted to see her the way she is now. That way I won't be able to kid myself into thinking that she's coming back."

Joanna saw the terrible emptiness in Daniel Berridge's eyes. She knew part of the pain had nothing whatever to do with how Trina Berridge looked now—had nothing to do with the indignities that had been inflicted on her body during and after her death. Her husband's hurt came from what had gone before, from the quarrel that had sent Trina Berridge into the desert in the first place. Hoping to ease the man's pain, Joanna found herself admitting to this stranger something she had mentioned to no one else, not even to Marianne. It was something so hurtful that she barely acknowledged it herself.

"Andy and I fought too," she said quietly.

"Excuse me?" Berridge said.

"Andy," Joanna said. "My husband. We had a big fight the morning he was shot. It took me months to learn that I had to let it go, Mr. Berridge. I can never take back those angry words, but the words aren't what killed him. The two aren't related."

The combination of surprise and aching distress that flashed across the man's face told Joanna she was right, that she had unearthed part of what was adding extra weight to an already overwhelming burden of grief.

"But it is my fault," he insisted. "We had a fight, she walked out, and now she's dead. If I had just kept my mouth shut—"

"If it hadn't been Katrina," Joanna heard herself saying, "it would have been someone else."

"What do you mean?"

"We're dealing with a monster here, Mr. Berridge. I believe he was out hunting, looking for someone to kill. My guess is your wife walked into his range finder and he blew her away. That same night he also shot up some of Alton Hosfield's cattle and an irrigation pump over on the other side of the cliffs but still on Triple C property. He probably gave the same amount of thought to killing your wife as he did to killing the cattle."

"But how . . ."

"He's a serial killer, Mr. Berridge. We're pretty sure of one other case and have tentative links to at least one more. There may be others as well, ones we don't know about yet."

"But how can this be? I had no idea there were others. If he's been operating around here, how come nobody ever heard anything about him?"

"We told your sister earlier, but it must have been after you left the lobby. Once these cases hit the media, as they probably will, either this afternoon or tomorrow morning for sure, you need to know that everything about this case is going to come under intense media scrutiny. Your years of relative anonymity here will be at an end."

"They already were," he replied.

"What do you mean?"

"A few months back, this guy showed up here at the ranch unannounced. I don't remember his name now, but he said he was writing a book on failed sports stars." He paused and frowned in concentration. "What was the title? I'm sure he thought it was real catchy. That's it. *Losers Weepers* was the name of it. All about sports greats or near greats who, for one reason or another, hung up their cleats or gloves or whatever and went home without ever living up to their supposed potential."

"And did you talk to him?"

"For a few minutes, but when he finally explained what he was after, I told him to take a hike."

"What was he after?"

"He wanted to know why I quit."

"And did you tell him?"

"No," Berridge said. "But I'll tell you. I lost my nerve. It was during the Indy. We were going around the track on a yellow. I wasn't even going that fast—seventy or so, maybe. And I was feeling great. I'd had the lead for twelve laps until somebody else spun out on the third turn. I was coming past the place where the safety team was cleaning debris off the track. And then my left rear tire flew off. For no reason, although they said later that I ran over a piece of metal that exploded the tire and tore the wheel right off the axle. It hit one of the safety guys full in the face. Broke his neck. He died instantly. I remember seeing his kids on TV that night, three little girls. The oldest was eleven; the youngest, seven. I haven't been in an Indy car since then. It just wasn't worth it to me. If I could kill somebody going seventy, what the hell could I do at two hundred?"

"But your wife wanted you to go back to it?" Joanna asked.

Berridge nodded. "Trina was really offended by the book and by my being included, with or without an interview. She went behind my back. She started calling up some of our old friends from racing, trying to see if she could put together a deal—a car, a sponsorship, all of that. She almost made it work, too. Two weeks ago, I happened to answer the phone in the middle of the day. Usually I'm outside then. This time, though, when nobody else answered, I picked it up. And I recognized the guy's voice the moment he opened his mouth—Tom Forbes. We used to be buddies when I was on the circuit. Now he's team manager for my old sponsor.

" 'How're you doing out there, Bud?' Tom says to me. That's what he always called me—Bud. 'I hear you're think-ing about coming back into the fold.' I didn't know what to tell him. That was the first I had heard anything about it. But as soon as I talked to Trina, I figured out where it came from. I told her no deal, and that's when the fighting started. I knew right then it was just a matter of time."

"That's when you started shopping around for a replace-ment cook?" Joanna asked.

"That's right." He paused. "Racing gets in your blood. It can be dangerous as hell, but it's also glamorous and exciting. And you can make a hell of a lot more money by winning a single race than you can grubbing out an exis-tence here for five or ten years. What Trina didn't under-stand is that I like this better. I like taking the time to plant something and then having a chance to watch it grow. I like taking something apart—like a broken bread machine—and putting it back together so it works like new."

The plank door slammed at the front of the ranch house. Joanna looked up and was surprised to see a collection of several people—young men, mostly—staring at them. Daniel Berridge saw them, too. "I'd better go," he said. "And I'm doing better now. Thanks for letting me talk. I guess I needed to."

Joanna nodded. In a few minutes of not asking questions, she had learned far more about Daniel Berridge than might have emerged in even the most focused of interrogations. By talking to him about Andy—by revealing her own dark secret—she had created a bond between them, a human con-nection, that left her utterly convinced that the man had no involvement in his wife's death.

Turning the Blazer to drive back out of the yard, Joanna tried to catch a glimpse of Rattlesnake Crossing's current crop of temporary residents. For Apache-warrior wannabes, the group of mop-haired, mostly blond young men standing on the porch looked disturbingly normal and ordinary.

When Joanna had crossed Pomerene Road earlier to bring Berridge home to Rattlesnake Crossing, the four-way intersection had been empty. Now, though, a white Nissan was parked there—a Nissan Sentra with a *Bisbee Bee* logo plastered on the door.

Not Marliss again, Joanna thought despairingly. *Not twice in one day.*

She would have tried to drive right on by, but Marliss Shackleford had seen the Blazer coming toward her. She clambered out of her car, waving frantically.

Joanna slowed and rolled down her window. "Is something the matter?" she asked.

"Is this where it all happened?" Marliss pointed up the now well-worn dirt track that led off toward the cliffs. "Is this where you're finding all the bodies?"

"From right here, this is a crime scene," Joanna told her. "That means it's off-limits for everyone but investigating officers."

"But what happened out here?" Marliss demanded. "Tell me. Back in town we're hearing all kinds of awful rumors. Is it true there's a serial killer on the loose in Cochise County?"

"As you know, Chief Deputy Montoya is in charge of media relations. I believe he's scheduled a news conference for later today. In the Quarter Horse over in Benson. If you want information, I'd suggest you be there."

"The *Bee*'s reporters will be there to cover the news conference," Marliss replied indignantly. "I'm a columnist, Joanna. My job is to cover the human-interest part of the story. The angle. Most of the time, angles have nothing to do with the pablum that's dished out at official news conferences."

"We're not exactly on the same wavelength, then, are we, Marliss?"

"What do you mean?"

"You say your job is to find an angle," Joanna told her. "Mine is to enforce the law. Between the two, I don't think there's a lot of common ground."

Marliss Shackleford's jaw stiffened. Joanna Brady had landed a blow, and both women knew it.

"My, my," the columnist said, her voice dripping with sarcasm. "Are we power-tripping or what?"

"You're welcome to call it whatever you want," Joanna returned. "As you said, I'm merely doing my job."

"And getting a swelled head in the process," Marliss added. "It might be a good thing if you took a good, long look in the mirror once in a while, Joanna. Maybe you'd see how you're treating some of your old friends. Maybe you'd come to your senses."

"Who are you trying to kid, Marliss? The two of us have never been friends, and you know it. And if you ask me, I don't think we're likely to be buddies in the future, either. So give it a rest. Forget the phony friendship stuff. Stay away from me and stay away from my crime scenes."

"Why, I'll . . ."

As Joanna drove away, she glanced in the rearview mirror. Marliss Shackleford stood frozen in a billowing cloud of dust, her mouth open in astonished but silent protest.

Within half a mile of driving away, Joanna regretted what she'd done. She understood at once that she had taken a bad situation and made it infinitely worse. If Marliss Shackleford had been gunning for Sheriff Joanna Brady before this, now the columnist would be downright rabid.

Way to go, girl, Joanna scolded herself. *You and your big mouth.*

CHAPTER FIFTEEN

Half a mile down the road, Joanna was so caught up in mulling over the confrontation with Marliss Shackleford that she barely noticed an early-eighties F-100 Ford pickup coming toward her. Only when the truck wheeled in a sharp U-turn and came speeding after her with its lights flashing on and off did she pay attention. She pulled over immediately. Stepping out of the Blazer, she was standing on the shoulder of Pomerene Road when the pickup stopped beside her. There were two men in the truck— Alton Hosfield, owner of the Triple C, and a younger man who looked to be in his mid-twenties.

"Sheriff Brady, what the hell is going on out here?" Hosfield demanded, leaning forward to speak across the young man in the passenger seat. "The phone's been ringing off the hook. My ranch is crawling with people I don't know, but I can't get any of them to talk to me. I think I deserve some kind of explanation."

"We're conducting a homicide investigation," Joanna said. "Two actually. One body was found up on the ledges just below the cliffs last night. Another was found by Search and Rescue this morning."

"Two homicides," Hosfield echoed. "On my property? You can't be serious."

"I am," Joanna returned. "Katrina Berridge was the cook at Rattlesnake Crossing, just up the road. From the looks of it, the weapon that killed her may very well turn out to be the same one that killed your cattle and wrecked the pump. The other victim, Ashley Brittany, was a biology student from N.A.U. in Flagstaff. She was down here doing a master's degree internship."

Hosfield rammed the pickup into neutral and then climbed out. He came around the front of the truck, clutching a frayed Resistol Stetson in his hands. Meanwhile, his passenger stepped out of the truck as well.

"This is my son Ryan," Alton Hosfield said. "Ryan, this is Sheriff Brady."

Nodding politely in Joanna's direction, Ryan doffed his Denver Rockies baseball cap. He was tall and lean like his father, but his bright blue eyes, unruly mop of long blond hair, and finely chiseled features bore little resemblance to his red-haired father's craggy features. Had Joanna encountered Alton and his two sons on the street, she would have known at once that Alton Hosfield and Jake were father and son. Ryan, on the other hand, didn't look as though he was remotely related to either his father or his half brother.

Joanna acknowledged the polite greeting by offering her hand.

"Glad to make your acquaintance," he said.

Joanna turned back to Alton Hosfield, whose face was knotted with a puzzled frown. "Why does the name Ashley Brittany sound familiar to me?" he asked.

"As I said, she was a student intern," Joanna told him.

"Working on a project for the U.S. Department of Agriculture."

"Wait a minute," Ryan offered helpfully. "I think I remember her. Wasn't she the cute little blonde who came around earlier this summer, talking about how we needed to get rid of all the oleanders in the yard because they were damaging the environment and killing off wildlife?"

Comprehension washed across Alton's tanned features. "That's right," he said. "The oleander lady."

"You knew her, then?"

"I talked to her that one time," Alton admitted. "Long enough to tell her to get the hell off my property. She showed up in one of those little Toyota 4x4s, wearing her ID badge around her neck and packing a laptop computer. Ryan's right. She was real full of business, too. She had been up to the house and had seen the oleander we have there—oleander my grandmother planted. Next thing I know she shows up in her shorts, a tank top, and tennis shoes and wants me to get rid of it. Wants me to pull it out by the roots. 'Whatever you do, don't burn it,' she says to me. 'The smoke's poisonous, too.' Give me a break!"

"So what happened?" Joanna asked.

"I told her to take a hike. I told her if she wanted to do something useful, to get her ass up to Montana or North Dakota and do something about leafy spurge. Now, there's something the Feds ought to be worrying about. We've had oleander around the house for seventy-five years and it's never killed even so much as a damned horned toad to say nothing of cattle or deer. Now, leafy spurge, that stuff's a killer."

"Leafy spurge?" Joanna repeated. "I've never even heard of it."

"So far," Hosfield said ominously. "That's because it hasn't shown up in Arizona yet. But that's what I told this woman—girl, really—that if she wanted to do something useful, she should go to work on the spread of that. *Euphorbia esula* is nightmare stuff. That's the whole problem with the Feds. They get all hot and bothered about things that aren't important, like oleander, for God's sake, and totally ignore the kind of thing that will put me and hundreds of people just like me out of business."

"Well, I can tell you that Ashley Brittany is out of business," Joanna said quietly. "Somebody shot her and then buried her under a pile of rocks up there on the ledge just under the cliffs. When's the last time you saw her, Mr. Hosfield?"

"I only saw her the one time, and I'm not sure when it was. A month ago? Three weeks, maybe? All I remember is, the river had flooded one of my pastures. I needed to get the cattle moved to higher ground or they were going to drown. And here's this little twit of a girl who wants me to drop everything else and chop down a bunch of oleander. Give me a break!"

"What happened?"

"I ran her off. I told her she must have missed the sign when she drove onto my property, or maybe she couldn't read it. But I told her that the little plastic badge with the USDA printed on it meant she was persona non grata on the Triple C and that she'd better get the hell out."

"And she left?"

"You bet."

"And you never saw her again?"

"Sheriff Brady, I already told you . . ."

"Let me ask you another question, Mr. Hosfield. Have you seen any other strangers around here in the last couple of weeks—somebody who looked like he didn't belong?"

"On the Triple C?"

"Yes. Or anywhere in the neighborhood for that matter."

He considered. "Well," he said, "there are those stupid pretend Indians. Seems like there's always one or two of them wandering around where they're not supposed to, either on foot or riding horseback. Other than that, I don't guess I've seen anybody. But then, Ryan and I have had our hands full, too. I haven't been on the west side of the river since we finally managed to move the stock over here. With the river doing its thing all summer long, we've been keeping most of the stock in fenced pastures on this side. That way, we can get trucks to 'em if we need to."

"So you haven't seen anyone?" Joanna asked.

"Like I told you, nobody except those yahoos from Rattlesnake Crossing," Alton answered.

"What about you?" Joanna turned to Ryan. "Have you seen anyone?"

"No, ma'am," he replied. "Not a soul. Dad and I are working pretty much sunup to sunset, so I don't have time to see anybody."

"There you are," Alton said with a shrug.

"Well," Joanna concluded, "keep your eyes open, and don't hesitate to call if you see anyone or anything suspicious. Right now my detectives are all tied up with crime-scene investigation. When they finish up with that, they'll be around asking questions. Detectives Carpenter and Carbajal will be spearheading the investigation, but they may be joined by officers from Pima and Maricopa counties as well, just so you'll be prepared."

"All right," Alton Hosfield said, clapping his hat back on his head. "I'll expect 'em to be dropping by in the next day or so. In the meantime, Sheriff Brady, I appreciate your taking the time to bring me up to speed. I was beginning to feel just a little paranoid." He paused and grinned. "If you ask Sonja, she'll probably tell you maybe even a bit more paranoid than usual. See you around."

With that he turned on his dusty Tony Lama boots and returned to his truck. Joanna went back to the Blazer.

It was so late in the afternoon when she reached Benson that she should have driven past the ongoing press conference at the Quarter Horse Cafe without a trace of guilt. She had already put in a very long day after several other very long days. But her father, D. H. Lathrop, had imbued his daughter with his own fierce work ethic. In addition, Joanna Lathrop Brady had been raised in her mother's spotless household, where free-floating guilt outnumbered dust motes three to one. So she *did* drive past, but not without suffering a few guilty pangs over the fact that she was somehow shirking her duty.

She was still battling her attack of guilt when she reached the Rita Road overpass on I-10. That was when inspiration struck. *Belle Philips.* As soon as the woman's name crossed her mind, Joanna reached for her radio. Then, realizing that a dozen reporters probably had their all-hearing scanners tuned to Cochise County frequencies, she fumbled for her phone instead.

Dispatcher Tica Romero took the call. "Where's Detective Carbajal?" Joanna asked.

"Still at the Triple C crime scene, as far as I know," Tica replied. "Do you want me to put you through to him?"

"No. Ask him to contact me by phone rather than radio. Cell phones may not be one hundred percent secure, but they're better than broadcasting everything we say over the airwaves."

"I'll have him get right back to you," Tica said. And she did. Joanna was on the horn with Jaime Carbajal before she had made it as far as Tucson's Wilmot Road.

"What's up, Sheriff Brady?" he asked.

"Jaime, have you had a chance to interview Belle Philips yet?"

"Are you kidding? We've been so busy since the medics hauled her away in the ambulance that I've barely given the woman another thought. Why?"

"Where is she?"

"University Medical Center," he replied. "At least that's where I understood they were taking her."

"It happens that I'm on my way there myself," Joanna told him. "That's where Marianne Maculyea and Jeff Daniels' daughter had surgery today. I was thinking, though, as long as you and Ernie are still tied up with the crime scene, I could just as well stop by and see Ms. Philips. She might actually know something about her husband's business."

"It couldn't hurt," Jaime agreed.

Armed with both official and unofficial reasons for being in Tucson, Joanna fought her way through rush-hour traffic and drove straight to the hospital. After stopping in the gift shop long enough to buy a small bouquet of daisies, she headed upstairs. As the elevator rose through the building, Joanna was grateful that the pediatric ICU was in a different part of the hospital from the adult surgical ICU, where Andy had died. That meant Jeff and Marianne would be in a different waiting room.

Expecting to find one or the other of them inside, Joanna stepped off the elevator and pushed open one of the swinging doors that led into the waiting room. To her surprise, the first person she encountered was Butch Dixon. "What are you doing here?" she asked.

He had been working on a small laptop computer. As soon as he saw Joanna, he closed the lid. "I've been waiting for you," he said.

"What's going on? Are you on your way back to Peoria?"

"Not exactly," he replied. "When Kristin called and said you were coming here to visit Jeff and Marianne, I decided

I would, too. That may be the only way I'll have a chance to see you—to turn up wherever you are—sort of like a bad penny. You're not avoiding me, are you?"

"No. Of course not." Joanna was flustered by finding him there. To her consternation, she could feel a hot-faced blush blooming at the base of her neck. "And we did have lunch today," she reminded him.

"That wasn't what I call having lunch," Butch objected. "You breezed in and sat down, but before we had a chance to exchange two words, that woman . . ."

"Marliss," Joanna supplied. "Marliss Shackleford."

"Whatever-her-name-is showed up and monopolized the conversation for as long as you were there."

"I'm sorry," Joanna said. "That's what she's like. Pushy."

"And you're skittish," Butch said.

She nodded. "Well, I suppose I am. I'm afraid people will talk, I guess. Afraid of what they'll think."

"What will they think?"

"That you and I are involved. Seriously involved."

"Are we?"

Butch was making it tough for her. Standing there with the little vase of daisies in her hand, while she fielded his questions like a complete ninny. "Yes, we're involved," she said. "But I'm just not ready to be serious. You understand what I mean, don't you?"

"I'm trying," he said. "So far, the signals are a little mixed. Look, Joanna, I want to have a chance to talk." He glanced around the waiting room. "As far as I'm concerned, this isn't the place to do it. How about dinner? Eight o'clock. I'll pick you up here, and we can go someplace nice. The Arizona Inn is just a few blocks away . . ."

Along with the hospital itself, the Arizona Inn was another place that held painful memories for Joanna Brady. She'd been there, in the dining room talking to Adam York of the DEA when Tony Vargas had walked into Andy's hospital room to finish the job he had started a day earlier in a wash off High Lonesome Road.

"No," Joanna said quickly. "Not there."

"I'll figure it out, then." Butch stood up and headed for the door. "See you here at eight. No excuses."

Joanna nodded. "But where are Jeff and Marianne?"

"Jeff's in Esther's room for this hour's ten minutes' worth of visiting. He should be out any time. Marianne's at their hotel taking a nap. See you."

Butch turned and walked out, leaving Joanna still standing and holding the flowers. She wasn't exactly alone. There were at least two other clumps of people, family members commiserating in low, solemn voices. A chill ran down Joanna's spine; she knew the kinds of crises they must be enduring where the only thing they could do was to keep their long, helpless vigils—waiting, hoping, and worrying.

Jeff Daniels burst into the waiting room. "Joanna," he said. "You're here."

"How's Esther?"

"All right so far," he replied. "They're keeping her pretty well sedated."

"And Marianne? How's she?"

"She's hardly slept for days," Jeff said. "I finally convinced her to go back to the room to nap. I called and found out she'd left a wake-up call for five. I canceled it. I want her to sleep until she actually wakes up. She's been running on adrenaline for months now, ever since the girls got here. She's tough, but the strain is starting to show."

"In other words, she's a wreck," Joanna concluded.

Jeff managed a rueful grin. "We both are," he agreed.

Looking down, Joanna remembered the flowers. "These are for you," she said, handing them over. "They're for all of you. I brought them, but they were Jenny's idea."

"Thanks." Jeff put the vase down in the middle of a small conference table that sat next to the vending machines. "We're not allowed to take flowers into the ICU itself," he explained. "But if we leave them here, everyone can enjoy them. Besides, for the next day or two, we'll probably be spending more time here than anywhere else."

Stuffing his hands in his pocket, Jeff sighed. "It was nice of Butch to stop by. He and I had a good visit. Just guy stuff—cars and baseball, mostly. But I was glad to have a chance to think and talk about something else. I can only deal with this for so long before I start to lose it." He broke off and shrugged. His eyes welled with tears. "Butch is a nice guy, Joanna. A real nice guy. You're lucky he's around."

"I know," she said. That was part of the problem. Butch Dixon was a very nice guy.

The door to the ICU waiting room swung open and several people came in at once. Joanna recognized them all—people from Bisbee's Canyon United Methodist Church come to offer prayers and moral support.

"It looks like you have another whole batch of company," she told Jeff. "I'll leave you to visit with them."

"You don't have to go."

"No," she said. "There's someone else in the hospital I'm supposed to see. I'll come back a little later when I finish up with her."

After pausing long enough to say hello to the newcomers, Joanna hurried back down to the lobby and was given directions to Belle Philips' room. Since Belle was a possible homicide suspect, Joanna had briefly considered posting a guard outside her hospital room, but then, with all the confusion of dealing with multiple cases, she had forgotten about it. Seeing Belle swathed in bandages and with casts on both an arm and a leg, Joanna realized that a guard wouldn't be necessary. Belle lay like an immense beached whale on her hospital bed, gazing up at a wall-mounted television set.

She flicked her eyes away from the set as Joanna entered the room. "I can't never answer any of these questions, can you?" she asked.

Jeopardy! was playing on the screen. "I can some of the time," Joanna replied, "but I don't watch it very often."

"I suppose not," Belle said. "You're a busy lady."

They were quiet, letting the television fill the room with low-level noise while Joanna searched for some way to start. "I'm sure this will be painful for you, Ms. Philips, but I need to talk to you about Clyde."

Belle bit her lip and nodded. "It's all right," she said. "I don't mind. What do you want to know?"

"When's the last time you saw him?"

"Saturday," she said. "He came by the restaurant and I cooked him breakfast."

"What about Sunday?" Joanna asked.

"I never saw him on Sunday," Belle said.

"But you did go by the house," Joanna pressed.

For a long time Belle Philips didn't answer. "Yes," she said finally. "I did go by, but I didn't see him."

"Did you go into the house?"

"Yes, but he must have been asleep," Belle said. "I didn't wake him up and I didn't see him, neither. I went in and came straight back out."

"If you didn't go to see him, why were you there?" Joanna asked.

Belle sighed. "I needed money," she said. "To pay my utilities. So I did that sometimes, when I was short. Went by and helped myself to a dollar or two. He always had money in his wallet. And he never seemed to miss it. Leastwise, he never complained about it. But I never killed him,

Sheriff Brady. I never did nothin' to hurt the man. You're not sayin' I did, are you?"

"No," Joanna responded, "I didn't say you did. I'm just trying to understand what all was going on in Clyde's life the last few days before he died. We don't have autopsy results yet, but Dr. Daly—the investigator for the medical examiner's office—thinks Clyde may have committed suicide. What do you think?"

"He never," Belle said flatly. "Clyde never would of done that, not less'n he got a whole lot sicker than he was already."

"You knew he was sick, then?" Joanna asked.

Belle shrugged. "I guess."

"With what?"

"Who knows? All I know is, the last few months he was always tired. Just dragging. Like he could barely stand to put one foot in front of another. Losing weight no matter how much food I stuffed into him. But Clyde wasn't one to go to doctors much. Didn't believe in 'em."

Joanna stared. Dr. Daly had taken one look at Clyde Philips' body and suspected that the man was suffering from AIDS. If Clyde didn't go to doctors, was it possible that he himself hadn't known what was wrong with him? Or was his former wife the one who didn't know?

"So as far as you know, Clyde didn't have a personal physician?"

"If he did, he never told me. And what's the point? Even if he was sick when he died, once he's dead, can't see how it matters."

It matters, all right, Joanna thought, *to anyone else who's ever been with the man. It matters to you.* She said, "So after you moved out, Ms. Philips, did you maintain any kind of relationship with your former husband?"

"I cooked for him," Belle admitted. "Did his wash.

Cleaned for him when the house got so filthy that I couldn't stand to see it. He paid me for it, too, for doing all those things, but I probably would of kept right on doin' even if he hadn't had no money to pay me."

"But you and he weren't . . . well . . . intimate."

Belle's laugh was hollow. "We weren't hardly ever what you call intimate when we was married, so why would we be after we was divorced? He told me real early on that I wasn't his type. That I wasn't no good in the bedroom department. So I put as good a face on things as I could and acted like we was just like any other normal married couple. You know, complainin' about it sometimes the way women do, about their husband all the time wantin' 'em to come across. That kind of thing. 'Cept in our family, it was me all the time doin' the wantin' and him sayin' he had a headache."

And that's probably a good thing for you, Joanna thought.

For a few minutes the television set droned on overhead while Joanna considered her next question. "Pomerene's a small town," she said finally. "It's the kind of place where people know things even though they may not necessarily want to. So do you have any idea who any of Clyde's partners were after you left?"

For the first time, Belle Philips' eyes strayed from the flickering television screen. "Sex partners you mean? I can't rightly say I do. And even if I did, I don't know that I'd say. Since Clyde's dead, what people say about him now really don't matter. But I draw the line at spreadin' gossip about the livin'. Gossipin' ain't my style."

"What made you divorce him, then? Did you leave because he was getting sick?"

Belle sighed. "Clyde was sick a long time before I divorced him, and not with nothin' catchin', neither. I just always kept thinkin' I could make him better. Fix him, like.

They're all the time tellin' folks that at church, sayin' that the unbelievin' spouse can be saved by the believin' one if'n they just pray hard enough. I prayed. Lord knows, I prayed for years, but it wasn't never enough."

"What do you mean he was sick then?"

"Sheriff Brady, the man is dead. Can't we just let sleepin' dogs lie?"

"No, we can't, Belle," Joanna returned. "You just told me yourself that you don't believe Clyde committed suicide. If that's the case, then he was murdered. Somebody else did it—some unidentified person put that bag over his head and closed it up tight. In order to find out who that person is, we need to know everything we can about Clyde himself. Everything. Good and bad."

"But he's already dead," Belle objected stubbornly. "What does it matter?"

Joanna took a deep breath. Maybe Dr. Daly was right and Clyde Philips had committed suicide. Even so, someone who knew him—someone who might have discovered the body before Belle had—could have stolen the guns. And Joanna was convinced that person with the guns was responsible for what had happened at the Triple C. One way or the other, Sheriff Brady needed Belle Philips' cooperation.

"It's not just Clyde," Joanna said. "It could be that other people are in danger as well. Someone wiped out Clyde's gun shop."

"Wiped it out? What does that mean?"

"I mean all of Clyde's guns are gone, Belle. A whole shop full of guns is empty. And all the paperwork that went along with them is missing. If Clyde didn't sell those guns, then someone stole them—probably the same person who killed him. Not only that, there's a very good chance that one of those weapons was used to murder someone up on the Triple C night before last."

"Someone else? Who?"

"A lady from Rattlesnake Crossing. Her name's Katrina Berridge. So far, we have possible links from that case to two others, not even counting what happened to Clyde. His death would make it four. We have to find out who's doing this, Belle. Find him and stop him. Whatever you can tell us about Clyde may help lead us to the person or persons responsible."

Again there was a long silence. "Boys," Belle said at last.

"Boys?" Joanna echoed.

Belle nodded sadly. "Clyde liked boys. If he had been messing around with other women, maybe I could of handled it. But boys was somethin' else. It just beat all."

"You're saying Clyde Philips was a pedophile?"

"That's a pretty highfalutin-soundin' word, Sheriff Brady. I don't know exactly what it means, but if it means someone who likes to screw boys instead of women, then that's right. Clyde was one of them. I didn't catch on to it for a long time. I s'pose you think I'm just stupid or somethin'. And maybe I am. I thought he just liked havin' all those young folks around on account of us not havin' any kids of our own. And then when I finally did figure it out, my pastor kept telling me to love the sinner and hate the sin. So that's what I did. For as long as I could stand it. But he kept goin' up to Phoenix and hangin' out with them boy prostitutes. Finally I just gave up. Gave up and got out, especially seein' as how I'd come into a little bit of money to help me get set up on my own."

Belle lapsed into silence once more, and Joanna had the good sense to realize that her questions were plumbing the depths of an open wound. "Do you know any of their names?" she asked.

Belle blinked. "Only one," she said.

"Who's that?"

"Talk to Ruben Ramos," Belle replied.

"Ruben Ramos? You mean Chief Ramos over in Benson? You're saying the Benson police chief is one of Clyde's friends?"

Belle shook her head slightly. "The chief's son. Ask him about his son. Ask him about Frankie."

That was what Joanna had come to Belle's room looking for—a single name that would put her inside Clyde Philips' circle of intimates. Now that Joanna had one, she rose to go.

"Before you take off, Sheriff Brady, tell me what I'm s'posed to do."

"About what?"

"About a funeral. I ain't Clyde's wife no more, but there ain't nobody left but me to plan a service. That's pretty hard to do with me lyin' here flat on my back."

"The body's been transported to the morgue here in Tucson," Joanna told her. "It's over at the Pima County Medical Examiner's office. Dr. Fran Daly is the investigator who'll be doing the autopsy. When that's done, she can release the remains to whatever funeral home you choose. You'll have to let her know which one."

"I ain't worried about no funeral home," Belle said. "It's what comes later's got me spooked."

"Later? What do you mean?" Joanna asked.

"The funeral part is what bothers me. What do I do? Go ahead and have a regular one in church with a casket and all that? Or what?"

"That's up to you, of course. You said something earlier about your pastor. Ask him. I'm sure he'll be happy to advise you, and he could probably conduct an appropriate service for you as well."

"You mean in the church?"

"Why not?"

"Clyde never went to church. Never so much as set foot

inside one, not even when we got married. A justice of the peace did that."

"Check with your pastor," Joanna urged. "I don't think Clyde's attendance will matter. Besides, funerals are for the living. Have the kind of service that will give you the most comfort. And remember, the last I heard, churches were supposed to welcome sinners."

"That's true," Belle Philips said. "But only up to a point. My pastor talks a good game," she added. "But when it comes to livin' it, he sometimes falls a little short."

Don't we all, Joanna thought. *Just ask Marianne Maculyea.*

After leaving Belle's room, Joanna walked as far as the elevator before turning around and walking back to the nurses' station, where a young man stood perusing a chart. His name badge read "Tony Morris, R.N." Finally seeming to sense Joanna's presence, he looked up. "May I help you?"

"You do blood work when patients come in here, don't you?"

"Yes. Why?"

"And you check for AIDS and HIV?"

"Yes."

"Do the patients know that?"

"They should. It says so plain as day right there on the admission form."

"If someone tested positive, would you let them know?"

Tony Morris's hackles seemed to rise. "Look—"

Joanna cut him off by handing over one of her cards. "I'm not faulting your procedures," she said. "You know Belle Philips, the lady down the hall with casts all over her body?"

Tony Morris nodded.

"There's a good chance that her former husband had AIDS when he died," Joanna continued. "I just talked to the woman. I don't think she has a clue about what was going on."

"You're saying her husband might have infected her and she has no idea."

"That's what I'm afraid of."

The nurse shook his head. "Christ," he said. "People like that deserve to be shot."

Maybe nobody shot Clyde Philips, Joanna thought. *All the same, it sounds as though he got what he deserved.*

CHAPTER SIXTEEN

Back in the ICU waiting room a few minutes later, Joanna found that Jeff Daniels was still involved with friends from Bisbee. Moving away from the group, she settled onto a couch in the corner and called the Pima County Medical Examiner's office. Joanna more than half expected to be told Fran Daly wasn't in, but to her surprise, the woman picked up her own line after only one ring.

"Don't tell me somebody down there has found another body," Fran grumbled when she realized Joanna Brady was on the line. "How long before Doc Winfield comes back?"

"He's due in on Monday."

"Thank God for that," Fran said, "although, at the rate things are going, you people could probably have another three or four cases stacked up for me by then. What do you want?"

"I'm calling about the Clyde Philips case," Joanna said. "Have you had a chance to work on the autopsy yet?"

"Sure," Fran said. "I tossed him in the van when I went hauling ass out to the Triple C. I've been working on it in my spare time. Give me some slack, Sheriff Brady. You know what I've been up against."

"Sorry," Joanna said, "but I just finished talking to Clyde's ex-wife, Belle Philips. She doesn't believe her husband committed suicide. She said that she knew he had been dragging around some in the last few months, but I don't think she had any idea he might actually have been sick, and I don't think the possibility of HIV or AIDS ever crossed her mind. She also doesn't think he ever went to a doctor. According to her, he didn't believe in them."

There was a long silence on the other end of the line. "Are you saying Clyde himself might not have known he had it?"

"It's possible," Joanna allowed. "Belle also told me that Clyde was a pedophile, although that's not the word she used. Wittingly or not, he could have infected any number of other people."

"Including his ex-wife. What a bastard! I was going to put the autopsy off until tomorrow," Dr. Daly said, "but I suppose you want it done right away."

"Actually, yes," Joanna replied. "I really would appreciate it."

"Give me your number," Fran Daly said with a weary sigh. "I'll give you a call as soon as I finish."

After she hung up, Joanna sat for a few minutes. Her initial impression had been that Fran Daly was something of a pill. In two days of working with her, she had discovered that, personality conflicts aside, Dr. Daly was nothing if not a consummate professional. The fact that she was willing to go ahead and work on an autopsy even after spending the whole afternoon in the broiling heat of a crime scene was impressive. It showed a dedication to her work that went above and beyond the call of duty.

For the better part of the next two hours, Joanna stayed

at the hospital, visiting with some of Jeff and Marianne's other friends, and with Marianne herself when she showed up at the hospital about a quarter to eight. She looked better than Joanna had expected—the extended nap had done her some good—but she was still a bundle of high-strung nerves.

"I knew you were coming, Joanna," she said. "I meant to be back here sooner so we'd have a chance to visit, but Jeff called the hotel and canceled my wake-up call. He said he thought I needed the rest more than I needed to see you."

"I'd say he was right," Joanna said.

"You've talked to him, then?"

"A little. He's been so busy meeting and greeting that I haven't had much of a chance. How are things really?"

Marianne shook her head. "Everything looks okay at the moment, but there's always the possibility that Esther's body will reject her new heart. That's the big worry right now. That and the risk of her coming down with some kind of secondary infection."

Joanna reached across the space between them, took Marianne Maculyea's hand, and squeezed it. "It's going to be all right," she said. "I know it is."

"Thank you," Marianne said, squeezing back. "I hope so."

Just then Hal Hotchkiss, one of the old-timers from Canyon United Methodist, broke away from the group gathered around Jeff. He came toward Marianne with his frail, liver-spotted hands extended. "Well, Reverend Maculyea, the missus and I had better head on back home pretty soon. It's a long trip, and I don't much like driving after dark anymore. My night vision just isn't what it used to be."

"Thank you both so much for coming all this way," Marianne said, somehow summoning up the strength to sound like the gracious Reverend Marianne Maculyea of old. "I'll just go over and say good night to Beverly before the two of you take off."

While Marianne wandered away with Hal, Joanna stayed where she was, watching the interactions of the Bisbee people who had gathered there. The other two family groups in the waiting room were much smaller and much quieter. Joanna found herself wondering where those other people were from. If they were from Tucson, presumably their friends wouldn't have had nearly so far to come in order to visit the hospital. *Maybe,* Joanna theorized, *the smaller the distance, the fewer the visitors. Or maybe it's just the difference between living in a city and living in a small town.*

She was still mulling over that idea when the door from the corridor swung open and in walked Butch Dixon. He saw where Joanna was sitting, but instead of coming directly to her, he stopped off at the group surrounding Jeff and Marianne. He stayed there for several minutes, chatting and being introduced around, before breaking away and approaching Joanna.

"Ready?" Butch asked.

"Ready," she said.

"You wouldn't like to wear a bag over your head or something, would you?" he teased. "That way people wouldn't know we're together."

"Don't be ridiculous," she said. But as they walked across the room and out the door, she was aware of any number of inquisitive eyes watching their every move. *Maybe that bag wouldn't have been such a bad idea after all.*

They rode together in Butch's car, a Subaru Outback. "This smells new," she said.

"It is," he told her. "I just picked it up from the dealer last week."

"I didn't know you were planning to buy a new car."

Butch looked at her and grinned. "I wasn't," he said, "but life is full of surprises."

They drove down Grant to Miracle Mile and then pulled into a place called La Fuente—"the fountain." At almost eighty-thirty on a weekday summer evening, the Mexican-style eatery was hardly crowded. They were shown to a small candlelit table near the bar. "Do you want something to drink?" Butch asked. "A margarita, maybe?"

"Iced tea for me," Joanna said. "I still have to drive all the way back home. It wouldn't do for the Sheriff of Cochise to be driving around in a county-owned vehicle with a hint of Jose Cuervo on her breath."

"Iced tea it is, then. I was hoping for a roving band of mariachis, but unfortunately, they only play on weekends."

Just then a young Hispanic woman, dressed in a peasant blouse and a colorful skirt, showed up at the table pushing what looked like a salad cart. "Guacamole for your chips?" she asked.

"Sure," Butch said. "Why not?"

The young woman made the dip table-side, expertly peeling and pitting avocados. She mashed the peeled fruit in a small stonelike bowl and then added salt and pepper, tomatoes, onions, lime, and chili pepper. When she finished and was leaving the table, Butch slipped her a generous tip.

Joanna dipped a tortilla chip into the light green mixture and tasted it. "Delicious," she announced.

"When the ingredients going into a dish are that fresh," Butch told her, "it would have to be good."

The tea arrived and the waiter took their order—*flautas* for Joanna and a combination plate with *chili relleño*, taco and beef tamale for Butch. "So what's up?" Joanna asked, once the waiter had left them alone. "You've been hinting around that you have some kind of big news. Spit it out."

"I sold the Roundhouse," Butch Dixon answered.

"You what?"

"I sold it." Butch grinned. "Two weeks ago, this developer came around wanting to buy the place. He told me he wants to build a new resort hotel complex right there in the middle of downtown Peoria to draw on all the snowbirds that come down to the Phoenix area for spring training. Over time, he and his partners had managed to go around picking up pieces of property.

"From what I can tell, they bought most of them for a song—all except mine, that is," he added. "When the guy first showed up, I wasn't aware of what had gone on, but I found out about it over the next few days. The next time I saw him, I was loaded for bear. And in view of the fact that I was the only person standing in the way of his putting together this multimillion-dollar venture, I was able to strike a pretty good deal—for me and for the folks who used to work for me as well. They all walked away with a very nice severance package. Like I told the developers, none of them *asked* to be laid off. That was the only way I'd go for it."

Butch was clearly proud of himself. Joanna, on the other hand, was stunned. "So it's gone?" she asked.

"The building's still there, but it's closed," he replied. "The developers must have greased the planning-and-zoning skids pretty good, because the use permits are already posted on the door. It was written into the contract that I had to vacate the premises within three days of closing, and they had the check to me so fast it made my head spin. We had one last party—sort of a drunken variation on a going-out-of-business sale. Then I packed everything else up, put it in storage, and I was out of there, just like that."

So that's why the phone was disconnected when I called, Joanna thought. "But Butch," she objected aloud, "if you don't have the Roundhouse to run anymore, what are you going to do instead?"

"Write," Butch answered. "Mysteries, I think. I was an English Lit major. I always wanted to write. In fact, I've been writing some over the years—scribbling away for my own amusement and pleasure, even though I've never had anything published. But I always said that if I ever had the opportunity, I was going to do it full-time. Now I have all the time I need. I'm retired at age thirty-four, and if I play my cards right, I won't ever need to have a regular job again. So I bought myself a little laptop computer, and I'm in the process of getting started."

"How wonderful," Joanna said. "You'll get to live your dream. But speaking of living, what about that? If you don't have the building anymore, you don't have your upstairs apartment, either. Where are you going to live?"

Butch looked at her and grinned. "Bisbee," he said.

Joanna could barely believe her ears. "Bisbee?" she echoed hoarsely. "No!"

"Bisbee, yes," he returned smoothly. "There are seventy thousand people in Peoria these days. That's about sixty thousand people too many for me. So I've bought a house out in Saginaw, Bisbee's neighborhood. One of those old-fashioned Victorian places with a tin roof, a wraparound front porch, and a stamped tin ceiling. This fall when school starts, if you're busy and Jenny needs somewhere to go after school, she can just walk up the block and come visit me. I promise to have plenty of milk and cookies on hand with very limited amounts of television viewing."

"You've already bought a house?" Joanna demanded. "How could you?"

"To quote an old friend of mine named Mike Hammer," Butch told her, " 'it was easy.' I called up a lady at Copper Queen Real Estate and told her what I wanted. By the time I showed up in town day before yesterday, she had narrowed the field down to three possibilities. The one in Saginaw is the one I chose. It's vacant. Since I'm paying cash and there won't be a mortgage involved, the closing should be pretty fast. But still, I won't be able to move in for several weeks. There's some work I want to do on it first—plumbing, painting, cabinetry. That kind of thing is always easier to do if the house is empty. So I plan to stay in the hotel until it's all finished."

Listening to him, Joanna was so astonished that she could barely comprehend the words. "You're moving to Bisbee?"

"I *have* moved to Bisbee," he said.

Joanna was thunderstruck. "But why didn't you tell me in advance? Why didn't you let me know?"

"Because then I would have been asking you for permission and you might have said no. I decided to present it as a fait accompli." His face darkened, "From the looks of things, it's probably a good thing I did."

"Your dinner, señorita," the waiter said, appearing at Joanna's elbow. Then he set another plate in front of Butch. "The plate is very hot, señor. Now, will there be anything else?"

Joanna shook her head wordlessly.

"I don't think so," Butch told him. "This will be fine."

The waiter walked away and Butch turned back to Joanna. "You're looking at me like I'm an invader from outer space."

"Why did you do it?" she asked. "Why did you go behind my back like that?"

"Because I care about you," he said simply. "I know what my feelings are for you and I hope, given time, you might feel the same way about me."

Joanna opened her mouth to speak, but he stifled her with a wave of his hand. "I'm not asking for any kind of promises from you," he added. "I know you need time, but

I also don't think that with me in Peoria and you in Bisbee, you're going to know me well enough to make a wise decision one way or the other. My mother told me years ago, 'Distance is to love as wind is to fire. It blows out the little ones and fans the big ones.' That sounded good to me at the time when the young woman I thought was the love of my life had taken off with somebody else. I thought she'd come to her senses and come back to me. She didn't. And now that I'm older, it doesn't sound smart."

He paused, then sighed. Again Joanna started to speak, but he waved her off and continued. "You're so busy down here, Joanna. There's your work and your friends and there's Jenny to take care of. I was afraid I'd get lost in the shuffle. That if I was always two hundred miles away, you'd put me out of your mind and never give me a second thought. Now that I think about it, after living through the last two days, it may not be all that easy catching up with you with both of us living in the same town.

"But I want to give it a chance, Joanna," he murmured. His eyes darkened in the soft glow of the candle on the table. "I'm a two-time loser in the love-and-war department. I want to get it right this time. I promise not to rush you, not to push you, but please, let me be here. We'll be friends to begin with. We'll have an opportunity to get to know one another. I've already met some of the people in your life, but this will give me a chance to get to know them better. Like Jeff Daniels and Marianne Maculyea, for instance. They both seem like very nice people, and today is the first time I've ever been able to talk to Jeff one-on-one. That's what we need to do, Joanna. We'll let some time pass, and then we'll see where things go from there. Fair enough?"

When Butch stopped talking, a sudden wave of silence washed across their table and swallowed it whole. He was right, of course, and Joanna knew it. Had he broached his plan to her in advance, she never would have agreed to it. She had liked the status quo and wouldn't have minded if things had gone on that way indefinitely. She had enjoyed the *idea* of having a boyfriend, but she had wanted to dodge the complications that would have arisen from having him too close by. She could talk to Butch—she loved talking to him about anything and everything—but because he had been safely out of sight most of the time, she hadn't had to examine her own heart and feelings too closely. She had felt she could be friends with Butch Dixon without being disloyal to Andy—to Andy's *memory*.

"Well," Butch said finally, "can't you say something?"

"I don't know what to say."

"Try," he said. The eyes he turned on her were bleak and almost devoid of hope. He had the forlorn look of a convicted felon waiting for the judge to issue an order of execution.

"It's just that . . . well . . . I'm surprised, is all."

"But you don't hate me for doing it?"

"No, of course I don't hate you. I'm glad for you."

He settled back in his chair with a sigh of relief. "That's all I need to know for right now," he said. "Don't say another word. Give yourself some time to get used to the idea. In the meantime, let's eat some of this food before it gets cold. It's been a long time since Daisy's."

Joanna picked up her fork, but she didn't touch her food. "Speaking of Daisy's, there are people around, like Marliss Shackleford, for example, who are going to make a huge deal of this. You just don't know what it's like to live in a small town . . ."

"That's all right. I have a pretty thick skin, and I suspect Sheriff Joanna Brady does, too."

"Maybe," she said. "I hope so." The waiter walked by. Joanna raised her hand enough to catch his eye. "I've changed my mind. I think I'm going to have a margarita after all. Blended," she added. "No salt."

"I believe I'll have one, too," Butch Dixon told the waiter. "Make mine the same way."

Despite a somewhat rocky start, Joanna and Butch went on to have a good dinner. Maybe that one margarita did make a difference. They talked about Jenny and her visit to her creepy cousins in Oklahoma. They talked about Eleanor and George Winfield and postcards Joanna had received from the pair of honeymoon cruisers. They talked, too, about Joanna's late-afternoon run-in with Marliss Shackleford.

They followed dinner and that one margarita apiece with several cups of coffee. By eleven o'clock, they were on their way back to University Medical Center when Joanna's cell phone rang.

"I have some bad news and I have some worse news," Dr. Fran Daly said. "Which do you want first?"

"Start with the bad," Joanna said.

"I was right about Clyde Philips having AIDS," she said. "He had a full-blown case of it, but there's no sign in his blood work that he was undergoing any kind of treatment. So you were right, too. He probably hadn't been to a doctor. Let's hope his ex-wife . . ."

"Belle," Joanna supplied.

"Let's hope she hasn't been to bed with him in the too recent past."

"Let's hope," Joanna agreed. "You'll probably be hearing from her before I do. She's supposed to call you about releasing the body and making funeral arrangements."

"Do you want me to tell her?" Fran asked, "Or do you want to do it? You've obviously met the woman. I haven't."

"Maybe not," Joanna said, "but in this instance, I don't think your being a stranger is as important as the fact that you're a doctor. I think it'll be better if that information comes from a physician. If nothing else, you can at least advise her to have herself checked out."

"I suppose you're right," Fran said. "I'll see what I can do."

"If that's the bad news, what's worse?" Joanna asked.

"I was wrong about his committing suicide," Fran answered. "I found blunt-instrument trauma to the back of his head."

"Couldn't he have fallen and injured himself that way?"

"Not six or seven times. None of those blows looked like enough to kill him, but they probably rendered him unconscious. The bag and the belt were probably added later to finish the job. I'd say you'd better check both of them for prints."

"We will," Joanna said. "I'll have my evidence techs go to work on them first thing tomorrow morning. What about time of death?"

"Sunday night or Monday morning. The room was cool enough that it slowed decomposition."

The call ended a few seconds later, and she switched off the phone.

"Bad news, huh?" Butch asked.

Joanna nodded. "Very bad news," she replied. "For several people," she added. "One of our recent murder victims turns out to have had AIDS, and there's a good chance he didn't know it. That means that most likely none of the people who've been hanging around with him knew it, either."

"Too bad for them," Butch observed.

After that, Butch and Joanna drove for several blocks in silence.

"Life used to be much simpler, didn't it?" Butch Dixon said at last. "Back in the old days, I mean."

"Yes," Joanna agreed. "Much simpler."

They reached the hospital parking garage a few minutes later. "Just let me out here," she said.

"Are you going back up?"

Joanna thought about it. "No," she said finally. "I think I'll just get in my car and go home."

"Drive carefully," Butch said.

"You, too."

"See you tomorrow, then," he added. "Maybe we can get together after work and I can show you the house."

"Okay," she said. "I'd like that."

Sitting there with her fingers on the door handle, Joanna was wondering what to say next when Butch leaned over and kissed her. It was a gentle kiss, but one that was spiced with a combination of tequila, salt, and cilantro and more than a trace of salsa. It was a soul-warming kiss that drew her into it, and before Joanna thought about it, she was kissing him back.

CHAPTER SEVENTEEN

When Joanna left University Medical Center, she had every intention of going straight home. But as she drove down I–10 toward Benson, she couldn't get what Belle Philips had said out of her mind: "Talk to Ruben Ramos."

Because of the Arizona Organization of Chiefs of Police, Joanna did know a little about Benson's police chief, Ruben Ramos—the broad outline, at any rate. She knew, for example, that he was Benson-born and -bred. He had started out as a lowly patrolman in Benson, joining the city police force right after high school and commuting on a part-time basis to the university in Tucson, where he had eventually earned a degree in criminal justice. He had risen through the ranks and had been chief for five or six years. Other than that, she knew almost nothing.

Turning off the freeway, she started down the hill into Benson. A few seconds later, she spotted a city patrol car parked off to the side of the road just beyond the bowling alley. She drove past, then reconsidered. After making a U-turn in the middle of the highway, she drove back up the hill to the patrol car.

"Can I help you, lady?" the officer asked, shining a flashlight in Joanna's eyes without bothering to set foot outside the comfort of his air-conditioned vehicle.

Joanna whipped out her badge. "I'm Sheriff Brady," she said. "I was wondering if it would be possible to talk to Chief Ramos."

"Is this important? After all, it's the middle of the night."

"You have a dispatcher, don't you?"

"Yes, ma'am."

"Have Dispatch call Chief Ramos on the phone. Tell him I have to talk to him and that I'll be glad to come by his house if need be. Tell him it's about his son."

With a shrug of his shoulders, the officer reached for his radio. After several exchanges back and forth, he returned it to its clip. "The chief says he'll come here. He wants you to wait."

That struck Joanna as odd. Had she been awakened in the middle of the night by a fellow law enforcement officer needing to speak to her in person, she would probably have asked him to stop by the house or the department. A middle-of-the-night rendezvous in a deserted summertime parking lot would not have been her first choice.

A minute or two later, an emergency call of some kind came in. With lights flashing, the patrol car sped off to answer it, leaving Joanna alone in the lot. She waited there for another five minutes or so until an unmarked, two-year-old Crown Victoria pulled up beside her. She recognized Ruben Ramos as soon as he rolled down the window.

"Let's cut to the chase," he said without preamable. "What's Frankie done now?"

"I'm sure by now you've heard about Clyde Philips—"

"Look," Ramos interrupted, "when you're a cop, you raise your kids under a damn microscope. And with three of the four, it worked fine. But Frankie's something else. I

240

just didn't want it on his record, okay? The kid's got a hard enough row to hoe without that."

"You didn't want what on his record?"

"It wasn't that big a deal," Ramos continued. "Booze only, no drugs, nothing like that. If there had been drugs there, too, well, that would have been another story. But kids have been getting adults to buy their booze ever since Prohibition went out the window. Frankie was drinking. So what? He would have had a Minor in Possession and that would have been the extent of it. And Clyde would have been charged with providing alcohol to a minor and maybe an open container. I talked to a few people," Ruben added. "And the paperwork ended up not going anywhere. Maybe it was illegal. Hell, I know it was illegal, but I don't know too many fathers who wouldn't do that for one of their kids. If they could, that is."

Taken aback, Joanna realized there was a yawning gulf between what she had come to discuss with Chief Ruben Ramos and what he *thought* she had come to discuss. "You think that's what this is all about?" she asked. "That I asked to see you because your son was caught in possession of alcohol?"

"Isn't it?"

Joanna shook her head.

Ruben stared at her, his eyes narrowing. "Wait a minute here, you don't think Frankie had something to do with what happened to Clyde Philips, do you? You can't be serious. It couldn't be." He looked incredulous.

"Tell me about the MIP," Joanna said.

"Somebody put you up to this, somebody who's out to get me," Ramos muttered. "Who is it? Somebody on the City Council? I probably shouldn't even be talking to you without having an attorney present."

"Chief Ramos, I am not out to get you. I'm dealing with

a series of homicides—four, to be exact, including Clyde
Philips. A serial killer is loose in Cochise County. I need
your help and your son's help as well."

"What kind of help?"

"You've told me yourself that Frankie had some connection to Clyde Philips. I suspect the killer did, too. All I want
from your son is for him to give us the names of some of
Clyde's other pals. Was there anyone besides Frankie involved in the incident where your son wasn't arrested?"

Ramos shook his head. "No, it was just the two of them.
They were driving back to Frankie's place and Clyde missed
a turn. They went into a ditch. No damage. According to
what I was told, Clyde wasn't all that drunk. It wasn't that
big a deal. At least that's what Eddy said."

"Eddy?" Joanna repeated. "You mean Eddy Sandoval?"

"Come on, Sheriff Brady," Ruben Ramos said. "Don't
climb Eddy's frame about all this. He and I go back a long
way. He knew about some of the problems Alicia and I have
had with Frankie. He was just trying to help out."

Joanna wasn't impressed. "Look, Chief, if I've got a deputy looking the other way at drunk-driving offenses, then
my department has a serious problem, one I need to address.
But for right now, catching a killer takes precedence over
everything else. Just tell me what happened."

Ruben Ramos sighed. "It was June," he said. "Right after
school got out. Frankie had just graduated. Not top in his
class. Not even in the top half, but he did graduate. And I
told him—I told all my kids—that as long as they were
going to school, they had a place to stay. And the other
three all took me at my word. They all graduated from college. One of 'em is even working on a doctorate at San Jose
State. But Frankie wasn't having any of it. He said he didn't
want to go to college, and he sure as hell wasn't athletic
enough to get himself a scholarship the way my other son

did. So I told him fine, do it your way. But I also told him that once he was out of high school, he was out of the house, too. I thought that as soon as he had to cut it in the big, cruel world, maybe he'd come to his senses and get his education same as I did."

Ramos paused, shook his head, then continued. "So Frankie graduates and he gets himself this little nothing job working for a roofing contractor. I told him the morning after graduation that he had two weeks to find a place to live. And he did, too. Next thing I knew, he was living in this wreck of a mobile home over in Pomerene. The place is a dump, but it was the best he could afford. He told me Clyde Philips owned the place and he was letting Frankie work off part of the rent by doing odd jobs around his gun shop—cleaning, sweeping, that kind of thing. The good thing about it was Frankie could work there at nights or on weekends when he wasn't doing his regular job.

"Alicia and I were real happy about that—more power to him. He was making his own way, maybe learning something useful. I was happy about it right up until Eddy Sandoval called me because he'd found Clyde and Frankie in that ditch, with Frankie drunker'n a skunk. Eddy called me as a favor and asked me what I wanted him to do about it. I told him if he could see his way clear to let it slide, I'd really appreciate it."

"Then what happened?" Joanna asked.

"I talked to Frankie about it. I tried to explain to him what a stupid thing that was for him to pull. I told him a Minor-in-Possession conviction would screw up his insurance premiums and all that other stuff for years to come. He just sat there with that damned nose ring on his face, staring at me like I didn't know what the hell I was talking about, like I was some kind of moron. That's the problem with kids—they always think they know so much more than their parents do.

"I just gave up after that. I told him if it happened again, he was on his own. I wouldn't lift a finger to help him. And that's that," Ruben finished. "The long and the short of it. I've barely seen him since then. Neither has his mother."

For a time, Joanna didn't know how to respond. Despite Ruben's protestations of having washed his hands of responsibility for his son, he was obviously still very concerned. He had volunteered the story of Frankie's MIP thinking that was behind Joanna's midnight visit. She agreed the man had every reason to be worried about his son, but not for any of the reasons he *thought*. Compared to the specter of AIDS, dodging a moving violation was trivial. And what was worrying Joanna right then was what other things Frankie might have done for Clyde Philips besides sweeping in order to work off his rent. Was he only a part-time janitor, or was there a sexual relationship as well?

"Tell me about your son," she said at last.

Ruben shrugged his shoulders. "What else do you want to know?"

"What's he like?"

In the dim light of the bowling alley parking lot, Joanna saw the pained expression that flitted across Ruben Ramos' broad features. "I wanted Frankie to grow up," he said hopelessly. "All I wanted was for him to be a man. People used to tell me how sweet he was. I didn't want him to be sweet. I didn't want my son to be a sissy, but he is."

"What about Clyde Philips?" she asked. "What did you know about him?"

"Nothing much," Ruben replied. "He owned a gun shop and he's dead. I hear he liked to party—at least he used to a while back. I've been told that in the last little while he had let up on the drinking. I figured liver damage probably got to him. That's what happens to guys who hit the sauce real heavy. And the night of the wreck, Frankie claimed Clyde hadn't had all that much to drink."

"Clyde Philips didn't have liver damage," Joanna said quietly. "He had AIDS. The medical examiner called me with the autopsy results just an hour or so ago."

For a moment Ruben Ramos didn't make the connection. "You mean AIDS—the disease queers get?" he asked.

Joanna nodded. "Homosexuals, needle-using drug addicts, prostitutes." She paused, not wanting to ask the next question, but knowing she had no choice. "Is there a chance Clyde Philips and your son were lovers?"

For a second there was no reaction at all, followed by a one-word explosion. "No!" Then, after another long, heartbreaking pause, Ruben nodded. "Probably," he said in a whisper. "I wondered about that—suspected it—but I didn't want to believe it. I guess I thought if I ignored it long enough, it would go away. I always thought it was my fault Frankie turned out the way he did. I wondered if it was something I said or did to him when he was little. I tried to help him, really I did."

"Chief Ramos, I—"

"He was arrested one other time," Ruben went on. "Besides that MIP thing over in Pomerene. One other time that I didn't mention. Because I was ashamed to—ashamed that a son of mine would turn out that way and do such a thing."

"What kind of thing?" Joanna asked.

"He was arrested in downtown Tucson," Ruben Ramos said. "For soliciting an act of prostitution. With a male undercover cop. I got him out of that scrape, too. But I warned him if he ever did it again, I'd kill him myself." Chief Ramos took a deep breath. "What do you want me to do?"

"I need to talk to Frankie," Joanna said. "As I told you

earlier, we have reason to think that the Philips murder is linked to several others—two here and one near Phoenix. At least one of those cases includes weapons that may have been taken from Clyde's gun shop. That means the killer might be a customer of Clyde's or else an acquaintance. So far, all the paperwork is missing from the shop, right along with the guns. If Frankie worked there, he might be able to help fill in some of the blanks."

Ruben straightened his shoulders. "All right, then," he said. "Let's go talk to him. We'll wake him up. Do you want to take both cars?"

"Sure," Joanna said. "That's probably a good idea. You lead; I'll follow."

At that time of night there was very little traffic. To reach Pomerene, they had to drive from the bowling alley parking lot on the far west side of the town, through Benson, and all the way out to the other side of town. In the process, they didn't meet a single vehicle. Even the Benson patrolman Joanna had spoken to earlier seemed to have disappeared entirely.

Once in Pomerene, they drove past Rimrock, the street where Clyde Philips had lived. A quarter of a mile beyond that, Ruben Ramos' Crown Victoria turned left onto a track that was more alley than it was street. The track led back through fender-high weeds and grass until it stopped in front of a deteriorating mobile home. There were no lights on, nor were there any vehicles parked in front of it.

"That's funny," Ruben said when Joanna joined him outside his Ford. "Frankie has an old VW bus. I wonder where it is."

Watching her footing, Joanna followed Ruben onto a sagging wooden deck that had been tacked onto the front of the building. Metal columns that had once held an awning of some kind still stood upright, but the awning itself was long gone. Ruben stomped across the porch and pounded on the metal door. "Frankie," he bellowed. "Come on out. I've got to talk to you."

There was no answer, so Ruben knocked again, harder this time. The aging structure seemed to shudder beneath the powerful blows. "Frankie, I said get your ass out here! Now!"

Joanna said, "It's all right. We can come back later with a—"

Just then Ruben grabbed the doorknob and yanked it toward him. With the hinges screeching in protest, the door came off in his hands. Ruben Ramos marched inside, switching on lights as he went. Joanna followed at his heels as he charged from room to room.

"Frankie, where the hell are you?"

The place had clearly been closed up for days, and it was an oven. A messy, moldy oven with dirty dishes and leftover food rotting on the counters and in the sink. They went through the entire place, but it was empty. Nobody was home and there were no clothes in any of the closets or drawers.

"I think he's gone," Ruben said. "Moved out."

"Looks that way," Joanna agreed.

They were retracing their steps through the house, and Joanna was thinking about the possibility of returning the next day with a search warrant when a scrap of paper caught her eye. Moving it with the toe of her shoe, Joanna dragged it out from under the couch far enough to be able to read it. The paper turned out to be an invoice—from Pomerene Guns and Ammo to the City of Lordsburg—for a sniper rifle priced at forty-five hundred dollars.

Standing behind Joanna, Ruben Ramos read it over her shoulder. "Damn," he muttered finally. "It figures. You said the paperwork was missing from the gun shop, didn't you?"

Joanna nodded.

Ruben looked around the bleak living room one last time. "So whatever's happened, Frankie's probably in on it."

"That's how it looks," she said.

"Well, I'd better go, then," the chief of police said. "For one thing, I need to tell Alicia so she'll know what we're up against. Then I'll call Marv Keller."

"Who's he?"

"The roofing contractor Frankie was working for. Obviously Frankie's taken off. Marv will be able to tell us when he bailed."

The shift from father to cop was subtle, but it was there nonetheless. In a world of good guys and bad guys, Frankie Ramos had removed himself from his father's team and thrown in his lot with the opposition. That meant he was pitting himself against his father and everything Ruben Ramos stood for.

Leaving things as they found them, they left the trailer then and walked back out into the night air. While Ruben tried to reposition the door against the wall, Joanna reached into her purse and pulled out her phone. "Call Marv Keller now," she said.

The hand that took Joanna's cell phone was visibly trembling, but by the time Chief Ramos spoke, he had himself under control. "Hey, Marv," he said. "Sorry to wake you, but this is important. Have you seen Frankie? He seems to be among the missing."

Unable to hear the other side of the conversation, Joanna waited until Ruben ended the call and gave the phone back to her. "Well?" she said.

"His last day of work was Friday. Came in and didn't say anything about not coming back, but Monday morning, somebody who claimed to be a friend of Frankie's called to say that he was quitting because he'd gotten another job with a contractor in Tucson. Marv said he didn't question it, because when a guy quits, he quits, and there's nothing he can do about it. He said he mailed Frankie's last paycheck here on Monday afternoon."

Joanna looked back at the darkened mobile home. *Where does that leave us?* she wondered. *Is Frankie Ramos another victim, or is he a killer? Which is it?*

"My detectives will get a search warrant and be here first thing in the morning," she said.

Ruben looked at her questioningly. "What about the door?" he asked.

And there was Joanna Brady, stuck in the same gray world of neither right nor wrong, the same one that had trapped a deputy named Eddy Sandoval when he had tried to help a friend, the father of a wayward son.

"The way I remember it," she said, "the door was already off its hinges when we got here."

"Thanks," Ruben Ramos said. "I'd better go."

Joanna stood on the porch and watched him make his defeated way back to the Crown Victoria. An hour earlier, the man had been at home with his wife, peacefully asleep. Joanna's phone call had summoned Ruben Ramos out of dreamland and dragged him into a waking nightmare. First she had forced him to look at the very real possibility that his son might have been exposed to the AIDS virus. Now she had presented him with the likelihood that Frankie Ramos was a serial killer as well.

"Chief Ramos," Joanna called after him.

"What?"

"Did your son ever spend much time around Phoenix?"

"Not that I know of," he said. "Tucson's easy to get to from Benson. Phoenix isn't. Why?"

"Just wondering," she told him.

He drove out of the weed-choked yard. Feeling the

weight of the man's heartbreak, Joanna had all she could do to climb into the Blazer to get herself home.

Why is it people want to have kids? she wondered as she drove. *Parenthood sure as hell isn't all it's cracked up to be.*

Joanna pulled into the yard at High Lonesome right at one-thirty. As usual, the dogs were glad to see her. But dogs were like that. It was their nature to always be glad to see whoever happened to come home, late or not. But thinking about Ruben and Alicia Ramos' mixed results in the parenthood department had made Joanna consider her own parental efforts.

Right now, coming home in the middle of the night was fine—Jenny was in Oklahoma with her grandparents. But what if Jenny had been at home? She was still too young to be left by herself on a long summer's day. And yet Joanna's job required her to put in those long hours.

When she had first been elected sheriff, there were a few none-too-subtle puns about her being the "titular" head of the department. The only way to stifle those criticisms and to prove her detractors wrong had been to do the job and do it well. She had pulled the long shifts when necessary and had worked her heart out, making sure her officers had the equipment and support they needed to do their jobs.

In the process, Joanna had really earned the title of sheriff—made it her own. But she had done so at considerable cost, both to herself and to her daughter. Working hard made people expect that she would continue to work at that same level. In fact, that was what she herself expected. But what kind of long-term family crisis was being created by her doing an outstanding job at work? Ruben Ramos had supplied an answer that came chillingly close to home.

According to Ruben, three of his four kids were fine. Frankie, the youngest, was the joker in the deck, the loser. Had Ruben failed Frankie as a father *because* of his job? Because he had been so focused on moving up the ladder in the Benson Police Department? The other three kids were evidently older. Maybe they'd had the advantage of a less distracted, less work-involved father. Maybe that was why they were upstanding, productive citizens, while their baby brother was a suspect in a serial murder case.

But what were the implications in all that for Joanna and for Jenny? Ruben had four chances to succeed as a father. When it came to being a mother, Joanna Brady had one— Jenny. What worried her now was that perhaps, by doing a good job at work, she was damning Jenny to a lifetime of alienation and failure. Of all the things Ruben had said, one had rung especially true. Cops' kids did exist under a microscope. For good or ill, members of the community tended to exaggerate whatever they did. The bad things were worse and the good things were better if your parent—your father, usually—was a cop. That had been as true for Joanna as it was for Frankie Ramos.

And so that night, as Joanna Brady crawled into bed, she included any number of parents in her prayers—Ruben and Alicia Ramos along with Jeff Daniels and Marianne Macul-yea. Her own mother, Eleanor Lathrop Winfield, made the list, as did Joanna Lathrop Brady.

CHAPTER EIGHTEEN

The alarm went off at six-thirty the next morning. Joanna punched it and decided to snooze for just a minute or two more. She woke up when the phone rang. "Are you coming in for the briefing or not?" Dick Voland growled. "With four people dead so far, you can pretty well figure things are a little hot around here this morning."

Joanna turned over and stared at the clock in total disbelief. Nine-thirty. She had slept three hours longer than she had intended. "I'll be right there," she said, scrambling out of bed as she spoke. "And yes, we definitely need that briefing."

Oversleeping was bad enough. Oversleeping when she was the boss was inexcusable.

As she threw on clothes and makeup, nothing went right. The first two pairs of pantyhose she put on both had runs. And no matter what she did in front of the mirror, it was going to be a bad-hair day. On her way to the Blazer, she noticed that Kiddo was in his corral, happily munching oats out of his feed trough. That meant that Clayton Rhodes, her handyman neighbor, had already stopped by that morning to do the chores and feed the animals. *Too bad he didn't wake me up at the same time,* she thought.

Driving to the justice center, she felt half sick and more than a little disoriented. Too many days in a row with far too much to do and not enough rest had taken their inevitable toll. Her already shaky sense of well-being went even further downhill when she encountered half a dozen media vehicles and out-of-town television remote-broadcasting vans parked in the driveway. Squeezed in among the vans was a small white Nissan bearing the *Bisbee Bee*'s logo.

That's just what I need this morning, Joanna thought grimly, *another dose of Marliss Shackleford.*

Joanna threaded her way through the vehicles toward the rear parking lot. She pulled into her reserved slot, the one directly in front of the private entrance that opened straight into her corner office. Letting herself in via that solitary door, she felt a debt of gratitude—and not for the first time—to whoever had designed that entryway; it allowed her to come and go at times like this without having to deal with what was sure to be a media mob scene in the lobby.

On an almost daily basis, she tried to remind herself that the media were not the enemy, but saying that didn't necessarily make it so—not on mornings like this.

She picked up the phone as soon as she reached her desk. "Send in Deputies Voland and Montoya," she told Kristin. "And Detectives Carpenter and Carbajal."

"All at the same time?"

"You bet," Joanna said. "There's no reason to go over all this stuff more than once if we don't have to."

It took a few minutes for the four officers to assemble, dragging along both extra chairs and coffee. The mood in the room was grim as Joanna called the meeting to order by turning to Dick Voland. "Did Ruben Ramos turn in a missing-persons report on his son this morning?"

Voland nodded. "I've issued an APB on Frankie Ramos and his VW bus."

"Good," Joanna said, turning to the others. "All right, then, guys, here's the score—four people dead and one missing. It's time to get a handle on this thing. Where do we stand?"

As lead detective, Ernie Carpenter took the floor. "Jaime and I spent half the night trying to make connections between victims, trying to see where they come together, who knew who, that kind of thing. As far as we can tell, Rebecca Flowers, the girl up near Phoenix, isn't connected to anybody. Maricopa County faxed her autopsy results overnight. She was found weeks after she died, so there's no way to tell an exact time of death, but they're estimating mid-April to first of May, two years ago. After that, there's nothing until this summer, when Ashley Brittany disappeared."

"Do we have an exact date on her disappearance?" Joanna asked.

"The last her parents heard from her was on the second Sunday in July, when she called them at home in Van Nuys, California, and said she was going hiking. They didn't start to worry until the next Sunday came and went and she didn't call. Her camper and pickup were later found abandoned in Redington Pass, so that's where the search for her was concentrated. Because there was no sign of foul play, Pima County treated the incident as a missing hiker. They searched for her for days, but if you remember, that's about the time the rains were getting serious. Pima County finally abandoned the search a week or so later."

"But we do know that she had been working here in Cochise County," Joanna said.

All eyes in the room focused on Joanna. Ernie Carpenter's bushy eyebrows knitted together in a puzzled frown. "We do?" he asked.

Joanna nodded. "I talked to Alton Hosfield yesterday," she said. "I ran into him on the road as I was leaving for Tucson. He called her the oleander lady and said he threw her off the Triple C. He said something about her wanting to chop down his grandmother's seventy-five-year-old oleander."

"All right," Ernie said, scribbling a note to himself. "Alton Hosfield. We'll check that out. If Ashley Brittany had been to the Triple C, chances are she went to the other ranches in the area as well—Rattlesnake Crossing, Martin Scorsby's pecan orchard. Right there along the river, there are a dozen big spreads plus God knows how many individual houses. If Brittany was doing an agricultural survey of some kind, we're going to have to talk to all of 'em. Even with the addition of those two guys from Pima County, that could take weeks."

"You'd better get started, then," Dick Voland told him.

"What about using patrol deputies to help out?" Joanna asked. "Can you spare any for this?"

The Chief Deputy for Operations glowered at the Chief Deputy for Administration. "That depends on whether or not Mr. Purse Strings can turn loose some payroll."

Joanna smiled. "You'll find the money, right, Frank?"

"Right," he said.

"Go on, Ernie."

"Chronologically, Clyde Philips is next, but in terms of effort, I think we need to go directly to Katrina Berridge. For one thing, we need to interview all the people who are currently staying at Rattlesnake Crossing. According to Crow Woman, this session ends on Sunday morning. That means most of the visitors who were there on the day the Berridge woman disappeared will soon be heading back home—to Germany, mostly. So if we're going to interview them and find out what they know, we need to do it ASAP. Clyde Philips' neighbors in Pomerene are going to be around for a whole lot longer than the foreigners are."

Joanna nodded. "So you'll do the Rattlesnake Crossing interviews first and the others later."

"Right," Ernie said. "We'll be starting on those first thing this morning."

"Maybe not first thing," Joanna remarked. "Where do you and Jaime stand on paperwork?"

"Look, Sheriff Brady," Ernie said, "Jaime and I have spent the better part of the last two days crawling on our hands and knees all over the San Pedro Valley. When do you think either one of us has had time to finalize our reports? They're done in rough form, but they're not ready to turn in—at least mine's not."

"This is going to be a complicated, high-profile set of cases," Joanna said. "Our work here is going to be in for all kinds of public and judicial scrutiny. I want the reporting process kept up-to-date. I want the last two days' reports completed and on my desk before you leave the department this morning," she concluded.

Ernie Carpenter wasn't accustomed to going head-to-head with Joanna. "With all due respect," he said, "I think it's more important to get on with the interviewing process than it is to finish up a bunch of worthless reports that nobody ever reads."

"Most of the time I'd agree with you, but not this time. You're going to have to humor me on this one, Ernie," Joanna stated firmly. "I said I want those reports, and I mean it."

The two detectives exchanged disgusted glances. "All right," Ernie agreed, leaning back in his chair and folding his massive arms across his chest. He didn't say, "It's on your head." He didn't have to.

"Who's next?" Joanna asked. "Jaime?"

"Well, like Ernie said, Maricopa County sent down the Flowers autopsy. Doc Daly was busy overnight, too." Jaime Carbajal picked up two file folders and waved them in the air. "She faxed us the autopsy results on both Ashley Brittany and Clyde Philips. I imagine she'll get around to Katrina Berridge sometime today. When the doc and I were working the Philips crime scene, she told me that, just from looking at him, she suspected Philips had AIDS."

"That's right," Joanna said, "And since we were operating on a mistaken assumption of suicide, how well did you have the evidence techs go over Clyde Philips' house?" Joanna asked.

"Maybe not all that well," Jaime admitted. "There was a lot going on that day."

"So have them do it today. I want every inch of the house dusted for prints, and the gun shop, too."

"All right," Jaime said.

"We'll also need a search warrant for Frankie Ramos' mobile home. Have the evidence techs go over that one as well." Joanna turned to Frank Montoya. "What's going on with you?"

"One way or another, it looks like we've got a serial-killer feeding frenzy going on in Cochise County. What am I supposed to tell that army of reporters outside in the conference room?"

"Tell them as little as humanly possible," Dick Voland advised.

Frank ignored him. "Do we let them know that we've made definite links with three of the four and tentative links with the fourth? And what about this Frankie Ramos thing? I'm afraid if we let that out, we'll have a case of mass hysteria on our hands. People will be seeing serial killers under every prickly pear."

"Considering the way things are going," Dick Voland observed, "they wouldn't be far from wrong."

Ernie spoke up. "We're sure Ramos is connected?"

Now it was Joanna's turn to provide information. "Clyde Philips owned the mobile home where Frankie Ramos was living. Frankie also helped out in Clyde's gun shop. But I suspect there was more to their relationship than either of those things."

"More?" Ernie asked.

Joanna took a deep breath. "I talked to Belle Philips last night," she said. "She divorced Clyde because he liked boys instead of women."

The room fell absolutely silent. Ernie was the first to speak. "You think the two of them—Clyde and Frankie— were . . . involved?"

Joanna nodded.

"But didn't Doc Daly's autopsy confirm that Clyde Philips had AIDS?"

Joanna nodded again. "And if Frankie found out about it, or if he had discovered that he, too, was infected, that could certainly provide a powerful motive as far as Clyde's death is concerned."

There were nods all around. Dick Voland frowned.

"Jaime, didn't you say that Doc Daly had already figured out the AIDS angle right there at the scene?"

Carbajal nodded.

"How'd she do that?"

"There were lesions on his body that she recognized."

Voland sighed. "I guess the woman's a lot smarter than she sounded the first time I talked to her on the phone. Speaking of Dr. Daly, though, what's the deal with her? Are her charges going to us or to somebody else?"

"Comes out of the medical examiner's budget," Frank Montoya said. "The board of supervisors authorized all that before Doc Winfield ever left town. Of course, at the time, nobody anticipated that there was going to be quite such a rush on her services, but . . ."

"Well, I'm certainly glad to hear that," Voland said. "At least the Patrol budget isn't going to have to take it in the shorts when it comes to paying the bill. That's what I've been worried about."

They all laughed at that, and the mood in the room improved immeasurably. For a change, bickering about budget constraints was a bright spot in the morning's proceedings, rather than a drag. But after that one bit of levity, they came right back to the task at hand.

"Getting back to the press conference . . ." Frank began.

"Dick's right," Joanna said. "Give them the names and background of each of the victims, but for right now it might be best if you didn't say much more than that. The investigation is continuing, et cetera, et cetera, et cetera. You know the old song and dance."

Frank Montoya grinned. "I'm a whole lot better at it now than I used to be."

Joanna looked around the room. "So, we're all on track for today?" The officers nodded. "Any other unfinished business?"

Voland raised his hand, holding up a fistful of computerized incident reports. "Another would-be naked-lady truck hijacking. It happened about midnight last night over by San Simon. This one was reported by a lady trucker who didn't stop. Once again, though, by the time a deputy showed up, the supposed hitchhiker was long gone. This time she was traveling east to west, just inside the Arizona/New Mexico border. It seems to me, if we're going to catch these guys, maybe the department should lease a truck, have a deputy drive, and have another one in the sleeper. We could have them spend a day or two driving back and forth between Tucson and Lordsburg. Let's say the truck stops for the hitchhiker. Then when the accomplice shows up, the guy in the sleeper is there to arrest him. What do you think?"

"Sounds like a good idea to me," Joanna said.

"Sounds expensive," Frank Montoya said.

On that final note, the meeting broke up. Frank was the last to leave the room. Joanna stopped him before he made it into the reception area. "Pull the door shut again for a minute," she said. "I need you to do something for me."

"What's that?"

"As soon as Ernie and Jaime turn in their reports, I'm going to have Kristin make copies of everything they've given me, including the autopsies. Once I have all that pulled together, I want you to fax it to the profilers at the FBI. But this morning, before you even go talk to the reporters, I want you to contact the Profiling Unit and let them know the stuff will be coming. That way, maybe they can have someone on standby ready to handle it. I also want you to tell them that any further communications about these cases should come directly to me, either by discreet calls on my cell phone or on my private line. I don't want calls from them going through the switchboard."

"How come?" Frank asked. "Surely you don't think someone from the department is involved in this case, do you?"

Joanna shook her head. "No, but I don't want any inadvertent leaks, either. If the press gets wind that the Feds are involved, we'll have a media stampede on our hands and panic besides. As far as I know, we've never had a serial killer loose in Cochise County before. The fact that we're calling in the FBI would scare people to death."

"Gotcha," Frank replied. "I'll get on it right away." He

walked as far as the office door, then stopped without opening it. "What about Alcohol, Tobacco and Firearms?" he asked. "With that whole shopful of guns gone missing, shouldn't we notify them as well?"

"Check with Dick on that. He was supposed to notify them yesterday. If he did, they aren't exactly beating a path to our door."

Frank shrugged. "It figures," he said.

Once Frank had left the room, Joanna settled down and tried to get a handle on her own paperwork. Since she was a firm believer in her mother's old adage about sauce for both the goose and the gander, Joanna started the process by doing her own contact reports, covering her conversations with Alton Hosfield, Belle Philips, and Sarah Holcomb.

The one with Sarah bothered her. Looking at what she had written, Joanna couldn't help thinking that she had blown that interview. Sarah had become so defensive when she realized that Belle Philips might wind up being a suspect that the flow of information had simply dried up. *Maybe I need to take another crack at her,* Joanna thought. *Maybe that's something I can do while everybody else is out interviewing the people at Rattlesnake Crossing.*

She moved from the contact reports directly into the unending stack of daily correspondence. She felt as though she was making great progress until Kristin reappeared with that day's collection. The top item on the stack was a copy of the *Bisbee Bee.*

"I wouldn't read that if I were you," Kristin warned as Joanna reached for the paper.

"That bad?"

Kristin nodded. "That bad."

Picking up the paper, Joanna turned immediately to Marliss Shackleford's column, "Bisbee Buzzings."

Anyone who's had the misfortune of having to deal with the Cochise County Sheriff's Department of late probably already knows that's one part of county government where the word "public servant" has fallen into disuse.

Someone needs to remind Sheriff Joanna Brady that she serves at the direction and will of the people who elected her. She also needs to understand that if a crazed killer is plunked down in their midst, the people have a right to demand to know what's going on.

She needs to understand as well that declaring the entire Triple C Ranch east of Benson as an off-limits crime scene is not the way to conduct an effective investigation. Hello, Ms. Brady. Are you listening? Banning reporters from doing their job is no way for you to do yours.

Joanna tossed the paper in the air. It sailed briefly on the current from the air-conditioning duct. Then, in a move not to be duplicated, it landed directly in the trash. "Good shot," Kristin said. "Looks like you filed it right where it belongs."

"Thanks, Kristin," Joanna said. The secretary started toward the door. "Have Ernie and Jaime dropped off their reports yet?" she asked.

"They just did."

"Good," the sheriff said. "Copy it all—autopsy reports, crime-scene reports, everything—and bring it to me right away."

By eleven-thirty, the whole stack of material landed on Frank Montoya's desk. He was just starting to fax it when Joanna left for lunch. She grabbed a quick combination breakfast/lunch at Daisy's and was back at her desk working and not watching the clock when the phone—her private line—rang at two-thirty.

"Sheriff Brady?" someone asked.

"Yes."

"Monty Brainard here, FBI. Excuse me, but is this a home phone number?"

"No. It's a private line in my office. If you don't mind, I'd rather not have your calls come through the switchboard. I'm trying to downplay this as much as possible. The less attention we call to the idea of a serial killer, the better. If people around here get wind that your office is involved . . . Well, you know the drill."

"I certainly do," Brainard replied, "although I'm not sure how much help we'll be able to give you. As I told the fellow who called me about this earlier—Mr. Montoya, I believe—we're so slammed here at the moment that I can't promise much more than just a cursory treatment. For more than that, you'll have to go through official channels and get on waiting lists and all that. Since you've sent me the info, however, I can probably give you a quick-and-dirty assessment, although I don't know how helpful it'll be.

"Do you want me to give it to you, or should I pass it along to your lead detective—Mr. Carpenter, I assume?"

"I'm sitting here with pad and paper at the ready," she told him.

"Okay, then," Monty Brainard said. "Here goes. In my opinion, you're dealing with a young white male, late teens, early twenties at the most. He's totally self-absorbed. He has no concept that anyone else actually exists. As far as he's concerned, his reality is the only reality."

"You think he's white?" Joanna asked. "You're sure he's not Hispanic?"

"Maybe," Brainard returned. "Hispanic is possible, I suppose, but my gut instinct says no. This is a loner of a young man with some severe issues when it comes to relating to the adult authority figures in his life. He hates women and men just about equally, but I find the fact that he didn't mutilate the male victim telling. There's probably still a sense of fear or awe about adult males. He's primally targeting women, but he's doing it to get back at the authority figure. Most likely that's his father, but it could be a stepfather or a grandfather, too. Maybe even a mother's boyfriend, but I doubt it.

"Then there's the burial motif. Let me see . . . yes, he did the rock-pile trick with two of the victims, both Flowers and Brittany. If your people hadn't found the Berridge woman when they did, he probably would have pulled the same stunt with her. I'm sure there's a message in the burial routine, but right now, on such short notice and with the information available, I can't decode it.

"The other ingredient, of course, is the scalping. Once you find him, you can pretty well count on finding a trophy room as well. It's going to be ugly."

Joanna's lunch turned sour in her stomach while Monty Brainard paused. "Am I going too fast?" he asked.

After one or two false starts, Joanna's years of taking shorthand dictation had come back to her and was serving her in good stead. "No," she said, mastering her queasiness. "I'm fine. Go ahead."

"Okay. From what I can see, there don't seem to be any connections at all among the women. Is that right?"

"That's correct."

"So they're probably crimes of convenience. He killed them for the same reason some people go out of their way to climb mountains—they were there. The rage was building for a long time, but the first victim, the one in Phoenix, was most likely his first real taste of blood. After that, there's a long pause. I suspect he was out of circulation for a time.

Maybe even incarcerated. The lack of fingerprints leads me to think that, too. Your perpetrator is wearing gloves. I'd guess he knows his fingerprints are on record somewhere. He also knows that if your investigators find them at a crime scene, you'll be able to find him, too. Anyway, he was locked up until sometime earlier this year. Probably until just before this new set of killings started.

"Unfortunately, Sheriff Brady, I believe not only are you dealing with a serial killer, your guy is in what we call the subcategory of spree. In other words, now that he's started on his tear, he's not going to stop until he's caught or dead. I don't happen to think he's particularly concerned about getting caught, either. To paraphrase Margaret Mitchell—frankly, my dear, I don't think the son of a bitch gives a damn. Which is why the stolen gun collection scares the hell out of me. Is that true? Does he really have access to a whole arsenal of weapons?"

"Sad but true," Joanna replied. "And unlimited ammunition as well."

"Great. Well, be advised, Sheriff Brady. He's liable to stage one hell of a grand-exit spectacle. He'll probably try taking along as many people as possible, including any he's missed so far—like specific family members, for example. Killing all these other people may just be leading up to the main event. Working up his courage, as it were." Monty paused. "What kind of guns?"

"Some of everything," Joanna said. "Including the possibility of several fifty-calibers."

Monty Brainard whistled. "Boy, oh boy, you'd better watch your guys, then. Don't send anybody up against him who isn't armed with the same kind of firepower."

"Great," Joanna said. "You wouldn't happen to be in a position to lend my department a couple of fifty-calibers, would you?"

"Not personally," Brainard said, "but I can put your request to the local agent in charge out there and see what he can do. Want me to have him give you a call?"

"Yes, that would be fine. Only give him the same two numbers Frank Montoya gave you."

"Will do. Hope this was a help."

"It is and it isn't," Joanna replied. "I feel like I'm climbing up a really tough cliff. Now I've turned over a rock and come face-to-face with a rattlesnake."

"There's one big difference between the guy you're looking for and your everyday, garden-variety rattlesnake," Monty Brainard told her.

"Oh? What's that?"

"As I understand it, a rattlesnake only kills when it's cornered. This guy is looking for kicks. So good luck, Sheriff Brady. You're going to need it."

"Thanks," Joanna said. "I know."

CHAPTER NINETEEN

For several minutes after getting off the phone, Joanna simply sat and stared at the instrument. Her conversation with Monty Brainard had opened a gate, leading her into what seemed like the valley of the shadow of death. It had allowed her a nightmarish glimpse of someone totally evil. What she couldn't reconcile in her mind was Ruben Ramos' view of his son with what she had heard from the FBI agent.

Yes, Ruben and Frankie were estranged. But were they that estranged? And if Frankie had just graduated from high school, that meant he was only eighteen now. That would have made him sixteen at the time Rebecca Flowers was killed. Would a sixteen-year-old "sissy" have done such a thing?

And what about Brainard's claim that between that first killing and the next ones, the killer had most likely been incarcerated somewhere? Surely if Frankie Ramos had already been shipped off to juvie for the better part of two years, Ruben Ramos wouldn't have been so concerned about his being charged with either solicitation or minor in possession.

Then there was the nagging question of ethnicity. Brainard had claimed the killer had to be white. Joanna Brady had never met Frankie Ramos, but she had no doubt he was Hispanic. Maybe when it came to sorting white from Hispanic, the agent was just flat mistaken. After all, nobody ever claimed that criminal profiling was an exact science.

Joanna sat there for some time longer with her door shut and without the phone ringing off the hook for a change. Most of her departmental troops were out in the field doing their respective jobs. It was hardly surprising, then, that the Cochise County Justice Complex seemed unnaturally quiet.

In the brooding silence, letting her mind wander and wool-gather, Joanna Brady remembered something Belle Philips had said the night before: "Clyde liked boys." She hadn't said that he liked a single boy. She had used the plural. More than one. Several.

Joanna's heartbeat quickened in her breast. Maybe that was why Brainard's assessment wasn't adding up. Maybe he wasn't wrong, after all, because there was another boy involved in all this. Maybe Clyde Philips had kept a whole stable of young men around him. If so, Joanna had an idea of someone who might know—Clyde's neighbor, the talkative Sarah Holcomb.

The only question in her mind was whether or not Sarah would talk to her. Joanna's last contact with the woman had gone offtrack so badly that she was half tempted to have one of the two detectives do the honors. After a moment's consideration, however, she realized that both Ernie Carpenter and Jaime Carbajal were far too busy. Both of them were probably up to their eyeteeth interviewing the soon-to-be-departing guests from Rattlesnake Crossing.

No, Joanna told herself. *This is something I can do.*

"Kristin," she said after grabbing up the phone, "if anybody needs me, I'm on my way to Pomerene to see how things are going. I'm forwarding my private calls to the cell phone, so you don't have to worry about trying to catch them."

"Any idea when you'll be back?"

Joanna glanced at her watch. It was almost three. "Probably not much later than six," she said.

Once in the Blazer, she turned on her emergency flashers and went streaking up through Bisbee and out the other side of the tunnel. It was another broiling-hot August afternoon. After five days of no rain, the summer monsoon season seemed little more than a distant memory. The desert was a hazy, blazing furnace. At the base of the Mule Mountains, looking out across the flat plain that stretched from Highway 80 all the way to the booming metropolis of Sierra Vista, Joanna spied a troop of dust devils twirling across the desert. They looked like so many reddish-brown soldiers jogging, zigzag-fashion, in the same general direction.

Once on Rimrock in Pomerene, Joanna pulled up into the welcome shade of the two tall cottonwoods that overflowed Sarah Holcomb's tiny front yard. Next door, parked in front of Clyde Philips' house, sat one of the department's evidence vans. Joanna was relieved to see it. That meant her people were still working. Ongoing progress was being made.

Joanna's knock on Sarah Holcomb's door brought the lady herself. "Oh, it's you again," she said with a disdainful sniff. "I thought you said next time you'd send one of your detectives. What is it you want?"

It wasn't a particularly welcoming or auspicious beginning. "My detectives are all pretty much occupied at the moment," Joanna began.

"I should say so," Sarah Holcomb huffed. "We're havin' a regular crime wave around here lately. Yes, indeed, folks is just droppin' like flies. I don't remember us havin' this kind of a murder problem back when we had a man for a sheriff. Do you?"

"You're absolutely right, Mrs. Holcomb," Joanna said placatingly. "The kind of situation we're dealing with at the moment is absolutely unprecedented. And that's what I wanted to talk to you about."

"Well, come on in, then," Sarah said, tapping her cane impatiently. "No sense standin' here in the doorway and lettin' the cooler work on coolin' down the outside."

Once in the living room, Sarah motioned Joanna back onto the overstuffed and utterly uncomfortable sofa, while she herself perched on the frayed arm of a worn, chintz-covered easy chair. With the cane resting beside her, she peered peevishly at Joanna. "You know, I'd a lot druther be talkin' to a detective. Like one of those guys on the TV. I specially like Colombo, that fellow with the old wrinkled trench coat and the bad eye. To look at him you'd think he's dumb as a stump, but that's what trips people up. They end up tellin' him all kinds of important stuff even though they don't mean to. That's how he catches them.

"So now, then," she continued, "let's get on with it. I don't have all day to sit around jawin'. Why don't you just come out and tell me what it is you want to know."

Please, God, Joanna prayed, *let me look dumb enough so Sarah tells me what I need to know, too.* She said, "Were you aware that someone was working for Clyde—cleaning his shop, that kind of thing?"

"Sure. Clyde called him Frankie. Don't know his last name. Nice-enough-lookin' little guy, no bigger'n a minute. Came over almost every night. Used to be he'd just show up every now and then, but since the first of the summer, I'd say he's been comin' here most every day."

"But when I was talking to you the other day," Joanna

countered, "how come you never mentioned anything about him?"

"As I recall the exact conversation," Sarah pointed out, "you wanted to know if I'd seen anythin' out of line. Anything unusual. Well, sir, Frankie and that little VW bus of his was here all the time. So that wasn't a bit out of line, then, was it? That's just plain ol' business as usual. I'da thought it was unusual if he didn't show up, which he did."

"He was here Saturday night?"

"Yes."

"What about Sunday?"

"I already told you, Sheriff Brady. I was in Tucson Sunday night. I had a doctor's appointment on Monday morning. So Frankie might've been here Sunday night and then again, he might not. I've got no way of knowin' either way."

"But you haven't seen him since then, right?"

"What makes you say that? I saw Frankie just this morning, as a matter of fact. Me and my cane was out taking our daily constitutional when he come barreling down Pomerene Road like the very devil hisself was after him. I waved, but him and that old van of his went by me in a cloud of smoke and dust. I don't think he even saw me standin' there. Get thinkin' about it, the sun was glarin' off the windshield so bad I'm not sure if it was Frankie driving. Maybe it was that friend of his."

"What friend?" Joanna felt her whole body come to tingling attention. She forced herself to stay relaxed. If she seemed too eager, Sarah Holcomb might spook and clam up once again.

"Don't rightly know his name, neither," Sarah said. "Don't think I ever heard him called by anything at all. He was just a guy who'd show up with Frankie now and again. He'd hang around out in the gun shop while Frankie done his chores. I never saw him lift a finger to help, never carry anythin' in or out or nothin', but I guess he kept Frankie company."

"Can you describe him?"

"Long drink of water. Sort of stringy yellow hair. Scrawny. Looked to me like he could have used a square meal or two. If I'da seen him on the street, I'd most likely've headed in the other direction. Looked like a no-account to me. I mean, here's poor little Frankie working his tail off, and that other lout never offered to help. Where I come from, friends pitch in when there's work to be done."

"So do you think this friend was from around here?"

"Can't say, but I suppose so, if he was hanging around here all the time. With the price of gas these days, that most pro'ly means he wasn't from too far away. But I don't know him, if that's what you mean. He's not one of the little kids who grew up in the neighborhood and went to school here and all like that. But then, neither was Frankie. Seems to me like there was always bunches of strange young 'uns hangin' around over to the Philips place. Not allus the same ones, mind you. Different ones would come and go from time to time. They sorta come in waves. Frankie and that friend of his come in the last wave. First time I seen Frankie was earlier this spring. The other one showed up a little later."

What was it Monty Brainard had said? Joanna wondered. *Something about the killer being locked up until just before the killings started? With a recently arrived friend, that would work. It would make sense.*

Her mind had gone off on such a compelling tangent that Joanna briefly lost track of what was being said. It took some effort to return to the interview. "So you saw Frankie's VW this morning?" she asked, hoping to smooth over the rough spot.

"What's the matter?" Sarah demanded indignantly.

"Didn't I say it in plain enough English to suit you? Yes, I saw his van as clear as I'm seeing you."

"Which way was it going? Toward Benson or away from it?"

"Toward. Good thing I was walkin' on the left-hand side of the road. That way I saw him comin' and was able to get out of the way. Otherwise I'da been road kill and you coulda put me on the list with all them other folks as has been killed around these parts lately," she added meaningfully.

"Going back to the friend," Joanna said. "Can you tell me what kind of vehicle he drove?"

"Nope. I only ever saw him gettin' in and out of Frankie's little brown-and-orange van."

"Is there anyone else around here who might have seen this friend or who might be able to tell us more about him?" Joanna asked. "We need to know who he is and where he comes from."

"Beats me," Sarah Holcomb said. "I reckon the only way to do that is go up and down the road askin' everybody you meet." She smiled brightly. "But that's what detectives get paid to do, ain't it?"

"Yes," Joanna agreed. "It certainly is."

The conversation might have drifted on indefinitely if Joanna's cell phone hadn't chosen that moment to crow its distinctive ring from deep in the bowels of her purse.

"My land!" Sarah proclaimed when Joanna extracted the handset and answered it. "A phone in a purse! What will they think of next!"

"Sheriff Brady?" Tica Romero said urgently.

"Yes. What is it?"

"We've got a problem. A Southwest Gas guy was out checking the natural gas pipeline along the San Pedro, somewhere between the bridge and Pomerene proper. He just called in to say he found a car—a wrecked brown-and-orange VW bus. He thinks there's a body inside, but since the van's hanging half on and half off the riverbank, we won't be able to get to it without a wrecker."

"Damn!" Joanna exclaimed. "Has anybody called Ruben Ramos?"

"Yes, ma'am. He's on his way."

"So am I," Joanna said. "What about Dr. Daly at the medical examiner's office up in Tucson?" she added. "Has anybody called her?"

"Chief Deputy Voland did that already. She's coming, too." Tica paused. "When is Doc Winfield due back?"

"Monday. Which may be fine for some people—like my mother, for instance—but it's not nearly soon enough for me."

Joanna ended the call and then turned back to Sarah Holcomb. "I'm sorry," she said. "I'm going to have to go."

"I heard you say somethin' about callin' in the medical examiner. That means somebody else is dead, don't it?"

There wasn't much point in denying the obvious. "I'm afraid so."

"Who is it?" Sarah asked.

"We don't know yet, not for sure," Joanna replied. "And we can't release any kind of information until after we have a positive ID."

"You just go ahead and play coy if you want to," Sarah Holcomb returned, "but I've got a real bad feeling about all this. It's Frankie, isn't it?"

"Really, Mrs. Holcomb, I just can't say."

Sarah Holcomb, however, was undeterred. "And if he is the one," she continued, "I'm likely the very last person to see him alive. Which means, I suppose, there'll be another whole set of dumb questions. Right?"

"Maybe," Joanna said noncommittally while edging toward the door. "If that's the case, we'll be in touch."

"Well, if'n you do, get 'hold of me in advance to set up an appointment," Sarah Holcomb admonished. "That's the proper way to do things."

"Right," Joanna said, making her escape to the gate. "We'll definitely phone you in advance."

"And another thing, Sheriff Brady," Sarah called after her from the porch. "You do know what this country needs, don't you?"

With one hand on the relative safety of the Blazer's door, Joanna turned back. "No," she said. "What's that?"

"Another president like Richard Milhous Nixon," Sarah Holcomb replied staunchly. "Now, there was a man who believed in law and order." With that she and her cane disappeared into the house, slamming the door behind her.

Once the Blazer started, Joanna breathed a sigh of relief. *Next time anybody has to talk to Sarah Holcomb,* she told herself, *I'm sending in the reinforcements.*

Back out on Pomerene Road, she came across the Southwest Gas guy in only a matter of minutes. He was standing on the shoulder of the road and waving both arms frantically to flag her down.

"I'm Sheriff Brady," Joanna told him, displaying her badge. "Is anybody else here yet?"

"Not so far. Name's Heck Tompkins. I'm a pipe inspector for Southwest Gas. With all the rain we've had the last few weeks, we try to go over the whole pipeline at least once a week, especially the parts of it that are so close to the river. That's where I was going when I saw the car—down to the river to check on the pipe. It's just over there."

Hobbled by her heels, Joanna limped across the rough terrain and over a low-lying hill until she was close enough to catch a glimpse of the dangling VW. One glance was enough to tell her that Tompkins' assessment was right. With the riverbank as eroded as it was in that spot, it was far too dangerous to try to get much closer to the vehicle than ten to fifteen feet away. But it was also possible to see the shadow of a figure slumped over the wheel on the driver's side.

Oddly enough, Joanna felt nothing but a sense of relief at seeing the body, a sense of closure. Whatever Frankie Ramos had done—whatever nightmares had driven him to commit his heinous crimes—he'd at least had the good sense to end it once and for all. It was over. Cochise County's first ever "spree" killer was out of commission. Joanna could hardly wait for morning to come so she'd be able to call Monty Brainard back in Washington, D.C., and tell him.

A tow truck dispatched from Benson was the next to arrive. The young driver was eager to get hooked up to the VW so he could tow it out and go on to his next call. "Sorry," Joanna told him, "this is a crime scene. You'll have to wait here until the medical examiner gives you the go-ahead."

"Says who?" the driver asked.

With an acne-covered face and close-set eyes, the tow-truck driver barely looked old enough or smart enough to drive. "I do," Joanna said, flashing her badge. "My name's Brady, Sheriff Joanna Brady."

"Oh," he said, blinking. "All right, then. I'll wait."

Chief Ruben Ramos' dusty Crown Victoria was the next vehicle to arrive on the scene. He jumped out of the driver's seat and was on his way across the hill toward the van before Joanna managed to head him off.

"This is a crime scene, Ruben. We have to wait for the medical examiner," she said, placing a restraining hand on his arm.

Ruben stopped and turned toward her. His face, glistening with sweat and tears, was wild with grief. "But what if Frankie isn't dead?" he demanded. "What if he needs help?"

"It's too late, Ruben. That car's been here for a long time, hours most likely. Look at the tracks. The wind has all but obliterated them. And all the windows are rolled up. It's probably two hundred degrees inside that vehicle. Frankie may have been alive when he went over the edge, but he isn't now."

Ruben Ramos' shoulders slumped. Shading his eyes with one hand, he stared at the VW for the better part of a minute, then turned and retreated to the road. There the group stood waiting in uncomfortable silence. To Joanna's surprise, the next arrival was none other than Dr. Fran Daly.

"We've got to stop meeting like this," the medical examiner said, climbing out of her van. "What have we got this time?"

For the next hour or so, a surprisingly agile Fran Daly dared the eroded riverbank to take crime-scene pictures. All the while pictures were being taken, all the while the tow truck was dragging the VW back onto solid ground, Joanna continued to hold tight to the fantasy that it was all over, that her "spree" killer was no more.

That theory began to fall apart as soon as the door to the van was opened wide enough to allow her to catch a glimpse of the person slumped behind the steering wheel. The plastic bag over the head and the belt fastened around the neck were easy enough to recognize. Still, they *could* have meant something else. They could have meant that Frankie Ramos had taken his own life.

But when Ruben Ramos asked that the bag be removed so he could make a positive ID, all hope for an end of things evaporated.

Once Fran Daly uncovered the bloody mess, Frankie's father uttered an awful groan and then simply crumpled to the ground. Standing beside him, Joanna reached out and tried to break his fall. So did Heck Tompkins. Between the two of them, they probably helped some.

And then, while Dr. Fran Daly abandoned her forensic duties and rushed over to administer first aid, Joanna sprinted back to her Blazer to radio for help.

Cochise County's spree killer was no longer neglecting to mutilate his male victims.

CHAPTER TWENTY

It was only eight o'clock when Joanna stopped at the end of her mile-long driveway on High Lonesome Road. Putting the Blazer in neutral, she climbed out and then trudged across the road to pull that day's worth of personal mail out of the box. Three bills, two catalogs, and a postcard from Jenny. In the bright August starlight, she couldn't quite make out the background on the picture, but the foreground was clear enough. It featured a unicorn—a lovely white unicorn.

Back in the Blazer, Joanna switched on the reading light and studied the picture. Then she read the message:

Dear Mom,

This is the prettiest unicorn I've ever seen. Grandma and I got it at a drugstore in Tulsa.

The G's said to tell you that we'll be home sometime on Sunday. I don't know what time.

I love you and I miss you. And I miss the dogs and Kiddo, too. Don't forget to give him his carrots.

Love,
Jenny

P.S. Guess what? I kicked Rodney in the you-know-what and now he's being nice to me.

Reading the postcard, Joanna didn't know whether to laugh or cry. She ended up doing neither one. Instead, she dropped the mail, postcard included, beside her purse on the seat and headed up the drive toward her house.

In all the time she'd been sheriff, Joanna Brady had never been as discouraged or as beaten down as she felt that night. She had returned from the latest crime scene near Pomerene feeling totally helpless. She had stood on the sidelines and watched while EMTs from the air ambulance service loaded Ruben Ramos on board to airlift him to the cardiac care unit at Tucson Medical Center. And then she had watched the technicians from the Pima County Medical Examiner's office load yet another dead citizen from Cochise County—some other person she, Sheriff Joanna Brady, had failed to serve and protect—into the meat wagon to be hauled off to the Pima County morgue. Once again Fran Daly had scheduled an autopsy for early the following morning.

And all the time this was going on, all the while those necessary and official tasks were being done, Sheriff Joanna Brady had stood apart from the action and wrestled with her own demons and with the grim knowledge that somewhere nearby, a killer waited, coiled and deadly as a rattlesnake, waiting to strike again.

"You'd better go home," Ernie Carpenter had said to her at last. "There's nothing more you can do here."

When he said that, Joanna hadn't even bothered to argue. Without a word, she had simply dragged her weary body into the Blazer and driven away. That late-summer night was devoid of all humidity. Consequently, the desert cooled rapidly. She left the windows open, hoping to cleanse the smell of death from her lungs, and from her soul as well.

Soon, though, she found herself shivering—whether from actual cold, simple exhaustion, or a combination of both, she couldn't tell. When that happened, she rolled up the windows and opened the vent.

Halfway up the dirt track to the house she realized that the dogs hadn't come running to meet her. That was odd. They almost always did. *Has something happened to one of them?* she wondered. *Tigger probably tangled with the porcupine again.*

Then she caught a glimpse of the house through the forest of mesquite and saw that the whole place was ablaze with lights. Her first thought was that Jim Bob and Eva Lou must have changed their minds and brought Jenny back home earlier than they had anticipated. Except that when she came into the yard, rather than the Bradys' aging Honda, she spotted Butch Dixon's Subaru parked in front of the gate.

What's he doing here? she wondered irritably.

Once she had accepted that there was no way she'd be getting back to Bisbee in a timely fashion, she had called Kristin and asked her to track down Butch and tell him what was happening. She had wanted to let him know that once again, through no fault of her own, she wouldn't be able to make their early-evening date.

That had been hours ago. She might have been happy to see him at five or six, but she wasn't the least bit thrilled at the prospect of seeing him now. She was sweaty and dirty and tired. The night before, she had washed the clothing from her crime-scene investigation bag, but oversleeping that morning meant she hadn't had time to dry the clothes and repack them. She had ventured out to the Frankie Ramos crime scene dressed in her regular work clothes. In the course of walking the rock-strewn riverbank, she had broken the heel on one shoe. That accounted for what looked

like a severe limp. One stocking, the third pair she had put
on that morning, had snagged on a mesquite tree branch,
leaving it with a three-inch-wide ladder run that went from
mid-thigh all the way down to her ankle.

When the motion-detector yard light came on, Butch and
the two dogs materialized all at once from the relative
shadow of the front porch. The dogs gamboled and Butch
sauntered toward the Blazer to meet her. Joanna climbed
out of the truck, slamming the door behind her.

"Long day," Butch observed. "It's about time you got
home." He grinned so she would know he was just kidding.

Temper, temper, Joanna warned herself. She wanted to be
glad to see him. Maybe she *was* glad to see him, but she
was too tired, too depleted. Joanna Brady was a foot soldier
in the war against good and evil, and evil was definitely
winning.

"What are you doing here?" she asked.

Standing with hands in his pockets and managing to look
both foolish and contrite at the same time, Butch shrugged.
"When Kristin called, I had already made up my mind what
we were having for dinner. Or supper. Which do you call
it?"

"Dinner."

"Well, dinner, then. So I thought, why not go ahead and
bring it on out here and wait for you? I used the dog-turd
key—that turd is *very* realistic, by the way—and let myself
in. I hope you don't mind."

"Mind?" Joanna returned. "Why should I mind?"

"But you look worn out," he said. "And from what I
heard on the radio, I can understand why. This is probably
a bad idea. Tell you what, I'll just go straighten the kitchen
back up, wrap up the bread, and then I'll go."

Joanna was torn. She wanted Butch to leave, to go away

and leave her alone. Unaccountably, she also wanted him to stay. "You mean dinner's already on the table?"

"Pretty much. It's no big deal. It's the kind of supper my mother used to make on hot summer nights back in Chicago—chef's salad, some fresh-baked bread . . ."

"You baked bread?"

"Actually, I cheated. I bought one of those ready-to-bake loaves from the store. I have my own bread machine, but it's locked up in the storage unit at the moment. Still, you can't beat the smell of fresh-baked bread to make a person feel all's right with the world."

They had been walking as they talked. When Joanna opened the back door, the two dogs darted inside. She followed, drawn forward by the magical scent of newly baked bread. As her mouth began watering, it suddenly occurred to her that at almost eight-thirty at night, maybe she was more hungry than she was tired.

"It smells wonderful," she said. "Don't go."

"Really?" Butch asked.

"Really. Just give me a chance to clean up and change." Stripping off her blazer, she left it on the dryer. Then she walked into the kitchen, removing her underarm shoulder holster with her Colt 2000 as well as the small-of-back holster that held her Glock 19. She loaded both weapons into the deep bread drawer beneath the kitchen counter and then dug her cell phone out of her purse.

As she plugged the phone into the battery recharger on the kitchen counter, she realized Butch was watching her— watching and frowning. "What's wrong?" she asked.

"That's where you keep all that stuff, right there in the kitchen? Shouldn't the guns be locked up in a cabinet or something?"

"Andy always used to lock up his gun when he came home from work, but Jenny was a lot younger then. Jenny and I talked about it a few months back. She knows enough to leave the guns alone, and when we're rushing around here to leave in the morning, it's a lot more convenient for me to finish cleaning up the kitchen and then grab them on my way out the door."

"Oh." That was all Butch said, but it seemed to Joanna that she noted a trace of disapproval in the way he said it. That got her back up. *What right does he have to come barging into the house, uninvited, and start criticizing the way Jenny and I live together?* She was about to say something about it when she looked through the kitchen doorway and caught sight of the dining room table. It was set with good dishes, cloth napkins, champagne glasses, and an ice bucket with a chilled bottle of champagne.

"The idea was to celebrate buying my house," he said apologetically. "The current owner gave me permission to go there and have a picnic supper on the front porch. Since there's no furniture inside, it had to be an outside paper-plates-and-plastic-forks kind of affair. Once I got here, though, and had real dishes and glassware to work with, it turned into something more elaborate. Would you like me to pour you a glass of champagne?"

Butch stopped talking abruptly, like a windup toy whose spring had come unwound. Joanna had been ready to nail him for what she regarded as uncalled-for interference, but her momentary anger dissolved in the face of his sudden stricken silence.

Why, he's nervous, Joanna realized. *He's almost as nervous and unsure of himself as I am.*

"No champagne until after I shower," she told him.

A few minutes later, standing under a soothing stream of hot, steamy water, Joanna felt the awful events of the day slowly drain out of her body. In her mind's eye she kept replaying that little scene in the kitchen and Butch's unspoken disapproval as she put the guns away in the drawer. Initially the incident had made her cross, but in retrospect it opened a window onto a whole series of bittersweet memories.

The day Jenny was born, a little girl from Douglas—a two-year-old toddler—had died as a result of playing with her father's loaded pistol. While Joanna had been in the early stages of labor at the Copper Queen Hospital in Bisbee, Andy had been down in Douglas at the Cochise County Hospital, taking a report from the bereaved parents. That little girl's death had made a profound impression on Andrew Roy Brady, new father and rookie cop. From then on, whenever possible, he had left his .357 closed up in his locker at work. The .38 Chief, his backup weapon, he had kept in a locked drawer of the rolltop desk in the bedroom.

Only now, long after the fact, did Joanna realize how conscientious Andy had been about that. He had never once complained about the day-to-day inconvenience. He had simply done it. It struck Joanna that, in that regard, Butch and Andy weren't so very different.

Stepping out of the shower, she toweled her hair dry and applied a few strokes of makeup. Then, wearing a comfortable short-sleeved blouse and a pair of shorts, she emerged from the bathroom and headed straight for the kitchen, where she retrieved the two guns from the drawer and started back toward the bedroom.

"You're right," she said in answer to Butch's raised eyebrow and unasked question as she hurried past. "You and Andy are *both* right on this one, and I'm wrong. Even though Jenny and I talked this over, I should have been keeping the guns locked up all along."

Butch followed her as far as the bedroom door. "Look," he said, "I didn't mean to sound like I was telling you what to do . . ."

"It's okay," she said. "When you're right, you're right. Now, didn't somebody say something about champagne?"

"Coming right up," he said. "Do you want to sip it first, or would you rather eat?"

"Eat, I think," she told him. "Until I smelled that freshly baked bread, I didn't have any idea how hungry I was."

In the dining room, the candles were lit. Butch held out the chair for Joanna to be seated. He poured a glass of the sparkly golden liquid and handed it to her, then poured one for himself.

"To your new house," Joanna said, smiling and lifting her glass to his.

"Yes," he responded. "To my new house."

There was a momentary silence; then they started talking at once. Butch said, "I hope you like—"

And Joanna said, "I'm sorry I—"

They both dissolved into nervous laughter. "All right, now," Butch said. "One at a time. I hope you like chef's salad."

"I love chef's salad," Joanna replied. "And I'm sorry I didn't get to see your house today. Maybe tomorrow."

"Given what's been going on around here, I won't hold my breath," he said. "It's been real bad for you, hasn't it?" He handed her a basket filled with thick slices of the freshly baked bread. She took one slice—still slightly warm to the touch—and slathered it with butter, nodding as she did so.

"This afternoon I thought I had it all figured out," she told him. "Then the whole thing fell apart on me. By the time it was over, it turned out that what I thought I knew I didn't know at all."

"Do you want to talk about it?" Butch asked.

"Not really. I guess what I need to do now is just forget about it. Try to keep work at work and home at home."

Butch passed her a bowl of dressing. "It's Roquefort," he said. "My own recipe."

"Homemade?"

"But of course. If it's any consolation, the same thing happened to me today. What I thought I had all figured out for Chapter One wasn't figured out at all."

"So you've started, then—writing, I mean."

"Everybody always says make an outline," Butch said. "So I tried that. I worked on the damned outline for a solid week and wasn't getting anywhere. Then I finally figured out what the problem is. I've always *hated* outlining. Always. So I threw out the outline and started over from scratch."

Dipping a sprig of asparagus into the dressing, Joanna took a tentative bite of her salad. "This is delicious," she said, savoring the tangy flavor on her tongue.

"See there?" Butch said with a grin. "I'll bet you thought I was just another pretty face." And then they laughed some more.

"Seriously, though. You said you were going to write mysteries," Joanna said. "What kind?"

"Well," Butch said, "that's what I thought I had figured out. I thought I'd write books about a kind of tough-guy cop. Now I'm not so sure."

"Why? What changed your mind?"

"You."

"Me?" Joanna said. "How come?"

"Because from what I've seen in the last few days around here, being a cop is a whole lot harder than I ever thought. And I'm not so sure I want to write about a tough guy, either. There are a lot of those in fiction, you know."

"Are there?"

"Sure. So maybe I'll write a book with a female protagonist instead."

"I see. A lady detective." Joanna thought about that for

a time before she spoke again. "Have you always liked mysteries?" she asked. "Did you read all those old books when you were a kid, the ones about the Hardy Boys and Nancy Drew?"

"I was a boy, I'll have you know," Butch replied indignantly. "I wouldn't have been caught dead reading a Nancy Drew."

"But you did read the Hardy Boys," Joanna persisted.

"Of course. Didn't everybody?"

Again silence filled the room and they ate without speaking. Joanna, wanting to keep things light, tried drawing him out. "Have you chosen a pen name yet?"

"Since I haven't written Chapter One yet, that seems a bit premature. So no, I haven't."

"Well, you should," she said. "When it comes time to start, that's what's supposed to go on the title page—the book's title and the author's name."

"Butch Dixon," he said slowly, sounding it out. "That doesn't have much of a ring to it. Sounds like somebody who'd write auto-repair manuals. No. Butch Dixon isn't going to cut it. And Frederick Dixon isn't much better."

"Then what's your middle name?" Joanna asked.

"Why do you want to know?"

"I just want to, that's all."

Butch sighed. "I hate my middle name," he said. "I haven't had enough to drink to start telling people my middle name."

"You're not telling people," Joanna objected. "You're only telling me."

"Wilcox," he said with a glower. "Not two l's like the town. One l."

"Why don't you use your initials, then?" Joanna suggested. "If you're writing about a female protagonist, people might think you're a woman. Let's say Faye Wanda Dixon."

Butch choked on a sip of champagne. "Faye Wanda!" he repeated. "That's awful."

"But you see what I mean."

"Okay, F. W. Dixon, then. That's all right, I suppose. But doesn't it sound familiar? I'm sure I know of a writer by that name."

When they finally managed to dredge the name Franklin W. Dixon out of their Hardy Boys memory banks, they gave up eating altogether and collapsed on the floor amid gales of helpless laughter. Joanna couldn't remember laughing like that in years. It felt good. What remained of her day's awful burden lightened and disappeared entirely.

"No wonder the name sounded familiar!" Butch gasped, wiping the tears from his eyes. "We were just talking about him. And I can still see it now, the name and the initials printed on the skinny little spines of those tan-and-brown books. What's funny is, I already owned both the F and the W and I didn't even realize it. And you're right, of course. Good old Franklin W.—F. W.—was a woman masquerading under a man's pen name, right?"

"Right," Joanna agreed. "Turnabout's fair play."

Eventually they got up, cleared the table, and loaded the dishes into the dishwasher. With the kitchen cleaned up and the dishwasher running, they took their last glasses of champagne out onto the front porch to sit in the swing and watch the stars. It was chilly enough outside to make Joanna wish she'd brought along a sweater.

Butch noticed her rubbing her arms. "It never gets this cool in Phoenix during the summer," he said. "Too much humidity. Too much pavement."

"Are you going to miss Phoenix?" she asked.

"I wondered about that, but don't think so." He paused. In the interim, a roving band of coyotes howled back and forth across the valley.

"See there?" Butch added. "You don't hear very much of that in Peoria anymore. No, I don't think I'll miss the city at all."

"So that's why you were so busy the last few weeks? You were working on the deal to sell the Roundhouse?"

He nodded.

"I was worried," she said. "Especially when I called and the phone was disconnected. I thought maybe . . ."

"Maybe what?"

"I thought maybe you'd taken up with some other woman."

"That was bothering me, too," he said glumly. "I wasn't hearing much from you, either. You kept saying you were helping out a lot with Ruth and Esther, but I was obsessed by the idea that some other guy had moved into the picture."

"So we were both . . . well . . . jealous."

"I guess so."

"Don't you think that's funny?" Joanna asked.

"No," Butch said, shaking his head. "It's not funny at all. I'd hate like hell to lose you, Joanna." His voice seemed to break when it came time to say her name, as though he could barely stand to say the word aloud. Surprised, Joanna turned to look at him, but he kept his gaze averted.

"You mean that, don't you?" she said.

There was real wonder in her voice. After months of bantering back and forth, after months of what she had regarded as just having fun, she had finally caught a glimmer, a hint, of the depth of feeling Butch Dixon kept hidden under layers of jokes and easy laughter.

"Please, Joanna," he groaned. "Let's just drop it. I promised last night that I wouldn't rush you, and I'm not going to. I just want to be here, that's all. I'm not asking for anything more than that. I'm not making any demands."

She moved closer to him on the swing, letting the bare skin of her leg meet up with the soft, worn denim of his jeans. Then she reached out and took his hand. "I wouldn't want to lose you, either," she said. She raised his tightly clenched fist to her lips and kissed the back of it. Under that light caress she felt the tension recede from Butch's hand and body both.

"Wouldn't you like to come inside?" she whispered.

"No," he said. "Really. I think I'd better go. Now, before things end up getting out of hand."

For months Joanna had determinedly refused to acknowledge the aching tensions and urgent sexual needs of her body. By denying their very existence she had managed to survive, had managed to keep the fires inside her banked, her longings under wraps. Now, though, to her utter amazement, Butch Dixon had broken through her resolve, and had let a demanding and insistent genie out of its carefully bottled imprisonment. After months of self-denial, Joanna Brady suddenly realized that she was still young and still alive. It was time.

Letting Butch's hand fall back in his lap, she reached up and brushed her lips across the firm muscles of his jawline. "Things are already out of hand," she whispered. "So maybe we'd both better go inside."

CHAPTER TWENTY-ONE

The dream overtook Joanna hours later. The sky overhead was deceptively blue as she walked across a grassy field. Far away, under a tree, stood a group of boys. "What are you doing?" she called to them. "What are you up to?"

They didn't answer, but even without being told, Joanna somehow knew. They had captured a frog from a nearby stream, and she hurried forward, determined to rescue the creature. In order to save it, she had to move faster, but her feet and legs seemed mired in mud or deep, river-bottom sand.

"You stop that now!" she shouted. "You shouldn't do that. It's not nice."

One of the boys turned and peered at her over his shoulder. Then his mouth twisted into an ugly, gargoylelike smile. He laughed and pointed, and the other boys looked, too, while Joanna churned forward, propelled by a terrible sense of urgency mixed with an equal amount of dread.

She reached the outside of the tightly knit circle. "Let me in," she shouted. "What are you doing?" As she tried to see over one boy's shoulder, he seemed to swell before her very eyes, growing upward and upward until he towered over her. She went to the next boy, and the same thing happened. One at a time, the boys transformed themselves into huge, thick-limbed giants. They closed ranks and shouldered her out of the way, but now there was a sound coming from inside the circle—a terrible whimpering.

"Please stop now," Joanna pleaded. "Please. Didn't your mothers teach you any better than this?"

One of the giants whirled around and glared down at her. "Mothers?" he said. "Mothers? We don't need no stinkin' mothers." He laughed. Then, with a shrug, he turned and walked away. One by one, the others followed. Joanna watched them leave. Only when the last one had disappeared beyond the crest of a hill did Joanna turn her attention to the bloodied form of the unfortunate creature they had left behind.

At first she couldn't tell what it was. But when she stepped closer she realized it was a child: Jenny. A Jenny with no arms or legs, lying helpless and screaming in the gore-covered grass.

The horrifying dream dissolved as suddenly as if someone had flicked a switch. In the nightmare's absence, the keening, awful scream remained.

"Joanna," Butch said, gently shaking her naked shoulder, "wake up. You're having a bad dream." He reached over and flipped on the bedside lamp. "Are you all right?"

"Yes," she said, "I'm okay," but her heart was hammering inside her chest. Sweat-soaked bedclothes clung to her naked body. Unbidden tears filled her eyes while a sob choked off her ability to speak.

Butch encircled her with both arms and held her against his chest. "Do you want to talk about it?"

Joanna took a deep breath. "He disables his victims," she

said. "He cripples them and then he leaves them to bleed to death. After they're dead, he mutilates the bodies."

"Someone in your dream did this?" Butch asked. His warm breath lingered on her ear.

"No," she said. "The serial killer we're tracking. The real one. I talked to an FBI profiler named Monty Brainard. He says we're dealing with a spree killer."

"But the killer was in your dream?"

"No, there were boys in my dream. I thought they were pulling the legs off frogs. But when I got close enough to see, it turned out they had Jenny."

"Boys had Jenny, not the killer," Butch mumbled. He sounded half asleep. "I don't understand."

"I do," Joanna replied determinedly. "Frogs and snails and puppy-dog tails, that's what little boys are made of. The profiler is right. The killer's a boy, and we've got to find him before he kills somebody else."

"Don't worry," Butch said, sounding now as though he was more than half asleep. "It was only a dream. We'll talk about it in the morning." With that he reached across and switched the light back off.

Joanna could tell by the way Butch had spoken that he was already drifting off. She waited until he was snoring softly before she eased her way out of his grasp, pulled on a robe, and crept out of the room. The clock in the kitchen said 4:15 as she turned on the kitchen light. After starting coffee, she slid into the breakfast nook to wait.

In the familiar confines of her kitchen, with the lights on and with coffee slowly bubbling into the pot, the dream receded from her consciousness, but it left behind a strange sense of both uneasiness and comprehension. Monty Brainard and her subconscious mind had dealt with the same problem and arrived at the same answer. The killer was a young man, little more than a boy. A man/boy with no sense of right or wrong, and with a video-game player's concept of life and death.

Intuitively, Joanna suspected that whatever his name, he was most likely the person Sarah Holcomb had identified as Frankie Ramos' loutish friend. With Frankie dead and unable to tell them who the friend was, Joanna knew they would have to come up with some other way of finding him.

There was always a chance that the evidence techs would discover a usable fingerprint. In the old days, latent fingerprints could help convict a known perpetrator, but they had been virtually useless in identifying unknown criminals. Now, though, with the help of AFIS—the Automated Fingerprint Identification System—that had changed. By using computers, it was possible to compare points of similarity on unidentified prints to those of millions of prints, often booking prints, that had already been loaded into the system. With the computer searching for similarities, it was sometimes possible for a crime-scene fingerprint to lead directly to a named suspect.

AFIS made the odds of that happening better, but it wasn't foolproof. For one thing, assuming Monty Brainard's assessments were right about the killer's previous run-ins with law enforcement, his prints were likely to be in the system. The problem was, he was also being extremely cagey about not leaving prints behind. Even if a usable print existed at one of the crime scenes, Joanna knew her people were utterly overwhelmed by the avalanche of crime-scene evidence that had come in over the past few days. It might take weeks or months to sort through it all. In the meantime, how many more victims would die?

So how do we do this in a timely manner? Joanna asked herself. *How do we sort through masses of crime-scene evidence to identify the killer?*

When the coffee finished brewing, she poured a cup.

Then after donning a warm jacket over her robe, she took her coffee cup out to the porch. There, sitting on the swing and soothed by the companionable presence of both dogs, Joanna considered the problem.

Monty Brainard claimed the killer was a loner. Maybe Frankie Ramos had been his one real friend—a fatal offense which had also qualified him as victim. But were there other acquaintances, other people who ran in the same crowd? They might not have been as close to the killer, but that didn't mean they didn't know him. Whoever those people were, they might very well suspect what the killer had done. They'd be scared now, worrying that perhaps they, too, had moved from the role of pal to potential victim.

The answer, when it came, seemed to materialize directly out of the steam wafting from Joanna's cup of coffee—Deputy Eddy Sandoval. Quietly easing the door open so as not to disturb Butch, she retrieved the portable phone from the living room and went back outside. Sitting on the swing, she dialed the department's number. Stu Farmer, the night watch commander, took the call.

"You're up bright and early this morning, Sheriff Brady," Stu told her.

"Funniest thing," she said. "I can't seem to sleep."

"Wonder why," Stu replied. "Now, what can I do for you?"

"What time does Eddy Sandoval come on duty today?"

"Hang on," Stu said. "Let me check the roster." Joanna listened to several minutes of clattering computer keyboard keys. "Here it is. He works three to eleven today. Want me to have him check in with you as soon as he comes on shift?"

Joanna didn't want Eddy Sandoval to have any kind of advance warning that she was about to land on him. "No," she said. "That's all right. I may be stuck in a meeting about then. It wouldn't do to have him waiting around to hook up with me. I'll contact him once I'm free."

"Anything else I can do?"

"Actually, there is. I want you to run a check on Clyde Philips."

"Philips? The guy who's dead?"

"That's the one," Joanna said. "I want to know what, if anything, is on his sheet."

"Will do. After I run it, want me to call right back with the information?"

"No, that's okay. Just put it in an envelope and leave it on Kristin's desk. She'll give it to me as soon as I come in tomorrow morning."

"Begging your pardon, Sheriff," Stu Farmer said, "it's almost five. That's *this* morning."

"Right," Joanna said. "This morning."

She put down the phone and sat waiting for the sun to come creeping up over the Chiricahuas and for the mourning doves to send their sweet daytime greetings across the waking desert. The tops of the mountains were just turning gold when the screen door squeaked open behind her. With wagging tails, both dogs went to greet Butch.

"Do you always get up this ungodly early?" he asked, easing himself down beside her. Barefoot and wearing jeans but no shirt, he had already poured himself a cup of coffee.

"You bet," Joanna said. "My folks always told me that the early bird gets the worm."

Butch groaned. "I suppose it'll wreck the analogy if I point out that the poor dead worm is also an early riser. How are you feeling?"

"Okay."

He reached over and ran his index finger along the rim of Joanna's ear. "I was hoping for something a little more effusive than that. Something on the order of 'wonderful' or 'fantastic.' " He paused. "Not feeling any regrets, are you?" he added. "I mean, you're not sorry I stayed over, are you?"

Joanna thought about that before she answered. She hadn't ever really contemplated the possibility that someone besides Andy might share the bed that had once been theirs. The likelihood of that had seemed so remote, she had succeeded in ignoring it entirely. When long-buried urges had overcome her the night before, they had taken her by surprise and created such blinding abandon that there had been no room for either guilt or regret.

She smiled at Butch and rested one hand on his knee. "I believe my heart is remarkably guilt-free."

"Whew," he sighed in obvious relief. "Am I ever glad to hear that! When I woke up and found you gone, I was afraid you were out here brooding and wishing some of what happened hadn't."

"No," Joanna said, "not at all. But be advised, we won't be able to pull stunts like this once Jenny gets home. To say nothing of my mother. Eleanor is going to take one look at my face and know I've been up to no good, although as far as I'm concerned, she and George don't have much room to talk. And then I'm worried about what my in-laws might think—that somehow I'm not honoring their son's memory. I wouldn't want to hurt Jim Bob's and Eva Lou's feelings."

"Me, either," Butch agreed. "What that means, then, is that as soon as all these people show up on the horizon, you and I are going to have to be the very souls of discretion. Absolutely above reproach. Over and above the people you've already named, are there any others we need to worry about offending?"

"I don't know about offending," Joanna said. "But there might be spies."

"Who?"

"Marliss Shackleford, for one."

"You mean she might have a paid informant on tap at the Copper Queen who could provide nightly bed checks to make sure I'm properly locked in at night and staying in my designated room?"

Joanna giggled. "Maybe not, but only because she hasn't thought of it yet. If she did, I wouldn't put it past her. It sounds just like her."

"Great. Big Sister is watching." Butch stood up. "How's your coffee?" he asked.

"It's fine."

"No, it's not fine. It's almost empty. Let me get you some more."

Butch disappeared into the house. He returned a few minutes later, wearing a shirt, carrying both cups filled to the brim. They sat quietly for a while, letting the morning age around them, watching the sky turn from lavender to orange to blue.

"Bartenders don't see many sunrises," he said. "It's pretty, but it still seems like an odd time of day to be up."

"Early morning is when I do my best thinking," Joanna told him. "It's my most creative time."

"Really. Well, there may be a lesson in that. Our new friend F. W. should sit up, take notice, and start setting his alarm." He looked off across the valley. "Not a cloud in the sky," he noted. "Does that mean the rains are over? Have the monsoons come and gone for the summer?"

"I don't know. Before the end of August, they could come back and take another crack at us."

"Let's hope," Butch returned.

Joanna took one of his hands in hers. "There are other things we should probably be talking about," she ventured quietly. "Other things that need discussion besides the weather."

"Like what, for instance?" he asked.

"Like why you got divorced," she answered. "Like why you got divorced twice."

He winced and made a face. "Just lucky, maybe?"

She squeezed his hand. "No jokes, *please.*"

"It wasn't really two divorces," he said. "The first one was an annulment. Debbie's parents got that one on religious grounds. We weren't much more than kids, either one of us. Looking back, I'm sure it was just as well."

"And the second one?"

"That one was ugly. Faith—I always liked the irony in that name—left me for my best friend," he said. "Worked me over real good in the process—mentally, financially, you name it. She managed to convince all concerned, including most of my relatives, that the whole deal was my fault. That I had somehow caused my wife to fall in love with somebody else."

"No wonder you took Jorge Grijalva's part," Joanna remarked, referring to a man who had been the prime suspect in the murder of his estranged wife, Serena. It was during the course of that investigation that she had first encountered Butch Dixon.

"Right," he said. "No wonder."

"And are they still together?" Joanna asked.

"Who?"

"Your former friend and your former wife."

Butch shrugged. "Beats me, although I suppose so. There weren't any kids, so Faith and I don't exactly stay in touch. I could probably ask my mother, though. The two of them are still thick as thieves. I'm sure my mother would be more than happy to give you an update."

"I'll pass," Joanna said with a smile. "But even with that bad experience," she added, "you're still willing to give romance another try?"

Butch looked at her. "You mean with you?"

Joanna nodded.

"I didn't have a choice," Butch told her. "You walked into the Roundhouse. I'm a sucker for redheads. As soon as I saw you, I was smitten. That's why they call it love at first sight."

"Come on," Joanna said. "Don't give me a line . . ."

"It's no line," Butch insisted. "The moment I saw you, my goose was cooked. 'Butch, old boy,' I told myself, 'here's the one you'd better not let slip away.' And nothing that's happened since has changed my mind."

He swallowed the last of his coffee. "So how about letting me whip you up a little breakfast?"

"You'll spoil me."

He grinned. "That's the whole idea."

"Well, Jenny's been gone for a week now. I doubt there are any groceries left in the house."

"Not to worry. I know there's still some of my bread left over from last night. And I believe I saw both milk and eggs in the fridge. With bread and milk and eggs, I can make dynamite French toast. What time do you have to be at work?"

"Eight."

He glanced at his watch. "Hey," he said, "as far as I'm concerned, eight is still a very long time from now."

"What's that supposed to mean?"

Butch put one arm around her shoulder and pulled her close to him. "Guess," he said.

Hand in hand, they rose and, with no further discussion, made their way back into the bedroom. Afterward, with time growing short, Joanna disappeared into the bathroom while Butch went to start breakfast. By the time Joanna was dressed, the homey fragrance of frying bacon filled the house.

Out in the kitchen, Butch was standing watch over the

stove as Joanna attempted to slip by him to collect another cup of coffee. He turned and touched her cheek with a glancing kiss as she went past. "Nice perfume," he said.

Joanna took her coffee and ducked into the breakfast nook. She had barely seated herself when Butch set a plate of food in front of her. "See there?" He beamed. "Admit it. There are some definite advantages to becoming involved with a man who's run a restaurant most of his adult life. I make a hell of a short-order cook."

"I notice you have one or two other talents," she said. "I can see why a girl might want to keep you around."

Joanna had managed barely two bites of French toast when the telephone rang. Realizing she'd left it on the counter in the bathroom, Joanna hurried to answer it.

"By the way," Butch called after her, "it drives me crazy when I cook food for people and they let it get cold. Did I ever tell you that?"

Coming back with the still ringing phone, Joanna held a finger to her lips to silence him before she answered. "Hello."

"Joanna?"

"Yes, Jeff, it's me. How are you? You sound awful."

"We've had a pretty rough night here," Jeff Daniels told her. "Esther's come down with pneumonia."

"Oh, no!" Joanna managed.

"The doctors don't know whether they'll be able to save her," Jeff continued. "Because of the transplant, they've pumped her full of immune suppressants. But now . . ." His voice trailed off.

Joanna took a deep breath. "How is Marianne doing in the face of all this?" she asked.

"Not that well. Right now she's down in the room with Esther. She didn't want me to call you, Joanna, but I thought I'd better. It's bad, real bad. I tried calling her folks. I talked to her dad on the phone, but not her mother. Even after all these years, Evangeline is still so pissed at Marianne that she wouldn't talk to me. I know she won't come, not even if Marianne needs her."

"Well, I will," Joanna said at once. "I'll be there as soon as I can."

She put down the phone and looked across the kitchen at Butch, who was still flipping French toast on the griddle.

"Esther has pneumonia," she heard herself say. "She might not make it. I've got to go to Tucson."

Butch took the last two pieces of French toast off the griddle and turned off the heat. "I'll go with you," he offered.

"No," Joanna said. "You don't have to do that."

"Yes, I do," he insisted. "I want to. Your car or mine, or do we have to take both?"

Joanna Brady knew she was tough, knew she was a survivor. But she also knew that this was one trip she shouldn't make alone.

"Let's go in mine," she decided. "That way, if I have to be in touch with the department, I can use either the radio or the phone. And the siren," she added. "If need be."

Butch's eyes met hers across the kitchen, then he nodded. "Right," he agreed. "The siren."

CHAPTER TWENTY-TWO

As they drove up through Bisbee and over the Divide, Butch sat quietly on the rider's side of the Blazer watching the desert speed by outside the window. "What are their families like?" he asked finally.

"Jeff's and Marianne's?"

Butch nodded and Joanna made a face. "I've never met Jeff's folks. They live back East somewhere—Maryland, I think. Marianne's parents, Evangeline and Tim Maculyea, came from Bisbee originally, but they moved to Safford after the mines shut down. They still live there."

"Safford," Butch mused. "That's not too far away, so they'll probably show up to help out, too."

Joanna shook her head. "I don't think so," she said. "Safford may not be that far away in terms of mileage, but emotionally, it could just as well be another planet. That's what Jeff was telling me on the phone. He called the Maculyeas and told them what's happening with Esther. I guess Tim was okay on the phone, but Evangeline wouldn't talk to Jeff and she won't come see Marianne, either."

"Why not?" Butch asked.

"Because Marianne's the black sheep in the family," Joanna replied.

"Black sheep!" Butch echoed. "The woman's a saint. She doesn't smoke or drink or use bad words. Not to mention the fact that she's a minister. What makes her a black sheep?"

"She's a Methodist."

"So?"

"Evangeline is a devout Catholic. She's been bent out of shape ever since her daughter left the Church. She hasn't spoken to Marianne since. The same thing goes for Marianne's two younger brothers. They don't speak to Jeff and Marianne, either. I don't think Evangeline Maculyea has ever laid eyes on Jeff Daniels, even though he's been married to her only daughter for more than ten years."

"I suppose that means she hasn't laid eyes on her grandchildren, either," Butch surmised.

"Right," Joanna said.

"That's a shame."

"No," Joanna disagreed. "That's a tragedy—all the way around."

As she drove, she kept one eye on the speedometer and the other on the clock. As soon as it was eight, she picked up the radio. "Put me through to Dick Voland," she told Dispatch. "He should be there by now."

It took a few minutes to track the chief deputy down. "Where are you, Joanna?" he asked.

"I'm in the car and on my way to Tucson," she said. "Jeff Daniels and Marianne Maculyea's baby has taken a turn for the worse. I've got to go see them. I'll need you to handle the morning briefing."

"No problem. I can take care of that. Anything in particular you want me to cover?"

Joanna thought about mentioning her Eddy Sandoval idea, but then she reconsidered. That was something she'd need to handle herself. But she did have another suggestion.

"I want you to have someone pick up the last three or four years' worth of high school yearbooks from both Benson and St. David. Have someone show them to Clyde Philips' next-door neighbor, Sarah Holcomb. She should look through them and see if any of the pictures match up with any of the 'young 'uns,' as she calls them, who used to hang around Clyde Philips' house."

"Okay," Dick Voland said. "I'll have someone get right on it. Jaime or Ernie, most likely."

"Whoever you send, tell them that once Sarah finishes examining the pictures, I want her to go visit her daughter, who lives somewhere up in Tucson. I want her to stay there until we put this case to rest."

"You think she's in danger?" Dick asked.

"Absolutely. If there's even a remote chance that she can identify the killer, she's as much a threat to him as Frankie Ramos was."

"What if she refuses to leave?"

"Then put a guard on her house. Park a deputy on her front porch twenty-four hours a day if you have to. I don't want anything to happen to the woman."

"Mounting a twenty-four-hour guard is going to cost money. Frank Montoya'll shit a brick over that idea."

"Well, then," Joanna said, "send him to talk to her."

"Frank? But he's not even a detective."

"He's a trained police officer, Dick. I'm sure he's fully capable of showing her a montage of photos and getting her reaction. He can do that every bit as well as a detective can. Aren't Ernie and Jaime totally overloaded at the moment?"

"Well," Voland conceded, "I suppose they are."

"Besides," Joanna added, "we both know that when

Frank's budget is on the line, he can be amazingly persuasive."

"I'd prefer to call it amazingly obnoxious," Voland returned, "but you're right. If anyone can charm the old lady into leaving town for the duration, Frank Montoya is it. Especially when there's overtime at stake. I'll have him go to work on it first thing this morning. As soon as the briefing is over. Anything else?" he asked.

"You tell me."

"I'm just now collecting my copies of the overnight incident reports. It doesn't sound like anything out of the ordinary."

"Good," Joanna said. "Keep me posted. If I'm out of the car, I'll have my cell phone with me. You'll be able to reach me on that."

"Right," Dick Voland said. "In the meantime, I hope things work out all right for Jeff and Marianne's little girl."

"I hope so, too." Joanna said the words, but deep in her heart she feared it wasn't to be.

The trip from High Lonesome to Tucson should have taken about two hours. It was accomplished in a little less than ninety hair-raising minutes. And if Butch Dixon had any objections to the way Joanna drove, he had the good grace to keep quiet about it.

As they walked from the hospital parking garage toward the lobby entrance, a wave of panic suddenly engulfed Joanna. She hesitated at the entryway, unsure if she was capable of facing what was coming. On her previous visit, Esther's situation hadn't been this bad. Now it was like having to relive everything that had happened to Andy.

Somehow, without her saying a word, Butch must have sensed what was happening. He reached out, captured her hand, and squeezed it.

"You have to do this," he said. "Jeff and Marianne are counting on you."

Bolstered by his words, Joanna took a deep breath. "I know," she said. "Thanks."

When they entered the pediatric ICU waiting room there was a lone figure in it, an elderly gentleman standing next to the window, staring down at the hospital entrance far below. It wasn't until he turned to face them that Joanna recognized Marianne's father, Timothy Maculyea.

"Mr. Maculyea," she said, hurrying toward him, "I don't know if you remember me. I'm Marianne's friend Joanna Lathrop—Joanna Brady now. And this is my friend Butch Dixon. Butch, this is Mr. Maculyea."

The older man held out a massive paw of a hand—the permanently callused and work-hardened mitt of a former hard-rock miner. "Tim's the name," he said to Butch. "Glad to meet you. I came as soon as I heard, but—" He stopped and pursed his lips.

"How are things?" Joanna asked.

He shook his head. "Not good," he said. "Not good at all."

"Where's Jeff?"

"Down in the room. It's the ICU, so they let only one person in at a time."

"And Marianne?"

Tim Maculyea swallowed hard before he answered. "She's down in the chapel," he said, his throat working to expel the words. "I haven't seen her yet. She doesn't know I'm here."

"And Mrs. Maculyea?" Joanna continued.

Tim shook his head once more. "Vangie isn't coming. She's always been a stubborn, headstrong woman. Not un-like her daughter."

Joanna turned to Butch. "I'd better go check on Marianne," she said.

He nodded. "Sure," he said. "You go ahead. I'll stay here and keep Mr. Maculyea company."

Minutes later, Joanna stepped into the hushed gloom of the dimly lit chapel, a small room that held half a dozen polished wooden pews. Marianne Maculyea, her head bowed and her shoulders hunched, sat in the front row. Silently, Joanna slipped into the seat beside her. Marianne glanced up, saw Joanna, then looked away.

"It's bad," she said.

"I know," Joanna murmured. "Jeff told me."

"Why?" Marianne whispered brokenly. "Why is this happening?"

"I don't have an answer," Joanna said. "There's never an answer."

Marianne put her hand to her mouth, covering a sob. "I thought she was going to make it, Joanna. I thought it was going to be all right, but it's not. Esther's going to die. It's just a matter of time. A few hours, maybe. A day at most. All her systems are failing."

"Oh, Mari," Joanna said, barely able to speak herself. It was what she had expected, yet hearing the words tore at her heart. "I'm so sorry. I don't know what to say, what to do . . ."

Marianne breathed deeply, fighting for control. "Joanna, I need a favor."

"What?"

"Promise me that when the time comes, you'll officiate at the service."

"Me?" Joanna was aghast. "Mari, you can't be serious. I'm not a trained minister. Surely one of the other pastors in town would be glad to step in . . ."

Marianne Maculyea shook her head fiercely. "No," she

said, "I don't want one of the other pastors. I want you. If one of them had nerve enough to mention the word 'faith' in my company or during the course of the service, I'd probably go berserk. Besides, none of them knows Esther, not really—not the way you do. You were there the day we brought the girls home from the plane, Joanna. We're still using the diaper bag you gave me to take to Tucson that morning. In fact, that's what we brought with us to the hospital to carry Esther's things—" Unable to continue, Marianne broke off in tears.

"Please," she added after a pause. "Promise you'll do it."

"Of course," Joanna said. "Whatever you want."

"Thank you."

For the next several minutes the two women sat together, lost in their own thoughts, neither of them saying a word. Joanna was the one who finally broke the silence. "Your father's upstairs," she said gently. "Butch and I ran into him in the waiting room."

"And my mother?" Marianne asked woodenly.

"No," Joanna said. "I'm sorry."

"That's all right," Marianne said. "It figures. How long has my dad been here?"

"I don't know. He was in the waiting room when we arrived."

Marianne sighed and stood up. "I'd guess I'd better go see him, then. Are you coming?"

"Yes I am." Joanna said.

The morning passed slowly. Several times Joanna tried calling Jenny, but there was no answer at the farm, and once again, she didn't want to leave this kind of disturbing message on anyone's answering machine.

Word of the impending tragedy had spread throughout Bisbee, so in the course of the morning, more and more people showed up—some of whom, in Joanna's opinion, had no business being there. She and Butch found themselves running interference, trying to keep the group of sympathetic well-wishers from completely overwhelming Jeff and Marianne.

At twenty after one that afternoon, Jeff emerged from the ICU, sank onto a couch, covered his face with his hands, and announced to the room, "It's over. She's gone."

Trying to stifle a sob of her own, Joanna buried her head against Butch Dixon's chest. There was nothing more to be said.

For the next half hour Butch and Joanna helped herd people out of the waiting room. When Marianne finally emerged herself—dry-eyed, despondent, and empty-handed except for the diaper bag—there were just the four people left in the room: Joanna and Butch, Jeff Daniels, and Tim Maculyea.

Marianne spoke only to Jeff. "I want to go home," she said. "Please take me home."

Jeff reached in his pocket and fished out a set of car keys, which he immediately handed over to Butch. "Marianne and I will take the Bug," he said. "We have to go by the hotel and check out on our way out of town. The International is parked behind the hotel on the corner of Speedway and Campbell. Butch, you're sure you don't mind driving it back to Bisbee?"

"Not at all. I'll park it on the street somewhere near the Copper Queen. And if I'm going to be out, I'll leave the keys at the desk."

"Good," Jeff said. "Thanks." Then, with a gentle hand on Marianne's shoulder, he guided her out the door. She moved stiffly, like a sleepwalker. It broke Joanna's heart to see the vibrant and loving Marianne Maculyea, a woman whose very presence was a comfort to those in need, so bereft and comfortless herself.

Hands in his pockets, Tim Maculyea stood to one side and watched them go. "It's rough," he said, shaking his head and swiping at tears from under his thick glasses. "It's awful damned rough." He turned to Joanna. "Marianne didn't happen to tell you when the services would be, did she?"

"No, she didn't," Joanna replied. "But I'll call you as soon as I know. What about your wife? Will she come?"

"I doubt it," Tim said sadly. "I'll see what I can do, but I'm not making any promises."

At two-thirty, Joanna dropped Butch off at the Plaza Hotel so he could take Jeff's International back to Bisbee. "You've been a brick today," she told him as he climbed out of the Blazer.

He looked at her and smiled. "Glad to be of help," he said, and then he was gone.

Once alone, Joanna headed back toward Bisbee. She tried to switch gears—to make the transition from private to public, from Joanna Brady to Sheriff Brady. But it didn't work very well, at least not at first.

Not wanting to broadcast everything that had gone on over the police band, she used her cell phone to check in with the office. She wasn't surprised to hear that everyone was out. In fact, considering that week's impossible caseload, Joanna would have been disappointed if her officers hadn't been.

"I can have one of them call you as soon as they show up," Kristin Marsten offered.

"No," Joanna said. "Don't bother. I'll be there in person soon enough. One other thing, though. Did Stu Farmer leave an envelope for me? It was supposed to be on your desk when you came in this morning."

"It was there, all right," Kristin answered. "There was a

piece of paper inside with Clyde Philips' name on it, and nothing else. It's a rap sheet with nothing on it."

"Nothing? Not even a minor vehicle mishap?"

"Nothing at all. I figured you'd know what it means."

"I'm afraid I do," Joanna said grimly. "It means there's a serious problem in my department, and I'm going to fix it."

When her cell phone rang barely a minute later, Joanna assumed one of her several officers had turned up at the Justice Complex and was returning her call. She was startled to hear a man she didn't know announce himself to be Forrest L. Breen, FBI Agent in Charge, Phoenix.

"Monty Brainard must have called you," she said. "He told me he was going to."

"Yes," Breen replied. "With some wild-assed idea about your department wanting to borrow some weapons. Fifty-calibers, I believe."

"Well, I—"

"I told him I'd get back to you, Sheriff Brady. I can see from the news reports that you and your people have your hands full right now, but you have to understand the agency's position. If you want to call us in officially, that's one thing. I can have people there in jig time. But the other is out of the question. Bisbee and Phoenix may be from the same state, but we're not exactly neighbors. And borrowing a fifty-caliber weapon isn't the same thing as borrowing a lawn mower or a cup of sugar. You do understand what I'm saying, don't you, Ms. Brady?"

Yes, Mr. Breen. I certainly do, you overbearing asshole, Joanna thought. "Of course," she said.

"So," Breen continued quickly, before she had a chance to finish her response, "as I said, if you'd like to call us in, I'll be glad to send in a team, along with someone to take charge of the entire operation and personnel who are actually qualified on the kinds of weapons we're talking about. Otherwise . . ."

Like hell you will! "Thanks, but no, thanks," Joanna said curtly. "I don't believe I'm interested." She ended the call then, hanging up on Mr. Overbearing Agent-in-Charge Breen before he could say anything more.

Joanna was still steamed about both Agent Forrest Breen and Deputy Eddy Sandoval when she drove through Benson some twenty minutes later. There, next to the curb outside the Benson Dairy Queen, she caught sight of Eddy's parked cruiser. *Speak of the devil!* Joanna thought.

Executing a U-turn, she drove back and pulled up beside his vehicle. "Meet me at the Quarter Horse," she told him. "I need to talk to you."

"Sure thing," he said.

Ten minutes later, Joanna had ordered a sandwich and was drinking a cup of coffee when Sandoval came sauntering into the restaurant. At the Triple C crime scene two days earlier, the man hadn't seemed nearly as large as he did now, walking across the tiled restaurant floor to her booth, pushing his paunch ahead of him. "What's up, Sheriff?" he asked, slipping into the bench opposite her.

Joanna had used the intervening minutes to plan her approach. She had decided not to soft-pedal any of it. "You've been with the department for a long time," she said for openers. "I'm assuming you'd like to continue."

A veil of wariness closed down over Deputy Sandoval's eyes. "What's this all about?"

"Frankie Ramos."

Joanna waited, giving the name a chance to settle between them. After it did, she waited some more, not offering any explanation, leaving the officer to wonder and squirm under her withering scrutiny.

"What about him?" Eddy asked finally.

"I understand you and Ruben are old buddies."

Sandoval bristled then. "I don't know what Ruben told you," he began, rising off the bench, "but I—"

"Sit, Eddy," Joanna commanded. "You and I both know what he told me. And you know what you did, so let's not play games."

Reluctantly, he settled back down. "Frankie's dead," he said. "So what do you want? My resignation, is that it?"

"I may want your resignation eventually. But right this minute, what I want is information."

"What kind of information?"

"Did you ever break up any parties at Clyde Philips' house over in Pomerene?" she asked.

Eddy Sandoval's eyes flickered and then slid sideways toward one of the many horse pictures painted on the wall. "A few, I guess," he admitted.

"How many would you say? Two? Five?"

"I don't know. I don't remember exactly."

"And how many of those show up in the official log?"

Sandoval dropped his eyes and stared down at the table-top. His finger traced a chip in the edge of the Formica. "Probably none," he said.

"Why not?"

"Who knows? Maybe I forgot. But I don't have to answer any of this," he added sullenly. "I've got a right to an attorney."

"You *do* have to answer, Eddy," Joanna said. "You have to because lives are at stake. Now tell me, was there anyone else in Clyde Philips' car the night you failed to arrest Frankie Ramos for that MIP?"

Eddy hung his head. "Yeah," he said at last. "There was one other guy there, a buddy of Frankie's, I guess. Last name of Merritt."

"What about this Merritt kid?" Joanna asked. "Was he

of age, or was he a juvenile, too? And if so, did you write him up or not?"

Eddy continued to stare at the table and said nothing.

"That's answer enough, I suppose," Joanna said.

"When I looked the other way, Clyde was always good for it," Eddy mumbled.

"Good for what?"

"I don't know, some ammo now and then. A gun, I suppose. Nothing big. Just little stuff."

"And you somehow never wrote up any of those citations."

"Yeah," he said. "I suppose that's it."

"What about Ruben Ramos?" Joanna asked. "Did you make him pay, too?"

Eddy straightened up. "Ruben's a good friend of mine," he said. "We've been buddies a long time. I never charged him nothin'."

"What about the other boy? What was his name again, Merritt?"

Eddy shrugged. "He's over twenty-one, so all he was looking at was an open-container. I went out to see his folks but ended up talking to his stepmother. I could see right away that wasn't going anywhere, so I gave it up."

"Who's his stepmother?"

"Sonja Hosfield," Eddy Sandoval said. "Out at the Triple C. As far as she's concerned, that boy could be drowning, and she wouldn't lift a finger to drag him out. I just let it go."

"Merritt Hosfield?" Joanna was puzzled. "I don't remember Sonja Hosfield mentioning a child by that name."

"Ryan Merritt," Eddy returned. "Lindsey Hosfield was all screwed up when she left Alton. Took back her maiden name when she got a divorce and changed the kids' names, too. Changed them legally. That's the kind of thing women do sometimes when they're really mad."

As the connections came together, Joanna's neck prickled with hair standing up under her collar. Ryan Merritt! She remembered meeting Alton Hosfield's son Ryan two days ago. He had given the impression of being a fine, upstanding, hardworking young man. She remembered the polite way he had doffed his hat upon being introduced to her.

But what if that politeness is all façade? she wondered. *What if a cold-blooded killer lurks behind those clear blue eyes?*

Joanna held out her hand. "I want your badge, Mr. Sandoval," she said. "Your badge, your gun, and your ID. As of this moment, you're on administrative leave. Hand them over."

Sandoval drew back in surprise. "Wait a minute, Sheriff Brady. You can't do that."

"Yes, I can. Watch me. I don't know about criminal charges. Right now you're out pending the formality of a dismissal hearing. You're to drive your county-owned vehicle back to your house and park it. I'll send someone out there later on this afternoon to pick it up."

Eddy hesitated, then grabbed his badge and wrenched it off his uniform. Reaching into his pocket, he pulled out his ID holder and slammed both of them down with a blow that sent dishes skittering across the table. The gun he slapped into Joanna's outstretched hand.

"There! Are you satisfied now?" he demanded furiously. "But you're not going to be able to nail me on any of this, Sheriff Brady. You never read me my rights. My attorney wasn't present during questioning. You won't be able to use a single word I said against me."

The old Joanna might have been intimidated by Eddy's show of physical force. The new one held her ground.

"Maybe," she replied, keeping her eyes focused on his florid face while she gathered up his credentials and weapon and shoved them into her purse. "But I don't think I'll have to stoop to that. I'm betting there are plenty of other irregularities that'll turn up in this sector, and I can assure you, Mr. Sandoval, I'm not going to rest until I find them."

CHAPTER TWENTY-THREE

Back in the Blazer, Joanna gripped the steering wheel with both hands and wondered what to do next. She opted finally for calling the department. "Who's in?" she asked Kristin.

"Nobody. Chief Deputy Montoya expected to be back by now, but the lady he was supposed to get to send to Tucson wouldn't go. He's been stuck at her house all afternoon."

"And not very happy about it, either, I'll bet," Joanna surmised. "Can we raise him on the radio?"

"I can't," Kristin said, "but I'm sure Dispatch can."

"Never mind," Joanna said. "I'm already as far as Benson. I can be in Pomerene by the time Dispatch gets us linked together. There are two things I need you to do for me. Number one, send a deputy over to Eddy Sandoval's place to pick up his cruiser. Then tell the patrol duty officer that Sandoval is off the roster until further notice."

"All right. Anything else?"

"Yes. Ask the records clerk to run a check on someone named Ryan Merritt. I don't have a date of birth, but he's probably around twenty or so."

"Just here in Cochise County?" Kristin asked. "Or do you want a statewide check?"

The very fact that Kristin had asked the question was a sign that she was becoming more savvy. In the early days of Joanna's administration, the recently elected sheriff and her newly assigned secretary had been at loggerheads more often than not. Now Joanna sometimes found herself wondering if Kristin Marsten had actually grown that much smarter in the intervening months or if the changes in Kristin were a reflection of changes in Joanna herself.

"I'm glad you asked, Kristin," Joanna said. "A statewide check is what I need."

"Do you have an address?"

"No. He's currently living on the Triple C spread up in Cascabel. That address would be somewhere on Pomerene Road, although I can't give you the exact number. Before that, he most likely lived somewhere else. Try the Phoenix metropolitan area or maybe even Tucson."

"Do you want me to call you back on this, or can it wait until you get into the office?"

"Call me back," Joanna said. "I need the info ASAP."

Leaving Benson, Joanna drove straight to Sarah Holcomb's house in Pomerene. She found Chief Deputy Montoya dozing in the shade of one of Sarah's towering cottonwoods. Frank might have tried to convince Kristin that he was suffering, but in actual fact, it was clear to Joanna that he was being treated like an honored guest. An old Adirondack chair and matching footstool had been moved from the elderly woman's covered back porch to the shady front yard, along with a small wooden table. On the table sat a metal tray laden with napkins, a tall ice-filled glass, a generous pitcher of iced tea, and a platter of cookies.

Joanna parked the Blazer and went over to where he was

sitting. "Hey, Frank," she said. "Wake up. No fair sleeping on the job."

He came to with a start. "I wasn't really sleeping," he said. "Just resting my eyes."

"Sure you were. I thought you were supposed to be guarding her. As in making sure nobody comes anywhere near her."

"I am," he said. "Nobody can get past me."

"I almost did," Joanna told him. "And what's the deal with all the cookies and the iced tea? I've interviewed this woman twice so far, and she's never offered me so much as a piece of gum."

Frank shrugged. "What can I tell you? Sarah must like me."

"Did you bring the yearbooks?"

"Yes," he said. "We've already been through all of them. We did that over lunch, to no avail. She claims she didn't recognize anybody."

"Where are they?"

"The yearbooks?"

Joanna nodded.

"In the back of my car," Frank said. "If you want to see them, I'll be glad to go get 'em." He headed for his Crown Victoria, his Civvy, as he affectionately called it.

Through overuse compounded by an error in purchasing, the Cochise County Sheriff's Department was long on Crown Victoria-type cruisers and short on four-wheel-drive vehicles. Because his position as chief for administration called for very little field work, Frank now drove one of the Ford sedans despised by the other deputies. With some money and a little technical know-how, Frank Montoya had managed to turn his departmental Crown Victoria into a credible mobile office.

"Here we are," he said, putting the books down on the

table. "Eight yearbooks in all. Four from St. David and four from Benson."

Taking the top book off the Benson pile, Joanna quickly thumbed through it, checking each class listing for Ryan Merritt. "Are you looking for someone in particular?" Frank asked when she finished thumbing through the first book and started on the second.

"Yes," she said. "His name's Ryan Merritt. He's Alton Hosfield's son, Sonja's stepson."

"If you don't mind a little help," Frank suggested, "we can probably hurry this job along."

There was only one unchecked yearbook remaining, the last one from St. David, when Joanna's cell phone crowed. As she juggled it out of her purse, Frank made a face.

"You're the sheriff," he said. "Couldn't you find a ring that sounds a little more dignified?"

Joanna ignored the gibe. "Yes," she said into the phone. "What do you have for us, Kristin?" Seconds later, she held the phone away from her mouth. "Don't you have a mobile fax rigged up in your Civvy?"

"Sure do," he said. "It's hooked up to a slick little laptop."

Joanna went back to the phone. "Yes, Kristin," she said. "Go ahead and send it to Chief Deputy Montoya's mobile fax machine. Does it include a mug shot? Great. What about fingerprints? Amen. Send the whole thing. And thanks, Kristin. Good work."

"Send what whole thing?" Frank Montoya asked as he gathered and restacked the collection of yearbooks.

"Ryan Merritt's rap sheet," Joanna said. "It even includes a mug shot."

"The fax does have a small problem at the moment."

"What's that?"

"The printer went off-line. I sent it in for repairs. Whatever material Kristin sends will show up on the screen, though. We can look at it there."

"Look at it nothing," Joanna said. "We're going to show it to Sarah Holcomb."

"Showing a single photo like this isn't going to comply with the montage requirements," Frank began. "Shouldn't we—"

"Lives are at stake," Joanna interrupted. "Bring it."

Within two minutes Frank and Joanna were sitting in the front seat of Frank's Crown Victoria, peering through the glaring afternoon light into the dimly lit computer screen.

"There's too much light here," Frank said. "We'll have to take it inside to be able to see it." He unplugged the laptop, folded it under his arm, and carted it out of the car and up the steps onto Sarah Holcomb's front porch. She answered his knock with a charming smile that faded as soon as she caught sight of Joanna.

"Why, Deputy Montoya," she said, returning her gaze to his face, "is there something more I can do for you?"

"Yes, Mrs. Holcomb, there is. I have a computer here with a picture I need you to take a look at. If you don't mind our coming in to show it to you, that is. There's too much light outside for you to read the screen."

"That beats all," Sarah said. "Never heard of havin' too much light to read by. Usually it's the other way around. Is this somethin' that's on what they call the Innernet? One of those chat-room kinds of things? Although how people can sit around havin' a chat inside a computer is more'n I can figure."

"It's a little like the Internet," Frank allowed, "only it's not exactly the same thing. May we come in?"

"Sure," Sarah said. "You could just as well."

Frank led the way into the house. Rather than being bullied onto the unsittable sofa, he headed for the dining room

table. Sarah followed, brandishing her cane more than leaning on it. "You're sure this won't scratch the finish or
nothin'?" she asked as Frank started to put the laptop down
on her highly polished table.

"No," he said. "It'll be fine."

"And won't you need a place to plug it in?"

"No, ma'am. It works off a battery."

"Like a flashlight, you mean? Lordy, Lordy, what will
they think of next!"

It took the better part of a minute for the computer to
reboot and re-create the file. Sarah watched the process in
abject astonishment. Once Frank had called up the proper
files, Joanna glimpsed a fax cover sheet followed by two
more pages. The fourth page held a picture. Maybe it wasn't
quite as sharp as it might have been with the help of a good
laser printer, but the likeness was close enough for Joanna.
She recognized Alton Hosfield's son at once. The likeness
was close enough for Sarah Holcomb, too.

"That's him, all right," she said. "That's little Frankie's
friend. How'd you find him? And what's his name again?"

"Merritt," Joanna said. "Ryan Merritt."

Sarah shook her head. "Never heard tell of no Merritts.
Must not be from around these parts."

He's from around here, all right, Joanna thought. *From far
closer than anyone ever imagined.*

"So, then," Sarah was saying, "is that all there is to it?
Is that all I have to do?"

"No, Mrs. Holcomb, it isn't. I'm going to have to insist
that you spend at least tonight and maybe tomorrow night
as well in Tucson with your daughter."

Sarah tapped her cane on the floor. "Now, see here, Sheriff Brady. Mr. Montoya said that as long as I had someone
here to look out for me—"

"That's not going to cut it anymore, Mrs. Holcomb. The

man you've just identified is the prime suspect in five murders. That's five, as in one, two, three, four, five. At the moment, you and a discredited police officer are the only people who can link him to two of the dead. And if you're our only witness, I want to be damned sure nothing happens to you. Now, I can understand if you don't feel up to driving yourself at the moment. In fact, I'll be more than happy to have one of my deputies drive you there. Otherwise . . ."

"Otherwise what?" Sarah asked.

"I'll have no choice but to place you in protective custody. Mr. Montoya will drive you over to Bisbee to the Justice Complex and lock you up for the night."

"You mean in a cell?" a shocked Sarah demanded. "In jail?"

"In jail."

"Why, that's outrageous. I never heard of such a thing."

"Please, Mrs. Holcomb," Frank said smoothly. "Sheriff Brady is right. I'm sure you'd be much more comfortable at your daughter's house. Won't you call her now and let her know you're coming?"

"She won't be pleased, havin' me show up like this on such short notice. She likes to have plenty of warnin' so she can get the house all spiffed up before I come to call."

"I doubt she'll mind that much," Joanna said, "once you explain all the circumstances."

After a flurry of phone calls back and forth to Tucson, Sarah reluctantly agreed to go see her daughter. Meanwhile, Joanna read through the rap sheet.

"So what's the deal?" Frank asked when he finally had Sarah packed, loaded, and backing her Buick Century out of the drive and onto the street.

"Ryan Merritt's juvenile record is sealed," Joanna said. "I have no idea what he did to land himself in the slammer for twenty-one months prior to his eighteenth birthday.

They let him out of Adobe Mountain and he was loose for a total of three months before he was arrested again on a parole violation. Because he was no longer a juvenile, he ended up serving the rest of his sentence in Florence. He didn't get out of there until May fifteenth of this year."

"Does that mean he was out of juvie when Rebecca Flowers was murdered up in Phoenix?"

"We can't be sure because no one knows exactly when Rebecca was killed. But it looks right."

"So what do we do?" Frank asked. "Call in an Emergency Response Team and go stake out the Triple C?"

Joanna covered her eyes with her hands. "I'm thinking. I'm worried that if we try that, he might pull the kind of stunt Monty told me about."

"The FBI profiler," Frank said. "The guy I called for you yesterday. You never said you'd talked to him."

"That's because I didn't tell anybody," Joanna said. "You're the only one who knows."

"Tell me," Frank demanded. "What did he say?"

"Let's see . . . that the guy was young and white. That he'd had problems with authority figures. That he'd been in and out of prison and had no compunction about killing or hurting people. Monty also said he was probably leaving a message for us in the way he posed his victims. How does this sound to you, Frank? I think scattering dead bodies all over his father's property qualifies as a pretty strong message.

"Monty Brainard also said that our boy probably no longer cares whether or not he gets caught. He thinks he'll opt for going out in a hail of bullets, taking as many people with him as possible."

"Including his family."

"Right," Joanna said.

"But if we go up against him, he may very well be armed

with some of Clyde Philips' fifty-caliber sniper rifles. Our guys won't be, so what are we going to do?"

"I don't know," Joanna said. "We can't pick him up for questioning because what we have now is strictly circumstantial. If we don't come up with enough to charge him, God only knows what will happen if we have to let him loose again. The problem is, the longer we wait to arrest him, the more danger his family is in. Sarah Holcomb told us Frankie Ramos was Ryan Merritt's friend. Look what happened to him."

For a long time neither Joanna nor Frank Montoya spoke. In the silence, there was nothing to be heard but the buzzing of a thousand locusts. High above them, a jet from Davis-Monthan Air Force Base arched across the blue sky, leaving behind a narrow band of condensation. *Not the writing on the wall,* Joanna thought. *The hand of God writing on the sky.*

"I have to warn them," she said.

"Warn who?" Frank asked.

"The Hosfields. I have to let them know."

"But if you warn them, aren't you warning Ryan, too? What if they tell him we're after him and he takes off? He might get away."

"But what if we're right about him? What if we keep our mouths shut long enough to collect evidence and he ends up killing his family before we actually get our act together? No," Joanna declared, making up her mind. "I'm going to go talk to them right now."

"Alone?"

"Look," she said, "the Triple C has been crawling with cops for days now. If a single officer shows up to talk to Alton and Sonja Hosfield, that's one thing. If a whole armored division shows up, that's something else. If I had killed three people in as many days and left a couple of other stray corpses lying around here and there besides, I'd head for the hills if I saw two or three cop cars drive into the yard all at once."

"You're right," Frank agreed. "Only one cop car, then, but with two cops in it. You and me, Joanna. Both of us together."

Joanna nodded. "Fair enough," she said.

Frank frowned. "But what if it goes bad? What if all hell breaks loose and he comes out with all barrels blazing?"

"That's what we have the cell phone for."

"By then it may be a little late to call for help."

"Who says we have to wait to call?" Joanna demanded. "We're going in the Blazer and I'm going to drive. While we're headed that way, you'll be on the horn to Dick Voland to bring in officers and position them as our backup."

They headed for the Blazer, climbed in, and fastened their seat belts. "Shouldn't we have Dispatch send for Eddy Sandoval? I don't know exactly where he is at the moment, but chances are he's closer to Cascabel than any of the other deputies."

"We can't call Eddy," Joanna said.

"Why not?"

"Because I just fired him."

"Oh," Frank Montoya said. "I see. Care to tell me about it?"

"Later. Talk to Dick first."

Frank did. Voland was back in his office at the justice complex when Frank finally reached him. After letting loose with a barrage of objections, Dick Voland finally gave up trying to talk Joanna out of her plan of action and began establishing contingency strategies. By the time things were settled, the Blazer had already turned off Pomerene Road onto the Triple C. When the Hosfields' tin-roofed Victorian came into view, nothing at all seemed amiss.

"It looks almost idyllic, doesn't it?" Joanna said.

"Right," Frank Montoya said. "And so did the farm-house in Truman Capote's *In Cold Blood.*"

"I never read that," Joanna said.

"You don't have to," Frank told her. "We're living it."

As they drove into the yard, Joanna looked around anxiously, trying to catch sight of the faded blue panel truck Ryan Merritt had been driving three days earlier. There was no sign of it, or of the ATV, either. The door to the building where the truck had been parked stood wide open, and the space inside was clearly empty.

While Joanna was parking the Blazer outside the gate, the front door of the house opened and Sonja Hosfield, with a purse slung over one shoulder, came striding across the porch. Joanna was so relieved to see the woman alive that she had to restrain herself from running up to Sonja and giving her a hug.

"Good afternoon, Mrs. Hosfield," Joanna said, rolling down her window. "This is my chief deputy Frank Montoya."

"I'm glad to meet you, Mr. Montoya," Sonja said. Then she spoke directly to Joanna. "I wish you had called to let me know you were coming. I would have told you not to bother. Alton had a meeting in town this afternoon, so it's the cook's night out tonight. We're meeting in Benson. Alton's supposed to take me to dinner. In fact, I was just on my way out the door when you drove up."

"And your sons?" Joanna asked.

"They're gone, too. They left a couple of minutes ago, as a matter of fact. Ryan offered to take Jake up into the hills to do some target shooting."

Target shooting! Joanna thought. *With twelve-year-old Jake!* As her heart filled with dread, some of it must have surfaced on her facial features. Sonja covered her mouth with her hand.

"What's the matter?" Joanna asked.

Sonja shook her head. "I probably shouldn't have mentioned it."

"Shouldn't have mentioned what?"

"Target practice. You see, Ryan's been in some trouble with the law. It happened before he came here to stay with us, but I remember Alton saying that he's not allowed to have access to guns. Still, since the boys were just going to be on our own property, I didn't think it would matter that much."

Sonja stopped talking and stared questioningly into Joanna's face. "I mean, Ryan hasn't done anything wrong, has he? They won't put him back in jail for that, will they?"

"They might." Joanna opened her car door and stepped down onto the hard-packed ground. "It might actually be far worse than you think."

Behind her in the Blazer, she heard a series of cell-phone beeps as Frank Montoya redialed the department. "Houston," he said to Dick Voland. "We have a problem."

CHAPTER TWENTY-FOUR

Sonja Hosfield stood absolutely still. "What is it, Sheriff Brady?" she asked. "What's going on? What's Ryan done now?"

"You gave him a weapon?" Joanna asked.

"I . . . yes. I told him he could use his dad's deer rifle. He caught me so much by surprise when he asked that I just said yes without thinking."

"What do you mean he caught you by surprise?"

"Ryan offered to take Jake along for the evening. All on his own, without my even suggesting it. I was pleased. The whole time he's been here, he's barely acknowledged his little brother's existence, while all Jake wants is to be included in what the big guys are doing. I was thrilled Ryan was willing to have Jake go along. Since they were just going to be right here on the ranch, I didn't think it would hurt anything. Sort of like Jake riding the ATV, even though he's too young to have a driver's license on a regular road. Not only that, having the two of them go off by themselves meant that Alton and I could have dinner alone for a change.

Almost like a date. I may have graduated as a Home Ec major, but I don't have to prove it by cooking every meal every single day."

Frank got out of the Blazer. "Dick's gathering up everybody he can, including the Emergency Response Team. They're on their way."

Sonja looked alarmed. "Do you have any idea where the boys were going?" Joanna asked.

"I don't know," Sonja said, shaking her head. "They loaded Jake's ATV into the back of Ryan's truck. I told them to stay away from those areas where all those investigators have been working the past few days, but they could be anywhere else. It's a big ranch." She paused and frowned. "Sheriff Brady, I heard him say something about an Emergency Response Team. That means something's happened, something bad. You've got to tell me what it is."

"Where does your stepson stay?" Joanna asked. "Does Ryan have a room here in the house?"

"No, we have a little building out behind the barn, a combination house and toolshed. Back in the old days when Alton could still hire them, *braceros* used to stay there year-round. Now we usually hire people who live elsewhere. The place isn't much, but when Ryan came to live with us this summer, he wanted to stay there. He *asked* to stay there. So that's his home—when he's home, that is. He spends a lot of time in town with friends."

"What friends?"

Sonja shrugged. "I don't know, really. I've never met any of them. Remember, I'm only a stepmother. He doesn't tell me any more than he absolutely has to, but his dad probably knows."

"Could we see his room, Mrs. Hosfield?" Joanna asked. "If you'd be good enough to allow us access so we don't have to go tracking down a search warrant, it could save everybody a whole lot of time and trouble."

"Why would you need a search warrant?" Sonja said. "Of course you can see it. There's nothing there, nothing to hide. It's just a little apartment with a bed, a dresser, and a refrigerator."

She led them across the yard to the far side of the building where the truck had been parked. Half of it was a garage/toolshed. The other half of the building served as living quarters. When Sonja tried the door, it was locked. "That's funny," she said, looking back at Joanna. "There's nobody on the ranch except us. Why would Ryan need to lock his door?"

"Break it down, Frank," Joanna ordered, drawing her Colt. "That's all right with you, isn't it, Mrs. Hosfield?"

"Why, of course . . . if you think it's necessary."

The door shuddered under the first two blows from Frank Montoya's shoulder, but it didn't give way until he slammed into it a third time. It splintered into pieces that fell out of the jamb.

"Wait here," Joanna said, and then she stepped inside.

The room was hot. It was also dark and gloomy. The only light came from a single dingy window shrouded by dirt and cobwebs. Unfortunately, there was an odor in the air—a heavy, coppery smell that was all too familiar.

It took several seconds for Joanna's eyes to adjust to the dim light. When she could see, she noticed a terrible dark smudge on top of the narrow cot—a smudge and a small, still figure. Hoping that it wasn't what she thought and yet knowing it was, Joanna moved gingerly across the room to the bed.

"Don't let Mrs. Hosfield come in here, Frank," she warned. "There's a body in here. Keep her outside!"

"What is it?" Sonja called from outside the broken door. "For God's sake, someone tell me what's going on!"

Sickened, barely able to breathe, Joanna stood over that terrible scene and came face-to-face with the appalling knowledge that they had arrived too late. She reached down and touched Jake Hosfield's lifeless wrist. The body was still warm to the touch, but the boy was dead. The cute kid with the bright red hair was dead, and his hair was . . . gone.

Joanna closed her eyes. In her mind's eye she tried to replay the past few hours—the confrontation with Eddy Sandoval, the time spent thumbing through the yearbooks, the time it took rebooting the computer, the few minutes spent arguing with Sarah Holcomb and making sure she was safely out of town. All those moments and minutes had added up into too many. For Jake Hosfield, those seemingly inconsequential decisions had made all the difference—the difference between life and death.

Squeezing her eyes shut to squelch the tears of rage that were forming and then holstering her weapon, Joanna wheeled and sprang back across the room, almost without touching the bare wooden floor. Outside, Frank stood just in front of the single wooden step with his fingers buried deep in the flesh of Sonja Hosfield's upper arm. For a second, Joanna thought he was physically restraining her, when in fact he was simply holding her upright. As soon as he let go of her arm, she sank down on the rough plank step like a lifeless doll.

"Not Jake," Sonja sobbed. "It can't be. Please, not my Jake."

Joanna saw the woman's mouth move, but she heard nothing. Something had happened to her in that darkened, bloody room. In those few seconds standing at Jake Hosfield's deathbed, she had confronted her own culpability. As sheriff, Joanna had sworn to save people like Jake from people like his half brother. That was her duty, her responsibility. She had failed, and that failure made her deaf to Sonja Hosfield's scream, inured her to the poor woman's pain, and galvanized her to action. If she paused for even a moment to give comfort, she wouldn't be doing what had to be done.

"Frank!" Joanna barked. "Give me the phone!"

Removing it from his jacket pocket, Frank tossed the phone to her. She caught it in midair and was dialing almost before it ever settled into her hand.

"Mrs. Hosfield, how long ago did Ryan leave?" she asked as her fingers raced across the keypad.

"I don't know. Ten minutes? Not much more than that."

"And did you see which way he turned when he reached the road?"

"No."

Frank said, "We didn't meet him along the road between here and Pomerene, so he must have gone the other way." Joanna nodded her acknowledgment as the emergency dispatcher answered the phone.

"Cochise County nine-one-one. What are you reporting?"

"This is Sheriff Brady. Put me through to Pima County nine-one-one. We've got a mutual-aid situation here. I've got to have help. Stay on the line so you'll know exactly what's going on. That way I won't have to repeat it."

"Yes, ma'am."

The connection was made within seconds, although it seemed much longer than that. A moment or two later, another voice came on the line. "This is the Pima County Sheriff's Department watch commander, Captain Leland White. What do you need, Sheriff Brady?"

"I'm out at Cascabel," she said. "I'm on the Triple C with a homicide that's happened within the last half hour. We've got a multiple-homicide suspect fleeing north on Pomerene Road heading for Redington. Once there, he may turn west and shoot through the pass between the Rincons and the Catalinas. Or he might go straight on north toward Oracle. The third option is that he may hole up someplace to fight it out. I'm sure he thought he had several hours' head start on us. I'm betting he's making a run for it."

"What's his name?"

"Ryan Merritt."

"Age?"

"Twenty-two. But you can get all the specifics off his rap sheet. He's listed."

"You want us to post an APB on this guy?" Captain White asked.

"Yes, but when you do, remember, the suspect is armed and extremely dangerous. He may be in possession of one or more fifty-caliber sniper rifles with a kill range of a mile or more. But what I really need from you is a helicopter. Does your department have one?"

"No, we don't, but the City of Tucson does. When we need it, they charge us an hourly rate. I forget how much."

"It doesn't matter. Whatever it is, we'll pay it. We've got to have one."

"All right," Leland White said. "But we'll have to move fast. It won't be long before we lose the light. What kind of vehicle is he driving?"

"Blue Ford panel truck. Nineteen-sixties vintage with an ATV loaded into the back. Can't tell you the exact model." Joanna held the phone away from her mouth. "Mrs. Hosfield, is the truck licensed to your husband?" Sonja nodded dumbly.

"Captain White? Okay, the truck is licensed to Alton Hosfield of the Triple C Ranch in Cascabel. You should be able to find the details from the DMV. I have one officer with me. We're going to leave the Triple C and head north as far as Redington. If we don't catch up to the suspect before then, we'll wait at the junction there in hopes the helicopter will be able to point us in the right direction. And that's all I want from the chopper—directions. Tell the pilot he is not to make contact. If possible, I don't want Merritt to know we're after him. We'll be better off if he keeps moving. If he stops, he'll have time to deploy those rifles and tripods. If he does that, we could have wholesale slaughter on our hands." *As if we don't already.*

"But going after him with only one officer . . ." White began.

"One is all I have right now," Joanna said. "And one is a hell of a lot better than none."

"What about roadblocks?"

"I've got reinforcements coming from Bisbee, but it'll take time to put them in place. They'll establish a roadblock on Cascabel Road between here and Pomerene, but if you could set some up on your end, that would be great."

"Okay. You've got it. I'll get Tucson on the horn right now. How do I get back to you after I talk to them?"

"By radio," she said. "I'm using my cell phone at the moment, but I don't know how much farther into the mountains we'll still have a signal. Cochise County Dispatch, were you listening to this whole thing?"

"Yes, ma'am."

"Pass all that information along to Dick Voland. And contact Fran Daly at the Pima County Medical Examiner's office. Tell her we're going to need her services down here one last time. Have her come out to the Triple C, to the little combination toolshed/apartment out behind the house. That's where the latest victim is."

"Will do. Anything else?"

"Not now. We're heading out."

All the while she was talking, Joanna and Frank had both

been moving back toward the Blazer. Now, with the call finished, Joanna started to climb into the driver's seat.

"Take me along," Sonja Hosfield said from two steps behind her. "I want to go, too."

"No," Joanna replied. "That's impossible."

"Please."

"Absolutely not. Out of the question. This is a potentially lethal situation, Mrs. Hosfield. We can't possibly have civilians along—"

"Sheriff Brady, what if Ryan comes back?" Frank interjected. "What if we're wrong and he isn't heading out of Dodge? We can't just leave Mrs. Hosfield here alone with no way of defending herself."

"You have a car," Joanna said to Sonja. "Drive into Benson. Find your husband and tell him what's happened."

"But she's unarmed," Frank pointed out. "Ryan may have taken a position somewhere between here and there. If so, he could ambush her along the way."

Joanna thought about that—about the possibility of adding yet another victim to Ryan Merritt's terrible death count. "All right," she said, relenting. "No more arguing. Get in back, Mrs. Hosfield. When I give an order, you follow it. Understood?"

Sonja nodded mutely and reached for the door handle. "There's a milk crate in the backseat with a Kevlar vest in it," Joanna continued. "Take that out and put it on." *Not that a Kevlar vest is going to do anybody much good,* she thought. *Fifty-caliber bullets will go through bullet-resistant vests like they're made of paper.*

Once in the Blazer, Joanna fastened her seat belt, switched on the ignition, and slammed the vehicle into gear. "Frank, there's an Arizona atlas in the pocket behind my seat. Get it out and let's see how many places he could turn off between here and there."

While Frank dragged out Joanna's dog-eared copy of the *Arizona Road and Recreation Atlas* and flipped through its pages, she raced the Blazer down the narrow private road that cut through Alton Hosfield's irrigated pasture, past a placid herd of calmly grazing Herefords. *Their lives haven't changed,* Joanna thought, *even though everything else has.*

"How could he kill his own brother?" Sonja Hosfield was asking from the backseat. Under such appalling circumstances, Joanna found the woman's voice unnervingly calm—far steadier than anyone would have expected. "How could he do that?"

How could Cain kill Abel? Joanna wondered. She said, "As far as we can tell, your stepson is a natural-born killer, Mrs. Hosfield. So far, we're fairly certain that he's killed six people—five of them in just the last week. There could be more, though, other victims we as yet know nothing about."

"Six people!" Sonja whispered. "I tried to tell him, but . . .

"What are you talking about?"

"My husband. Before Ryan ever came here, I tried to tell Alton that boy was trouble, but I never dreamed, never imagined, that he could do something so . . . appalling. His mother's a mess, and I was afraid he would be, too. That we'd have to watch him constantly. Alton told me I was imagining things. He said all the boy needed was a chance and that I was being paranoid."

You weren't paranoid, Joanna thought. *Not at all.*

"But Alton's Ryan's father, and he was determined to try, so I went along with it," Sonja continued. "He felt so guilty about what happened between him and Lindsey. She was Alton's first wife, you see. One of the world's worst mothers. She put Alton through hell, and the kids, too. Ryan and Felicia—Ryan's younger sister—practically had to raise themselves. Lindsey gave them no supervision, no guidance, and once she left, she pretty much cut off all contact between Alton and his children.

"It's no wonder Ryan got in trouble, then. We didn't even know about it when he was locked up the first time and sent to Adobe Mountain. They let him out on parole and he was locked back up again within minutes. That was the first we heard anything about it—the second time, when they put him in Florence."

"For what?" Joanna asked. "What was he locked up for the first time?"

"Nobody ever told us. The first we knew there was a problem was when Ryan wrote to Alton from Florence and asked if he could come here when he finished serving his sentence. I was against it. I was afraid of the kind of influence someone like that might have on—" Sonja's voice broke. "On Jake," she finally said. "I was so afraid of what might happen to Jake."

They rattled across the cattle guard and turned north. "But your husband let him come anyway?" Joanna asked. "Over your objections?"

After a few moments, Sonja regained control enough to answer and nod. "Alton thought we could help. Thought the combination of living out here, doing hard physical labor, and having a loving family around him would somehow remake Ryan. Fix him. Make up for all those years of neglect. Once Ryan got here, Alton tried to explain that he had fought for custody when he and Lindsey divorced. That he had wanted to keep both Ryan and Felicia with him here on the ranch. He tried to explain that those were different times back then, when men didn't get awarded custody no matter what.

"And Ryan did seem to listen. I mean, he wasn't nearly as bad to be around as I had thought. Once he knew what was expected, he pitched in with work around the place.

Alton said he was a good worker. He didn't know much about living on a ranch, though he was willing to learn. But when he wasn't working, he didn't hang around with us. He wasn't much interested in having a family kind of relationship."

Sonja lapsed into silence, and Joanna looked at her watch. How long it would take for the helicopter to cross Redington Pass depended on the chopper's speed and the physical location when it was contacted. Tucson had expanded to fill a wide swath of valley from east to west and north to south. A location on the far west or north side of town could add as much as twenty miles to the distance.

"What are you seeing?" she asked Frank who, in brooding silence, was studying the map.

"There are little roads that lead off into the mountains, but they mostly don't go anywhere. We should probably put a roadblock up on Muleshoe Road between the Nature Conservancy Center and Willcox. Then, up beyond Redington, there are forest service roads as well. The real problem, though, is that since he has access to an ATV, there's no reason he couldn't go right around whatever roadblocks we do throw up."

"Good point," Joanna said. "But go ahead and call for them anyway. And while you're at it, see if you can get a fix on the helicopter's location. The sun will be going down pretty soon. When it does, we'll be screwed."

Speeding along the deserted road, Joanna kept up the velocity as much as possible. At fifty miles an hour, the washboards disappeared, but loose gravel made the twisting corners as slippery as icy pavement. At that rate they were fast coming up on Redington, coming up on the place where the road would split off in different directions. There Joanna would be forced to make a critical decision. Depending on which fork she chose, she would either be right on Ryan

Merritt's fleeing trail or off in the hinterlands and headed in the wrong direction.

While Frank repeatedly attempted to contact the helicopter by radio, Joanna glanced in the rearview mirror and caught sight of a now dry-eyed Sonja Hosfield staring out the window. "Did one of my deputies come see you a few weeks back?" Joanna asked. "Somebody named Eddy Sandoval?"

"Yes. It wasn't very long after Ryan got here. Deputy Sandoval came by one afternoon while Alton and Ryan were working in the fields. The deputy didn't say straight out what he wanted or what it was all about, but he hinted around that it had something to do with Ryan. I put my two cents' worth in right then and there. I told him Ryan Merritt was an adult and responsible for his own actions; that if Ryan got himself in trouble again, he'd have to get himself out of it. I gave Ryan the same message later that night. I wanted him to know that if he screwed up, he was on his own. That his daddy wasn't going to fix it for him."

The speeding Blazer arrived at the first junction just outside Redington. There was nothing for Joanna to do but pull over and wait for information from the helicopter while Sonja Hosfield went on talking and unburdening herself.

"It sounded good," she was saying. "I really read him the riot act. I told him if there was even a hint of any more trouble, he'd have to find himself some other place to live. I meant it, too. I meant every word. The only problem is, I never would have been able to make it stick."

"Why not?" Joanna asked.

"Because Alton wouldn't have backed me up on it. He would have come to Ryan's rescue again. He loves him, you see. Ryan is his firstborn son. Alton loves him to distraction, no matter what. And that's why my little Jake is dead now. It isn't fair. How can that—"

A voice cut in on them from the radio in the dash. "Sheriff Brady, can you read me?"

"Yes."

"This is Todd Kries with the Tucson PD," a voice said over the rattling racket of a flying helicopter. "Hold on. I think maybe we just got lucky."

CHAPTER TWENTY-FIVE

"I'm looking down on a light blue, older model panel truck."

Awash in relief, Joanna rammed the Blazer into gear. "Which way?" she demanded. "Ask him which way." Frank relayed the question.

"Toward the pass," Kries answered. "Up Road Three-Seven-One, Redington Road, almost to Piety Hill."

"Can you find that on the map, Frank?" Joanna asked.

"It's right here," her chief deputy said, using his index finger to point to the spot. "According to this, it looks to be seven or eight miles beyond the Redington junction."

"Can you tell what the situation is on the ground?" she asked.

"I was told to make just a single pass," Todd Kries said, "so that's what I did. It looks like he's down in a wash. He may have a flat tire. The truck is sitting funny, like maybe it's jacked up or something."

"And the ATV is still in the back?"

"Can't tell. The back doors are open but I can't see inside.

What do you want me to do now, Sheriff Brady? I'm alone at the moment, but if you'd like me to, I could go back as far as Tanque Verde Road, where Pima County is setting up a roadblock. They're supposed to be bringing in some sharpshooters. Maybe I could fly one of them out here with me, along with some additional fire power, too."

"Good idea," Joanna said. "Do that. It'll give my deputy and me a chance to get closer. But don't go in until I give the word, understand?"

"Got it. You don't have to convince me," Todd Kries said. "If the guy's packing a fifty-caliber, I'm not in the market to be a hero. I've got a wife and two point three kids at home."

Joanna jammed the gas pedal all the way to the floor. She was just getting up a head of steam when the Blazer rounded a curve and came face-to-face with a small herd of foraging cattle. The Herefords—wild-eyed yearlings, mostly—seemed astonished to find a vehicle bearing down on them on that seldom used road. They stood in the middle of it, stricken and staring, before finally kicking up their hooves and leaping out of the way at the last possible second.

Out of the corner of her eye Joanna saw Frank Montoya grip the hand rest as the last calf, bare inches from the Blazer's front bumper, dashed to safety. "Hold it there, fireball," he said. "If we're going to be in a fight, I'd as soon be alive when we get there."

Usually Joanna would have balked at the idea of somebody backseat driving, but this time she knew she was pushing the envelope. "Sorry about that," she told him. "I'll slow down."

"Thanks." Picking up the radio mike, Frank checked in with Dispatch. "Did everybody hear what's going on with Pima County?" he asked.

"We've got it," Larry Kendrick said. "We'll pass the word on to everybody else."

"What are you going to do?" Sonja Hosfield asked from the backseat.

Trying to listen to the radio transmissions, Joanna was annoyed to have Sonja talking to her. Carrying on a conversation was an unwelcome distraction. She answered all the same.

"We're going to try to get as close to Ryan's truck as we can. When we stop and Chief Deputy Montoya and I jump out, you're to stay put, Mrs. Hosfield. Understand? Under no circumstances are you to set foot outside the car until either he or I give you the all-clear."

Sonja, however, gave no indication she had even heard. "Is Ryan going to die?" she asked.

"That depends," Joanna said.

"On what?"

"On how well we plan the confrontation, for one thing," Joanna told her. "It depends on whether we're able to get there before he knows we're coming. And," she added pointedly, "it depends on whether Frank and I have any distractions."

"I don't want him to," Sonja said. "Live, I mean. If Jake's dead, Ryan should be dead, too."

"That'll be up to the courts," Joanna said. "To a judge and a jury. Based on what I know about Ryan Merritt, he sounds like a good candidate for death by injection. Or at least life without parole."

"I want to see him dead now," Sonja insisted.

"Please, Mrs. Hosfield. I can't talk anymore. I've got to concentrate. Frank, what are you carrying?"

"I've got my nine-millimeter," he said. "And my Glock."

"Great," Joanna said. "Between us we have two Glocks, a nine-millimeter, and a Colt 2000. That's not much when you're stacking them up against a deer rifle, at least one fifty-caliber, and God knows what else."

"So we're a little outgunned," Frank returned. "Maybe even *seriously* outgunned. We'll just have to play it smart."

"Great. Any bright ideas?"

"We could always wait," Frank suggested. "Give our reinforcements a chance to come on-line."

"Waiting would also give Ryan a chance to take up a defensive position and dig in. No, that won't work."

"So we keep going instead," Frank said. "We get as close as we can, then we ad-lib like crazy."

"Did you ever take any drama classes in school?" Joanna asked.

"Drama?" Frank echoed. "Me? Are you kidding?"

"Well, I did. At good old Bisbee High. Mr. Vorhees, the drama instructor, always used to tell us, 'Ad-libbing is for amateurs.' "

Even though she had to fight to keep the Blazer on the washboarded road, Joanna glanced in Frank Montoya's direction long enough to catch some of the heat from the scathing look he leveled in her direction.

"With all due respect," Frank returned, "when Mr. Vorhees said that, I doubt he was looking down the barrel of a Barrett fifty-caliber."

Surprisingly enough, Joanna and Frank both laughed then, hooting and giggling. *Sonja Hosfield probably thinks we're nuts,* Joanna thought. But she understood the tension-easing and lifesaving power of laughter in situations like this. It was a way to take the pressure off long enough to stay alert and alive.

"How much farther?" Sonja asked.

"We can't tell," Joanna said. "We probably won't know until we get there."

Just then Todd Kries' voice boomed out of the radio and

made her jump. "Sheriff Brady, I'm coming back now. I've got myself not one but two armed deputies. Both of them with high-powered rifles and night-vision sights for when the sun goes down. We're just now crossing back over the top of the pass. How close are you and where are your reinforcements?"

"The reinforcements are still a long way out," Joanna told him. "They're passing Cascabel now. As for me, I don't know where the hell we are. The speedometer is showing seven miles since we turned onto Redington Road. Maybe we've already missed him. He may have finished changing his tire and moved on."

"I don't think so. I've been keeping an eye out for traffic on the road. According to my estimate, you're almost there. Do you want me to go in and take another look?"

"No," Joanna said. "Hang back a little. The sound of a helicopter can carry a long way out in the middle of nowhere. Wait until Frank and I have actually made visual contact. As soon as we do, I'll call you in."

"Okey-dokey," Todd Kries said. "We'll just sit up here and twiddle our thumbs until you give the word."

The Blazer rounded a sharp curve. After that the road dropped away like a plunging roller coaster. At the bottom of the steep drop, sitting crookedly across a sandy wash, was Ryan Merritt's blue truck.

"We've got him," Frank shouted into the radio. "Come on in, Officer Kries. Bring in your troops. Now's the time."

Earlier, Todd Kries had said the panel truck was sitting crooked. It still was. At first Joanna thought it might be stuck in the sand rather than up on a jack. And there, plain to see, was Ryan Merritt himself, standing at the back of his truck and trying to wrestle the ATV out of the bed through the open back doors at the end of the truck. As the Blazer came over the rise, he must have heard the sound of an approaching vehicle. He turned briefly and looked at them, then turned his attention back to the truck. In the next few seconds Joanna realized that they had arrived just at the critical instant of his unloading the vehicle. He was balancing most of the ATV in midair. Had he relaxed his hold, he might have dropped it.

As he continued to wrestle the ATV, Joanna slammed on the brakes. "Hit the bricks, Frank. I'm right behind you."

To Joanna's dismay, Frank didn't respond with instant compliance. Instead, he thumbed down the speak button on the radio one more time. "We're out of the Blazer, Kries. I'm going right. Sheriff Brady's going left. Tell those sharpshooters of yours to go after *him*, not us."

With that Frank threw the radio down and bailed out of the truck. Joanna paused long enough to look back at Sonja. "Remember, stay down!" she ordered. "If you see things are going bad—if you see that Frank and I are losing it—put the Blazer in reverse and get the hell out of here. Understand?"

Sonja nodded wordlessly.

Leaving the engine running and drawing her Colt, Joanna dropped out of the Blazer. She hit the ground rolling, shoulder first, and came to rest against a pillow-sized boulder. The force of hitting the rock knocked the wind out of her lungs and sent the Colt spinning away from her hand. Only when she had retrieved the gun did she realize how badly she had hurt her shoulder. Her whole arm was numb. It was all she could do to maintain her hold on the Colt's grip.

Seconds later, still rubbing her bruised shoulder, she heard the clatter of an arriving helicopter. Good as his word, Todd Kries had already dropped over the mountains and was bringing in his two sharpshooting deputies as promised.

Way to go, Todd, Joanna thought, but before she could

finish that train of thought, the engine of the ATV surged to life. Moments later, it came roaring down the road.

"Joanna," Frank shouted, "look out! He's coming your way!"

But then Joanna realized that Merritt wasn't coming toward her at all. He was actually aiming for the Blazer. In a flash of intuition, she realized that her four-wheel drive vehicle was what he was really after. A fateful flat tire had disabled Ryan Merritt's main means of escape. He had other transportation. For off-roading, the ATV was great, but long-term, it wouldn't move far enough or fast enough for him to get away. And it wouldn't carry any kind of payload, either.

As those thoughts flashed through Joanna's mind, she also realized that because the road was terribly rough right there, he was being forced to use both hands to drive. Both hands. For those few seconds, then, Ryan Merritt wasn't armed.

Measuring the distance between him and the Blazer and between herself and the Blazer, Joanna knew it would be a foot race—a life-and-death foot race. She also knew she had to get there first. Placing second wasn't an option. If Ryan beat her, the Blazer would be his. It was sitting there running with the key already in the ignition and with Sonja Hosfield trapped in the backseat.

He wouldn't hesitate at killing Sonja, any more than he would hesitate at killing someone else, Joanna thought.

Sometimes during the summer, before diving into the icy-cold, well-water depths of the Elks Club pool, Joanna would stand on the diving board and gulp a single preparatory breath. She did that now. Then she pushed up off the ground and propelled herself toward the Blazer.

She beat him there by mere inches, flying horizontally into the open driver's door from five feet away and sliding all the way across the seat. The knuckles of her fingers slammed against the door handle on the passenger side. Once again the Colt was knocked from her hand. This time it landed on the floorboard. By the time she had groped around and found it, Ryan Merritt was already behind her at the open door. And now he, too, was armed. He was raising the deer rifle to aim it when the deafening sound of a gunshot exploded in Joanna's ears.

She looked on in horror while a shocked expression froze on Ryan Merritt's face. The bullet smashed into his forehead, leaving a seemingly small hole. Then it exploded out the back of his head in a shower of gore. The half-raised deer rifle clattered to the ground. It fell backward, away from the open door. And so did he.

At first Joanna thought that Frank must have raced back to the far side of the Blazer and fired the fatal shot from there. But then she saw him. He was still yards away. The shot had come from much closer than that.

The sound of the shot reverberated in Joanna's ears. The smell of cordite stung her nostrils. Puzzled, she raised herself up and turned around. In the backseat of the Blazer sat Sonja Hosfield. A small but deadly and still smoking pistol was gripped in her trembling hand.

"I wanted him dead," Sonja said simply. "Ryan deserved to be dead, and now he is."

"But where did the gun come from?" Joanna asked. "I thought . . ."

"It was in my purse," Sonja Hosfield explained. "It's always in my purse. I've carried it for years."

"You'd better hand it over," Joanna said. Without a word, Sonja Hosfield complied.

The next few minutes were a blur of activity. But when there was a pause in the action, Joanna tried to slip away on foot, putting a little distance between herself and the din of arriving emergency vehicles. Some thirty feet from the roadway, she sank down on a boulder. She had retrieved her cell phone from Frank. Unfortunately, her attempt at a discreet exit hadn't gone unnoticed. She had removed the phone from her pocket and was punching numbers into the keypad when Frank Montoya came surging through the undergrowth.

"What's the matter?" he asked anxiously. "Are you all right?"

"I'm okay," Joanna said shakily, holding up the phone so he could see it. "But if you don't mind, I need a little privacy—to call my daughter."

CHAPTER TWENTY-SIX

Afterward, Joanna barely remembered the rest of that Friday night. She finally went dragging home sometime around midnight. There was a message on the machine from Marianne saying that if it was all right with Joanna, the services for Esther would be Monday afternoon at three o'clock.

She stood in the shower until she ran out of hot water, but no amount of showering could wash away the horror of what Fran Daly had shown her when she met up with the medical examiner in the hot little room behind the garage on Alton Hosfield's Triple C. Monty Brainard's assessment had been right on the money.

The frost-covered freezer compartment of Ryan Merritt's refrigerator was his trophy room. There, wrapped in separate plastic sandwich bags, Fran Daly had discovered the frozen, bloodied remains of four newly harvested human scalps. A few feet away, in the bottom dresser drawer, she had found one more, much older than the others.

"What do you think?" Fran Daly had asked, opening the drawer and shining a flashlight so Joanna could see inside.

Joanna had sighed. "I think we just found the rest of Rebecca Flowers," she had said. "The poor little runaway from Yuma."

After the shower, Joanna went to bed and tried to sleep, but without much success. She found herself almost wishing that Butch had come back to the house so she could have cuddled up next to him. It wasn't that her body was chilled; her soul was.

Butch called the next morning as Joanna was getting ready to leave for work. "How about breakfast?" he asked.

"I can't," she told him. "I have to be in the office in ten minutes."

"Are you okay?"

Joanna closed her eyes, grateful that he had asked the question, while at the same time wondering what about her voice had given her away.

"No," she said. "It turns out I'm not all right. But I have to go in all the same. We've got a whole lot of cleaning up to do around the department this weekend. It'll probably take most of the day."

"Dinner, then?"

"I think so," she said, "but call me later, just to be sure."

During the morning briefing, Joanna learned from Dick Voland that more than thirty thousand dollars in cash had been found packed into the back of Ryan Merritt's truck. "Since we didn't find any guns other than his father's deer rifle and the one fifty-caliber in his truck, I think it's safe to assume that he unloaded most of the weapons from Clyde Philips' shop. We don't know where yet, but I've got ATF chasing after them. The agent in charge wanted to know how come we hadn't clued his office in earlier."

"You mean you hadn't?" Joanna asked.

Voland looked at her sheepishly and shook his head. "I

told him I put on too much Vitalis and it must have slipped my mind."

In spite of herself, Joanna smiled. "How'd that go over?"

Voland grinned back at her. "Not too well," he said. "But what could the guy say?"

"Not much." Joanna turned to the others. "Now, have we had any luck sorting out the connections between Frankie, Clyde, and Ryan?"

Ernie nodded. "As a matter of fact, we have," he said. "The evidence techs were going over Frankie Ramos' VW bus here in the impound lot when they found an unfinished letter addressed to his folks. Here's a Xerox copy."

Dear Mom and Dad,

I'm sory for all the trubble I caused. Clyde was nice to me but he was getting sicker and sicker. I tried to take him to the doctor but he wuldn't go. Ryan said we should take the stuff from the shop and cell it. He said he had frends from Florens who wuld buy guns and stuff, but Clyde hurd and was mad as hell. Ryan hit him and put him to bed I thought he was dead but he wasn't. When Ryan saw he was still breathing he wanted me to hit him to, but I culdn't. I put a bag over his head. Mom, pleese ask God to forgiv me.

I'm scarred of Ryan. He sez he's comming tonite to giv me the mony. But I don't want it. What shud I do? I can't tell what

The letter ended in mid-sentence. "That's all there is?" Joanna said.

Ernie nodded. "That's it."

"Has Ruben Ramos seen this yet?" she asked.

"No," Ernie answered. "Not yet."

"You'll take it to him?"

"Right away. As soon as we finish up here."

"And stay with Ruben after he finishes reading it," Joanna added. "He may need someone to talk to."

Later, when the briefing had finished with the one set of cases and moved on to more routine matters, Frank Montoya brought up the issue of Eddy Sandoval's dismissal. Firing a deputy put a real crimp in Dick Voland's Patrol Division. It also meant that Frank's carefully contrived work roster for the following month would have to be redone. Neither of the two chief deputies was happy about that, but neither of them faulted Joanna for her decision.

Hours afterward, Joanna had just put down her phone for what seemed like the tenth time and was reaching for her office bottle of aspirin when the private line rang.

"Joanna," Eleanor Lathrop Winfield said the moment her daughter answered, "you'll never guess what happened!"

"What?"

"We're here in Seattle getting ready to catch our plane back to Phoenix when there you are!"

"Mother," Joanna said, "I haven't been anywhere near there. Believe me, I've been stuck right here in the office all day long."

"Not in person, silly," Eleanor said. "Your picture. It's right here on the front page of the *Seattle Times,* along with a big article that was continued two pages later. What in the world have you been up to while we've been gone? I've read the article and so has George. We can hardly believe it. And the article calls you a hero. Whatever happened to the word 'heroine'? I think it's ever so much nicer. 'Hero' makes you sound so . . . well . . . masculine. In my day, a woman who wrote books called herself an authoress, not an author. That sounded much more ladylike, too, if you ask me."

Joanna sighed. "I didn't write the article, Mother. As a matter of fact, who did?"'

"Someone from the *Bisbee Bee*," Eleanor answered. "The article and picture both must have been picked up by the wire services."

"Marliss Shackleford didn't write it, I hope."

"Heavens, no. She's nothing but a columnist. No, I think it was probably Kevin Dawson, the son of the publisher. Anyway, I have to go now. They're calling our plane. We won't be in until late tonight. Will I see you tomorrow?"

"I doubt it, Mother," Joanna said. "I'll need to spend time with Jeff and Marianne tomorrow before Jenny and the Gs get home. The funeral's Monday."

"Funeral!" Eleanor exclaimed. "What funeral?"

"Esther's," Joanna said wearily.

"Esther? You mean Jeff and Marianne's little girl?"

"Yes. She died yesterday afternoon at University Medical Center in Tucson. She had surgery and then she caught pneumonia."

Eleanor was outraged. "Joanna Brady!" she exclaimed. "Why on earth didn't you call and let me know?"

"It turns out I was a little busy." And then Joanna almost did it again. She was on the verge of apologizing when she caught herself and realized that she didn't have to. There was nothing to apologize for. "Besides, Mother," she added, "you were on a ship, so you weren't exactly available. Remember?"

"Oh," Eleanor Lathrop Winfield said. "I guess that's right."

An hour later, Joanna picked up the phone, called the Copper Queen, and asked to be put through to Butch Dixon's room.

He came on the line and greeted her. "Does this mean you've surfaced?"

"For the moment. Do you have any plans for the evening?"

"Hopes, yes," Butch said. "Plans, no."

"How'd you like to come on out to the house? We'll

cook dinner together. And bring your jammies," she added with a nervous laugh.

"Wait a minute, does that mean dinner might turn into another sleepover?"

"It might," she conceded. "Jenny comes home tomorrow afternoon. That's when I turn back into a pumpkin."

"When should I show up?" Butch asked.

"Make it an hour," Joanna said. "I still have to go to the store and buy groceries."

"Make it half an hour," he countered. "*I'll* go buy the groceries."

Butch was as good as his word. He showed up with his Outback loaded with groceries five minutes after Joanna had walked into the house and kicked off her shoes. They had an early dinner, listened to Patsy Cline, and were in bed but not exactly sleeping when the phone rang at a quarter past ten.

Joanna groaned first, but she answered.

"Sheriff Brady?" Tica Romero said. "I'm sorry to bother you at home, but we have a problem here."

"What kind of problem?"

"There's a convoy of eighteen-wheelers parked in front of the department. We've got a man and woman screaming something about unlawful imprisonment, and then there's a whole bunch of pissed-off truckers who claim the woman— who happens to be married to one of them—is the naked hitchhiker who's been running the honey-pot deal out on I-10. What should we do?"

"Call Dick Voland," Joanna said. "Tell him I'm under the weather. He'll have to handle it."

Butch grinned as Joanna set down the phone and switched off the light. "Under the weather?" he teased.

"Well," she said, "maybe I meant under the covers."

EPILOGUE

The Monday after Ryan Merritt's death was hot and muggy. It was like the aftermath of any other natural disaster. The end of Cochise County's spree killer brought with it a flurry of funerals.

Early that morning, Clyde Philips was laid to rest in the Pomerene Cemetery after a moving service conducted by Belle's pastor at the First Pentecostal Church of Pomerene. And up the road at the Triple C, after a service in the Benson L.D.S. church, Jake Hosfield was laid to rest in the family plot. Alton had wanted to bury Ryan Merritt—a boy the tabloids were already labeling the "Cascabel Kid"—in the family plot as well, but his wife wouldn't hear of it. After a brief but heated battle Alton had acceded to her wishes.

When the younger boy's service was over, Alton took off alone on what had once been Jake's ATV. He rode it all the way to the edge of the river, stopping only when he was sure he was safely out of Sonja's sight. Then he spent a heartbroken half hour scattering the ashes of his other son, his firstborn. As he scattered the ashes, he also turned loose his lifelong dream of one day handing over his hard-held family spread to one or both of his sons. A lesser man might have taken his own life that afternoon, but that wasn't Alton Hosfield's way. When he finished what had to be done by the river, he went back to the house and his wife and tried to go on.

A few miles away, across Pomerene Road at Rattlesnake Crossing Ranch, Daniel Berridge and his sister, Crow Woman, conducted a private ceremony for Katrina Berridge, burying her in a grave the two of them had spent the night digging by hand. A photographer for *People* magazine tried to crash the ceremony, only to be driven off by what he later called "a shovel-wielding maniac in a black squaw dress and moccasins."

After a short service at a funeral home in Tucson, Ashley Brittany's remains were shipped back to her home in southern California for final burial. Ruben and Alicia Ramos heard an aging priest celebrate their son's burial mass at a small parish church in Benson.

The last of the funerals that day, the one scheduled for three o'clock in the afternoon at Bisbee's Canyon United Methodist Church, had nothing at all to do with the Cascabel Kid and everything to do with Joanna Brady. She sat by the pulpit, nervously aware that she was sitting in Marianne's accustomed spot. Eventually, looking out at the sea of familiar faces and listening to the soothing notes of the organist's prelude, she began to feel a little better.

Esther's casket was tiny and white. Dwarfed by banks of flowers, it was covered by a blanket of white roses interspersed with sprigs of greenery and baby's breath. While Joanna watched, a rainbow of midafternoon sunlight splashed in through the stained-glass window and transformed the delicate white petals into a kaleidoscope of breathtaking colors—jewel tones of red and green, blue and gold.

Moments before the three o'clock starting time, the last few people began filing into the front pew, the one that had been reserved with bands of black satin.

Jeff and Marianne were there with their other daughter, Ruth. As usual, Ruth was being a two-year-old handful. It took the concerted efforts of both Angie Kellogg and Dennis Hacker to keep her corralled in the pew. Seeing Angie there in the front row, Joanna couldn't help wondering how many times in her life the woman had actually set foot inside a church. But then, she was there for the same reason Joanna Brady was—because Marianne Maculyea and Jeff Daniels were her friends.

Beyond Dennis Hacker, at the far end of the pew, sat Butch Dixon. Beside Butch, huddled under the protective wing of his arm, sat Jennifer Ann Brady.

At last the organist stopped playing. In the hushed and expectant silence of the room, with no other sound but the distant rumble of the air-conditioning unit, Joanna knew it was time for her to stand and speak. She had expected her knees to knock, her hands to shake, and her voice to quiver, but none of that happened. She was doing this for Marianne. She was doing this because a friend had asked it of her as a favor. And that, Joanna realized, taking hold of the pulpit with both hands, was what made doing it possible. When Joanna Brady conducted Esther Maculyea-Daniels' funeral that afternoon, she did so with a poise and confidence that surprised her almost more than it surprised her mother.

"The first hymn today isn't listed by number in your program," she said. "I didn't think that was necessary, because it's one we all know by heart."

Down in the front pew, Butch Dixon shook his head and tapped his ear. Seeing that, Joanna knew she needed to readjust the volume. Clearing her throat, she spoke more clearly, more firmly into the microphone. "This particular song was one of Esther's favorites. It's the one her parents sang to her when she was restless and unable to sleep. Please join me in singing 'Jesus Loves Me.' "

Joanna had stayed up half the night on Sunday, writing and rewriting the service, searching her heart, hoping to hit on just the right combination of hope and comfort. Now, as Jeff Daniels and Marianne Maculyea rose from their seats and joined hands to sing, Joanna allowed herself to believe that she had achieved her goal.

Enough time had elapsed since Andy's funeral that she could no longer remember any of the specifics of that service. What she was left with was the sense that whatever words Marianne Maculyea had spoken that day, whatever songs had been sung or Scriptures read, they had all been exactly right. And maybe, she hoped, that would be true here as well. Perhaps, once the pain had lessened some, Jeff and Marianne would feel that way about this service. Maybe, in the long run, what was said or sung wouldn't matter nearly as much as that beautiful rainbow splash of stained-glass color reflecting off the snow-white petals of the roses.

The voices of the congregation rose in unison, finishing the first verse of the childhood hymn and marching inexorably into the second:

Jesus loves me. He will stay
Close beside me all the way.
If I love Him when I die,
He will take me home on high.

Up to then, Marianne had been singing right along with everyone else, but at that point her voice faltered. She stopped singing and turned into Jeff's arms, burying her head against his chest. That moment of parental inattention was all the restless Ruth needed. Determined to escape the confines of the pew, she slipped away from her parents, dodging past Angie Kellogg and Dennis Hacker as well. The escape-bent child might have made it all the way to the side aisle if Jenny hadn't reached out, caught her, and dragged her back.

Wrestling the wriggly child into her own small lap, Jenny whispered something into Ruth's ear. Joanna more than half expected the toddler to let loose with a shriek of objection. Instead, nodding at whatever magic words Jenny must have uttered, Ruth snuggled close to Jenny's chest. With a contented sigh, she stuck one chubby thumb into her mouth and closed both her eyes. Instead of only one child sheltered under Butch Dixon's protective arm, now there were two.

The whole small drama played itself out in less time than it took the congregation to reach the end of the chorus. Watching it, Joanna was struck by her daughter's quick-thinking action and also by her kindness. Without any adult prodding, Jenny had seen Ruth making a run for it and had done what needed doing. There was an unflinching responsibility and a resourcefulness in Jenny's action that struck a responsive chord in Joanna's heart—something Joanna Brady recognized in herself.

Through the years, looking in wonder at her fair-haired, blue-eyed daughter, Joanna had thought of her as Andy's child. Jenny was, after all, a mirror image of her father. But seeing Jenny then, with Ruth nodding off in her lap, Joanna realized that Jennifer Ann Brady was a chip off more than one old block. She was her mother's daughter as well.

Joanna's eyes flooded with unwelcome tears—tears that were as much joy as they were sorrow. At the same time her heart was overflowing with sadness for Jeff and Marianne and Ruth, at the same time her whole body ached with hurt for their awful and wrenching loss, Joanna nonetheless felt a certain motherly pride. Looking down on Jenny, she could see into the future enough to know that her daughter was growing up to be a kind, loving, and caring person. Like her mother, she would someday be known as someone who was true to her friends and could be counted on for help in a time of crisis.

The song ended. The last note lingered in the hushed sanctuary as Sheriff Joanna Brady moved once more to the pulpit. There, resting on the polished dark wood, lay Marianne Maculyea's worn Bible. The book was open to the third chapter of Ecclesiastes. Taking a deep breath, Joanna steadied her voice and spoke.

"The Scripture today comes from the old Testament, the Book of Ecclesiastes, Chapter Three, Verses One to Eight. 'To every thing there is a season, and a time to every purpose under heaven'."

The words were familiar to her. Joanna had heard them time and again over the years, and yet this time when she read them aloud in that hushed, listening church, it seemed as though the words were intended for her alone. They were speaking about the triumphs and tragedies of her own life: ". . . a time to weep and a time to laugh; a time to mourn and a time to dance . . ."

For the first time she understood, to the very depths of her being, that without surviving terrible sadness, she might well have been blind to the astounding miracle of joy. The one made the other possible.

Finished with the Scripture reading, Joanna sat down while choir director Abby Noland stepped forward to sing a solo rendition of "Amazing Grace." Sitting at the front of the church, Joanna found her eyes drawn to Jenny—to Jenny and the now sleeping Ruth. Rather than smiling, Joanna reached up and tugged at her ear. With that simple gesture, a silent signal passed between mother and daughter. Like the signal television actress Carol Burnett had often sent to her grandmother, Joanna sent an unspoken "I love you" to Jenny.

Jenny sat with her chin resting on Ruth's tousled hair. Over the sleeping toddler, Jenny beamed back at her mother and tugged at her own ear in reply.

Yes, Joanna Brady thought, smiling an almost invisible smile. *Definitely a chip off the same block.*